BACK TO PARADISE

A novel by Dan Churach

Cover design and artwork by Janice Wentworth

This novel is a work of fiction. Any names, characters, businesses, places, events, locales, and incidents are either the products of the author's imagination or used in a fictitious manner. Any resemblance to actual persons, living or dead, or actual events is purely coincidental.

DEDICATION

To Kathy and Tom, …the best sister and *hānai* brother anyone could ever have. Thanks for all your support over the years.

CONTENTS

DAN CHURACH

ACKNOWLEDGMENTS

I would never have learned what Hawaiian culture was all about without many of our friends and *hānai* Hawaiian family. *Mahalo* especially to Val De Corte, Janice Wentworth, Barbara Hallacher, Bill and Jackie Parecki, Steve and Su Welsh, Joe and Kathy Halbig, Bruce and Tina Davis, Ian and Angie Midson, Martha Fontana, Dee McCall, Ray and Ester Kottke, Michael and Gale Clark, Earleen Grune, Ernie Kho, and Leon Hallacher. I also thank the hundreds of students I learned from over so many years in *Hawaii nei*. Your love and spirit will remain with us always... *mahalo nui loa*. Most of all, thanks to the love of my life, my wife and my *kuuipo*, Karn.

PROLOGUE

"Love All that You See with Humility. Live All that You Feel with Reverence. Know All that You Possess with Discipline."

— Kahuna Hale Makua

DAN CHURACH

Present Day

Uncle Kapena was a *kahuna*, a Hawaiian elder who lived his entire life in the little beachside community near Hilo. Many locals would go to him for comfort, advice, for help when making decisions, and for questions of the old, Hawaiian way. The *kahuna* was a special part of the *keikis* learning of the ancient ways and how they fit with modern life. In the truest sense, the *kahuna* was a teacher and helped so many young people learn how to be 'human'. Uncle Kapena's family was much bigger than that as understood by *haole* convention since his *hānai* family reached friends and community members beyond any biological prerequisite of Western culture. In fact, a *hānai* family transcends any age, biological, religious, or educational barrier and simply connected those members of extended 'family' in spiritual, life-long relationships. Uncle Kapena might not have been of the same blood as Wailani, but he was every bit as much of a *hānai* grandfather to her as he sat on a grass mat under a clump of coconut palms talking story with his *hānai* granddaughter.

* * *

Wailani quietly pulled her smartphone from her bag and shifted it into the shade to better see its screen.

"Put that away, Wailani." Uncle Kapena's voice wasn't loud, but its meaning was clear.

"But I just wanted…"

Kapena interrupted her. "The ways of the old and the ways of the new may coexist quite nicely, but there is a time and a place for everything. When you asked me about Hawaiian ways, it is NOT the time to be looking at a smartphone."

Wailani turned her eyes away from Kapena out towards an old post protruding from the sand. "I'm sorry, uncle."

He smiled. "No need." Kapena's eyes followed Wailani's as he looked at the post. For a moment, they both noticed a Hawaiian owl perched on the post. "Are you looking at *pueo*?"

"I am, uncle. He looks as though he is listening to us."

"He is."

"Uncle, the *pueo* is an owl – surely he can't be listening to us." She started to giggle but was quickly interrupted.

"On the contrary… *pueo* IS listening to us." Uncle Kapena nodded towards the old fence post. "You say that *pueo* is merely a dumb animal. Don't you think *pueo* just might be much more than that? Don't you think that WE should be listening to *pueo*?"

"I don't know, uncle." Wailani was a bright teenager, but she was uncertain of where Kapena was going with his comment.

"*Pueo* has a very special meaning to the Kealoha family. *Pueo* had a very, very special meaning to your *tutu*."

"The *pueo* and grandma?" Wailani always wanted to know more about her *tutu*, but mostly the family never talked about her since she went away.

"Oh yes." He saw her face light up at the mention of her *tutu* and knew she was ready to learn the full story, no matter how incredible it might seem to her. "Do you know what an *aumakua* is? I hope that fancy high school you go to teaches some Hawaii culture to you, no?"

Well yes, we do have Hawaiian Studies classes, and I think I know what an *aumakua* is. Isn't it like a ghost or something… of someone who has died, right?"

"Ghost? Well, not exactly a ghost. An *aumakua* is more like a…" Wailani's smartphone beeped. Kapena spoke with a gentle but firm tone. "I will tell you all about *aumakua* and *pueo* and your *tutu*, but you have to turn your cell phone off now, Wailani."

She was embarrassed. Quickly, Wailani pulled her phone from her bag and followed her uncle's wish.

"When we are done here, remind me to tell you of how the Kealoha family is very much involved with that smartphone of yours." Kapena shifted his position. He had a feeling this conversation could go on at length. "You have the right idea about an *aumakua*, but we really wouldn't call it a ghost. You see, ancient Hawaiian culture most certainly believed in a life after death, the same as you probably learn about over there at Saint Joe's School." Kapena scratched his chin, considering his words carefully. "But the Hawaiian beliefs find the line between living and dead much more porous than Western-style religions do."

"Porous?"

"Yes… Hawaiians believe that when you die, that spirit can come back in a different form and can go back and forth between the living and the dead. That line between here and the other world has holes in it through which spirits can pass back and forth."

"That is like a ghost." Her eyes seemed like big saucers at the thought.

"Well… but not in the spooky sense like a Halloween ghost, Wailani. An *aumakua* can manifest itself as an animal, a special place or as a person. Sometimes an *aumakua* can go back and forth amongst all three forms. Though any animal can be an *aumakua*, many times in the Islands, they are taking the form of *manō* – a shark, or *pueo* – the owl, or *io* – the hawk… Actually, there is no limit here to what form or forms it may take, but whatever body or object the *aumakua* may take, the fact is that it usually is a relative who has passed that line between living and dead. In a sense, it is like a family god, returned to the living to guide, to help, and most of all, to inspire. An *aumakua* is somewhere between heaven and earth, but he always guards over the family. Probably at Saint Joe's, you learn the Christian concept of a 'guardian angel'… that is as close to the Hawaiian *aumakua* as we can get."

Wailani listened to every word Kapena spoke but kept her eyes glued on the *pueo*. "Why did you say that *pueo* had such a special meaning to *tutu*?"

"Well, because *pueo* always looked over your *tutu*… over *tutu* and over all the Kealohas. *Pueo* is our family *aumakua,* and he watches over us now."

"Oh, Uncle Kapena, do you really believe the old Hawaiian legends?"

"I certainly do, Wailani. I do, your *tutu* did, and Malia does."

"Mom? Even mom believes how special the *pueo* is?"

"Yes, yes – even Malia."

"Well then why did *tutu* just go away... disappear? Wasn't *pueo* watching out for her?"

"Of course he was, but don't believe for one minute that you can out-think the *aumakua*. *Aumakua* knows so many things that we don't know, and we could never know why he allowed that to happen. I only know that *pueo* was watching and did what was best of *tutu*."

"You say that *pueo* watches over our family... the WHOLE family?"

"Of course."

"Well, how about *tutu's* fellow? Why didn't *pueo* look after my granddad?"

"Oh he did, Wailani, he did. He looked over *tutu* and granddad very closely... more than you could ever know. You are old enough to hear the whole story, my dear Wailani. Do you want to hear... at least as much as I know?"

"Oh yes, Uncle Kapena. Please tell me what you know of *tutu*."

PART ONE

"Life is paradise, and we are all in paradise, but we refuse to see it."

— Fyodor Dostoevsky

1
Friday, February 8, 1957

"Would you answer that phone, honey? I'm just getting your lunch onto the table."

"Sure, mommy." The young boy quickened his step as he managed to free one arm from his winter coat. He reached the telephone on the third ring-ring. "Hello."

There was no immediate answer. And eerie feeling flushed through the boy as he momentarily hesitated, distracted by the unexpected fragrance of some unknown, unseen blossom.

"Hello. Hello. Is anybody there?"

A man's voice began to mumble. "Is... is..."

Again, the boy waited, the out-of-place scent of flowers confusing his brain. "Wait - I'll get my mom." He set the phone on the table. "I guess it's for you, mom."

He finished pulling his other arm from his coat, his thoughts occupied by the sweet, tropical smell that filled his head. That's crazy, the boy thought — there are no fresh flowers in Philadelphia during the wintertime.

2
Wednesday, February 3, 1999: 4:00 P.M.

"Hello." Benjamin Decker nearly lost his balance while leaning over his partially packed suitcase lying open on the bed. On his second attempt, he nearly yelled into the phone. "HELLO! Who is this?" An irritating click announced another wrong number — an all too frequent occurrence during the past six or seven weeks. He placed the receiver back on the hook and continued packing. He couldn't put the thought out of his mind that maybe these weren't really wrong numbers.

"Who was that, dad?" Bonnie Decker came walking into the second-floor bedroom with a stack of freshly laundered underclothes and set them down next to the suitcase.

"No one. Well, I guess it was someone, but they just hung up again."

"Maybe it's one of Lisa's friends."

"Come on, Pumpkin. All her friends are fully aware of the fact that she's away at college. And besides that, why wouldn't they at least leave a message? I should ask you if you've made any strange friends lately."

"Oh, come on, Dad — none of my friends would just call and hang up like that."

"Maybe you have a secret admirer..."

"DADDY!" The cute, high school sophomore blushed at her father's teasing suggestion.

"Thanks for getting the laundry, Bonnie. I think I've pretty much gotten my things together here." He counted several pairs of jockey shorts and neatly placed them in his bag.

"Are you sure you don't need an assistant of some sort on this trip? I'd do it for really cheap!"

"I know you would, honey. And I wish I could take you along this time, but you know I can't. Believe me, I'll get you out to Hawaii eventually."

"Promise?"

"I promise." He rubbed the top of her head. "So, how was school today?"

"Well — actually, it was rotten!"

"Rotten? Aw, come on! Just listen to that tone of voice. I can't believe anything could be THAT rotten!"

"That stupid Mrs. Kozloski assigned us class presentations again, and you know how much I hate to talk in front of all those people."

"Now, now — isn't calling her stupid being a bit harsh?"

"Well, I mean why does she always want us to give oral reports? Liz says it's probably because she's just too dog-gone lazy to grade essay ones — like then she'd actually have to read them, even!"

"Oh, come on, pumpkin! I've known Sara Kozloski for years, and she's one of the hardest working teachers at Grovesnor High — and I know that YOU know that, too. She only gives you those kinds of assignments for your own good."

"Yeah, right — like I guess now you'll even tell me that eating spinach is for my own good too!"

"Now come on, Bonnie!"

"Oh, I know, I know — at least I think I know... But I still hate having to talk in front of the whole class like that. Sometimes — all the time — I get so nervous that one of these days I'm... I'm simply going to throw up!"

"I hardly think you'll go to that extreme. You know that it's perfectly natural to get nervous. The only way it gets any better is if you keep on practicing — keep forcing yourself into situations where you have to speak in front of a lot of people. You've heard your mom tell her stories about when she first began teaching." He shook his head as his mind suddenly seized the fact of just how fast youth gives way to middle age. "Oh god... can that possibly be over twenty years ago already? Anyway, she was scared to death to stand in front of her first class the year after we were graduated from college. I remember many mornings before school she'd be so nervous that her whole body would literally shake all over. I nearly had to force her to go in a couple of times. But that was only in the beginning — until she mastered her fear. You simply have to learn — like we all learned — that if you just challenge that fear and not back down from it, it'll eventually just go away. I know it's hard to believe, but it will — honest!"

"Sure, sure — I know. Eventually, it will... Like maybe in a billion years or so! Or maybe it will never, ever, happen for me. I'm not taking any chances. I've decided that when I get old like you..."

"Old like me?"

Bonny smiled and kept talking. "...I want to get some sort of job doing something somewhere in a secluded little office. I want a job in which I'll never, ever have to speak in front of more than two or three people at a time."

"Something... Somewhere... Sometime... I'm afraid it doesn't work that way, honey. You just can't plan things out that way. For goodness sake, look at me — an electrical engineer. I always thought that engineers worked in small offices and never had to talk to a lot of people — right?"

"Well, I... I sort of know what you're saying... And yet you're always giving talks. I mean, look at you now — going to Hawaii and all... and to speak to..."

"Exactly my point. I'm going to Hawaii to address a convention at which there'll be thousands of people in attendance. But do you think that when I was your age I ever even though of speaking in front of so many people? No way, Jose! When I decided to be an engineer, the last thing that ever crossed my mind was that I'd have to speak in front of such a large audience. And yet lately, I've been called on more and more to do just that. The point is that you just can't be sure when you'll have to make a presentation — a presentation upon which your whole career and livelihood may depend."

"Well, I never thought of it like that. Maybe Mrs. Kozloski is doing it for our benefit, but I still get really apprehensive just thinking about it. I guess I'll make it somehow, but..." Bonnie glanced down from the window to see Emily Decker's car dodge a snow bank as it turned into the driveway. "Hey, here comes mom."

* * *

"I thought I'd be home earlier, Ben. I got tied up after school and just couldn't get away until now. I would have called, but I simply couldn't."

He stood at the base of the stairs and looked at Emily, wondering why he felt so damned uncomfortable talking to her about all but the most trivial things anymore. "It's okay, Emily. I came home early to pack — got here about two o'clock or so, I guess. I'm just about done, too. Look, I still need to run over to

Corrigan's Drug Store to pick up a few odds and ends — toiletries and whatnot."

"Make sure you lay your travel folder on top of your carry-on, so you don't forget it."

"Yeah, yeah — I already did."

"Did my mom call this afternoon — after you came home to pack?"

"Your mom? No, not while I was here. Were you expecting her to call?" Ben once again tried to decipher his wife's face, but she quickly turned away.

"No, no — not really. Well... actually, I mean... I just thought she'd be calling about Sunday dinner…"

"You are going to Pottstown Sunday, aren't you — up to mom's house? With Bonnie going up to University Park to spend the weekend with Lisa, it's going to be pretty lonely around here. You may as well spend the day with your mother." He opened the hall closet and grabbed his jacket.

"I probably will, but I'm going to have to start putting a dent in that stack of term papers I have to grade." She nodded towards a report-filled cardboard box sitting on the dining room table. "I want to let her know I won't be over until early afternoon."

"So, give her a call."

"I will."

"Speaking about phone calls, we got another one of those wrong numbers a little while ago, though I'm not really too certain that it was a wrong number. They just hung right up — again."

Emily again avoided any eye contact with her husband as she brushed a non-existent wrinkle out of her skirt. "Probably just kids." Her tone of voice exhibited no concern.

"Yeah, sure. At least I hope so." Ben slipped into his coat and reached for the door. "Look, since you're the last one in the driveway, I'm gonna use your car. I'll be back in half-an-hour or so."

"Fine. Oh, by the way, I really don't feel like cooking tonight, and I doubt that you do either. I thought we could order a pizza for dinner — have it delivered. Is that all right with you?"

"Yeah, sure — sounds great to me. I know that Bonnie will approve — if she ever gets out of the bathroom long enough to eat some of it! How about double cheese, pepperoni, and mushrooms?"

"That's fine. I'll order in a half-hour or so. Will that give you enough time?"

"Yeah, that's okay. I can pick it up if you'd like."

"No, I know how much you have to do yet."

"Okay. I'd better get a move on so I'm back by then." He closed the side door and briskly jogged down the steps and onto the driveway.

As Emily grabbed the banister and started up the stairway, she was stopped on the second step by the ringing of the telephone. She quickly turned back and grabbed the receiver hanging on the kitchen wall. "Hello..." Her face immediately filled with a big smile. "Oh sure — I bet you do." She unconsciously looked around as if to assure her privacy. "You must say that to all your girlfriends. How are you, love? Yeah, I know. He did get home really early today — so he could get packed... Well, not tonight. No point in pushing it. I mean, we have this entire weekend plus all next week — Ben will be gone for ten whole days. And you know that when the cat's away..."

3
Thursday, February 4, 1999: 5:05 A. M.

Ben pulled his car onto the entrance ramp marked I-95 SOUTH — PHILADELPHIA. The airport was only about a forty-minute drive from their Bucks County home, but the threat of more snow and his 7:45 A. M. departure time had Ben and Emily out of the house extra early on this dismal morning.

"Aw man, I'd still have been tired if I could have slept in until noon today." He covered his yawn with his right hand while his left remained on the wheel.

"You've been pushing yourself, Ben. Maybe you'll be able to get some sleep on the plane."

"Maybe. I sure hope we don't have any delays getting out of Philly, especially considering the nasty weather forecasts."

"Yeah, I know you're looking forward to Chicago — well, at least to seeing Stosh, I mean. And your scheduled layover at O'Hare surely doesn't give you much leeway for any delays."

As Ben accelerated into the middle lane, he noticed the first flakes of snow fluttering through the beams of his headlights. "That's true — only a few hours. I've got to admit I'm really looking forward to spending a little time with him over a cup of coffee or two. I haven't seen him for... oh god, I guess it's about three or four years now. It'll be nice just talking a little...."

"Talking about us..." She was quite abrupt with her assertion.

He frowned as he briefly glanced over at his wife. "Now, just what in the hell is that supposed to mean?"

"You tell me. Janet and Tom Carleson saw me grocery shopping the other day, and they acted as though I had a deadly disease or something." Her tone revealed a simmering hostility.

"Hey, now wait one minute here, Emily. Maybe it's just too early in the morning, but I think I missed something. I'm not following this at all. First of all, you actually seemed to show some genuine concern about my physical wellbeing — I mean with my lack of sleep and all. Then the next thing you know — WHAMMO! You totally switch gears and start accusing me of god knows what! I mean, what the hell are you talking about anyway? Why the big huff?"

"You know exactly what I mean, Ben — I'm talking about the Carlesons! I don't know what you told those two, but they both acted so aloof, so — well... not the least bit like their normal selves. I can simply imagine what you've been telling them about me."

"Aw, get off that paranoid kick, Emily! I don't have to tell anyone anything. Don't you think it's pretty damned obvious even to a casual observer that we've really been growing in opposite directions as of late? I mean, for Christ's sake, we don't even wind up going to visit our friends as a couple anymore. It was awkward as all hell attending the Carleson's party the other weekend all by myself. I mean, YOU tell me — how does one explain an English teacher away on a weekend business trip?"

"And I suppose you're blaming THAT on me."

"I'm not blaming it on anyone. I merely mean it as a statement of fact. For Christ's sake, I AM still a human being, you know. Just because I studied engineering doesn't mean I don't have feelings." He continued staring at the road ahead as both the snowflakes and the traffic became heavier the closer they got to center-city. "You know, Emily, I still love you — I always have. But it seems that every time I get a chance to be with the family anymore, you have to go on some trip or work late at school or attend some meeting. I confess that I'm getting pretty damned tired of spending so much time alone — of always having to make excuses for why we're not together. And for that matter, even though I've never been much for jealousy or suspicion, it's getting more and more difficult not to wonder whether there's someone else."

"Oh, get off it, Ben! Need I remind you that when Lisa and Bonnie were both old enough to go to school, it was YOU who suggested I go back to teaching? And now you know damn well just how tied up I've been with all my administrative responsibilities and the work I put in on the curriculum and accreditation committees. Why didn't you just say no years ago if you didn't want me to work?"

"Why didn't I say no? Give me a break, Emily. What would it have mattered any? I wanted you to have the opportunity to develop your own career — not a separate life!"

Her only answer was silence. After fifteen more minutes of a conversation-less drive, Ben turned off the Airport Circle Drive and followed the signs marked PHILADELPHIA INTERNATIONAL AIRPORT — DEPARTURES. He pulled over to the unloading zone and parked the car. "Well, here we are. I'll just get my bags out of the trunk and grab a porter. This snow is starting to stick. You'd better get headed back to Grovesnor right away. It's hard to say just how bad this storm's going to get."

"Hopefully, they'll give us a snow day or at least let us go home early."

"Whatever. Just drive carefully, will you?

"Yeah, sure." Her tone left absolutely no doubt that she didn't believe — or accept — his concern.

Ben opened the trunk and yanked out his bags. A uniformed porter appeared seemingly from nowhere. "D'ya need any help, sir?"

"Please."

The burly man loaded his luggage on a cart and reached for his ticket folder. He opened it and fingered through the packet. "I don't imagine you'll be missing this snow in Hawaii. Check you right through, Mister... um..." He quickly glanced at the luggage tags. "...Mister Decker?"

"Yeah, I'd appreciate it. Ah, here — I'll take that carry-on bag."

The porter quickly wrote up baggage tags and returned Ben's ticket envelope with the stubs stapled inside. "You can just check the video display once you're inside the terminal building for that gate number, Mister Decker."

"Thanks a lot." Ben patted several crumpled bills in the man's hand and circled around to the driver's side of his car. He handed her the keys and leaned in the open window to kiss her on the cheek. "Look, Emily, I really meant it."

"Meant what?"

"I DO still love you."

"Right, Benjamin." She terminated her caustic response quickly by rolling up the window, briefly glancing at the rear-view mirror, and pulling away from the curb with a jerky squeal of her tires. He watched until her taillights disappeared into the mix of traffic and snowflakes and then slung his carry-on bag over his shoulder. Ben quickly stepped out of the cold, wet morning and onto a terminal escalator. Somehow, he felt the dismal weather quite appropriately fit his mood.

4
Thursday, February 4, 1999: 9:10 A.M.

"...Decker. Mister Decker, I'm so sorry to wake you, but we're preparing for our arrival in Chicago."

"Um, O'Hare? We're here already?" Ben rubbed his eyes and arched his back.

"Yes, Mister Decker. You were sleeping so soundly that I didn't want to disturb you. But you have to put your seat in the upright position now, sir. You know, federal regulations require that..."

"Ah... yes, I know. It's no problem." He righted his seat and checked his belt. A glance from his aisle seat toward the window to his right revealed a piece of the Lake Michigan shoreline below. At least the sky was a lot clearer for landing in Chicago than it had been for the take-off in Philadelphia two hours earlier. Thank god for small favors! Ben was always nervous enough about flying into and out of busy O'Hare without having bad weather to further complicate matters.

* * *

Looking down at the end of the jetway that connected the plane to the arrival gate, Ben thought that it sure looked sunnier than any February morning in Chicago had a reason to be. As he exited the ramp into the main concourse, he was impressed with the bright, airy feeling the arched glass ceilings always presented — what a marvelous piece of architecture. He quickly surveyed the masses of people waiting to meet arriving passengers and felt mildly disappointed at not immediately sighting his old college friend. He tried to move out of the busy stream of people long enough to get his bearings. Suddenly, he felt a strong hand grab his shoulder from behind and forcefully turn him around.

"Ben Decker! You old horse's ass, you! So how the hell are ya?"

"Hey, Stosh! Long time, no see, buddy! How's the old Polish stallion doing?" He immediately dropped his carry-on bag and embraced his lifelong friend in a tight bear hug.

"Come on, old buddy. Let's move over here out of this meandering mass of humanity." The two walked onto a people mover beltway and were whisked away toward the main terminal building. "We can get ourselves a cup of coffee at the restaurant in the central hub. Of course, by now you're probably all coffeed-out from the flight!"

"Not really. I slept almost the entire way."

"Aha! Sleep deprivation! Waking up too early in the morning, are you?"

"Well, I sure did today."

"Yeah, but waking up to catch a so-called business flight — and I use the term BUSINESS very loosely — a business flight to Hawaii doesn't sound too difficult to me. At least I think I could have somehow managed to get out of my cold bed this morning to head for the tropics." Stosh smiled a grin a mile wide. "Just how the hell do you get these kinds of tough assignments, anyway? Who do you think you're bull shitting with this business stuff?"

"Come on, Stanley. I mean, for Christ's sake..."

"Stanley, huh? Now it's Stanley, is it? I always know I got your goat when you start calling me Stanley..."

All right, honest — it really is a business trip. I've got to make a presentation to a group of buyers, and it will either make or break this new gadget we've developed." Ben patted his carry-on bag indicating its valuable contents. "Believe me, I could really use a Hawaiian vacation right about now more than anyone else I can think of. But regrettably, this trip won't allow me any time for R and R."

"My god, buddy, you make it sound so tough. I really offer you my condolences. We folks in the social services industry don't generally let ourselves get stuck with these kinds of lousy assignments that nobody else wants. You know — like flying off to such mundane spots as Hawaii. We always try to go for the really flashy locales. As a matter of fact, I'm just as happy as a pig in shit to tell you that yours truly is booked for a return engagement in the fabulous inner city this afternoon — another fun-filled day in the Chicago ghetto! Now, are you absolutely sure you don't want to trade assignments with me?" Stosh mockingly attempted to contain his smile as he stepped off the people mover and led the way toward the restaurant sign.

"You've got it all wrong, my friend."

"Yeah — RIGHT! So, where are you staying once you get to Aloha-land?"

"Well, I don't know how much time I'll actually be there, but my reservations are for the Hilton Hawaiian Village — the Rainbow Tower. I believe that's what they told me."

"Hey, what a great place! When Linda and I were still together — that's the only time I ever got to Hawaii — we stayed in the Rainbow Tower. It's a really nice place — and huge, too! I remember lying by that beautiful lagoon they have, sucking up some fancy tropical drinks and watching all the beautiful women wearing next to nothing."

"I'll bet Linda remembers that, too... I mean, you watching the bikinis!" Ben started to snicker.

"Give me a break, Ben old buddy. We were still on good terms back then. Anyway, I'm just trying to tell you what a nice place it is. And now you've got me more envious than ever!"

"I believe you. I only wish I had some time to enjoy the sights."

As they entered the restaurant, a hostess seated the two next to a window overlooking the busy tarmac outside. An army of baggage handlers, mechanics, security personnel, caterers, and other assorted attendants darted everywhere, busily servicing the endless array of aircraft constantly coming and going.

"Why don't you order breakfast, Stosh. Leading the life of the confirmed bachelor must result in a rather unexciting, helter-skelter diet. Seeing as how I got you to fight the morning traffic to meet me here, the least I can do is fill up that belly of yours."

"Don't kid yourself about the diet. Not having anyone around the house leaves me a lot of time to perfect my culinary skills. You'd be surprised at some of my exotic creations. After all, how do you think I've been so successful in developing this?" He patted his rather ample belly. "But nonetheless, if it really helps relieve any of your well-deserved guilt about leaving your old buddy behind here in this freezing hellhole we call Chicago, I'll take you up on the breakfast."

Both men briefly reviewed the menu and ordered their meal. As the waitress scurried off, Ben reached into his bag and pulled out a plastic case smaller than a standard notebook, but less than an inch thick. He held the matte-black case in front of him, it's sleek finish interrupted only by a small, green light blinking steadily in one corner. "This is it, Stosher." His face beamed with genuine enthusiasm.

"That's the miraculous gadget? Some kind of little laptop, huh?"

"Well, it's not really a laptop the way you're thinking, but it IS miraculous — the Alpha-Max 2000! This baby has more capacity than a hundred-thousand-dollar mainframe did only a few years ago — almost a terabyte of memory and pushing a thousand MIPS if that means anything to you."

"Tera-what? Honestly, it really doesn't mean jack to me. I only use a computer to word process reports, and that's about it. But it sure sounds impressive as all hell! Now, if the thing could only talk." Stosh laughed at the thought.

"Man, this is way more than a computer…" Ben turned to see that no one was within earshot. "…it's actually a computer inside of a phone." Ben set the shiny device on the table between them and tapped its surface. A female voice spoke in perfectly clear English, "You have twelve new messages, Mister Decker, but none of them are marked urgent or personal. Would you like me to respond to them for you?"

Ben looked up from the device enough to catch his friend's startled look. He spoke in an even tone to the piece of plastic as though he were speaking to another person sitting at the table. "Ah, yes, Alpha. I'd appreciate that. Keep monitoring messages for me and — unless there is an emergency — don't bother me until we get to Honolulu."

"Certainly, Mister Decker."

Ben tapped at the gadget again and lifted it in his hand. He looked across the table at his friend, slowly waving the Alpha-Max 2000 at him. "This little baby only weighs about half a pound. As you can see under this flap that there is a small keyboard, but she understands

English as well as you or I can speak it. She'll even read all my messages to me and take dictation for responses."

"How'd it know you had messages? I didn't see you call anyone?"

"That's the beauty of it, Stosher — the Alpha-Max 2000 is ALWAYS online. There is a built-in antenna, and we swung a deal with Tel-Fleet International."

"TFI? You mean the phone giant?"

"Yep. You could be anywhere on the planet and this little computer – actually, a telephone-computer – is in constant communications with the Internet."

"A telephone-computer?"

"Yep… she makes phone calls, too… phone calls, e-mail, notes, spreadsheets…"

"Holy shit!" Stosh's eyes went wide. "But… but it… SHE said SHE would respond…"

"Beautiful, isn't it? Once she's set up properly, Alpha can respond to routine messages without any guidance. I mean to respond to simple stuff. You know — requests for information, schedule changes, meeting arrangements — that sort of stuff."

"You keep calling it SHE?" Stosh was quite overwhelmed with an amazing piece of hardware. "It's not a… not a person, Ben."

"No, no — you're quite right. But I'll tell you this, she'll rapidly be thought of that way. This is state-of-the-art as far as artificial intelligence goes. All these decades, everyone was waiting for a robot that had arms and legs and looked like some tin beast out of the old sci-fi movies, and along comes Alpha-Max 2000. For those who like, SHE could easily be a HE. It's all a matter of programming." Ben flushed with pride as he spoke of his innovative creation.

"Damn!" Stosh rocked his head from side to side. "I'm sure that the finer details of your miraculous piece of electronics are way beyond my meager brain, but I know you've really come up with a winner. I mean, how many guys get the kind of national exposure you got in that piece on you in *NEWSWEEK MAGAZINE* last week. Now I know why you didn't want to tell them all the amazing details! Right on — my old college crony making the big time!" Stosh raised his clenched fist into the air to punctuate his praise.

"Yeah, well thanks. We did get some good ink there, and I appreciate your compliment. But with any luck, it's this trip that will really make or break it. What happens this week in the Islands will be very critical to our marketing plans. We've got a whole advance team out in Honolulu right now, setting up the groundwork and making the contacts. We're trying to swing a contract with a Korean firm to jointly produce them. Hey, we're talking some big bucks here — BIG BUCKS — upwards of something like a million units."

"Whoa! A million of these babies!" He extended his hand and gently touched the case of the computer-phone. "They've got to cost a fortune. Hell — how much will one of them go for?"

"You're going to be surprised… On a million units, we can get the retail price down somewhere around nine or ten grand!"

"I guess you're talking some major bucks here, old buddy." Stosh's finger flicked in the air as if he were manipulating some invisible abacus. "Whoa! You're talking into the BILLIONS here. Are you sure you don't need a social worker on this Hawaiian venture of yours?"

"Sorry, Stosh, but I don't really need a social worker. What I really DO need is a couple of months off — a real vacation. And in light of my personal life lately, I could also probably use the services of a good shrink."

"I've been telling you you've needed mental help since I've known you." Stosh's smile reached from ear to ear.

"But regrettably, my friend, at last, I actually agree with you."

A serious expression flooded across Stosh's face. "Hey, wait a minute here — you're serious, aren't you? By god, I think I detect something less than total satisfaction, old man. You're supposed to be at the peak of your career — on the top of the capitalistic heap, so to speak. Out of all our friends back in college, you've become the epitome of — please forgive me — the yuppie supreme. For crying out loud, you're right on the verge of being FILTHY rich…"

"Yeah, yeah, I know. That's what I keep telling myself. But believe it or not, it doesn't seem to help any. I guess money isn't all it's cracked up to be."

"It isn't, huh? Well shit — I'd like to find THAT out on my own! But you sure as hell know that no shrink will help you with over-work. You've simply got to slow down some."

"Oh, it's more... more than that — more personal. It's just that... Well... um..."

"Is it Emily?"

"I'm not saying it's all Emily. I mean, I'm not convinced that it's her fault. Hey, we BOTH decided to get married, after all. But god knows we certainly have had a breakdown in our relationship these past several years. Oh, you know... It involves the whole communication thing or — more specifically — the lack of it. We really don't talk about much that really matters anymore. And I've been determined to look at myself first — if there's something I can do to make it better."

"And?"

"And so far, I haven't come up with any bright ideas." Ben stopped waving the Alpha-Max 2000 and slipped it back into his carry-on bag.

"Is it nasty?"

"Nasty? Well no, not really nasty — at least not in any outward sort of way. We just don't see each other much at all anymore. Oh, we're basically humane to each other and only occasionally have any kind of major battles." Ben soaked up some egg yolk with his toast and downed it with a mouthful of coffee. "Talk about your damned-if-you-do, damned-if-you-don't scenario... When I was starting out and not earning much cash right after we got out of college, Emily always pissed and groaned about her having to work to help fill out the monthly budget. So wouldn't you know it — at last we pretty much have more money than either one of us ever dreamed possible, and now I just don't have enough time to be around the house anymore. And when I am there, she's not."

"Boy, ain't that everyone's problem — you either have the time with no money or the money with no time. But I can't believe you folks don't arrange to spend some quality time together? I mean nights, weekends..."

"Quality time! Sounds like some social worker's buzz word to me. Hell, I'd take ANY kind of time. I don't know what it is, Stosh, but lately — oh, the past few months in particular — Emily never seems to be around anymore. I've already confessed to my busy schedule, but — despite it all — I still make it a point to be around as much as possible. But she's got meetings for this and trips for that. It seems that just when I think I've finally set us on the proverbial easy street, there's no more US to enjoy it together. I mean, we don't even make love to each other anymore."

"Aw man, now that's REALLY nasty! Once Linda and I got into that damned asexual stage, we both knew it was time to say *adios amigo*. That's like owning a cow that you can't milk."

"Good one, Stosh. You have such a way with words. Any women's group worth its weight would have you locked up if they heard you make a statement like that."

Stosh dropped his head and, for a split second, nearly looked remorseful. "Well, I only meant... Oh shit — you know what I meant! So, are you seeing anyone else?"

"Oh come on, Stosh. You've known me longer than that. I'm a one-woman man, my friend — plain, old, monotonous monogamy to the extreme. I'm telling you, I still love Emily. But it's getting harder and harder for me to really LIKE her — to put up with the hurt. Lately, I've actually become more and more convinced that she's the one who is."

"Is? Wait a minute here, Ben — you're losing me. She's the one who is WHAT?"

"Seeing someone. Just a pile of circumstantial evidence — a lot of wrong numbers, unexpected weekend trips, late nights at school. I don't want to seem paranoid, but when I really think about it, I guess it's almost obvious what's going on. Yet as stupid as it sounds, I go out of my way NOT to think about it. I really don't want to find anything out — you know — to damage my ideals, my ego... I made my commitment twenty-some years ago and, to me anyway, that commitment is for life. I don't want another relationship, another woman."

Stosh was shaking his head. "Boy oh boy, that's old Benjamin Decker, ain't it? Your loyalty-to-the-extreme always was both your biggest strength AND your greatest weakness. This sure doesn't sound too good to me."

"I guess you can say that again, my friend, because it sure as hell isn't any too good at all."

"When I last talked to you at Christmas, I sort of figured something wasn't quite right between you two, but I never thought things had deteriorated this far."

"Well, they sure have."

"And the girls."

"I'm keeping my fingers crossed, but so far, all's okay with them. To this point, both Lisa and Bonnie are doing just fine."

"Do they know?"

"Oh, I'm sure they know that something's not just right, but I don't believe either one has any idea of just how much the relationship has disintegrated. I pray to god that they're old enough to deal with whatever winds up happening." Ben put his coffee cup down and grabbed the check as soon as the waitress appeared with it. He quickly glanced at the numbers and then reached for his wallet.

"So, what are you going to do?"

"I don't know, Stosh — I just don't know. By both interest and training, I'm an engineer. And an engineer tends to approach a problem from as logical a standpoint as possible — survey all the parameters, consider and test all options, and then make a rational decision and stick with it. And yet..."

"But for god's sake, Ben! We're not talking about designing some new circuit or building some new gadget here. Wake up, man! Can you try lightening up on that damned left-hemisphere-thinking-pattern of yours for a change! This is your wife we're talking about here."

"Stosh, Stosh, Stosh — slow down a second. That's my point exactly. Give me a little bit of credit here, will you? I fully realize that all the logic in the universe doesn't seem to mean a hill of beans in this situation. My gut response was to intellectualize my emotions, but that sure didn't prove successful. So, I guess my next line of defense has been to try to lose myself in my work. Well, I've sure been putting in long days lately, but as a therapy, it really sucks and has proven quite useless. In short, good buddy, I'm really lost as to just what to do, and I feel more depressed than ever."

"Oh boy..." Stosh shook his head from side to side. "I wish I could help you — tell you what to do. But hell, I ain't your shrink — just your friend... Maybe you two should just make it a point to chuck your busy schedules and go away together. I mean, go to some isolated, romantic spot in which just you and Emily could be alone together and maybe try to work this thing out."

"I practically begged Emily to come along to Hawaii — to spend a week or two hiding out on one of the neighbor islands together as soon as the convention is over. I mean shit — you'd think anyone would jump at the chance to mellow out a bit in paradise. But she just didn't want to hear about it — too many responsibilities to the rest of the world! You know — thanks, but no thanks."

"Sounds like a real bummer... So now what?"

"Who knows? Life goes on... I guess... I think I'm going to try to lose myself in a bundle of money and..."

Stosh was shaking his head. "It ain't gonna work — I can save you a whole lot of trouble and tell you that right here and now. That capitalism shit may work for some folks — at least in the short run — but I know you better than that, Ben... And I'm telling you that when you're dealing with matters of the heart, it just ain't gonna work. "

"Oh, I know you're right, but what the hell am I going to do? Look, believe me — the money's going to be there. The Alpha-Max 2000 will at least assure me of that." Ben placed several folded bills in the center of the table as a tip and glanced at his wristwatch. "Damn! I just got here." He stood, slung his flight bag over his shoulder, and looked at the numbers scrawled on his boarding pass. "Well, I guess I'd better be finding this departure gate."

Stosh looked up at his friend, almost in shock. "I'm totally at a loss here, my friend. I was so psyched to see you — it's been about three or four years, hasn't it? And in a mere hour-and-a-half of chatting with you, I'm totally bummed out!"

"Aw, man... Look, Stosh, that's not what I wanted to do at all. I'm sorry I got into this whole thing, but I just couldn't help but talk about..."

"Hey — it's okay." He stood and tried to reassure his friend. "What the hell are buddies for? I just wish I could do something."

"You can do something, Stosh."

"And what's that?"

"Just keep being my friend — and stay in touch."

"You too, huh?" A big grin came over Stosh's face. "Like send me a GOOD postcard from paradise, will ya?"

"Preferable with some Island women in scant bikinis on it, right?"

"Yeah, the Island women sound just fine, but you can hold the bikinis!"

5
Thursday, February 4, 1999: 11:50 A.M.

"Our flight time to Honolulu will be approximately eight hours and fifty-two minutes. Captain Bisset has advised me that he will turn off the seat belt indicator just as soon as we reach our cruising altitude."

Ben made himself comfortable in his window seat. He looked out over the big jet engine suspended beneath the wing and watched the brown, mid-western fields below as they receded into smaller and smaller squares, only occasionally interrupted by white pockets of snow. It never failed to amaze him just how flat this part of the country was, and how frigid and desolate it could look — at least at this time of the year. He couldn't help but think that the landscape appropriately matched his spirit right now — cold and dismal...

"...Islands before?"

"Pardon me." Ben blinked his eyes as he realized that the older man seated to his left was speaking to him. "I'm sorry. I must have been dozing... lost in my thoughts for a minute. Never mind me."

"That's perfectly okay. I only asked if you've ever been to the Islands before."

"Well, um... yes. Ur... no. Ur... Well, more precisely, I haven't really been IN Hawaii... I mean to really spend any time there. I've been to Asia — Tokyo, Seoul, Singapore — several times, but I've only flown into and out of Honolulu International — plane changes, you know. I've never actually been out of the airport area. And how about you — is this your first trip?"

"Oh heavens no. The wife and I have been making the trip just as often as we've been able to — since back in 1969. That's when we discovered the Islands." Giving absolutely no credit to either the early Polynesians or to Captain Cook, the older man proudly nodded at his lady companion. "Of course, now that we're retired and have more time, it's so much easier to travel. We just love Hawaii."

The smiling, gray-haired lady seated next to the aisle not-so-discreetly nudged her spouse with an elbow. "Ah sure... Sorry... I mean, um... I'm Martin... My name's Martin Penrose." He offered his hand to Ben. "This here is the wife, Betty Jo."

"I'm very glad to meet you, Martin. And you too, Betty Jo." He tipped his head towards the older lady. "I'm Benjamin Decker."

The motherly lady leaned forward and spoke up. "Surely you're not going on vacation all alone young man — are you?"

"Ah, yes... I'm afraid so. Ah... well, I mean, you're half right. I'm traveling by myself, but regrettably, this won't be much of a vacation. I'm on a business trip, actually."

"A business trip? Oh my... business in Hawaii... Whatever could that be? Your business, I mean?"

"Electronics. I'm making a presentation at an electronics convention in Honolulu. I'm an electrical engineer. You know — we design computers and what-not."

"How about that! They're everywhere! Even Dinghoffer is getting into that stuff now and, believe you me, they..."

"Pardon me?" Ben was totally lost by the old man's babblings. "I'm not familiar with any — um... was it Dinghoffer?"

"Oh sure — I'm sorry. That's Dinghoffer Dairy — the largest dairy processing plant in Milwaukee — actually, in Wisconsin. I spent forty-two years working there — made foreman on the pasteurization line for the last eighteen. They keep plugging in more and more computers and fancy-schmancy robot gadgets on all their lines. As I was saying, they even have computers now whose sole purpose is to check up on other computers. Ain't that just something else? Yeah, you computer fellows sure have changed the world these past several decades."

"Well, I'm not so sure we deserve all the credit — or blame, for that matter — but you're certainly right in saying just how much the world has been changing lately."

Ben was relieved when a pretty flight attendant mercifully interrupted the conversation and leaned over the three travelers. "Would any of you care for a cocktail, soft drink, any type of refreshment before our dinner service begins?"

Martin looked first at the attendant's name badge and then very slowly and deliberately pronounced her name as though he had just uncovered some great secret. "Mo-ni-ca. Good afternoon, young lady. Me and the Misses here will have a couple of them there fancy Mai Tai drinks." Betty Jo, silently maintaining her perpetual smile, nodded her approval at her husband's choice.

"And you, sir."

Ben couldn't help but notice the close resemblance of her short, brushed back blond hair to that of his own Lisa. Though longer hair was much more to his personal liking, he was constantly reminded by his two teenaged daughters that nowadays, the unisex look was THE style. "Could I have some sort of diet cola, please?"

"Why, of course. Here are our dinner menus. I'll be back in just a few moments to give you your drinks and to take your orders."

Ben selected the teriyaki chicken dinner, garnished with pineapple and papaya, and served with rice and vegetables. It proved to be typical airline fare — suitable to sustain life, but nothing at all to write home about. As hard as he tried, he had little or no success at diplomatically dodging much of the rambling conversation with the Penroses. They both certainly seemed to be nice enough people, but they simply never wanted to stop talking.

He decided to burn their names forever into his memory so that the next time he was in Wisconsin, he could be sure to avoid them.

At last, he actually welcomed the flight attendant's intrusion when she requested that all the window shades be lowered so that the in-flight movie could be shown. Though the last thing in the entire world that he wanted to do was to watch some overly boring, feature-length soap opera, Ben found himself putting on his set of earphones in self-defense. The movie proved to be quite the sedative, and he rapidly drifted off to sleep.

* * *

"...of you on the left side of our aircraft should just be able to make out the snow-covered summits of Mauna Kea and Mauna Loa on the Island of Hawaii — also known as the Big Island to residents. We will be landing in Honolulu on the Island of Oahu in about forty minutes. Our flight attendants will be around shortly to help you prepare for our arrival."

"I see you finally woke up, Benjamin." Martin finished wrapping up his earphones and tucked them into the seat pocket in front of him. "Well obviously, the movie didn't appeal much to you. I don't believe I ever saw anyone sleep so soundly in an airplane seat before."

Ben arched his back, stretched his arms, and let out a sigh. "You can surely say that again. I usually can't sleep for beans on a plane, but I've got to admit that that movie certainly did it for me — put me right out cold, just like a baby. Of course, now I'll really pay for it with a sore neck." Ben rubbed his neck hard, trying to exorcize the painful crimp that had developed during his nap.

"You need your rest, young man." Betty Jo leaned forward to make herself visible. "I used to always point out to my kids that when your body needs rest, it'll surely tell you so by making you sleepy. So like I said, you must have needed it. And by the way, you really didn't miss a thing — the movie really was lousy — simply awful."

"Well, that's good to know."

"Yeah, they just don't make movies anymore the way they used to. And now that the Japanese have even bought most of Hollywood, who knows where it will all end?"

Ben began to stand. "I don't mean to interrupt, but if you'll please excuse me, I'd better make a trip to the restroom before we prepare to land."

He stood but had to pause momentarily right in front of Betty Jo while waiting for two flight attendants to slowly make their way up the aisle, collecting an assortment of plastic cups, cellophane wrappers, and paper napkins. As he glanced toward the back of the wide-body plane, he was once again struck with amazement at the technological accomplishment of a jumbo jet. No matter how frequently he flew — and lately, that had been quite often — he simply couldn't help but marvel at the miracle of such a huge aircraft even getting off the ground. He finally made his way down the aisle and took his place in the short line of passengers waiting to use the lavatories. Surveying the mix of people proved fascinating. The milieu of colors and cultures were quite evident, but the overwhelming majority fell into one of two general categories — mainlanders going on vacation and local Islanders returning home.

He felt a bump of air turbulence as the intercom briefly hissed to life. There were a few seconds of barely audible static, and then just as quickly, the speakers went silent again. Finally, the crackle returned as a female voice spoke her practiced message. "Please notice that the captain has turned on the seat belt sign. Would all passengers please return to your seats at this time and prepare for our arrival." An attendant stooping down and stowing food trays in the galley right next to Ben looked up at him. "Oh, go ahead. You're the last one in line there. You still have a little time, but you'd better hurry."

"Thanks. I'll only be a minute." Ben heard the latch on the lavatory door begin to open just as his attention was caught by the profile of a beautiful island woman reaching into an overhead rack several rows in front of his position. He couldn't help but think of just how beautiful so many of the Polynesian people are, especially the women — this woman. Chauvinistic? He smiled to himself as he contemplated what Emily's reaction would be if she could only read his thoughts right now. He quite innocently and unconsciously continued to stare at the woman closed the bin and turned to sit down. ZAP! Time seemed to stop! As swiftly and surely as a lightning bolt, her eyes made solid, almost physical contact with Ben's. Her gaze unexpectedly jolted his entire being. At once he found himself paralyzed by — immersed in — an eerie, mystical encounter as her eyes studied him, captivated him, peered deep into his soul. But how could a mere glance penetrate so deeply his inner self? He was suddenly dizzy — overpowered by an acute feeling of *déjà vu* — and yet, *déjà vu* about what? Surely, he had never met her before. But he felt a... a what? A closeness? A bond? He somehow KNEW their lives were connected... but how?

He wanted his vision to linger, but just as suddenly as she had appeared, she was gone. Where? Did she sit down? Disappear? Had she really ever been there at all? Though he didn't at first realize it, he now became aware of the fact that he had been so enamored by her eyes that he couldn't even look enough beyond them to see the rest of her face. He simply HAD to walk past her seat to see if...

"Sorry, but you'll have to hurry, sir. We'll be landing in about ten minutes, and you have to get back to your seat. The captain is expecting some rather bumpy flying up ahead. Do you need any help? Are you all right, sir? Sir?"

The trance was snapped. His initial reaction was to resist the attendant's unwelcome intrusion into his — his what? Was this some sort of spiritual encounter? A psychic experience? A dream? Whatever it was, he wished he hadn't been yanked back to reality so quickly. But just as he considered his response, he heard a loud bang, and the plane began a wild, rhythmic vibration. Ben grabbed for the bulkhead in an attempt to steady himself, but almost immediately, the aircraft dropped and rolled to one side. He had been shaken by air pockets before, but never quite as severe as this one. The plane once again shook fiercely, eliciting several cries of panic from a disbelieving load of fellow passengers. He inadvertently looked up in response to the screams. Funny how some people react so frantically to what he was certain was merely a little bit of turbulent air. His thoughts began to return to her eyes. He swore he was connected to her eyes in some mystic...

BAM!!!

The whole craft shuddered furiously once again. As much as he wanted his thoughts to linger on those eyes, the circumstances simply wouldn't allow it. The big jet pitched to one side and rolled savagely back to the other, violently tossing its passengers about. Aw damn, he thought, talk about going from a fantastic dream to terrible nightmare in a split second. Please tell me the whole goddamned plane isn't going down! His knuckles strained white as he held onto the bulkhead with all his strength. Aw holy shit! Where's a safety belt now that he needed one? The rhythmic vibration grew stronger and stronger until, at last, a surge of terror flooded through his entire being. Was there any chance at all that the plane could withstand such force?

BAM!!!

Another loud bang shook the aircraft, and he sensed that he was lurching out of control toward the corner of the galley wall. He was aware of falling, but there was absolutely nothing he could do to prevent the impact. He automatically threw his hands in front of his face in an attempt to soften the blow, and yet he somehow knew that his effort was totally in vain...

* * *

"Mister Decker, are you okay? Mister Decker?" His head slowly moved back and forth as though he were trying out his neck muscles all over again. "Are you all right? We must have just hit an air pocket, and you really bumped your head here — you'll be all right." The woman was rubbing his head where he had hit it against the corner of the bulkhead.

Ben opened his eyes to see the attendant looking at him with deep concern on her face. He recognized her face, only something just wasn't quite right. He slowly looked around the plane. "Um... yeah — I'm okay... Ah... at least I think so, anyway..."

Ben studied her face. He was certain that she was the same attendant. Wasn't her name Monica? But now her blond hair was not in its same, short, punk rock style. It had been redone much longer, much straighter. It was shoulder-length and curled under at the ends, topped by an old-fashioned flight attendant's cap. Oh, come on! She simply couldn't have grown hair that fast. Aha — a wig! It must be a wig he told himself... or another stewardess? He visually searched for her nametag and read it aloud, "Monica?"

"Yes, sir — that's me. Are you sure you are all right? Are you feeling a little better?"

"But your hair..." He again shook his head from side to side. "Wasn't your hair shorter, much shorter? A different style, maybe?"

"No, no, Mister Decker. Look, let's not worry about my hair just now, sir. It's been this way for years. Now you just bumped your head here..." She extended her hand towards a metal serving cart next to the bulkhead. "...but I'm sure you're going to be all right. Here now, let me help you get back to your place."

The stewardess stooped down next to him to help him to his feet. Ben couldn't help but notice the old style, seamed nylons the young lady was wearing. As he rubbed his neck and began to take in his surroundings, he felt a surge of panic flush into his consciousness. "Hey — wait a minute! What is this? Something's terribly wrong here! Look, I'm telling you something's just not right!"

"Now, now — come on, Mister Decker. There'll be time for all that when we get into Honolulu. Let's just get you buckled up back in your seat."

As the two made their way down the aisle, Ben was very conscious of everyone watching him. But he was just as aware of the fact that the whole setting was wrong — all wrong. The cabin was small — much smaller than the jumbo jet he knew he was on — or had been on... And the noise was wrong — louder and different from that of the 747. Monica helped him into his spot, but it was obvious that that wasn't correct, either. There were only two seats on either side of the single, central aisle — not at all like the three-aisle-four-aisle-three configuration of the jumbo jet. And it appeared that no one was seated right next to him.

"Where are the Penroses?"

"Who, sir? The Pembrokes?"

"No, no — the Penroses — ur, Martin and Betty Jo, I believe. They were sitting right here next to me."

"You must be mistaken, Mister Decker. You were seated here all by yourself. We only have seventy-five passengers on board today, and we have no one by the name of Penrose — or Pembroke, for that matter."

Ben thought he'd never have wished to see the Penroses again, but he realized how quickly one's mind could change. He rubbed the small bump on his head again and looked out of the window. "Oh my god! That's simply not possible!"

"Not possible? What is it now?"

"The engines... they're... they're props..." Ben pointed at the two propellers spinning outside of his window. "This is a jumbo jet — I'm telling you we left Chicago on a jumbo jet!"

"A jumbo jet? Chicago? Well, I never heard of such a thing as a jumbo jet. Jets — sure... We're supposed to start flying jets in another year or so, but this is the pride of our fleet right now, sir. This is a Pan American Airways Constellation — Flight 511 out of San Francisco."

"I know I must be sounding totally crazy to you right now, but believe me, something's just not right here. I mean, like this has got to be a bad dream or something!"

"Look, sir, as soon as we land in Honolulu — and that will only be another hour or so — we'll get you to see a doctor, pronto. As a matter of fact, I can have the pilot radio ahead so that when we land, they..."

"No, no, no... um... Look, Monica, I'm all right — just a little shook up from the jolt to the head, you know." He was still massaging his bump. "Just let me get my wits about me here, and I'm sure I'll be as good as new by the time we land."

"How about aspirin — would you like a couple of aspirin?"

"Um... Do you have any ibuprofen?"

"What?"

"Ibupro... Um... Yeah, some aspirin would be just fine, thank you." The stewardess hurried off down the aisle as Ben tried desperately to collect his wits. A cabin of this vintage had to be thirty-five or forty years old — and yet it was brand new! The wide lapels on his coat offered discerning evidence that he didn't even have his own clothes on anymore. None of this could really be happening — could it?

The pretty attendant returned, holding a small tray with two aspirin and a paper cup filled with water. He threw the pills into his mouth, took a gulp of water, and swallowed them down. "Thanks — I really appreciate it. By the way, this still is Thursday, February the fourth, isn't it?"

The flight attendant's smile never left her face, but a look of concern became increasingly evident. "Of course it's February, Mister Decker, but... it's Thursday the seventh."

He smiled. He NEW it was the fourth because he had entered the date on the Alpha-Max 2000 several times today. Something very strange had happened, and he wanted to call as little attention to that as he could. "Of course... right... I'm... I'm just trying to get my bearings here. The bump really knocked me silly for a minute." He once again reached for his head.

Monica returned his smile. "Don't you worry, Mister Decker. Travel always seems to do that to people, and you know, I mean, it's a long way to the Islands. A little bump on your head can make you lose consciousness for a while, but look at the bright side of things — just how much time could you actually lose?"

6

Thursday, February 7, 1957: 3:15 P. M.

The fog had cleared from Ben's head, but he was still just as confused as ever about exactly what had happened to him. For the past twenty minutes, he had been quietly sitting in his seat, observing his unfamiliar surroundings, and getting lost in his thoughts. If he didn't know better, he could be easily convinced that he had somehow been thrown back in time. No way! All the end-of-the-world tabloid stories withstanding, he just couldn't buy into that sort of ridiculous thing. Hell, he was an engineer and was well aware of the fact that that just couldn't happen — absolutely could NOT happen! Actually, the more he considered the back-in-time option from the scientific point of view, he reminded himself that it was just downright, flat out impossible! Okay, chuck that alternative. But there still must be some logical explanation to this whole fiasco.

Could it be some elaborate hoax? Maybe this plane was some wealthy antique buff's idea of a good time. Or maybe it could be another one of those nostalgic, back-to-the-past events arranged like some sort of publicity stunt? But this entire setting — right down to the hairdos, the clothing, and the pillbox hats — all fit in with some bygone era. Whoever did this must have spent some really big bucks — BIG BUCKS — to pull off such an elaborate charade! It simply had to be something like that — some perfectly logical explanation. Of course, he still couldn't fathom what happened to the 747 he had been on. After all, he wasn't living in some sort of cheap, grade-B science fiction flick. A several hundred-ton jumbo jet couldn't just disappear into thin air. All right, Ben told himself, I'll just sit back and enjoy this wild caper while it lasts — eventually answers will come.

"We'll be landing in Honolulu in a short while. Please tighten your seat belts and make sure your cigarettes are properly disposed of in the ashtrays." The throbbing, rhythmic whine of the gasoline-driven propellers offered a much louder background noise with which the static-laden intercom had to compete. The stewardesses quickly patrolled the aisles, checking seat belts and passing out small packages of Chiclets.

Monica handed him his pack of chewing gum. "Here you are. Why don't you chew this, Mister Decker? It'll help keep your ears from popping."

Keep his ears from popping! Ben could easily sense the plane's rapid descent and now realized that he had been unconsciously holding his nose and blowing out to relieve the pressure as it built up in his middle ear. This was getting weirder and weirder! He finally spotted the first point of land from his window. That had to be Oahu, he told himself. Well, he would be the first to admit to his lack of expertise on the geography of the late-1990's Honolulu, but he had flown through here often enough to know approximately what the island should look like.

"Those of you on the right side of our aircraft can now see the windward side of the Island of Oahu coming into view below. Oahu is known as the Gathering Place and has the largest population of all the..." The attendant went on with her background data on the Islands. Ben unconsciously tuned her out since he had heard the spiel many times before.

He stayed glued to his window and concentrated on the unfolding landscape below. He could recognize the familiar greenness of the 'wet' side of the island, but he could spot little else of consequence to either confirm or deny this silly notion of somehow being in a different time. The land grew nearer and nearer until it nearly filled his field of view. The pilot trimmed their flight path until they were flying right along the shoreline towards Koko Head Crater. As the crater came into sight, he had an expansive view along the green, windward coast. The weather was quite clear with only puffy, white cumulus clouds hugging the tops of one of the two main mountain ranges that formed the island. He began to feel a bit queasy in his stomach as, no matter how hard he tried, he simply couldn't make out any of the scores of subdivisions and condominium complexes he knew had to be down there — somewhere. The urban sprawl had spilled into this area of Oahu decades ago.

The plane finally banked steeply to the right, revealing the impressive vista of Diamond Head in the foreground with the city of Honolulu stretched out behind, squeezed between the beautifully folded, emerald-green mountains on one side and the azure-blue Pacific on the other. Ben swallowed hard — the skyscrapers and freeways of the Honolulu he had seen from the air twenty times before were simply not there. Waikiki beach appeared nearly barren with only a handful of low-rise hotels perched on her white sands. He squinted to see what he wanted to see so badly. But no matter how hard he tried to see the Honolulu he knew, it was nowhere to be seen. It was quite obvious to him that something was terribly, terribly wrong.

"Please prepare for landing. We ask that you keep your belts fastened until we are completely stopped in front of the terminal."

As they flew near the center of the city, Aloha Tower stood out quite prominently with two rather large passenger liners docked at the pier right next to it. At least the downtown area itself was quite built up and obviously an urban center, but the low heights of the buildings remained conspicuously telling to Ben. Where did all the skyscrapers go?

The Lockheed Constellation circled over Pearl Harbor and banked back towards Diamond Head once again. No condominiums, no expressways, no Aloha Stadium! A startled Benjamin Decker maintained his watch out of the window as the plane continued its full flaps down descent until it finally touched down to a perfectly smooth, uneventful landing. The airliner taxied towards a quite modest, old-style wooden terminal building. He could see a portable stairway being pushed into place by two men of obvious Polynesian ancestry. Again, the stewardess spoke over the loudspeaker. "Thank you for flying on Pan American Airways. We ask you to fly with us again and hope you have a pleasant stay in the Territory of Hawaii."

PART TWO

"Hawaii is not a state of mind, but a state of grace."

— Paul Theroux

7

Thursday, February 7, 1957: 3:40 P.M.

As Ben stepped out onto the portable stairway, a fresh, gusty trade wind and a warm, tropical sun heartened him at once. He couldn't help but think that if this were merely a dream, the illusion certainly was pleasant enough. On his way down the ramp, he looked intensely for any telltale evidence that would punch a hole in the back-in-time scenario, but if such confirmation existed, it certainly wasn't very conspicuous. He was impressed by a wide array of old trucks, autos, and other maintenance vehicles, all scurrying about the tarmac to service an assortment of seemingly antique propeller-driven aircraft. His uneducated eye estimated that the newest piece of equipment within eyesight had to be at least thirty-five or forty-some years old.

Ben bounded off the bottom of the stairway and followed the line of disembarking passengers into the terminal building. He was overwhelmed by the sweet fragrance of countless flowers making up the beautiful leis being draped over many of the travelers' heads. A large wooden sign announced, 'ALOHA AND WELCOME TO THE TERRITORY OF HAWAII' and was signed 'Governor King'. He assumed the flow of passengers would eventually lead to the baggage area, and, in a shorter time than he predicted, his hunch proved correct.

An empty wooden bench offered as good a place as any to sit and attempt to collect his sanity while awaiting the luggage truck. He was more tired from the trip than he thought he would be, feeling as though he had been flying for days. He delighted in the fact that the bump on his head was nearly gone already, and he no longer felt any pain at all, just utter fatigue. Considering his exhausted state, Ben knew he simply had to take a nap before he made any decisions before he tried to face this problem head-on.

Ben placed his carry-on bag up on the bench right next to where he was seated and reached inside to find his baggage stubs. The ticket folder was right where he had put it back in Chicago, only to his bewilderment, the logo on it had been somehow transformed from its original United Airlines imprint to that of Pan American Airways. Upon a quick inspection of the ticket, it became quite apparent that it was a handwritten edition as opposed to his original computer printout version. And the price read $408 for the round trip. That simply was not correct — just flat out impossible! There was no doubt at all about the price. The $732 figure had been forever fixed in Ben's memory after the hassle he had to go through with a new hire in accounting before she finally realized who Ben was. Really — did she actually think this was going to be some sort of pleasure trip? Her boss knew damned well that he was making the trip for the sole purpose of selling the latest breakthrough in electronics, the Alpha-Max 2000. Now that his frazzled mind thought about it again, just who the hell was over in accounting, anyway? It must be Johnson — Karl Johnson. Well, he should make damned sure his new hires were aware of...

DAMN! THE COMPUTER-PHONE! The Alpha-Max 2000!

Ben immediately reached for his flight bag and zipped it wide open. The computer-phone just HAD to be in here somewhere! He reached in and hastily fumbled through his belongings — no Alpha-Max 2000! Holy shit! He simply couldn't have lost it — no way! The bag had been with him the entire time — except when he went to the restroom just before he hit his head. Maybe he should call the office. Of course — but wait, what time must it be back there? He glanced at his wristwatch. Oh wow — they got that too! His digital watch had been replaced with an old, wind-up, analog model. He finally noticed that even his bag was different — an older, all-leather model. Whoever was responsible for this had certainly been quite thorough up to this point. The whole thing reminded him of a plot from that old television series — the one where each week the stars created some very elaborate, high-tech hoax to trick a designated stooge into doing exactly what they wanted. Um...

wasn't it called *"Mission Impossible"*? Sure, that had to be it. He pondered the puzzle pieces — the Penroses suddenly gone, the missing Alpha-Max 2000, the convenient bump on the head... Yeah — that was exactly what he was involved in here — some sinister industrial espionage caper arranged to steal the Alpha-Max 2000!

Ben's train of thought was interrupted by the arrival of a small truck pulling three trailers loaded with suitcases and other assorted cargo. The crowd began to thin as people picked out and unloaded their baggage right from the carts. The more Ben considered it, he wasn't at all certain if the rest of his luggage would still look the same as it did back in Philly. His question wasn't answered for several minutes until most of the bags had been claimed. He began to check the nametags of each remaining bag one by one until he finally came across two side-by-side, monogrammed suitcases with his name on them. Ben grabbed the handle and then picked the first one up, casually setting it on the floor next to where he stood. As he reached for his second bag, a rather anxious looking, middle-aged man dressed in a dismally bland, dark-colored suit literally yanked the bag right out of Ben's grasp.

Ben was quite surprised and shouted at the stranger. "HEY, WAIT A MINUTE! That's MY bag you've got there." Ben reached to reclaim his bag.

"But initials are mine..." The man's English was broken, and his accent quite thick. He used his pointed finger to indicate the monogrammed initials BND inscribed just next to the handles.

"Hey, look — I'm really sorry, but there's some sort of mix up here." Ben at once began to fumble for his ticket folder to locate his luggage check stubs.

The aggressive character already had his stub out and, leaning over and checking the suitcase's tag, glared up at Ben. "Pardon, sir. I seem to have... have a mistake here." The voice was quite deep in pitch and anxious tone. Ben couldn't exactly place the accent but was fairly certain it sounded as though it had an Eastern European origin. The stranger released Ben's piece of luggage and pulled another, similar-looking bag from the mostly emptied cart. He nervously looked around as if he were checking to see who was watching and then quickly disappeared into the crowd of passengers looking for their bags. Ben couldn't help but think that anyone dressed in such a dull, baggy, brown suit seemed incredibly out of place here amidst all the brightly colored aloha wear. This guy couldn't be a tourist, could he? Ben slowly shook his head. No matter where he traveled, he was time and again reminded of the fact that it surely does take all kinds! He gathered his belongings and made his way through the busy loading area and out towards the curb.

"Taxi! Taxi!"

Ben spotted a short, man with Asian features standing next to his open cab door. The driver surveyed the crowd of arrivals, trying to find a fare. His eyes finally made contact with Ben's. "Taxi, sir?"

"Yeah, sure — can you get me into Waikiki!"

"You got it. Are these here all the bags ya got?"

"Sure are."

The cabby opened the rear door of the banged-up, seemingly antique Checker cab, and Ben slid into the back seat. The hustle and bustle of the crowded arrival area were immediately overwhelmed by the cab radio as it blared out Elvis Presley singing, *"Love Me Tender".* The driver carried the two bags around to the rear of the vehicle, hoisted them up and into the trunk, and closed the lid. As he got into the front seat and slammed the door behind him, he lowered the volume of the radio and turned around to face Ben. "Aloha! Welcome to Hawaii, sir. This your first trip to the Territory?"

"Um... Territory, huh? Ah, yeah — yeah, it is."

"I don't mean to be nosy, but ya never know. A lot of guys come back here... After the war, I mean — Navy guys, mostly. It's always nice to welcome them back to paradise."

"I can understand that — about being paradise, I mean."

"Well, not today it ain't. It's really windy and not too pleasant of a day. Of course, at least the rain's stopped."

"Oh yeah — did you have a lot of rain lately?"

"God, yes! It's been a really wet winter so far — of course, even more on the other side of the Island than here, but at least it's starting to clear up. Now, if we can get rid of this lousy wind and cold..."

"Cold! This feels just great to me." Ben nearly laughed at the thought of the Hawaiian cabby calling temperatures in the low seventies cold. This was a proverbial heat wave compared to what he had just left behind in Philadelphia yesterday — or was that today?

"So where to?"

"Waikiki."

"Yeah, yeah, but I mean which hotel? You're staying in a hotel, no?"

"Um... Sure... Well, er... I've got reservations at the Hilton Hawaiian Village — Rainbow Towers."

"The Rainbow Towers — no way, man! I mean, I'm sorry to sound so abrupt with you, but no you don't."

"What do you mean, I don't?"

"Must be some sort of mistake. You see, old man Kaiser just — hey, now wait a minute here! You ain't working for him, are ya?"

"For whom?"

"Old man... ur, I should say, Henry... MISTER Kaiser."

"No, no — nothing like that."

"Well, that Hilton Hawaiian Village place just ain't done yet. Oh yeah, they have some cottages over there, but no Rainbow Towers yet. Old man Kaiser ain't supposed to have the place finished enough for guests for a couple of months. Too bad — there are so many tourists here right now we could use the extra space. I got a cousin working construction over there, and he tells me that Kaiser is trying really hard to speed it up — maybe even open one floor at a time."

"Look, Mister... ur, um..." Ben's expression revealed his search for a moniker with which to address the cabby.

"It's Van — just call me Van."

"Okay, Van. Look, I must have been mistaken. My reservation is for the Royal Hawaiian Hotel." Ben was pretending to look in his flight bag as he somehow remembered reading that the Royal Hawaiian was one of the oldest hotels on Waikiki Beach — and the only other one he could remember by name."

"Now that's more like it. Yeah, the old Pink Palace is a very nice place. You'll really enjoy it there. Like I said, it sure is a good thing you got reservations. I'm sure they're all booked up." The cabby turned around and started up the engine. "I'll have you there in twenty-five or thirty minutes." He slowly worked his way into the traffic and headed away from the terminal building.

Ben was fascinated by the cars — every last one of them was from an era long gone by. He felt a nauseous twitch in his stomach as he realized the increasingly unlikely possibility that anyone could pull off such a wide-ranging sham. If this really were some sort of ruse, whoever was staging it was spending many times more money than the Alpha-Max 2000 was worth. They came to a stop at a traffic light, and Ben heard a newsboy hawking the afternoon paper. "Hey Van, would you mind telling him I'll have one of those papers."

"Sure thing, sir." He waved his hand at the child. "Hey Bra — da man like one paper he'a."

The boy handed the paper through Ben's open window. "How much?"

"A dime."

Ben handed the kid a quarter, and the boy started to dig in his coin pouch to find change. "Thanks, son, but that's okay — keep it."

The lad's face lit up as though Ben had given him a hundred-dollar bill. "Hey — thanks a lot, Mister!"

The light turned green, and the cabby pulled out as Ben scanned the front page. The headline was in red — *IKE TAKES STRONG STAND ON SUEZ CANAL CRISIS*. He hesitated at first and then looked up and read the paper's masthead — *THE HONOLULU STAR-BULLETIN*, Thursday, February 7, 1957.

8

Thursday, February 7, 1957: 5:10 P.M.

The cab pulled up in front of the classy, pink hotel. Ben couldn't precisely categorize the architecture, but his first impression convinced him that there must have been some Spanish influence in the original design concept. The grand old palace was quite tastefully adorned with open-air balconies and topped off with an elegant, pink bell tower.

A Chinese doorman opened the back door of the cab before the driver had finished unlocking the trunk. "Aloha, sir, and welcome to the Royal Hawaiian. Let me get a boy over here for those bags."

"Thank you." He slid out of the back seat and was at once captivated by the beauty of the setting. A variety of deep green foliage plants were everywhere, complemented by an endless spectrum of magnificently aromatic tropical blossoms. A sizable flock of gossipy mynah birds dashed and darted about the fronds of a hundred stately coconut palms, jockeying to claim any available roost upon which to spend the rapidly approaching night.

"This is just sensational — so this is the Royal Hawaiian, huh?"

"Yes, sir. She's the finest hotel in all the Territory — all the Pacific!" The doorman unconsciously thrust his chest out with obvious pride.

"How old is this place?"

"We're just celebrating our thirtieth anniversary this month."

After making sure the luggage was stacked on the bellhop's cart, Van walked back to where Ben was standing. "That'll be three dollars and fifty cents, sir."

Ben fished a five-dollar bill from his wallet and handed it to the driver. "Thanks a lot, Van. You've been very helpful."

"Thank you, sir. I hope you have a pleasant visit here in the Territory." He slid back behind the wheel, started the engine, and leaned out of the driver's window as he began to slowly pull away. He looked back at Ben and shouted out loud, "Aloha!"

* * *

"I'm so sorry, Mister Decker. I just don't understand how we could have had such a mix-up." The desk clerk's concern seemed so genuine that Ben was beginning to feel pangs of guilt for insisting that he had a reservation, even though he knew full well that he didn't.

"Do you have any room — any place at all? Even if you know of another hotel that might have something. I simply need a place to sleep."

The clerk scratched his forehead as he intently studied his room register. "Look, please wait here for just a minute. Let me check out a possibility or two for you."

The concerned clerk ducked into an office behind the main desk and pulled the door closed behind him. Ben turned around and leaned on the counter as he surveyed the ornately decorated lobby. Huge crystal chandeliers sparkled and reflected in a series of floor-to-ceiling glass mirrors. Many shades of pink, rose, and burgundy were tastefully mixed to compliment the surroundings. Large floral bouquets consisting of all kinds of cut orchids, anthuriums, ginger, and *ti* leaves were arranged exquisitely in vases set on rose marble-topped tables. A rather brisk trade wind blew through the open-air entrance, down the central corridor, and out over the poolside bar overlooking the world's most beautiful beach. The scurry of employees, local folks, and tourists offered convincing testament to the overflow business the Royal Hawaiian was enjoying.

Again, he swallowed a lump in his throat as he considered the past several hours. Could all this be fake? Antique aircraft, cars, trucks — all this assembled for some unknown, mythical plot to hoodwink him. And the thousands of people he had seen, complete with authentic fifties dress — every last one cast simply to deceive Benjamin Decker. Talk about creating paranoia in someone! This just couldn't be a trick! A scam of this size was much too involved to pull off successfully — wasn't it?

"Mister Decker." The clerk had returned to his window and stirred the would-be guest from his thoughts. As Ben turned back toward the clerk, he detected a more relieved expression on the man's face that at least hinted at some good news. "Mister Decker, I'm happy to inform you that we can at least accommodate you for tonight. We have only one room unoccupied at this point — and it's one of our best, I might add. But regrettably, it will not be available as of tomorrow afternoon. I hope that by then, we'll be able to find you some more long-term living arrangements."

"That'll be just great. At least I'll be able to get myself one good night's sleep. Besides that, I'm not exactly sure how long I'll be staying here in Honolulu anyway. I really appreciate your help, Mister, um..." Ben looked for some identification tag, but none was apparent.

"Oh, I'm sorry — I left my name tag at home. Palani — Palani Lembrose is my name."

"Well, thanks a lot, Palani. I can't tell you how helpful and reassuring you've been. Oh, by the way, is it possible to make phone calls from the room?"

"Why, of course, Mister Decker. Local calls you can now dial direct, but you'll need the operator to place any overseas phone calls."

"Thanks again."

Palani used his open palm to hit the bell sitting on the counter and looked over at a small assembly of white-jacketed staff members. "Bellhop!" A young man immediately came over to the desk and began to reach for Ben's bags. "Manny, would you please see to it that Mister Decker here gets settled into room 418." Palani once again looked at Ben. "I'll work on finding you something for the weekend and will send someone up to your room to let you know the arrangements later. *Mahalo* for your understanding."

"*Mahalo?*"

"Yes — thank you. *Mahalo* is Hawaiian for thank you."

"I should be the one thanking you." Ben smiled and turned away from the desk to oversee his luggage, but the two bags and Manny were already gone. He walked through the lobby towards the back, ocean side of the hotel. Next to a large, deep blue swimming pool was a thatched hut that housed a bar. Several people were seated at open-air tables, each of which had its own, thatched sun umbrella supported overhead. Looking beyond and out to the Pacific, he could see many surfers taking advantage of the lively south swell to close out their day riding the waves. The sun was still fully above the horizon, but Ben imagined that it wouldn't take long for the clouds stacked up in the distance to finally extinguish its red-yellow glow for this day.

He looked down at his key — 418 he reiterated in his head. Maybe it would be best if he went up to his room, took a hot shower, and took a short nap. He was certain he'd feel in much better shape to go get a snack in a few hours or so. With any luck at all, maybe he'd awaken from his sleep to discover that this was all just a bad dream.

9

Thursday, February 7, 1957: 7:20 P. M.

The shower felt magnificent, and the nap was even better. He figured that he was either totally exhausted or suffering from a bad case of jet lag. Of course, the more he considered it, the more convinced he became that it was a combination of the two. He hoped he would feel awake enough to nourish his growling stomach. At first, he continued to just lie on the bed and stare mesmerized at the spinning of the antique ceiling fan. Finally, he rolled over and hung his feet from the side of the bed, momentarily remaining motionless as he let the fog clear from his sleepy head. He had no doubt that the room was one of the Royal Hawaiian's best. It was very large and equipped with the finest of furnishings when compared to that of any standard hotel. There was a small anteroom with a closet, dresser, and adjoining bath right next to the entranceway. The nightstands featured small, fresh floral arrangements placed beside each table lamp. On an end table next to a rattan sofa was a clunky, old-fashioned dial telephone. And the entire wall opposite the hallway consisted of a floor to ceiling window with a glass door leading out to the balcony. The view looking out over Waikiki Beach towards Diamond Head was absolutely breathtaking, though the abundance of city lights that he knew should be there were still conspicuously missing.

He motivated himself enough to lazily saunter into the bathroom and search his travel bag for his toothbrush and toothpaste. Ben squeezed a little paste onto his brush and began to work on his teeth. "Oh god, is that me?" He blurted the question out loud as he peered into the mirror. Of course, what could you expect when looking at a fifty-year-old carcass that had been deprived of its much-needed sleep? Yet he was almost surprised to see that his general appearance was exactly the same as it had been back in Philadelphia so early this morning. Was that really this morning? Whenever — physically, he certainly didn't appear to be one day younger or one day older, for that matter.

He finished brushing his teeth and dabbed some water on his face. There was much to consider. Was Philadelphia — his late-nineties Philadelphia — only eighteen hours ago, or was it nearly forty years in the future? What a bizarre thought all this was. But he had to find out — he simply had to prove to himself whether this 1957 stuff was real or if it was just a big put-on or a sinister plot of some type. Of course, he still had absolutely no idea whatsoever of just how he could make that sort of determination.

Back in the anteroom, he yanked a pair of white Bermuda shorts from his bag and quickly stepped into them. He selected a red pullover shirt and was in the middle of slipping it down over his head when there was a knock on the outer screen door. "Just a minute! I'll be right there!"

Ben pulled his shirt down over his torso and let it hang out over his waist. "I'm coming." He went over to the entrance and unlocked the inner door. A gusty trade wind blew a mixture of sweet fragrances through the screen and into his room. He could only make out the shapely silhouette of a medium-sized woman with long, dark hair flowing down over her shoulders.

"Mister Decker? You are Mister Decker, aren't you?"

"Why yes, that's me."

"Aloha and welcome to the Royal Hawaiian Hotel, sir. My name is Leilani Kealoha, and I'm the customer service representative for the Royal Hawaiian Hotel." Her voice was quite melodic and remarkably soothing.

Ben fumbled with the latch on the screen until, at last, the door swung wide open. "Please come in." As the woman stepped in from the poorly lit hallway, Ben got his first look at her face. She appeared to be in her middle twenties, of some sort of mixed Polynesian extraction, and absolutely beautiful. She had exceptionally attractive features and incredibly tantalizing, dark brown eyes. Tucked behind her right ear was a beautiful, fragrant yellow-white flower that Ben knew at once he had smelled before. He was at once overwhelmed by her presence.

"Well, okay. I'm sorry that I'm so rushed, but we are really quite busy this week, you know. We have a totally full house."

"Sure, um... Busy... Yeah, I can certainly see that. Not here, I mean... Ah... not here — in the room... Downstairs, I mean — so many guests and all." Oh wow, he thought — why was his mind reeling like this? He was almost conscious of stumbling over his own words, helplessly babbling senseless chatter like a pimply-faced teenager talking to a pretty girl. Now that's one for the books — Benjamin Decker being totally mesmerized by a complete and utter stranger! "Look, I want to apologize for my incoherence. You see, I... I just woke up from a nap and..."

"Oh, for goodness sakes, Mister Decker, please don't worry about that. I should be the one to apologize. I'm really sorry about the mix-up… for having to bother you in your room like this. We just haven't been able to figure out exactly what happened. We tried to locate some record of a booking for you, but regretfully, we weren't successful. Who did you say your travel agent was again?"

"Um... Kauffman. The Kauffman Travel Agency at the Oxen Valley Mall back in Pennsylvania — ur, that's Grovesnor, Pennsylvania. Look, I'm sorry... that is, I must have inadvertently left the paperwork at home." Ben was trying to concentrate on the matters at hand — the need for a hotel room, his missing Alpha-Max 2000, the absurd notion that this was somehow 1957. And yet despite all these consequential issues, he couldn't focus his mind on anything other than his desire to make small talk with this woman. Out of the clear blue, Leilani had suddenly become the most alluring woman he had ever met. Surely, she was very beautiful — even to the point of being exotic — but he knew he just had to snap out of it and calm down. But alas, it was no use. As hard as he tried, he simply couldn't keep his eyes — and his mind — away from this enchanting woman. Thank goodness that thoughts were not visible!

"Oh boy, we really do have a problem here. That's the name that Palani gave me — he's one of our desk clerks. We just haven't been able to find that agency anywhere in our master travel guide downstairs. That supposedly lists every agency back in the States, but I don't know... Are you sure it couldn't be listed under a different name?"

"I... I don't think so..." Ben tried so hard not to stare, but his eyes were totally lost in hers. She looked somehow familiar, but he knew he couldn't have ever laid eyes on her before. And yet somehow...

"Well, it doesn't really matter at this point. We'll continue to work on finding some accommodation for the weekend. At least you can enjoy your stay here this evening, Mister Decker."

So beautiful — she's just so beautiful. He knew he was totally losing control of himself, and it embarrassed him — even terrified him — to be so far out of character. And yet, in some warped way, he looked forward to immersing himself in this terror! "I just can't tell you what a pleasure it's been. Ur, pleasure it is — staying here, I mean. I already know how much I'll enjoy it — the ah... beautiful room and all. And the view from the patio is simply magnificent."

"The patio?"

"Ah... the balcony."

"Oh, of course — you mean the *lanai*. Here in the Territory, we call a balcony or verandah by its Hawaiian name — *lanai*."

"*Lanai.* I see. Well, regardless of what we call it, the view is tremendous. Um... are you always this busy — being sold out, I mean?" Oh god, he didn't want her to leave. He was willing to make any kind of small talk that he could just to keep her a short while longer — maybe long enough to figure out why she looked familiar to him.

"Busy — yes. Sold out — no. Not usually, anyway. I just saw in the newspaper this week that during this past January, Hawaii set a new record for visitors — a little over seven thousand tourists in one month. Can you imagine that — seven thousand tourists! On top of that, military families have taken up many of the cheaper rooms in Waikiki. They have their own housing shortage. And adding to the chaos here at the Royal Hawaiian, we're also celebrating our thirtieth anniversary this month."

"Anniversary? Oh, yeah — the doorman mentioned that." Ben rubbed his head where he had bumped it on the plane.

"Are you all right, Mister Decker?"

"Yeah... sure. I guess I'm just more strung out from the trip than I had figured. Jet lag, I guess." Holy shit! That was it! She reminded him of the woman he had seen on the plane — right before he had hit his head. But she certainly WAS NOT the same woman. Leilani was younger, somehow different from the woman on the plane. And yet he was convinced they could have easily been related — maybe even sisters.

"Jet what?"

"Jet..." He suddenly realized that the term was several years away from coming into the vernacular yet. "Oh, um... Actually, it's nothing — Philly slang, I guess. I'm only trying to say I'm very tired."

"Sure — that's quite understandable. All the way from Pennsylvania — that must have taken you several days' worth of flying. I think that just the flight from San Francisco to Honolulu is over nine hours."

"Well, actually..." Ben wanted to share his predicament with someone, and the way he was feeling right now, Leilani would be the best of all possible choices. But he quickly decided that this simply wasn't the correct setting. "...actually, I took my time and spread the trip out over several days."

"Well, you really should get some rest."

"I certainly plan to do just that, but first I need something to eat. Do you have any suggestions for a good place to get some chow?"

"Sure do. Our Royal Hawaiian Galley downstairs serves great food."

"But you're not the least bit biased, are you?" Ben couldn't help but grin.

"Honest to goodness — they really serve great food, and the atmosphere is excellent."

"But I'm not ready for a big meal. I was really thinking about some sort of a snack — maybe a sandwich — and a cup of coffee."

"No problem — you can get a light meal there. And tell them that Leilani said to give you the best seat in the house."

"Leilani... Leilani..." He let her name roll off his tongue as he tried it out. "Leilani... What does it mean — you know, in English?"

"Leilani? Oh, it means majestic flower or heavenly flower — something like that." She dipped her head in obvious embarrassment.

"Gee, I didn't mean to make you feel self-conscious. But what a pretty name — so fitting. Leilani... It just has such a wonderful sound to it."

"Why, thank you, Mister Decker." If the light in the entryway had been brighter, Ben was convinced he would have caught her blushing.

"Please — it's Ben. I feel more comfortable with Ben."

"Then, Ben it is."

"And I'm going to take you up on your suggestion to try the Galley, Leilani. Um... how do you say it in Hawaiian? Is it my-hay-low?"

He could tell that it took all her self-control to keep from laughing. "You must mean *mahalo*?"

Ben couldn't help but laugh at himself. "Ah... I'm sorry — foreign language has always been my Achilles heel. I was trying to say thank you."

"Yes — that's pronounced ma-HA-low."

"Okay then — *mahalo* it is. I'll look forward to hearing from you, Leilani."

She turned, exited the door, and walked down the hallway. Ben stood by the door, frozen in a trance-like state, trying his best to understand why this woman's presence was so alluring to him. For crying out loud, he thought to himself, Leilani was an extremely good-looking woman, and he was only human. The day a man stops appreciating the beauty of an attractive lady should be the day after he died! And yet he knew he was only kidding himself. Something was still quite different here. Enjoy looking — sure. But he knew full well that he had never been one to get caught up in wild flights of fantasy simply because some attractive female batted her eyelashes at him. He was too much in control of himself to let that happen. Maybe that was why he prided himself so much on his loyalty. After all, Benjamin Decker wasn't some wet-behind-the-ears teenager, being held captive by some adolescent flood of male hormones.

Finally, several minutes after she had disappeared down the hallway, he closed the inner door. But even then, he found it quite impossible to get his mind off his visitor, constantly reminded by the wisps of heavenly fragrance she had left behind, floating on air as a subtle reminder of her visit.

10

Thursday, February 7, 1957: 8:10 P. M.

Ben walked into the Royal Hawaiian Galley and was immediately met by a hostess. "Aloha and good evening, sir. Welcome to the Royal Hawaiian."

"Aloha." The term felt more natural to Ben than he would ever have believed possible.

"How many will be at your table this evening, sir?" She looked past him as if to determine whether or not he had any unseen companions.

"I'm sorry to say, just one. Um... Miss Kealoha told me to ask for the best seat in the house."

"Oh, you know Miss Kealoha?"

"Well — kind of. Ur... it is Miss, isn't it?"

"Yes, it is." A smile crossed the hostess's face. Before Ben could explain his honorable intentions, she grabbed a menu and turned towards the dining room. "As far as the best seat in the house goes, it looks as though you're in luck. God knows — an hour ago, I'd have had trouble finding you ANY seat. Why don't you follow me?"

As the two walked through the sea of tables, Ben noticed that the peak evening rush had waned. Several spirited bus boys cleared away the spoils of many dinners, their work offering ironclad confirmation of the fact that it had been a bustling rush hour at the Royal Hawaiian Galley.

"How's this right here?" She extended her arm toward a table set for two next to the open-air end of the room overlooking a magnificent white sand beach, warmly lit by a score of flickering Polynesian torches.

"Oh, wow — this is just outstanding! Thanks a lot."

"You're welcome." She handed him an oversized menu. "I hope you enjoy your meal."

Ben seated himself and folded open the menu. He knew he only wanted something light — maybe a hamburger or a sandwich — but almost out of a sense of duty, he still began to review the wide variety of selections. A quick glance revealed full dinners ranging in cost from $2.49 up to $5.25. With prices like that in one of the most elite establishments in Waikiki, he couldn't help but be reminded of his predicament. That said, now that he had a chance to sit down for a moment and reflect on the happenings of the past twenty-four hours, Ben realized that he didn't even know exactly what his predicament was.

On the one hand, he had to consider this silly notion of somehow being transported back in time — an alternative he had already pretty much abandoned as impossible. And yet the only other option that made any sense at all — the industrial espionage scenario — seemed to require such an intricate strategy that only the most paranoid person would ever consider it a possibility. Two options and both were so preposterous that he couldn't wholeheartedly subscribe to either one.

He closed the menu and placed it on the table. To hell with logic! Oh sure, if only it were that easy. He couldn't help but think that the cold, analytical thought patterns of an engineer would curse him right to his grave. He was acutely aware of the fact that his innate nature simply loathed any quandary in which all the alternatives appeared equally absurd. There HAD to be a logical solution. Of course, he was making this negative assessment based on rather limited input. He was convinced that he needed to garner more information, but exactly how was he going to go about doing that? If he had ever needed a friend — someone to confide in — this was certainly the time. And yet now as he really considered his plight, Ben realized for the first time just how alone he was.

"Have you decided, or would you like me to come back in a couple of minutes?"

"No, no... I mean yes, um... I've decided. I'll have a... Er... Do you have bacon-lettuce-and- tomato?"

"Sure do. Rice, coleslaw, or French fries?"

"I'll have the fries."

"And anything to drink?"

"How about a cup of coffee — make it decaffeinated — and with cream, please."

"Decaffeinated?" Her inquisitive expression let him know in no uncertain terms that she had no idea just what it was he was asking for. "I'm sorry, but I'm not familiar with..."

"No problem. Don't mind me. I'm still trying to recoup from my journey. I only want a cup of coffee, please. Oh, and could I also have a glass of water?"

"Most certainly, sir." The smile had returned to the waitress's face as she finished writing his order and quickly walked away from Ben's table.

Ben turned his attention out towards the sea. Only the white tops of the waves reflected the light of a half-moon as they gently rolled over the reef and onto the torch-lit sand. He reflected on the fact that his waitress expressed total unfamiliarity with decaffeinated coffee. Of course, any good actress could feign surprise at...

"Here's your ice water."

Ben was somewhat surprised at the waitress's quick return. "Oh jeez, that was quick. Thank you."

She responded with a genuinely warm smile. "I'll get your coffee right away." The woman turned and retreated towards the kitchen once again. Though Ben had only been in Hawaii for a brief time, he couldn't help but be impressed with the unpretentious demeanor exhibited by everyone he had met so far. Was it a consequence of geography? ...socialization? ...tradition? Or was it attributable to an earlier, less complicated era? Whatever the cause, it certainly resulted in a conspicuously laid-back, innocuous lifestyle. It was difficult not to envy such a mellow, comforting way of life, even considering the inevitable drawbacks that...

"Good evening, Mister Decker."

Ben was jolted from his contemplation and at once reacted by snapping his head around as if to plainly announce his arrival back to the here and now.

"I'm sorry, Mister Decker. I didn't mean to startle you — honest. You must have been totally lost in your thoughts."

"Oh... Um... Miss Ke... Kealoha, ur... Leilani." Ben was as happy to see her as he was surprised. "You're absolutely right — I was... And for that matter, I guess I'm still trying to wake up after my nap. I'm sorry, but my mind must have been somewhere off in never-never land, totally lost in my thoughts."

"Only good ones, I hope."

"Well yeah, now that you mention it, they were good thoughts. I was just reflecting on my observation that everyone I so far have met in Hawaii has been so pleasant, so positive."

"It's the aloha spirit, Mister Decker. It IS real, you know."

"The aloha spirit, huh? And just what is the aloha spirit supposed to be?"

"Gee, I'm not sure exactly how to define it. I guess the aloha spirit is simply an attitude or an approach to interpersonal relationships that assumes the best about the other person rather than the worst. It's kind of like starting out by giving someone the benefit of the doubt — trusting them. And I'm happy to say, it almost always works."

"Now that IS refreshing." In any other circumstance, Ben knew he would have dismissed the idea as trite or superfluous, but somehow, he could sense her sincerity. "Um... Why don't you have a seat?" He stood and pulled the other chair out from the table.

"Well... Sure, why not?" She removed her small bag from over her shoulder, placed it on the table, and slid into the seat. "I was hoping I'd find you down here. I was just about ready to go home for the evening, but I thought I'd try your room first. Obviously, you weren't there. As you already know, we have no vacancy at the Royal Hawaiian for the weekend, but I think I've found you an alternative. The Moana Hotel — just down the street here — is going to set up a bunch of cots in a service area off their Banyan Courtyard starting tomorrow night. Now I wasn't able to actually confirm you there for the weekend, but I have a calabash cousin who is a desk clerk over there, and first thing tomorrow morning, I'll give him a call."

"I really appreciate your help so much, but I can go on over there in the morning and see if I can bunk there for a few nights. I really didn't want you to trouble..."

"Mister Decker, you're no trouble — no trouble at all. I really want to help. I mean, aside from doing my job, I really want you to have a pleasant stay here in the Islands."

"Well, hospitality like that is pretty difficult to argue with, so if you really want to..." Whoa! A caution alarm was blaring away loudly somewhere within his psyche. Was this woman for real? It was very hard not to be a bit suspicious. Could anyone be THIS nice? Could any stranger be so damned benevolent, so seemingly unselfish? A little voice was screaming out loudly in his brain to be careful — VERY careful. This woman could be a part of the mission-impossible plot he had considered. "Look, I'll make a deal with you."

"A deal?"

"Yeah. You can try to contact your… your… um… cal-a-something-or-other…"

"Calabash."

"Yeah, calabash — your calabash cousin in the morning if you agree to drop the Mister part and just call me Ben."

Her radiant smile stretched ear-to-ear. "Okay, Ben. We've got a deal."

"Now, will you let me buy you a drink?" Ben felt his stomach do a flip, almost as though he were a teenager asking a girl to dance for the first time.

"Well, um… I don't… I just don't know." The glow immediately drained from her face, and her words became very hesitant as she broke contact with Ben's eyes and stared directly at the wedding ring on his left hand.

"Oh, gee — I don't want you to get the wrong idea here, Leilani."

"But you're married, aren't you?"

"Well, yes… I mean, not really… Ur, I mean… Look — I honestly don't want you to misinterpret my intentions. I'm not making a pass at you or anything like that. I just thought that maybe you'd like to share a drink and some conversation with me. I can't really explain it, but I really feel very comfortable talking with you." Ben shook his head as soon as he heard his own words. "God, I must really sound pretty dumb here. Probably all the guys say that to you. I'm feeling, well… feeling really awkward here. Maybe you'd just care to talk some…"

She tilted her head into her hand in a quite conscious attempt to hide her blushing. Suddenly, Ben felt his heart sink at the thought of frightening her with his awkward words. But just as quickly, the smile returned to her face in an unspoken assurance that he had not offended her. "Well… sure, what the heck. I'm off duty now, and I'm not in that big of a hurry."

"How about one of these fancy Hawaiian drinks?"

"To be honest, I really don't drink alcohol. Um..."

"Hey, no problem — that's fine. How about a cup of coffee or something?"

"Iced tea — I'll have an iced tea."

Ben ordered her drink when the waitress brought his bacon-lettuce-and-tomato sandwich. He gestured towards his plate. "Would you care for anything? ...a sandwich? ...French fries? ...a piece of cake?"

"No, no — you just eat, Ben. I had dinner earlier, and I'm really just thirsty right now."

"Okay — whatever you say. So, have you lived here all your life, um... Leilani? Jeez — do you mind my calling you Leilani?"

"Heavens no — that IS my name. Anyway, I've lived here for the past several years — since fifty-two. I was born on the Big Island — in Hilo — and spent most of my life over there."

"The Big Island?"

"Ah, yeah. That's what we call the Island of Hawaii — it's really a big island, you know."

"I thought this was Hawaii?"

"Well sure, this is the Territory of Hawaii, but this island is Oahu, and you are in the city of Honolulu right here."

"Ah, right – I should have known that." Ben KNEW that he was aware of that.

"And the Island of Hawaii is called the Big Island. And Hilo is the largest town there, though god knows it's not really too large — pretty rural, actually. Anyway, I was in the first graduating class at Saint Joseph's High there. Do you believe it — they finally let girls in there." Her perfectly white teeth glistened. "The year after I got out of high school, I moved to California for ten months to live with my older sister, but I really never made the adjustment to living in the States. Just too fast for me, I guess."

"The States, huh? And then back to Honolulu?"

"Well, only after spending four or five months trying to find a job I liked in Hilo, but nothing ever came up. Hilo's mostly just a sleepy little plantation town, totally dependent on sugar. I want to do more with my life — grow beyond that whole little town mentality."

"So, you really didn't like it there." Ben took another bite of his sandwich.

"Oh no, that's not the case at all. I always like going back to visit my mom and younger brother and sister over there, but I still need to be away. I'm not exactly sure why. I guess it has something to do with Dad."

"Your Dad?"

"Yeah. He died during my junior year of high school — a really tough time for me. He spent thirty-some years giving his life to that lousy plantation — even lost a hand and three toes in a field accident back before the War. He was a very good man, but he wound up drinking himself to death. As you might guess, I am understating the point when I say it was a really unpleasant time for mom and us kids."

"I'm sorry, Lani. Ur... jeez — Leilani."

"Goodness, Lani is just fine. That's what almost all of my friends call me."

"Okay, Lani. Look, I'm sorry I interrupted you at such an inappropriate time..."

"No, it's all right. Surprisingly, I think I've turned it into a very positive part of my life — like trying to make the best of a pretty rotten situation. God, I sure learned! I learned more than I could ever put into words. I certainly never try to take anyone for granted anymore. It's taken me until now just to get over the worst of the hurt. But I'll never, ever forget..." She sipped on her tea. "I'm sorry — I must sound awful, rambling on so much about myself. I mean, we've only just met, and here I am, telling you my life story. You must think I'm terrible."

"No, no I don't — not in the least. I'm really interested — I mean about who Leilani is. I really find you interesting — really easy to talk with."

She blushed. "Oh, enough of me for right now. Now I'm really feeling as self-conscious as can be. How about you, Ben Decker? You're from, um — is it Pennsylvania? Boy, that's so far away."

"Farther than you may imagine."

"Do you have any keikis?"

"Keikis?"

"Children — I mean children?"

"Oh, sure. I have two girls. Lisa — my oldest — she's in her first year of college now. And Bonnie — she's a sophomore in high school."

"Both born before the war? Were you in the war?"

"The war? Oh, Vietnam? I was..."

"Where?"

"Vietnam. You know, over in Southeast Asia, near..." By reading the look on her face, Ben knew he was on the wrong track. "Oh my god, you mean World War Two, don't you?" Ben shook his head in disbelief.

"Come on, Ben. I know Pennsylvania is a long way from here, but it's certainly not THAT far. If your kids are in their mid-to-late teens now, they had to be born in the late-thirties-early-forties, right?"

Ben was saved from answering as the waitress came back to the table. "Anything else I can get for either one of you?"

"Leilani?" Ben looked across the table to see Lani shake her head from side to side. He pulled out his wallet. "No, that will be all."

The waitress finished scribbling on the check and placed it on the table. "*Mahalo.* Have a pleasant stay here in the Territory. See you tomorrow, Lani."

Ben left money for the bill and tip on the change tray as he stood, still shaking his head. "World War Two, huh... Aw, Lani, there's so much I have to try to figure out here. I need to talk to someone, but I fear you'll think I'm crazy."

"Crazy? I don't think you're crazy, Ben Decker. But you do sound as though you're very tired from your trip."

He walked to her side of the table and pulled her chair out as she stood. "Do you have to go right away?"

"Well — that depends. What do you have in mind?"

"Am I being too forward to ask you if you'd take a little walk right out here on the beach with me?"

"Well..." At first, she considered his invitation in expressionless thought, but in a matter of seconds, she beamed her brilliant smile at him. "Only if you promise to be good."

"I promise."

11

Thursday, February 7, 1957: 10:00 P. M.

As the two walked barefoot out onto a nearly deserted Waikiki Beach, Ben felt much more awake than his head told him he should be — and he felt much more apprehensive about Lani than his heart told him he wanted to be. Why did she seem so open, so trusting? Was she for real? Or was the problem with him? Was it his age? His relationship with Emily? Why was he so skeptical... so wary? Trust? Maybe he needed to develop some aloha spirit of his own. Maybe that would allow him to relax and at least enjoy whatever it was into which he had staggered. He took a deep breath of air. "Oh Lani, this is just magnificent — it makes just being alive more than worthwhile."

"It's one of the reasons I couldn't live in California."

"You mean the ocean?"

"Yep."

"But you have the ocean in California. Of course, I guess that depends on where your sister lives."

"Oh, she lives near the water — close to Ventura. But it's not really the same at all."

"How's that?"

"It's cold — the water's really freezing. A lot of times at night like this, I just like to go for a swim — really spontaneous like. And you just can't do that in California."

"Yeah, I guess the water is pretty chilly there."

"Chilly is an understatement. And then you have the fog... Too often the whole coast gets socked in with fog — I mean right along the shoreline. Oh, I guess even the fog has a certain beauty to it for those who appreciate it. But I grew up under the crystal-clear skies here in the Territory, and I really missed them back in California."

"Well, I can see how you could become so spoiled living in Hawaii that no matter where you went, you would always have the urge to come back to paradise."

"That's true — despite all this cold, winter weather."

"The cold, winter weather! Give me a break, Leilani!"

"Oh Ben, you silly *malihini*. It's winter here, and to us local folks, it's REALLY cold!"

"Lani, it's got to be seventy degrees out here right now. And by the way, what's a mal-a..."

"A *malihini* — a stranger or newcomer. Believe me — you are definitely a *malihini!*"

"Newcomer, huh? How about that — here I thought it was that species of warm water fish so popular in Island restaurants."

Leilani was totally unsuccessful at trying to suppress her laughter. "You're kidding, aren't you? The fish you're talking about is the *mahi-mahi*, Ben. A newcomer is a *malihini*." She continued her muffled laughter.

"Well, how am I supposed to know the difference? Hey, I'll take your word for it, but *malihini, mahi-mahi, mahalo*, whatever — they all sound pretty similar to this newcomer. No matter what you want to call it, this is still a perfect night to me." Ben kicked his thongs aside and stepped forward enough to let the incoming surge of the sea flow over his feet. A half-moon approached the horizon. "Oh wow! This water is so warm."

"That's one of the reasons I like to swim at night — especially this time of year. It's warmer IN the water than it is out of it." She already had her sandals off, and the two sauntered side by side through the swash. Leilani stared down at the sand. "Ben, um... Why are you here in Hawaii alone? I mean, if I'm too personal, just say so, but where's your wife?"

"Well, I'm here on business, and she's back in Philadelphia."

"Business? What kind of business are you in?"

"Oh boy, here we go." He knew perfectly well that he was treading on very dangerous ground. Trust her? Tell her the incredible truth? He couldn't help but think that maybe his being an engineer made this kind of dilemma extra difficult, and yet he figured that sometimes in life, he just had to act on a gut feeling and hope for the best. And right this very moment — at this precise second — he somehow intuitively knew that this was one of those times.

"Huh?"

"Um, I said here we go. I'm in the... ah... the computer business — I design kind of like computers."

"Computers? What's a — oh, I know! You mean like Univac?"

"Hey, that's good — ah... yeah! Like Univac, only no tubes — it's much more advanced."

"You must work for the government then, yeah? Isn't Univac a government..."

"Well, slow down here for a second. I never said I worked on Univac. That's an ancient prototype of what we're doing."

"Ancient?"

"We'll get to that part in a bit. Anyway, the government isn't even involved in my work — at least not directly, anyway. Actually, I own a piece of my own company — a private corporation."

"Your own company, huh? Wow! You know, I read the paper every day, but I never knew that these computer things were so advanced."

"Well, it gets a little more complicated than that, Lani."

"Complicated? Oh, you mean top secret or something like that — to hide the technology from the Reds and stuff."

"The Reds? Do you mean he's a communist? Um, not really... It's just that... Look, I'm not exactly what I seem to be. Um, time-wise, I mean..."

"Time-wise? You know, back at the restaurant, you seemed surprised when I mentioned The War. You even said I'd think you were crazy. What did you mean by that?"

Ben scratched his head and considered his situation. In his mind's eye, he saw the image of a man poised at the edge of a cliff, getting ready to leap. Once he started, he knew he'd be in free-fall until he reached the bottom. There could be no telling only half of this story. Trust, huh? He'd known this woman for a total of... a couple of hours... trust? Well, here goes nothing. "Okay, Lani, if you really want me to do this — I mean, to tell you this whole story..."

"Please. I want to know who Ben Decker is."

Ben let out a sigh. "Don't say I didn't warn you — you're definitely going to think I'm nuts."

"No, I won't — I promise."

Ben again expelled a gush from his lungs and replaced it with a deep breath of fresh air. "Okay, you asked for it! Actually, I don't really know where to start."

"Well, when in doubt, why not start at the most logical place of all — the beginning."

"I'm not sure I know just where the beginning of this entire episode is — or was..." Ben took another deep breath, rubbed his chin with his hand, and jumped from his imaginary cliff. He proceeded to tell her the entire saga, from his preparations for attending the convention to bumping his head on the airplane. They strolled as far as Fort DeRussy and turned to walk back, all the while Leilani quietly listened to every detail. By the time they reached the Royal Hawaiian Hotel again, the first quarter moon nearly lost its struggle to stay above the horizon. The last shimmering sparkles of moonlight danced their way across the ocean right up to the beach. Lani grabbed his hand and led him to a park bench situated directly under a clump of coconut palms. The couple sat in perfect silence as they peered towards the sea, both obviously reflecting on Ben's incredible story.

The silence lasted the several minutes it took until the last rays of moonlight were swallowed by the sea. Leilani traced a circle in the white sand with her dangling foot. "You know, Ben, I don't think you're crazy."

"Well, I appreciate that, but I'm not so sure that I have as much faith in my sanity as you do."

"Come on, Ben. There's got to be some logical explanation for all this. Maybe you have amnesia or something. I saw a movie once where..."

"No, no — I've been through it all several times already, and that can't be it. This is NO movie, Lani. I just don't know what's going on here — and to be perfectly honest with you — I'm scared as hell. I thank god that at least you have given me a chance to get this off my chest."

She extended her arm towards him and squeezed his hand. "I can't explain it, but even though I've only known you for a few hours, I feel as though we've been friends for a long, long time. This has never happened to me in my entire life — and certainly not this quickly. At first — when I noticed your wedding ring back at the Galley — I feared that you only wanted to take advantage of me. But I know now that's not the case. I can't explain it, but I can feel you in my heart, Ben Decker. I trust you, and I'll help you in any way that I can."

A gentle trade wind, warmed by the sea, stirred the palm fronds overhead. "I'm just so... well... Oh, Lani." Hard as he tried, Ben couldn't find the right words. He felt a tear pushing its way into the corner of his eye. "I... I know it's ridiculous, but I'm so afraid you'll get the wrong idea. It's just that... Well... Aw man, this is tough. For the first time in god knows how long, I feel like a silly kid falling in love with the prettiest girl in the whole school. But jeez-o-man, I'm nearly fifty years old, and I don't make a habit out of chasing after women. This has got to be a dream. None of this can be happening. I feel totally out of control, and I absolutely can't stand being unable to chart my own course."

"I better go, Ben."

"Jesus — I said the wrong thing..."

"No, no — nothing like that. God knows I want to stay with you, but my inner voice is telling me that maybe we both should have some time to consider what's happening, to think about what we've shared together here tonight."

"I... I know you're right, but I'm so damned afraid that I'll wake up in the morning to find that Leilani was only a dream. Oh god — I want you to be real so much."

"I'm very real, Ben." She leaned over and kissed him on the cheek. Ben responded by putting his arms around her and pulling her close to his chest. She raised her head from his shoulder and whispered in his ear. "Could any dream ever make us feel like this?" She snuggled even closer to him until she found his lips with hers and pressed herself tightly against him. The two kissed each other deeply.

They stayed locked in their embrace for seemingly minutes until, quite suddenly, Leilani sprang up and brushed her long black hair back into place using her hand. "Ben, you have to believe that I'm not like this... I mean, so quickly... Everything's happening here so... so fast."

"I..."

She leaned over and gently touched her index finger to his lips. "Please don't say anything — don't let the moment end. I'll see you in the morning — I promise."

"But Lani..."

"Please..." She quickly turned and ran off across the beach in the general direction of Diamond Head and was at once gone.

* * *

Ben remained on the bench in total silence. He kept his eyes fixed firmly on the nearly dark sea now illuminated only by the feeble glow of a thousand stars scattered at random across a perfectly clear sky. The night air had become cool, and yet every gust of the gentle trade wind blowing over the tepid ocean brought a surge of warmth onto the land and into his spirit. What had taken place on this beach tonight? Could it have been a dream? ...a hallucination? Or was it, in fact, a reality? For that matter, did it even make sense to try to analyze a feeling logically? At this point, he simply had no way of determining what happened here, but for whatever it was worth, he knew with his entire being that he wanted this night to be real. Oh dear god, he wanted Leilani to be real even more.

Lani, Lani... He caught himself reveling in — in what? In the infatuation of a teenager? His soul was on fire, but his cerebrum painfully battled confusion. An engineer needed facts — thrived on facts — not feelings. An engineer always remained in control, even under the most trying circumstances. An engineer always remained responsible and always remained true to his duty, never wavering from his obligation to solve the problem... to reach his objective. And Ben knew that, beyond anything else, he was an engineer. Yet he knew too well that he had totally lost control, lost even the most limited understanding of anything that was happening. But it somehow FELT wonderful and yet — damn it — he felt guilty for feeling such joy.

For nearly an hour, Ben sat still on the bench in an almost trance-like state. He remained a helpless spectator to the quarrel played out deep within his mind's eye, a quarrel between his intellectual self and his emotional self. And yet somehow, after all the analysis and cogitation, it suddenly dawned on him that just maybe he finally learned — learned a fundamental truth – that in matters of the heart, understanding has little or nothing to do with intellect.

At last, he stood and began to walk back to the Royal Hawaiian. The air blowing in from the sea felt so warm, so fresh. He didn't want this night to end. He stopped and turned for one last look, almost as if to forever fix this setting in his mind. A hundred yards away, near a clump of coconut palms, Ben spotted the silhouette of a sizable man, a lit cigarette dangling from his mouth, now standing where no one had been only a minute earlier. The eerie figure quickly and quietly slithered into the shadows and out of sight. Was this only a coincidence? Ben's gaze rose toward the sky. *Oh god, if you're there, please let Leilani be for real.*

It was after midnight by the time Ben finally crawled into bed. Despite his extraordinary predicament and his growing paranoia, as soon as his head hit the pillow, he fell sound asleep.

PART THREE

He that does good for good's sake seeks neither paradise
nor reward, but he is sure of both in the end.

— William Penn

12

Friday, February 8, 1957: 5:20 A. M.

Ben rolled over and grabbed for his watch, which he had placed on the nightstand — only twenty minutes past five. He had been absolutely convinced that he was going to sleep until noon. Of course, now that he thought about it, back on the East Coast it was already ten-twenty in the morning, and he was certain that his body rhythms had to still be functioning in that time zone. He stared at the ceiling as if to test his vision, and then, finding it quite muddled, he raised his hands in a vain attempt to rub away the fog in his eyes. He gathered his thoughts enough to remember that he was lying in a hotel room in Hawaii. Ben was abruptly reminded that he was still in the same quandary that he was last night. His consciousness began to run the script all over again: was this merely some kind of bizarre hallucination? How could he still account for the mid-flight transmutation of a 747 into an antique aircraft? How could anyone explain the incredibly detailed assortment of 1950's trappings? And then there was Leilani...

He sat up on the side of the bed and reached for the telephone. He couldn't help but think that if all this really were just some nostalgic dream, he still must be asleep. Though the plain black phone appeared to be brand new, its style was that of the old fashioned dial type — the kind he was sure no one even manufactured anymore. He was damned if he was going to have another day filled with the confusion and uncertainty of yesterday. It was time to get to the bottom of this whole fiasco, and he was determined to start finding some answers right here and now. He put the receiver to his ear and dialed the operator.

"Aloha and good morning. This is the front desk. Can I help you?"

"Good morning. This is Benjamin Decker in room 418. I'd like to place a long-distance call to the East Coast — um... Pennsylvania, please."

"One moment, please. I'll connect you with the overseas operator."

"Over-seas operator — good morning. How may I help you?"

"Yes, operator — ah... good morning. I'd like to place a call to Philadelphia, Pennsylvania."

"IS that a person-to-person or station-to-station call?"

Ben shook his head. He hadn't heard those terms for decades. "Person-to-person, please."

"Your name and room number, please."

"Sure. This is Benjamin Decker, and I'm in room number 418."

"And to whom would you like to speak this morning, Mister Decker?"

"I'd like to speak with William Katzenbach at the Penn-Comp Corporation. The area code is 215, and the phone number is 625-2991."

"Pardon me, sir. Did you say something about a code?"

"Um... yes. That was area code two one... Ah..." Oh wow! It suddenly dawned on him that the whole concept of area codes didn't even exist yet. "No, no... I'm sorry, ma'am. I'm just waking up here, and I'm a bit foggy yet. That number is 625-2991 — that's in the Philadelphia area, operator."

"What is the exchange?"

"Exchange? I only have that number, ma'am."

"Ah... Just one moment, please." Ben could hear a series of clicks and tweaks and a great deal more static than he was used to hearing on long-distance calls. Of course, all his mobile phone and long-distance business calls today... or in the future... use modern, microwave-satellite links that generally resulted in crystal clear connections. And then there was the Alpha-Max 2000 that was online all the time. If this 1957 scenario somehow proved correct, he was painfully aware of the fact that the Russians wouldn't shock the world with Sputnik for another eight months yet.

At last, he could just barely make out several distant rings, followed by a click and a female voice answering the phone. "Hello. This is the Southeastern Pennsylvania operator. What number are you trying to reach, please?"

Ben used his finger to trace a series of large question marks on his bedspread as he listened intently to his Hawaiian operator respond. "This is Hawaii calling for a William Katzenbach at 625-2991."

"In what city is that?"

"That's in Philadelphia — the Penn-Comp Corporation."

"And the exchange, operator?"

"That's the only number my party has, Philadelphia."

"Okay. One moment, please." Again, there was a succession of clicks and hisses.

"That exchange must be LOCUST. I'll try LO5-2991. Um... let me see..."

A whole series of clicks and hisses returned. He unsuccessfully tried to decipher the faint, unintelligible voices in the background. Maybe his paranoia was getting the best of him, but it sounded for all the world as if somebody were trying to tap his line. On the other hand, didn't old-fashioned over-seas cables sound just like this?

"I'm sorry, Hawaii — the number you have tried to reach is in a vacant series. And ah... Just one moment, please." Another minute or so of verbal silence passed. "Um... I'm sorry, but Philadelphia information doesn't seem to show any listing at all for that company. Would you please ask your party if they have an alternate number or if it could possibly be listed under another corporate name or in another town?"

"Mister Decker, do you know if..."

"Yes, operator. I heard the question, but no, I'm sorry, there is no other listing for that company." He was tempted to add that there wouldn't be any listing for at least another thirty years! "I'm terribly sorry for the inconvenience. Thank you so much for your trouble." Ben placed the receiver back in its cradle and stared across the room at the wall.

As an engineer, he was fairly used to dealing with complex problems with apparently contradictory inputs. Ninety-nine-point-nine percent of the time, the simplest alternative would prove to be the correct one. In light of all the complexities and convolutions involved with any of the back-in-time scenarios, that option seemed to be highly improbable. And because he had been carrying an extremely valuable piece of new technology, a more sinister plot seemed much more likely. At the very least, it was obvious that a financially lucrative motive existed.

Furthermore, didn't he "catch" the silhouette of someone who had been watching him last night? Even the unsuccessful phone call to Bill Katzenbach just now certainly piqued his suspicion. He simply had to believe that the mission-impossible-like, industrial-espionage plot was the most plausible.

Ben rubbed his hand across the stubble on his chin as he continued to consider his predicament. Until he had some honest-to-goodness proof, any theory was sure to have some weak points. But god knows this espionage scheme had several holes in it, each big enough to drive a truck through — or fly a jumbo jet through, for that matter! He couldn't shake the nagging notion that whoever was responsible for perpetrating such a complicated deception certainly had gone to a tremendous amount of trouble. That was the thing that bothered him the most. No matter how hard he tried, he just could not — even in his wildest dreams — conceive of any possible way that the Alpha-Max 2000 could be worth the kind of money this sham had to cost. Oh sure, the new computer-phone was a nifty piece of technology, maybe even a technological breakthrough of huge proportions... Still, new electronic systems were notorious for being on top of the retail heap for periods of time measured in months or — depressingly — sometimes only weeks. Really, wasn't this whole thing developing into a much too intricate plot to simply steal a prototype super-phone? It sure as all hell didn't seem very cost-effective.

Ben stood up from his spot on the side of the bed and ambled into the bathroom. He uncapped his toothpaste, ran a uniform portion of it along his brush, and proceeded to give his teeth a workover as he continued to ponder the alternatives. OK, he certainly had to somehow reckon with the high degree of difficulty involved, and yet, it surely wasn't an impossibility. Just go out and buy yourself some top-of-the-line, Disneyland-type engineers. With the proper planning and extensive enough resources, they could certainly turn the trick. It was entirely plausible to fake the old plane and cars and even the hotel — maybe by taking over an entire deserted island or something like that. It was even well within the realm of the tenable to feign a bogus cab ride from the airport, using the various matting and projection techniques that had bolstered Hollywood's special effects departments for the past umpteen years. Yet he still had to somehow explain such an exorbitant expense. And even if he could eventually account for the money, to Ben, the most disturbing part of all this still had to be explained. Exactly how was Leilani involved in all this? If all the 1957 Honolulu stuff really proved to be a big put-on, did that necessarily mean that Lani was simply acting out one callous part in this whole production? Well, if she were really just playing a cruel game with his emotions, she certainly had put on a command performance last night.

He took a big gulp of water and rinsed his mouth. As he looked at himself in the mirror, he tried to remember the statement Stosh made at O'Hare yesterday — or whenever it may have been when he had seen him last. Exactly how did he put it? Something like "your loyalty-to-the-extreme was always both your biggest strength and your greatest weakness." Maybe old Stosh was right on the money there. In a quarter-century of married life, Ben had never seriously considered another woman in any kind of romantic way. Oh sure, he certainly pleaded guilty to playing out in his mind the fleeting fantasies that he was certain all men endured — probably in many instances enjoyed. But not even one time during his entire married life did he ever actually contemplate any sort of intimate liaison with anyone other than Emily.

He pulled back the curtain, stepped into the tub, and adjusted the temperature using the two spigots. He quickly engaged the old-fashioned shower control and directed a hot stream of water right onto the nape of his neck. Oh, for god's sake, the more he thought about it, the more astonished he was regarding his encounter with Lani last night. The simple act of an embrace and passionate kiss was not the epitome of his amazement. After all, even at the ripe old age of almost fifty, all the hormones still flowed freely through his system, and a woman of Lani's beauty and presence were more than equal to stirring a corporeal quiver in the loins of any man. But what really boggled Ben's mind was the deep emotional feeling — almost a passionate commitment — that he was feeling for an almost total stranger. Now THAT was the out-of-character occurrence that simply couldn't have been predicted in any malevolent scheme. The woman had kindled a fire in Ben's heart that he knew was beginning to burn out of control with lightning speed. In barely half a day, his psyche had been consumed with the thought of her — maybe even to the point of being blinded by her. Of course, in many ways, having him fall madly in love with a beautiful young lady could have been the *piece de resistance* of any recipe created to pull the wool over his eyes. What better way to prevent someone from seeing the truth than to first make him blind. Aha, but the sheer genius of the method contained its fatal flaw — anyone carrying out such an involved conspiracy would certainly have studied Ben's history in great detail. And keeping that track record of incontestable fidelity in mind, any strategy that depended on him falling head-over-heels for a woman would have had to be discounted right in its embryonic stages.

The hot water massaging his weary frame helped to awake and rejuvenate his physical being. Even after he had finished rinsing all the soap from his body, he continued to delight in the pounding stream of invigorating water. No, Leilani was not any rogue. He was absolutely certain of that. She simply couldn't be a part of any sinister plot. After all, he was positive that she had been perfectly sincere with him on the beach last night. He felt that in his soul. Now, as for his being the victim of some corporate thievery conspiracy, he had to admit to being much less sure of himself. It was easy enough to fix a phone call to Bill Katzenbach. After all, considering what he had been through during the past day, a telephone call to his partner was obviously quite predictable. But if there really were some perverse stage master directing this entire production solely to bring about his demise, Ben was convinced that he could act in a more unpredictable, confounding manner. He could feel a smile creeping onto his face as he thought about meeting his adversary's challenge. Surely, he could put his unknown antagonists' mettle to a better test than he had so far.

He shut off the water, grabbed his towel, and dried himself thoroughly. With his towel wrapped around his waist, he fished his razor and a can of shaving cream from his toilet bag. Now that was funny — he hadn't seen one of the old, double-edged razors for years. He worked an ample amount of the lather into his skin and proceeded to shave the thirty-hour stubble from his face. Oh wow — come to think of it, did he, at last, find something his adversary had overlooked. He picked up the can of shaving cream and began to read its label: BURMA SHAVE. Hey, maybe he had found something — he hadn't seen a can of Burma Shave for twenty-five years. Did they still manufacture the stuff? He continued to read the small print on the label. Nah, no luck here — not one date anywhere to be found.

He finished shaving and went back into the bedroom area. It only made sense that they would have arranged for all his personal belongings to be screened for any telltale dates. Well, to keep "them" honest — whoever "them" might be — the least he could do was to check. He sat on the love seat, set his travel bag by his side, and opened it up. First, Ben inspected all the coins that had been in his pockets and all the bills in his billfold — every last date was pre-1957. Strangely enough, all his credit cards were gone. Apparently, in their place, he counted sixteen, one-hundred-dollar travelers' checks, every last one of them dated February 4, 1957, and signed Benjamin N. Decker. Well, thank goodness that his opponents were thoughtful enough to give him some spending money. Considering these 1957 prices, sixteen hundred dollars could more likely than not go quite a long way. He also still had his Pan American return trip ticket to Philadelphia scheduled for Saturday, February 16, 1957. He continued to go through his wallet and, to his absolute surprise, all his legal documents — driver's license, hospitalization card, Penn-Comp ID, and so on —

all were exactly the way they had been back in Philly, right down to and including the 1990s dates. Now that seems strange. Was that some sort of slip up? Now he might be getting somewhere — wasn't he? He could use the license to prove he was from the future. He slowly shook his head from side to side. Nah — the driver's license didn't mean a thing. After all, now that he thought about it, who would believe it was real? Oh sure, Lani would. But she already believed him, didn't she?

He closed the bag and scratched his chin. What to do now? Aha! This ought to fix them. A noticeable grin appeared on Ben's lips as he once again picked up the phone and dialed the front desk.

"Good morning and aloha — front desk. Can I help you?"

"I hope so." He now spoke in a clear tone that radiated confidence. "This is Ben Decker in room 418 again. Could I please have the overseas operator once more."

"Sure thing, Mister Decker."

Almost immediately, another voice came on the line. "Long-distance operator. How can I help you?"

"Hello, operator. I'd like to make a station-to-station call to Philadelphia, please."

"Name and room number, please."

"Yeah, sure — it's Decker, Ben Decker, in room 418."

"Um... 418. That's the Royal Hawaiian, isn't it?"

"Yes, madam."

"OK, Mister Decker. What is the number you would like me to try?"

"That's an area... um, that's in the Philadelphia, Pennsylvania area..." He could once again hear the old pulse digits being clicked off through the static. "...and the number is MAYFAIR - 63150." Again, Ben could make out another series of distant clicks and clacks. He leaned back in his seat and took a deep breath. His sense of smell was unexpectedly treated to a delightful, strangely familiar floral fragrance wafting through the open window. A rush of *deja vu* hit Ben over the head like a club. God — why did that smell seem so familiar? Though he had no idea from what kind of a blossom it came, he was certain the scent had been tucked away in his memory — for a long, long time.

His focus was once again drawn back to the phone by the sound of an almost recognizable ring-ring and a pause, a ring-ring and a pause. A tingle propagated down Ben's spine — had he made a mistake in placing this call? At last, the line was answered, and he could almost simultaneously hear the Hawaii operator click off her connection.

"Hello."

A large knot immediately made itself evident in Ben's throat. He unsuccessfully attempted to swallow the lump. As hard as he tried, he simply couldn't utter a single sound.

"Hello. Hello. Is anybody there?"

Finally, Ben struggled to barely sputter out a few feeble words. "Is... is...."

"Wait — I'll get my mom."

The brief pause seemed to last a lifetime. "Hello."

"Hel... hello. Is..." Ben tried to force the words from his mouth.

"Hello. Is anybody on the line?"

"Is... is... John... there?" The words barely passed his lips.

"I'm sorry — is this long-distance? I can hardly even hear you. Please speak up."

"John..." At last, the name loudly leaped off his tongue. "Can I speak to John?"

"Who do you want to speak with?"

"J... John..."

"Now Cyril, is that you? Cyril?"

Ben's face flushed white. He moved the receiver several inches away from his ear and looked at it as though it were an instrument of sadistic torment. The tinny, distant voice kept echoing out of the earpiece.

"Look, Cyril, you know that George is at work right now. Come to think of it, why aren't you at work today, Cyril?"

He fought his natural intuition that kept urging him to drop the receiver. He was at least determined to finish what he had started somehow. Slowly, he raised the phone once again to his ear.

"Cyril? Cyril... You sound so far away. Where are you, Cyril?"

He cleared his throat. "I'm terribly sorry, ma'am. I must have dialed the wrong number." He hung up the phone and, for what seemed to be a very long time, simply sat in the love seat and tried to analyze the incredibly bizarre experience he had just been through. At last, he felt as though he had collected his wits enough to get up and head back to the bathroom to get a drink. As he filled the glass, he glanced up at his likeness in the mirror. The image he saw looked like that of a man who had just seen a ghost! The reflected specter of his pale white face merely reinforced the terror that he felt deep inside. There was no longer any question at all in his mind. Though he had no idea of how it had happened, Benjamin Decker was at last absolutely certain he had somehow traveled back in time to 1957.

13

Friday, February 8, 1957: 6:35 A.M.

Ben stepped into the elevator and pressed the button for the lobby. Although he had been awake and functioning for well over an hour, he still felt a desperate need to get his morning fix of caffeine. As the doors closed, he was alone with his reflection in the shiny, brass doors of the elevator. As his vision remained fixed on his reflected image, he knew he needed to plan some course of action. Should he wait to return to Philly on his scheduled flight next week, or should he try to make earlier arrangements? Of course, what in god's name would he do if he arrived back in Pennsylvania, and it was still 1957? And in any event, what was he going to do about Lani? She was certainly real enough, and his feelings about her were just as genuine as genuine could be. Could he take her with him? For that matter, would she go? Oh god, how about Emily? ...and his girls?

The elevator eased to a stop, its indicator arrow marking the lobby. He kept watching his likeness in metal doors as they began to open onto the main floor. As if by magic, his reflected image disappeared and was replaced by that of a beautiful, Polynesian woman and her name spontaneously leaped from his lips. "LEILANI!"

She was standing right in front of the elevator, waiting for the doors to open. "BEN! I was just coming up to wake you. Oh, Ben." She threw her arms around him and squeezed him as tightly as she could.

"Lani, Lani, Lani... I was hoping so hard that I would find you down here. You must be psychic. Did you sense me thinking about you?"

"Well, I don't claim to be psychic, but I'm sure glad we ran into each other."

"But why are you here so early? I thought you didn't start work until nine o'clock."

"You're right, I don't start until then, but I've been awake for a couple of hours. I just couldn't sleep much at all, and I needed to see you. Oh, Ben, I don't want you to think I'm — you know."

They were still standing where they had met, right in front of the elevator, totally oblivious to the world. Quite suddenly and simultaneously, they both became aware of the fact that several people were trying to shuffle around them and get into the lift.

"Come on, Lani, let's get out of the way here." He gently placed one hand on her shoulder and ushered her away from the elevator. "Have you had any coffee yet? Any breakfast?"

"Not yet, but it sure sounds good to me — at least some hot tea, anyway."

"Whatever you say."

They walked towards the open-air coffee shop on the terrace fronting the beach. Ben's nose was once again attracted to the sweet, tropical fragrance emanating from the yellow-white blooms covering a compact tree growing by the patio. That positively was the source of the odor — and his reoccurring sense of *déjà vu*. He bent over and retrieved one of the yellow-white, five-petaled blossoms, lifted it to his nose, and breathed deeply. A broad grin spread across his face. "Maybe it's time to stop long enough to smell the flowers."

"Pardon me."

"Oh... um... nothing. It's just that this flower has such a magnificent odor — very alluring. I swear it's familiar to me — kind of a composite scent of all things Hawaiian. What kind of a flower is it?"

"Oh, that's plumeria, and I agree — it has such a beautiful fragrance. I frequently wear one behind my ear. You've probably smelled them at the airport, too. They're the lei-stringers' favorite flower."

"Yeah, that must be it — the airport. I wouldn't expect there'd be too many of these back in Pennsylvania." Ben handed the flower to Leilani. "A beautiful flower for a beautiful lady."

Leilani's blush was genuine. "Why, thank you, Ben." She tucked the flower behind her right ear and led the way and chose a small, round table that had an umbrella pole coming out of its center. It was the last table on the edge of the large, tiled area, right next to where the beach began. "How's this?"

"Just fine." He pulled a chair out, and she sat. Ben made his way around to the other side of the table, pausing for a moment to take in the view of the beauty surrounding him. Several beach boys could be seen in the direction of the Moana Hotel, readying their surfboards and outriggers in anticipation of hiring themselves out to the many tourists. He seated himself across from Lani. "Now then, what were you talking about back there — you don't want me to think what?"

"Oh Ben, you know..."

"Come on, Lani, I don't know. Tell me what you're talking about?"

"Well, I couldn't sleep, and I kept tossing and turning — all night long — and I kept thinking that you must have thought I was, well... you know..."

He could see her eyes getting moist, and he clutched her hand beneath the table. "For goodness sakes, Lani, I'm not going to bite you. What are you trying to say?"

She expelled a rush of air and squeezed his hand hard. "Oh Ben, I couldn't help imagining that you must think I am a really... well, like some kind of a loose woman — I mean like I was really promiscuous or something." The moisture in her pretty, brown eyes had finally given way to full-blown tears. "I'm just not like that, Ben. Honest to god I'm not..."

"Lani, Lani, Lani." Ben shook his head from side to side. "That's the absolute last thing that I thought about last night. I woke up quite early myself this morning, and believe me, that notion never crossed my mind."

"But you must think I'm always chasing after married guys. After all... I... um... I mean..."

"Oh, now I see. Look, Lani, get a hold of yourself here. I think no such thing. As a matter of fact, now that you mention it..." Ben pulled his wedding ring off his finger and handed it to Leilani. "Look on the inside of that and tell me what it says."

Lani wiped the tears from her eyes, held the ring in front of her, and read out loud, "ESH to BND, 10-31-72. This is your wedding ring, isn't it?"

"Well, if you want to call it that."

"What do you... um... Does this mean October of nineteen seventy-two?"

Ben nodded his head.

"But you said you were married for twenty-some years..."

"Well, I was... ur, I will be... Um... Look, Lani, what is today's date?"

"It's February 8, 1957."

"Don't you see — that seems just incredible to me. I don't pretend to have any idea about the hows and whys, but surely you can see the implications here, can't you?"

"Sure." Her tears had begun to dry up. "You're telling me that you really ARE from the... the future."

"Yes, I am. And something happened to me about an hour ago that has absolutely, positively convinced me that you are one-hundred percent correct."

"I'm correct?"

"Yeah — I mean correct about it being 1957."

"Hey, hold on here, Ben. Now I understand how confused and unsure you may be about what today is, but believe me, I'm not the least bit confused. I KNOW it's February 8, 1957, just as surely as I know my own name!" She looked at him very strangely. "There can't be any doubt about that — not to me, anyway. I haven't had any strange plane trips or suspicious bumps on the head. Certainly, I know what today's date is."

"OK then, surely you'll agree that I can't possibly be married. I mean, I haven't even met Emily Harris as of now, and the way things are going, it's doubtful that I ever will!"

"But how can all this be?"

"I told you that I don't pretend to know exactly how all this has happened, but one thing is certain: I used to be there — in the late 1990s, I mean — and now I'm sure as all hell here — smack dab in the middle of 1957!"

"I'll vouch for that. You said something happened this morning that finally convinced you. Just what happened? Why are you so positive?"

He shifted somewhat closer to her and turned his body directly facing her. He extended both arms, gently caressed Lani's hands, and peered directly into her eyes. He first exhaled and then inhaled quite deliberately. "I had the most uncanny experience a little while ago, and I swear that I feel funny even talking about it." He unconsciously looked around as though checking to see if anyone was listening.

"Ben, who are you looking for?"

"Oh, I don't know. Just being paranoid, I guess. After you went home last night, I noticed someone that may have been watching us on the beach. I guess I still need to convince myself that no one is keeping an eye on me."

"Most likely, you only saw some beach boy trying to walk off his insomnia." She looked around in the general direction of the beach. "Well, I don't see anyone listening in right now."

"I hope you're right." Then he leaned closer to her and continued in a very quiet tone. "I placed a phone call to the States earlier this morning — to Philadelphia."

"Surely you couldn't have talked to Emily."

"You're right — I couldn't have, and I didn't. I called my parents' home."

"Your parents? And?"

"And I spoke to my mother."

"You're sure? I mean, how can you be so sure it was really your mother?"

"Oh, I'm sure — absolutely convinced, for that matter. Look, it's a long story Lani, and I don't want to burden you..."

"Come on, Ben. You're not burdening me with it."

"Well, I'll try to explain it to you as briefly as I can. Obviously, you're convinced — um, you KNOW — it's 1957. After all, you live here. But I'm having all kinds of problems accepting this. I mean, you've got to admit that this has to be the most bizarre thing you've ever heard of in your life!"

"Admitted... But I DO believe that YOU believe it, Ben."

He squeezed her hands again. "Oh Lani, I'd just about be going out of my gourd without you to talk to. Anyway, my mind keeps trying to make some semblance of sense out of this whole fiasco. I mean, there's got to be some sort of logical pattern here. I keep coming back to this idea of a sinister plot that someone has put together to steal our latest electronic gadget."

"Well, I follow what you're saying, but you know that just can't be the case."

"Can't be? Why so sure?"

"Come on Ben! Wouldn't that mean you don't believe me? It would mean I'd have to be part of some plot! I'm just me, Ben — plain, old Leilani Kealoha."

"Obviously, all this has crossed my mind. But it's possible you became involved in this in a totally innocent way and still not be aware of a thing."

"Right! And I'd still be believing that it was — IS — 1957. Come on, Ben — there's just no approach you can take with this whole thing that will still allow you to have it both ways."

"Well, okay Lani. I guess ya got me there. I do believe you — now. But in my own mind last night — even this morning yet — I was still trying to sort through the possibilities. Anyway, I was fairly convinced that someone was trying to persuade me into believing that I had somehow been transposed back in time. So, I needed to find a way to discover a flaw in their plan — a chink in their armor, so-to-speak. Well, I knew that it was easy enough to fake me out on a supposed phone call to my partner, but I figured there'd be no way they could fool me if I called my folks — actually spoke with one of my parents."

"Why? Couldn't they have anticipated that?"

"Some things just can't be anticipated. You see, my father, George Decker, had two brothers — Cyril and Paul. For god-only-knows what reason, all three of the brothers always called each other John. I mean, conversations among the three were really something else to try to follow, because they all addressed each other as John. Now I'm telling you this as fact, and it's a rather minor point, but there's no way anyone could know this today — no way at all! Anyway, I made the call a little while ago and..." He cleared a rapidly developing lump in his throat and squeezed her hand in his.

"And what?"

"Well, my mom didn't answer the phone."

"Who did?"

Ben could feel the blood draining from his face. "I did." His tone was so feeble that Leilani couldn't hear him across the table.

"Ben — are you all right?"

He nodded in the affirmative.

"Who answered the phone?"

"I DID." It was though a dam had burst as he blurted out the words.

"Oh god. Did you speak with..."

"No, no... I... he... mom quickly got on the line. At least for starters, I was positive it was her voice."

"How could you be so sure?"

"Come on, Lani, we're talking about a mother here — and I was lucky enough to grow up in a really close-knit family. I mean, wouldn't you still recognize your own mother's voice, even if you hadn't heard it for years?"

"Well... Yeah, I guess I see what you mean, but I'm still not sure you could..."

"And then there was the... um... that." He pointed toward the flower she had placed behind her ear.

"You mean the plumeria?" Lani gently touched the flower with her hand.

"Yes — the plume... plumeria. Of course, I didn't know what it was called until just a few minutes ago when you told me. But believe me, this fragrance has been stashed away deep in the back of my brain somewhere for forty-some years. Isn't it funny how the mind can file away a simple odor for all that time and recognize it in an instant, releasing a flood of memories and feelings with it."

"I... I guess I know what you mean. But how do you know you remembered the plumeria from then. Maybe you smelled it on one of your trips to..."

"No, no, Lani. When the fragrance of that blossom hit my brain this morning — not to mention hearing my own voice answer the phone — it all came back to me. That precise same smell was in my mom's kitchen way back in 1957. I don't have any idea how that can be, but I remember that I even asked her about it."

"And?"

"No go — she didn't smell it. Only I did... but I KNOW I did. The rest of the phone call aside, the plumeria all by itself absolutely, positively convinced me that the conversation with mom was just as real as real could be." His pale face still attested to his shaken state of mind.

"But, you're implying that there's more?"

"Sure, there is. When she answered, I asked if John was there. Now no one could know what weird personal habits those three brothers shared forty-plus years ago. If anyone were putting on some big hoax solely for my benefit, they would have had to tell me I had the wrong number or something — no John lives here."

"I'll go along with that."

"Well, mom knew exactly who I wanted."

"How do you mean?"

"I mean, she just assumed that I was my Uncle Cyril and that I was asking for my dad — George. I'm telling you that she was absolutely convinced I was Cyril."

"So, did you talk to her?"

"Oh god, Lani, how could I? The whole notion of speaking to her is ridiculous. I mean, as far as she is concerned — you know it is 1957 — I'm not quite a teenager yet. God forbid if I'd have answered my own phone call!"

"Oh boy! I see what you mean..."

"It even gets worse than that. For crying out loud, I could barely get any words at all out. The lump in my throat was as big as a grapefruit."

"Because..."

"Because? Come on, Lani, you keep forgetting — I really AM from the future. You see, both my mom and my dad have been dead for almost twenty years. I may as well have been talking to a ghost!"

14

Friday, February 8, 1957: 7:40 A.M.

The waitress cleared away the last of the breakfast dishes. Ben broke small pieces from the crust of his toast and fed them to a couple of brightly colored finches that showed no fear of their human benefactor.

"Carlos will have your head if he sees you feeding the birds." Lani smiled broadly as she leaned back and sipped on her cup of tea.

"Carlos? Who's Carlos?"

"He's our food and beverage manager. It just drives him crazy when he sees tourists giving handouts to the feathered visitors. To him, the birds are just one more source of dirt for which he needs to schedule someone to clean up after."

"I guess I'll have to plead ignorance." He took a sizable gulp of his coffee. "Well, I hope you filled up. I still can't believe a woman as small as you are could possibly have eaten all that you did. I mean, where'd you put it?"

"Stop it, Ben. You're making me feel self-conscious."

"I'm only teasing you. But eggs, sausage, and all that butter on your rice and bread — aren't you the least bit concerned about your cholesterol level?"

"Cholesterol? What on earth is cholesterol?"

"You know, cholesterol — the fatty... um... Aw..." It suddenly dawned on Ben that he was reflecting on a health concern — or was it a fad? — of an entirely different time. "Okay, I get it — the fifties, huh. And you must have been wearing an I LIKE IKE button in the presidential election last fall."

"No, as a matter of fact, I liked Stevenson. But we couldn't vote here in the Territory anyway. Ben, why are you talking so funny? What is this co-les-traw stuff, anyway?"

"Col-es-traw!" Ben couldn't restrain his laughter. "No, no — it's cholesterol. Look, never mind. It's just one of the latest crazes straight out of the future. I'll try to watch myself."

Refusing to be deterred by his laughter, Lani covered her mouth as if to hide a yawn.

"Well, I see... So, conversation with me must just bore you to death."

"Oh Ben, now you know that's not true. I'm really tired. I'll bet I didn't sleep more than an hour last night."

"...worrying that you left a wrong impression on me."

"Yes. And just plain worried about you in general."

"In general? Now, what does that mean?"

"Oh, come on, Ben. In my entire life, I never felt — um... felt the way I did for you last night. So fast... ur, I mean it was just so fast... out of control... It was hard enough to try to get a hold of my feelings, but then all a sudden, it dawned on me that I had to deal with this whole back-from-the-future thing."

"How do you mean that?"

"Goodness sakes, Ben! You told me that you had to rule out in your mind that I was some sort of menacing collaborator in this far-ranging plot. I mean for crying out loud, how is some innocent girl from Hilo supposed to take this charming, sweet-talking guy from Philadelphia who just flat out tells me he came back in time over forty years. Just think about that for a bit — CRAZY or what? Now you have to admit, it's not every day an Island girl — any girl — gets that kind of line dropped on her."

"Hey, wait a second here! It's not a line, Lani..." Ben tilted his chair back on two legs as he contemplated her apprehensions. "Aw man, when you put it like that, I can see your point of view. I guess I've been so worried about MY believing YOU that I never really gave much thought to YOUR wariness about ME. But I'm telling you, Lani, all that I have told you is true."

"Okay, Okay — I do believe you. But give me a break, Ben. I sure had to go over that in my mind a few dozen times. As a matter of fact, wouldn't you think me strange if I didn't wonder at least a little bit about your story."

"Well yeah, I guess so. But all that's important now is that you trust me — believe me. You really do, don't you?"

"With all my heart. And you know what else I believe in for the first time?"

"What?"

"Love at first sight." She blushed and looked away toward the feeding finches.

"Oh, Lani." He leaned over and tenderly kissed her on her cheek. Lani put her arms around Ben's neck as they both closed their eyes, the small kiss impulsively escalating into a deep embrace. Neither noticed that one of the more opportunistic yellow and red finches had used the gentle moment as an invitation to land and nervously sort through the few remaining crumbs right on the table. The tiny bird, totally oblivious to the loving couple so near, anxiously picked at a crumb, hopped over a saucer, and found a rather large piece of crust. No sooner had it made the discovery, the finch was somehow airborne, miraculously maintaining a hold on the sizable strip of toast as though its life depended on it. Ben followed the finch's flight and noticed a much larger bird perched on the edge of a thatched shed behind the restaurant, its big eyes seemingly staring right at him. "What kind of bird is that, Lani?"

Lani looked up to the thatched roof. "That's *pueo*, a Hawaii owl." She smiled.

Ben teased her, "Jeez, I almost think that you know *pueo*."

She arched her eyebrows and beamed at him. "I DO know *pueo*. *Pueo* is my *aumakua*."

"Auma... help!"

"My *aumakua*. An *aumakua* is like my guardian angel."

Ben tilted his head. "Your guardian angel?"

The waitress quite audibly cleared her throat, tactfully looking at the bill pad she held in front of her. "Um... Excuse me. Will there be anything else here this morning, or should I total the bill?" She had obviously startled them both.

Ben quickly looked up, face flushed red just like a little boy who was caught with his hand in the cookie jar. So much for guardian angels. "Oh gee, ah... Yeah, I think that's it. Lani?"

Lani smiled and put her hand to her mouth as she nodded her approval. The waitress hastily retreated towards the kitchen. Lani could no0 longer suppress her laughter. "Oh Ben, I wish you could see your face. It's worth a million dollars."

"For Christ's sake, Lani! I'm not exactly used to kissing strange women in a public place all the time, you know."

"So now I'm a strange woman, am I? I guess you'll..."

"No, no, no. I mean — oh, you know exactly what I mean. Look, when do you have to be at work, anyway?"

"Not till nine."

"Nine, huh. Don't forget, you have to make that call to your cousin over at the Moana Hotel."

"What for?"

"Come on, Lani. You know doggone well that I still need a place to bunk, right."

"Yeah, right, so?"

"Well, surely you don't want me sleeping on a park bench, do you?"

"Come on, Ben. I thought that was all settled."

"Settled? How's that?"

"I thought you already agreed with me?"

"I'm not following you at all, Lani. Agreed with what? What am I missing here?"

"Come on, Ben. After all that you — we — have been through during the past day, there's no point in having you suffer through an open-air dormitory. My apartment is rather small, but my sofa is perfectly comfortable. At this point, you may just as well stay at my place."

15
Friday, February 8, 1957: 5:15 P. M.

The cabby placed the two suitcases on the curb as Ben searched his billfold for the fare. He looked up at the three-story, stucco-covered building. "So, this is the Kealoha residence, huh?"

"You can bet your bottom dollar, mister." There was an air of pride in Lani's voice.

"It sure is just as close to the Royal Hawaiian as you said it was. I know you felt funny taking a cab, but I really didn't feel like lugging these bags." He picked one up with each hand and looked to Lani.

"Yeah, it's exactly one mile. I nearly always walk. Once in a while — when we get a rainy day — I'll hop on the bus." She carried her handbag and his carry-on and led the way past the line of coconut palms and toward an outdoor stairway. They climbed two flights of stairs and walked along a narrow, open-air balcony. "Are you still alive back there, porter?"

Ben was nearly out of breath. "Just barely. I guess you could tell that I don't haul luggage for a living."

"Well, you'll be happy to hear that we're just about home." Lani only passed two or three more doors before she finally stopped, reached into her bag, and rooted around for a moment. "I know it's in here some. Aha — there it is." She fished a small keyring out, unlocked the door, kicked her sandals off, and stepped into the apartment. "Aloha and welcome to my humble *hale*."

"Let me guess — *hale* has to mean house, right?"

"Your mastery of the Hawaiian language is simply superb!"

"But my mastery of being a porter still leaves much to be desired." Ben dragged both bags in the door and, once inside, abandoned them abruptly. "I was getting a bit nervous when you couldn't find your keys. I thought sure as shooting that it was going to be the Moana dormitory for the TWO of us tonight." He started to chuckle.

"Oh, Benjamin!" She rolled her eyes towards the ceiling as she placed her bag on the wooden framed sofa.

He took a deep breath and began to survey the medium-sized, one-room, parlor-kitchen combination. The walls were constructed of plain cinder blocks, painted white and decorated at intervals with inexpensive but colorful five-and-dime store prints. The floor was covered with nondescript linoleum, brightened up here and there with several small throw rugs. Three windows and a large skylight gave the room an open, airy feeling. A small table, only large enough to comfortably seat two people, was placed right in front of a picture window looking out towards a view of the beautifully green, jagged mountains that formed the backdrop for Honolulu. Though quite simple, the apartment reflected a neat, well-organized occupant. "So, this is your place, huh? I really like it — very nicely done."

"Why, thank you, Ben. It's certainly nothing fancy, but it's all I can afford on my three-hundred-fifty-dollar-a-month salary."

"My god, Lani! You only get three-fifty a month!" Ben was shaking his head from side to side in disbelief.

"Hey, that's pretty good money around here. I was only getting two-eighty-five as a secretary in the personnel office. I just got the promotion to customer relations about a year and a half ago."

"Man-o-man, I'd better get used to 1950's finances." He looked down towards his feet. "Oh jeez, I still have my shoes on. From the looks of the piles of footwear outside all the doors, I guess I'm breaking a local taboo. Sorry." He bent down and started sliding his shoes from his feet.

"Oh, it's OK, Ben. Leaving one's shoes outside the door is a local custom — a throwback to Japanese tradition, I guess. But in Japan, they always covered their floors with grass mats. I guess the mats would have really taken a beating if folks wore shoes while inside — especially during their winters. No need here, though — don't worry about it."

"No, no, no. I don't want to be the least bit of trouble. You know, when in Rome..."

"Do as the Romans do. I know, I know. But remember, this is the Hawaiian Territory, not Rome."

"Nonetheless..." Ben walked back out the door and placed his shoes next to Lani's. "...woe be it me to..."

"Please bring the newspaper in with you."

He bent over to pick up the paper. As he straightened back up again, he inadvertently glanced down at the street. A big, local-looking man leaning on the corner lamppost quickly turned away as soon as Ben's eyes made contact with him. The stranger dropped his cigarette onto the curb, ground the butt out with his foot, and hastily started to walk away. Was this the same man he had spotted last night? Was he under surveillance? Well, he figured that there was no sense in troubling Leilani. He reentered the apartment and closed the door behind him. "So, where do you want to go for dinner tonight? The very least I can do is buy you a meal."

"Oh Ben, I'm so tired from last night's ordeal, I'd just as soon stay here — if that's OK with you." She took the paper from his hand and placed it on the end table. "I mean, I left home so early this morning that I wasn't even here by the time the morning newspaper came. Now that's really early! Why don't we just get cleaned up and relax around here tonight? God knows you must be tired, too."

"True, true, my dear. But we still need sustenance — we need to get something to eat."

"I'm going to make you dinner."

"Aw, I don't want you cooking. You just confessed to being weary."

"Oh, it's no problem. Since you mentioned Rome, I thought I'd make spaghetti. That's really easy, and I just love spaghetti. How about you?"

"Hawaiian spaghetti — now that sounds different! As long as you don't put any pineapples in it..."

"Pineapples?" She looked at him as though he had totally lost his mind.

"I guess that means no pineapples. Okay, you talked me into it."

"Great! Spaghetti it is. I'll get dinner together and, if you want to, you can go and get cleaned up. I mean, take a shower or a shave or do whatever it is men do when they get cleaned up."

"Whatever men do! My dear Leilani, what in god's name are you trying to say here?" Ben had a big smile on his face. Lani didn't.

"Well, I never... Ben Decker, I never, ever had a guy around my place before. Come on, Ben, I'm single. I told you that I'm not THAT kind of girl, and I don't appreciate you insinuating that..."

"Insinuating what? Boy oh boy! Touchy, touchy, touchy! I wasn't trying to insinuate a thing. Whatever happened to the liberated female?"

"The what?"

"The liberated... Oh man, there I go again. Sorry. I forgot women haven't been liberated yet. I'll bet you haven't even burned your brassiere or..."

"Benjamin! You'd better watch your language!" She grabbed the newspaper and mockingly began to hit him over the head with it. "Stop it, Ben. I don't know if you're just kidding or if you're trying to get fresh with me."

"I'm sorry, Lani. Honest. I'm not getting fresh with you. It's just that... Oh god, I better quit while I'm ahead. If anyone — even in her wildest dreams — would consider this to be ahead... well... It's just that it's so amazing how many ways the world has changed during the past four or five decades. I keep forgetting how, ah... well, um... how sheltered ladies used to be."

"Sheltered? I don't understand what you mean."

"You will, young lady. Believe me, in a few more years, you'll understand very well. Now, where's this bathroom in which I'm supposed to do whatever it is that men do?"

Lani was scratching her head as if she were trying to decide whether or not to wait until history played itself out or if she should press Ben for more detail now. "I'm starting to really wonder about you, Ben. Maybe I should reconsider all the trust I'm feeling for you." She shook her head and walked towards an open doorway. "This is my bedroom, and the bath is right next to it — over there. You can put your bags out of the way in this corner." She walked into her bedroom and pointed toward an open area on the far side of the room. "Over here." She opened a closet door. "Now, let me get you a clean towel."

16
Friday, February 8, 1957: 7:30 P. M.

The Hawaiian spaghetti turned out being as Italian as any he'd ever had. Ben insisted on finishing up the dishes while Lani took a bath. He cleaned out the sink and hung the dishtowel on its rack. He picked up the newspaper on his way over to the sofa and glanced at the masthead on the front page: *THE HONOLULU ADVERTISER,* "Aloha! Today is Friday, February 8, 1957." Ben scanned his way through the first section for a good fifteen minutes until Lani finally opened the bathroom door and promptly marched out, fully draped in an oversized pink bath towel.

"Aha, Leilani Kealoha! I caught you! If I didn't know better, I'd say that you stole that towel directly from... let me think now — could it have been the Royal Hawaiian Hotel?"

"I did not, you *kolohe*, you!"

"Hey, quit cursing me..."

"I'm not cursing, you RASCAL! Employees always get first dibs on any old linen. A single girl has to save her pennies wherever she can, you know."

"Yeah, yeah." He feigned an expression of disgust and shook his head as he dropped the newspaper onto his lap.

She totally ignored his tease. "Well, it looks as though you've been occupying yourself with the *ADVERTISER.* Don't let me interrupt. I still have to fix my hair and put something on. I'll be out in a few minutes." She entered her bedroom and pulled the door closed behind her.

Ben went over to the small, antique refrigerator, placed a few ice cubes in a glass, and filled it with water. He came back to the couch and returned to the paper. His quick survey of current events proved quite revealing: problems in the Middle East, questions concerning nuclear disarmament, political corruption in Washington, a four-person murder-suicide in Illinois. If he didn't see the datelines on many of these stories, he'd have thought this was just another 1990s newspaper. There certainly were differences in terms of money items — the Dow Jones closed yesterday at 468, Ike promised the inflation rate would be reduced from its "monstrous" one and a half percent, and sirloin steak was advertised for sixty-nine cents a pound. And yet once he got past the prices and the gadgets, he was absolutely amazed at how little the human condition had — will — really change during the next forty-some years.

The bedroom door opened, and Lani came out wearing a colorful Hawaiian print blouse and a pair of khaki shorts. She was still combing her long, black hair back over her shoulders as she sat next to Ben on the sofa. "I feel like a new woman — so refreshed."

"I'll vouch for that, lady. You sure look all revived and ready to go." He breathed deeply. "Ah! And you smell as fresh as a Hawaiian waterfall."

"A waterfall? And just how does a waterfall smell?"

"Fresh and clean — just like sweet Leilani."

"Why thank you, kind sir. It's just such a different analogy than the run of the mill comparison to a flower — a plumeria, no less."

"...only because I'm so different from some run of the mill guy."

"Oh, I see — you must use that line on all your women..."

"Hey, lady!" He gently pretended to hit her arm. "Now, I told you that I wasn't like that."

"Okay, Okay. So, what have you discovered in the *ADVERTISER* while I was soaking, anyway?"

"Well, I don't know if you're ready for this, but what I've discovered, my dear, is rather profound."

"Profound, huh? And what could that be?"

"Well, in my time — in the future — it seems as though there's a considerable yearning by so many people to return to the past, to do things the way they were done in the 'good old days', so-to-speak. People are willing to spend really big bucks to buy anything old — music, cars – even watching old TV shows. Anything able to feed the need for nostalgia is destined to be a best seller. Well, it's really interesting to sit down for a half-hour or so and read a newspaper from the 'good old days' firsthand. I'll tell you — I'm downright amazed."

"Amazed? How so?"

"I guess the nostalgic vision of many of my cohorts doesn't seem to come with twenty-twenty eyesight."

"Come on, Ben! Speak English, will you?"

"I only mean that so many people from my time think the world was somehow better in the fifties — that there were fewer problems or more solutions or whatever. But that's because human memory has such an effective screen built right into it."

"What sort of screen?"

"Well, call it a nostalgia screen if you want. You know nostalgia is a fond remembering of things in the past that, by definition, always includes ONLY the pleasant stuff. Our memories quite selectively filter out all the bad recollections and amplify the good. That's what is meant by the old phrase, 'time heals all wounds'. Obviously, time doesn't heal the wound — it FORGETS them!"

"I see what you mean. I guess it's no different now. If you looked at the entertainment section in the paper, you'd have noticed that. The war movies wind up being the most popular shows. Of course, they always seem to remember all the glory of war, but very little of the pain."

"Exactly the point, Lani. You folks living in the fifties have your own nostalgia. When you really think about it, you couldn't be any different in that respect. Hey, we're all human, and happy memories are the balm people of all generations use to soothe their past horrors. Oh, all the names and some of the places are different, but human nature surely hasn't changed one iota during the past — next — forty-some years. I'm downright convinced of that. And to tell you the truth, I find that both pleasantly reassuring on one level and scary as hell on the other."

"It must really be weird to see the world from two different positions in history almost simultaneously."

"Now there's an understatement if I've ever heard one!"

"You know, I'm a reader, and I consider myself a fairly well-informed person. Actually, I really did quite well in high school and all. And yet, I'm not really sure that I want to see into the future before it actually happens. It scares me to think about burning bras and all that..."

"Oh, Lani, don't lose any sleep over that. I just didn't mean it to..."

"Thank god!" She let out a rush of air to express her relief. "You were only kidding — women didn't really burn their bras then — did they?"

"Well, no... ur... yeah... I mean, I wasn't really exaggerating history or anything — there was a period of rebellion when a lot of women did actually burn their bras in protest, but..."

"Protest what? I like being a woman!"

"Well, I'm sure they did too, but it's just that many people — especially men — sort of took women for granted and treated them unfairly. I guess they still do in many ways."

"For example..."

"Well..." Ben rubbed his chin, trying to think of an appropriate illustration. "Ah... for example, why didn't you go to college?"

"Me? College?"

"Yeah, college. You're very bright — I'm certain you could have done well in college."

"Well, I don't know, really. I never actually thought about it. None of my girlfriends planned to go, and we never talked about it. You've got to admit, most women are too busy being mothers to go to college."

"Why? Because men want them to be that way?"

"Um... I don't think so..." Ben could see that she was seriously considering his question.

"Just imagine a time when almost all women like yourself will go to college — become doctors and lawyers and professors. Think of the time when women will finally have the chance to do anything they want, a time when some of the best academic schools in the country will be women's schools — schools like Smith College and Wellesley and... Ah, look, maybe it isn't such a good idea to get into all this. I'm not so sure I'm necessarily a qualified authority on the women's movement, anyway."

"Women's movement?"

"Keep reading the papers. In time, they'll give you a much better insight into the women's liberation movement than I ever could."

"You tease... Now you really have whetted my appetite. But I have the distinct feeling that I'll have to take your word for it." She got up and walked towards the refrigerator. "Would you like a Coke?"

"No thanks. I've been drinking ice water. You've got the best, tastiest water I've ever had."

"Ben..." She looked at him in a funny way as if to let him know she realized that he was kidding her. "You're always teasing me. Will you be serious? Now, do you want a Coke, or don't you?"

He couldn't hold back his laughter. "Lani, I'm not kidding you at all. I love this water. It's the best tasting stuff in the whole universe, as far as I can tell — no joking involved. If you only knew what Schuylkill Punch tasted like."

"Schuylkill Punch? That sounds just awful! What's that?"

"It IS awful! The Schuylkill River flows through Philadelphia, and at least some nearby towns back there draw their drinking water from it. That is, of course, after all the other towns upstream are finished dumping their sewage into it."

"Ew... Sewage?"

"Honest. And, to make the stuff potable, they have to put so much chlorine in it that it literally stinks. Yuck!"

"Now that's disgusting. But I never can tell if you're kidding or not. Are you telling the truth?"

He raised his opened right-hand high. "I swear. You know when you came out from your bath, I told you that smelled good. Again, I wasn't kidding you. In the Philadelphia of my time, you'd smell just like chlorine bleach after coming out of the shower. Believe me — it's just terrible! Enjoy your Coke, young lady. I want more water." He got up and filled his glass once again.

Ben returned to his spot on the couch. Lani sat facing him on the other end of the sofa with her back propped against one of its arms. She placed her classic shaped Coke bottle on the end table, tucked her knees into her chest, and grabbed them with her hands. "What's Emily like?"

Ben was taken somewhat off guard by the instantaneous change in topics. "What's she like? What do you mean?"

"I mean, is she pretty?"

"Well, yeah. Sure, she's pretty — oh, maybe about five feet two or so."

"Same height as me?"

"Yeah. Maybe a little bit taller. Ah... she has blue eyes and blond hair and a nice figure. Actually, she's like the all-American women."

"All-American?"

"You know — kind of like the type of women you'd see in the movies."

"Ah... Like Marilyn Monroe?"

Ben nearly laughed at the thought of what Emily's reaction would be to being compared to Marilyn Monroe — the antithesis of the liberated women. "Well — not exactly, but you have the right idea. And on top of all that, she's a very bright woman — just like you are."

"Did she go to... Oh, stupid question! Of course, she went to college. You said she was a teacher. Plus, you said ALL women go to college in your time."

"Well, not exactly all women go to college. But yeah, certainly Emily did. That's where we met."

"Same school?"

"Nah. She went to Temple University, and I went to Drexel — they're both in Philadelphia — right in the city. Ever hear of either one of them?"

Lani shook her head. "Not really. You said you just didn't have the same feelings for her anymore. Do you still love her?"

"Oh, Lani, do you really want to go through all this?"

"Sure. I wouldn't have asked otherwise."

"I guess it depends on what you mean by love. I don't dislike her — I care that she is safe and secure and happy, even. And I certainly care that my girls are okay. But if you mean love like in a romantic way — well, we're just not... Oh, I just don't know how to say it. We don't really share that special, ah... um..."

"I understand. When did it happen, Ben?"

"What?"

"When did the two of you fall out of love?"

"Oh boy, that's not the kind of thing I could easily put a date on. Jeez, I don't even know. It was a gradual thing — after a while, we just started doing less and less together. And before you knew it..." Ben snapped his fingers. "I mean, until you just asked when we fell out of love, I never really thought about it that way. But we surely have grown apart."

"That's so sad."

Ben's eyes gazed towards the floor as an expression of melancholy crossed his face. "That's very true. Believe me, it certainly wasn't the kind of development either one of us planned for. Actually, if you pardon my double negative, I haven't thought of us NOT really loving each other, cause in some ways, we still probably do. It's more like we just plain don't LIKE each other anymore."

"Now wait just a minute, Ben. Your double negative sounds more like double talk to me."

"No, no — I sure don't mean it to! You know, it may sound crazy, but I always thought couples basically had their terms all screwed up anyway. I mean, it certainly is possible to love someone and have no emotional involvement at all."

"What do you mean?"

"I mean in the Christian sense of the word love. How many times do you hear a minister, priest, or rabbi talk about loving your fellow man? You know, I'm not really a religious person in the go-to-church-regularly sense, I really do believe what I'm saying here with all my heart. I do love my fellow man and feel a great obligation to care about his wellbeing. However, it's quite obvious that this doesn't have to entail any sort of personal regard or sexual union or anything at all like that. As a matter of fact, the Christian kind of love I'm talking about doesn't really involve any emotion whatsoever. It's really quite possible to love someone and yet not necessarily like them at all. Are you following me?"

"Well, kind of..." She nodded her head and released one of her tucked up knees as she reached for her Coke.

"But the opposite case is quite impossible."

"The opposite?"

"Yeah, the opposite. All I'm trying to say is that it's just not possible to like someone if you don't love them, too. I mean, as far as romance and intimate relationships go, the really meaningful term here is like. Considering the perspective I just explained, I personally like far fewer persons than I love. And naturally, most of the emotional interactions are tied up with the people I like."

"You know, I never really thought of it that way before, but I think I agree with you. The only trouble is that it would really sound funny telling your husband that you liked him instead of saying you loved him."

He stared right into her big, brown eyes. "I like YOU, Lani. Now, does that sound so funny?"

She blushed. "Well, no but... Oh, Ben, you know what I mean..."

"Sure, I know what you're saying, but it sounds funny to you right now only because our terms have been so very poorly defined for generations upon generations. For crying out loud — just because poets write love poems instead of LIKE poems doesn't mean the entire concept is wrong."

She took a gulp of her soda and looked him right in the eye. "Okay, okay — you've converted me already. And you know what — I like you too, Ben. I mean... I like you very much." Her face was still flushed red.

"Oh, Leilani... You know that's the nicest thing you could say to me. And we've established that the feeling is mutual." He put his hand on her knee and gave her a gentle squeeze.

"Since you and Emily have fallen out of love — ur, find yourselves not really liking each other anymore — do you ever feel lonely?"

"I sure do. For crying out loud, I am human. But I spend a lot of time working. It's a great diversion, and it helps to take my mind away from thinking about her.

"So, who do you talk to?"

"No one, really. I'm not that close to anyone anymore."

"How about your friends from college?"

"Well, I still feel close to a few. At least there's one friend in particular that I feel more comfortable with than anyone else I can think of offhand. But heck, he lives in Chicago, and I rarely see the guy anymore. It's pretty hard spilling your guts to someone on a long-distance call."

"And I guess it must make it worse, even, living together like that."

"Worse? What do you mean?"

"I know I get lonely many times. Oh, I don't mean lonely like there's no one around the house or anything like that. I have several pretty good friends that I see fairly often, and we do oodles of neat things together. But I'm talking about feeling lonely for someone to share your life with, to be alone with, to... well... to love. I mean... to make love to... to... Oh, you know what I'm saying."

"Yeah, I know."

"Well, it must be worse living with someone that you used to be together with like that — in a loving kind of way. And all of a sudden you don't get together like... well, you know. Together like..."

"Like making love to each other."

"Yeah, that's it. It must be harder having your ex-lover right there to always remind you."

"Well, I sure wouldn't recommend such a living arrangement. As you have correctly surmised, it is a rather strange situation. And how about... Nah — it's none of my business..."

"Come on, Ben. You can feel free with me."

"Well... I just wonder about you. Like is there... Well, you know... do you have a... a friend — like a boyfriend, Lani? I mean, the friends you mentioned — don't you have a kind of special guy?"

"Not really. The friends I'm talking about aren't like that. We just have a group of maybe six or eight of us — guys and girls — but I'm not romantically involved with anyone."

"That's sad. For someone as pretty and nice as you are, that just doesn't seem right."

"Oh come on, Ben, I appreciate your kind words, but obviously life doesn't work that way. I just haven't met anyone that really ah... stimulates me, appeals to me..."

"Turns you on."

"Turns me on? Gee, I never heard that expression before, but okay — I never met anyone who really turns me on."

Ben thought he could almost notice that she dipped her head to hide her self-consciousness. "You know that thanks to you, Leilani, for the past twenty-four hours or so I really haven't felt that kind of lonely. I don't want you to get the wrong idea, but I just... well..."

"I feel really comfortable sharing my thoughts and feelings with you, too, Ben. Now, what's this about a WRONG idea?"

* * *

They watched *Beat the Clock* and *My Friend Flicka* on Lani's brand new, old fashioned, portable black and white television complete with a rabbit ear antenna on top. Ben was especially entertained by many of the local advertisements, particularly one touting the Liberty House department store was selling the "finest aloha shirts in all the Territory" for $2.98 each. "After all," the poker-faced announcer said, "it's better to spend the extra money knowing you're purchasing quality." Territorial Chevrolet was advertising their brand new 1957 Chevy at a list price of $1,559, and that wasn't even counting the trade-in. Lani fell sound to sleep on Ben's shoulder halfway through the Pan American World News broadcast. He was fascinated by the filmed highlights of the second Eisenhower-Nixon inaugural and dazzled by a clip of Ted Williams signing the highest contract ever offered an athlete — reportedly between $90,000 and $100,000. By the time the news had ended and *Night Owl Theater* came on the air, he too was ready to turn in for the night. He very gently lifted the sleeping beauty and carried her into her room, pulled the covers back, and carefully put her into her bed. Ben kissed her on her forehead and returned to the living area, quietly pulling her door closed behind him. He lay down on the sofa and fluffed up the pillow she had put out for him. The very last thing he was conscious of was the thought of just how Leilani could have truly shaken his deepest spirit so quickly, so completely. But he didn't linger on the notion for long at all. Within a minute or two, he was sound asleep.

17

Saturday, February 9, 1957: 7:20 A. M.

Ben lay on the sofa with his eyes half-open, immersed in his thoughts over just what he was going to do. He couldn't spend the rest of his life transposed nearly half a century back in time from where he was supposed to be. Sure, it was fun while it lasted, but somehow he couldn't picture going through the turbulent sixties, the me-first seventies, and — horror of all horrors — the greedy eighties all over again. And yet, the more he considered it, what choice did he have? He was an engineer and was painfully aware of the fact that there was absolutely no scientific reason he had been transplanted back in time in the first place. And based on that same rationale, there could be no justification for believing that he could somehow once again be dispatched through time — and on this occasion forward, no less — only to miraculously wind up back in the late-1990s just as though nothing had happened. And everyone would live happily ever after, amen! Yeah, right — in a pig's eye that was going to happen! But could he just continue to let himself be swept right off his feet, to fall deeper and deeper in love with? His thoughts were interrupted by the sound of the door opening.

"Well, look who finally woke up. I can't believe you carried me into bed last night without ever even waking me for a goodnight kiss." Leilani came into the apartment with both of her arms wrapped around a grocery bag. She dropped her keys on the table and placed the paper sack on the kitchen counter.

"How'd you ever sneak out of this house without me hearing you?"

"I forgot to tell you of my feline heritage!"

"Yeah, sure. Well, good morning to you anyway. And despite what you're supposing, I promise that I most certainly did kiss you goodnight. So, where've you been off to so early in the morning?"

"Early! First of all, I don't believe I slept as late as I did. I mean, I'm normally up by six or so, and today I slept in until ten 'til seven. That's late for me. Oh well, I guess I really needed it. Anyway, once I woke up, I thought I'd go pick up some fixings for a picnic lunch."

"Aha! Does that mean we have a nice morning out there in the real world — weather-wise, I mean?"

"A nice morning..." She went over and pulled the picture window drapes aside. "Just look at that, will you? It's a downright beautiful morning. The sun just came up a little while ago, and it's just begging us to go out and enjoy it. Don't you just love the *Koolaus* when they're so bright and green in the early morning sun?"

Ben sat up on the sofa and marveled at the view of the splendidly rugged, sharply pointed volcanic peaks reaching into the puffy white cumulus clouds that cloaked their majestic summits. The countless low-rise buildings that collectively comprised the city of Honolulu spread off into the distance. Many structures that were perched precariously on the hillsides seemed to grudgingly concede the city's containment by the mountains. "Well, now that you mention it, I can definitely understand your reverence of them. They certainly are beautiful mountains. So where, may I ask, does my dear Leilani propose to have this picnic you're talking about? Please don't tell me I have to climb any mountain this morning. I don't care how beautiful the weather may be, my mountain climbing days are long over."

"Oh, Ben — don't be silly! Well, I thought I'd take you to my favorite beach, or — more precisely — my favorite beach on the leeward side of Oahu."

"As if I were nearly discerning enough to be able to tell the difference. I mean windward, leeward, starboard, port — they're all the same to a Pennsylvanian."

"Yeah, right! That's fine until you get tired of being rained on over on the windward side. Remember, I grew up in Hilo."

"Am I supposed to know what that means?"

"Hilo — you crazy *haole* — has to be the epitome of all things windward."

"Interpretation, please..."

"Hilo is known for the six vees — very green, very clean, very sleepy, and very, very, very rainy."

"Aha... I think I gotcha. Now then, what's a *haole?*"

She smiled at him. "YOU are a *haole* — a crazy *haole*, no less! I guess the word actually means a stranger or foreigner, but Hawaiians have always applied the term to any Caucasians, even if they've lived here their entire life."

"So, it's finally come to this. Now you're condemning my ethnic or racial background."

"Oh, Ben — I am not! I'm only teasing you, and you know it! Besides that, I'm *hapa-haole* myself."

"Seems like I'm really getting a language lesson this morning. What's this *hapa-haole* stuff?"

"*Hapa* means half. I'm half-Caucasian — well, not literally half, but partly Caucasian. My dad was three quarter's Hawaiian and one-quarter English. My mom was Chinese, Japanese, Portuguese, and French."

"Wow! Talk about complicated family trees."

"It's not really unusual — actually, quite common — for folks born in the Territory to have incredibly jumbled ethnic bloodlines. There are obviously a lot of mixed marriages. Of course, when you think about it, almost every culture is represented somewhere in the Islands. Sailors, I guess."

"Sailors?"

"Yeah — sailors. Ever since Captain Cook invaded this paradise several centuries ago, travels of all nationalities have sailed through these Islands. And eventually, the sailors come back, get together with the girls and do what boys and girls do…" She smiled. "In the end, it seems as though most everybody comes to Hawaii wants to sooner or later get back to paradise."

"Back to paradise, huh? Makes good sense to me..."

"One way or the other, I always thought it was neat to have such a blend of cultures."

"Yeah, but I can see where it could definitely cause some real conflicts."

"Oh, maybe some, but nothing like the kinds of problems they're having back in the States. Most local folks here get along really well together — that's what we call the aloha spirit and..."

"Okay, Okay — I've heard about the aloha spirit already. For crying out loud, you ought to work for the Hawaii Visitors Bureau."

"Hey, wait a minute, Ben. I'm proud of our Island lifestyle AND the aloha spirit."

"All right, all right — don't get yourself all in a huff. I guess that so far, it all seems real enough to me."

"Seems real... Well, Ben Decker — it IS real. Goodness, compared to YOUR United States — I mean, four more colored people were lynched in Mississippi last week!"

"Colored? Lynched?"

"I read it right in the *ADVERTISER* yesterday."

"Oh my god, I keep forgetting that these are the good old days. But really, MY United States! Please don't blame the WHOLE problem solely on me. Somehow I think there's enough culpability to go around."

"I only meant it figuratively."

Ben shook his head from side to side, mumbling "the good old days" mostly to himself.

"Good? You say GOOD! I don't know about that! Look, can we talk about something else. This whole colored mess — the segregation problem, I mean — it just really depresses me."

Ben climbed off the sofa and began to fold his blanket. "Why don't you tell me what kind of picnic lunch you have in mind. I wish you had woken me earlier. The least I can do around here is to buy some of the food."

"Don't worry about it — you'll have a lot more chance to do that. You're not planning to go anywhere, are you." Almost at once, Lani reflected on what she just said. A look of concern quickly replaced her smile.

"Yeah, I do have big plans for travel. As soon as I get dressed and have some breakfast, I'm going to the beach."

* * *

Lani finished drying the last of the dishes, and Ben opened the bathroom door. "Now I put my bathing suit on under my shorts. That's what you wanted me to do, right?"

"Sure, that's best."

"How far is this beach?"

"It's really not that far at all — just down the end of *Kalakaua* Avenue."

"So, can we walk?"

"Well, we could. But since we have to carry the picnic lunch and other beach stuff, we may as well jump on a bus."

"Do we have beach towels?"

"I have mats." She opened a small closet near the front door and pulled out two rolled up grass mats. "Let me throw these in there too." She produced two pairs of old-styled swimmer's goggles and dropped them into the bag.

"Is that it, my dear?"

"That's it, Ben."

"Then, it's off to the beach we go."

18

Saturday, February 9, 1957: 9:15 A. M.

As the two of them stepped off the bus, Ben set the picnic basket and beach bag down for a moment, rooted around in Lani's canvass sack, and pulled out his pair of sunglasses. "The sun's incredibly bright this morning — February, huh?"

"Yes, February. What? You expected snow?"

"Snow! Now, who's being the silly holly..."

She chuckled. "It's NOT holly, you silly man — it's *haole*..."

"Um, yeah — *haole*... er, *hapa-haole*?" He snickered at the thought of a winter blizzard in Hawaii. "Haha… snow in Hawaii... now THAT'S funny!"

"Nah, nah… I said, SNOW! That's not the least bit funny. And it's certainly not the least bit unusual where I grew up on the Big Island."

"You're serious, aren't you?"

"Yes, I'm serious."

"Even though I've never been over there, I do remember reading that there are some big mountains on that island — YOUR Island."

"Sure are. *Mauna Kea* and *Mauna Loa* are huge mountains — both are close to three miles high. There's snow on them all winter long most years."

"That's really a strange thought — snow in Hawaii." He once again hoisted his load and followed Lani's lead.

"Kaluahole Beach is just down this right-of-way." She turned onto a sandy trail headed right towards the sea.

"Looks like there are some really great, old mansions around here."

"Yeah, sure are. Naturally, rich people own them all. I've been told that Kaluahole was the best beach on this entire end of the Island — fifty-some years ago. After the turn of the century, more and more of these estates were developed, and the sea walls and jetties they built robbed the beach of its sand. You'll see — it's still really nice, but the beach itself is a lot narrower than it used to be."

As they came around the last dense stand of coconut palms, a magnificent stretch of perfectly white sand came into view. "Wow! Losing sand, you say? Well, it sure looks big enough to me!"

They reached the end of the trail and stepped onto the sand. Ben once again dropped the beach gear and reveled in the sweeping vista. The pure white, fine sand beach was bordered by a nearly solid wall of stately green palms and fronted by the deepest, azure blue ocean Ben could possibly imagine. Only one group of three or four persons could be seen on the beach way off in the distance, but he spotted numerous surfers offshore, bobbing on their boards while waiting patiently for that perfect wave. "So, this is the narrow beach you're talking about, huh?"

"This is it. Do you like it?"

"Oh, Lani, it's the most beautiful beach I've ever seen — even in pictures!"

"I sure like this beach myself, but I can't wait to show you much nicer ones — a lot less crowded."

"This is crowded, huh? It amazes me that way back here in the fifties, some folks were already complaining about development. Oh, poor Lani, you have no idea what development is — yet..."

She had pulled the beach mats out of the bag and was unrolling them to spread on the sand. "How about if we set up back near the coconut trees. That way, if we get too hot, we can easily get in the shade."

"Sounds like a good idea to me."

The two mats were spread out side by side, and Ben used several fallen coconuts to weight down the corners and keep them from being blown by the gentle trade winds. He removed his shorts and pulled his shirt over his head. Lani had already stripped to her suit and darted towards the water at full speed while yelling back at him, "Last one in is a rotten egg!"

A rotten egg? Ben hadn't heard anyone say that for — well, now that he thought about it — most likely for forty years! He threw his shirt onto the mat and ran after Lani, who was already diving into the surf. Ouch! No wonder she was running — the sand was incredibly hot! He, too, hit the water at full speed and dove into the first wave he met. He quickly swam up beneath Lani and grabbed both her legs as he rose up out of the water, tumbling her right into another wave. She poked her head out of the bright blue Pacific and pushed her long, wet hair back over her shoulders. Able to see once again, she threw both of her arms around Ben's neck and cuddled up close to him as he stood in chest-deep water.

"This water is absolutely perfect — crystal clear, eighty degrees, and such a beautiful setting. Tell me I died and went to heaven."

"Sorry, honey, you didn't die, and this isn't heaven. Looks like you're stuck right here in Hawaii — with me, no less." She pulled herself up to his mouth and kissed his lips. Ben responded tenderly, clutching her tightly to his body and fully returning her passion. They remained tightly locked in their embrace for seemingly several minutes, until quite unexpectedly, the largest wave of the day crashed into the romantic couple and plunged them head over heels, arms and legs flying, into the soft sand below. As the two surfaced and looked at each other, they simultaneously both broke out in jovial laughter.

They both continued to bob up and down as each swell rolled by. Ben was captivated by the sight of the coconut-tree-lined beach that, from this offshore perspective, seemed to run right up to the base of Diamond Head Crater. "I still just can't really comprehend this whole thing, Lani."

"What, Ben? Do you mean the beach? …the weather? It sure is a beautiful day."

"Well, that's most certainly a part of it, yes. Hawaii has to be a special place for anybody — at ANY time. But to an east coast guy, no less, Hawaii seems just totally unreal — like some enchanted dream that exists only in the mind's eye. Even under the most adverse conditions, I'm sure these Islands would have a way of overwhelming the most contemptible of souls. But in my case, it's a whole lot more than just being here in Hawaii."

"You mean the whole time thing?"

"Well, sure. But in an even broader sense, I mean that I've been totally dumbfounded by this entire experience. Just put it all together once: being thrown back in time, finding myself here in Territorial Hawaii, feeling the uncertainty of the whole thing — that's got to be enough to stagger the most stable person. But…"

"But what?"

"But then, as if that weren't somehow enough, I wind up meeting you."

"Oh Ben, you make it — me — sound like such a... well, a... a real liability." An unmistakable but silent flash of outrage raced across her face.

"No, Leilani — that's not it at all. As a matter of fact, I'm trying to tell you it's exactly the opposite. You're... well, you um... kind of complicate..."

A complication! So, you find me to be a complication?"

Ben could sense that he was digging himself into a hole. "No, not at all. Now YOU'RE putting words into MY mouth. I only mean... well... that just maybe..."

"Do you find me attractive, Ben?" She self-consciously lowered her eyes to the water.

"Very."

"How about provocative?"

"Provocative? How do you mean?"

"Provocative — you know. How can I say it? Do I make you... well, you know... make you sort of get filled with desire?"

"Oh god — don't ask such a silly question?"

"It's not exactly silly — do I make you feel all mixed up inside? Ah... kind of quivery?"

"Mixed up inside? Kind of quivery? Now that is an understatement if I've ever heard one. I mean, for goodness sake, I AM only human, you know."

"But you don't understand. I don't mean — well, you know — male hormones and all that stuff." She self-consciously turned her eyes down toward the water."

"Oh my dear Leilani, I understand exactly what you mean only too well."

"You know, ever since I was in about the eighth or ninth grade, and these started to grow..." She briefly cupped her ample breasts, "...boys — er, men — always found me to be quite attractive physically. I don't want you to think I'm bragging about that. Actually, it really embarrasses me to be thought of in that way. But with you... What I want to know is if you find me really... well... provocative, stimulating — on the inside. Like in the sense that you feel moved by me emotionally, too, and not just sexually." She grabbed his hand and started to walk towards the shore.

"I thought that was obvious, Leilani. For goodness sake, I'd be lying if I didn't admit to finding you sexually attractive, but it's much deeper than that. For that matter, that's precisely what I mean when I said that YOU have been the most sensational part of this whole thing. You see, I really feel emotionally overwhelmed by you — I feel short-circuited and totally out of control."

"And that displeases you — being out of control?"

"I'm an engineer, Leilani. You've got to understand. By training, I tend to be a really cerebral sort of person — always in command of a situation. I'm the kind of guy who hates to fly in an airplane, not because of any fear of crashing, but because I won't be flying the machine by myself."

"But surely engineers have emotions too..."

"Certainly they do. But I've always been able to rule over my emotions — at least I've been able to keep them out of the way. That is until I met you. And that's what really boggles my mind."

"Me?"

"Well sure, but more specifically, I mean my reaction to you. You've got to understand that I'm not the kind of guy who runs around with a lot of different women. I never was that kind of person."

"Before you met Emily, you mean?"

He slowly nodded his head yes.

Did you ever used to..."

"Oh god no! That just wasn't — isn't — my personality. I met Emily in my freshman year of college, and that was that. Oh, I had a couple of girlfriends in high school, but none of them ever amounted to anything serious." A big grin forced its way into his expression. "Oh boy, if you only knew Shirley Ann Ingersol, you'd fully understand what I mean about nothing serious ever happening!"

"Shirley Ann Ingersol?"

"Never mind. She was just an old high school sweetheart — if you could call her that. It's really not worth any more explanation than that." He bent over and pulled two towels from the bag and handed one to Lani. "I'm only trying to tell you that I never was any kind of go-get-em, wild-eyed ladies' man. Conversely, I was — hell, still am — basically a pretty shy guy. So, when I finally met Emily Harris some twenty-five plus years ago, she became the sum total of all my romantic involvement — until you."

Leilani sat down on one of the mats and opened her picnic basket. "That's kind of what I meant — do you really feel, well... like... um, kind of like maybe romantically involved or..."

"Or like I'm falling in love?"

"Um... ah... well..."

"I guess I already answered that, Lani."

"But I want to hear what you mean very specifically. Do you sort of feel like maybe you could..."

Ben felt sorry watching her struggle with and tumble over her words and actually considered it his duty to try to end her emotional suffering. "Yes, yes, a thousand times yes! I plead guilty to falling head over heels for you, dear Leilani. I... I love you." Ben could hardly believe he heard himself clearly. It wasn't at all because he was unsure of his emotional self — he was unequivocally certain of his feelings. It was simply hard to accept that old, steady-as-a-rock Benjamin Decker had been totally blown away by a beautiful young woman. And worse yet, he'd only known her for a couple of days.

"Why are you so hesitant?"

"I'm not hesitant, Lani."

"Ben..." She looked at him with hurt in her eyes.

"Well, at least I'm not the least bit hesitant about YOU. I KNOW I LOVE YOU — absolutely, positively, no question in my mind about that. My only apprehension stems from the fact that this whole situation is so weird, so paradoxical. For Christ's sake, I haven't even met Emily yet — and I won't meet her for well over a decade. And yet we've been married for... for a quarter of a century. But now that I've met you, I probably will never meet Emily Harris. Of course, where's that leave Lisa and Bonnie? I'm babbling in circles because my head is jumbled and spinning in circles and..."

Leilani nearly knocked over the basket as she reached for his hands. "Oh Ben, I can hardly believe how fast this has all happened. I'm almost afraid that I'm going to wake up and find that you were only a dream."

He gave her a gentle kiss on her forehead. "No, believe me — this is no dream. We're really here together, Lani."

* * *

Lani crumpled up the last of the wax paper sandwich wrappers and tucked them away in the beach bag. With no warning, she sprung to her feet. "Let's go for a walk."

"To?"

"To nowhere — just down the beach. Come on, it'll help you digest your lunch."

"God knows, after eating a sandwich that size, we'll have to walk all the way to Hilo."

"I don't know about that. Two hundred miles of Pacific Ocean could slow us down a bit." She got to her feet and grabbed the two pairs of black runner goggles she had tucked into the beach bag.

"Hey, I don't know the first thing about diving."

"Oh Ben, you know how to swim, don't you?"

"I do."

"Well, I just want you to see all the fishes. They're especially neat down in that little pocket there where the beach ends, and the cliffs begin." She pointed towards a little cove off in the distance.

"I don't know, young lady — my eyes are pretty good, and I don't even see one fish."

She playfully poked him in his side. "Silly."

They walked hand in hand, strolling carefree through the swash zone. Ben occasionally bent over to pick up small pieces of broken coral that had been washed up by the tide, casually examined each piece, and then threw each out into the sea.

"You know, young lady, you're really lucky you were born out here."

"Lucky? How do you mean that?"

"I only mean you're fortunate to be able to enjoy this kind of natural beauty all the time. Of course, when you live in this fantastic setting permanently, I wonder if there's a tendency to kind of take it all for granted — to sort of overdose on so much beauty."

"No, I don't think so. Oh, naturally some people never appreciate anything. But it seems to me that most *kama'ainas* – local folks – realize what we have and try to take advantage of it."

"I've often had a similar thought about the climate. I mean, you must get spoiled having such a moderate climate. For example, even you were grumbling about how cold it was the other evening!"

"It has been cold, Ben — after all, it's winter!"

"See what I mean. And I guess you think it's hot in the summer, too."

"Well, of COURSE I do." She almost sounded offended.

"So — let me get this straight — sixty-five degrees is cold, and eighty-five degrees is hot, right?"

"Stop making fun, Ben!"

"Oh come on. I'm just teasing you. It is a rather blatant example of relative perceptions, though."

"I guess so."

"But I still need to ask one question that my buddy Stosh and I always used to wonder about."

"Stosh?"

"Yeah, Stosh — that's Polish for Stanley. Anyway, he's my crazy old college buddy from Chicago that I think I mentioned to you earlier."

"Okay, now I remember."

"Yeah, the old Polish stallion himself." Ben displayed a grin from ear to ear.

"Polish stallion?"

"Just an old nickname. Believe me, that part's not really important. Well anyway, we always used to wonder about life in the tropics. You know, to people who live their lives in temperate climates where winters can get very nasty, spring is always the most welcomed season — it's a symbol of rebirth and renewal that allows all life to grow and flourish once again. But in the tropics where you never have a winter, can there ever be a spring."

"Oh come on, Ben! Sure there's a spring. To start with, even though it may be quite different from yours, we still have winter. But spring in the Islands is just marvelous — the weather changes, and we get a lot less rain, the ocean and waves all change, the days are longer, the sun shines with much more intensity, many different flowers bloom. Even the plumerias you like so much bloom mostly in the spring and summer. Believe me — there is just as beautiful a spring here in Hawaii as there is in Philadelphia, and its arrival is anticipated all winter long by young and old alike."

"What was that?" Ben was pointing towards a streaking speck as it darted across the scraggly grass between two coconut palms.

"What? Oh — it must have been a mongoose. Do you mean to tell me that you never saw a mongoose before?"

"A mongoose? Now, where do you think I'd see a mongoose in Philadelphia? We have squirrels, and... Hey, now that you mention it, I have seen a mongoose before. Must have been several years ago, when we had the girls at the Philadelphia Zoo. Don't they eat snakes or something?"

"Jeez, I don't really know what they eat in — well, wherever they come from. I think I heard that once, though. But thank god we don't have any snakes at all in the Territory of Hawaii, so they sure don't eat them here."

"No snakes! Do you mean there are no snakes at all in Hawaii?"

"Not even one."

"I guess this MUST be paradise. Please pinch me to see if I'm really conscious..."

Lani did! She pinched his thigh and immediately sprinted away down the beach.

"OUCH!!! Hey, you lousy bum! I'm going to get you..."

Ben started to chase after her, but she quickly made a sharp right turn out into the surf. He dove in after her, but she was swimming her finest stroke towards an outcropping of rocks. Ben followed, but his out-of-shape, middle-aged body was simply no match for her youthful speed.

About a hundred feet out from the shore, Lani stopped, put her feet on the bottom, and turned towards Ben. "There's a pocket of sand over here. Be careful you don't tramp on the coral."

He finally caught up to her and cautiously tested the depth, almost surprised that the water was, in fact, shallow enough for them to comfortably stand. "You rotten bum! I don't believe you pinched me back there. And that hard..."

"Come on, Ben. You even said please when you asked me to do it!"

"Yeah, and I think you actually took a chunk right out of my leg..."

"AW — what a poor guy... Here, try a pair of these goggles on." Lani handed him a set of swimmer's goggles as she pulled the other pair over her own head. She pulled her long, black hair out over the top of the goggles' elastic band and let it drop back down over her shoulders.

"Like this?" Ben followed her silent instruction.

She answered by nodding her head in the affirmative and pushed herself off the bottom. She began to float, stretched out in a prone position. Ben watched and tentatively mimicked her lead. As he first put his head down, he was initially anxious about what he would see as he opened his eyes. Suppose there were man-eating sharks or giant squid out here! He was quickly reassured as several small, bright yellow fish swam past him. For all intents and purposes, the little fish were totally oblivious to the human invader swimming in their domain.

Ben was extra deliberate in making certain that Leilani never disappeared from his view, and yet the more he investigated, the more rapidly he gained confidence in his security. Within a few minutes, it finally crossed his mind that he was actually beginning to enjoy his swim. He hovered at the edge of the reef, dazzled by the thousands of fish visible in waters only ten to twenty feet deep. Though he had always enjoyed watching nature-oriented documentaries on television, he never imagined that so many schools of fish could be observed in such shallow waters, especially this close to shore. He discovered that by quietly floating in place, only poking his head up at intervals for air, he could follow small groups of variously colored fishes as they scurried back and forth across the coral heads, totally oblivious to their human observer. Suddenly, he was startled as a giant turtle rounded a column of coral and swam into view. Ben maintained his distance but watched in fascination as the three-foot-plus diameter turtle kept flapping his flippers and giving the distinct impression that he was flying through the water while surveying the reef below. To Ben's total surprise, Leilani swam into view some twenty feet behind the turtle, gracefully weaving her way through delicate coral outcrops that made up the reef. Her long hair streamed straight out behind her as she exhaled a rapidly rising cluster of bubbles that she promptly raced to the surface.

Ben stuck his head out of the ocean and treaded water. "So is the beautiful mermaid finished harassing that poor turtle."

"I was NOT harassing him — I was following him!"

"Yeah, yeah, I hear you!"

"You trouble maker, you! Let's swim back over there to the patch of sand from which we started."

Ben swam a hundred feet or so back to their starting point, all the while maintaining his watch on the reef below. When he finally reached the shallow pocket of sand, he cautiously planted his feet firmly on the bottom. Lani had already reached the spot and was removing her goggles. She ducked her head under the water and reemerged using her hands to push all her hair back over her shoulders. "So, how'd you like my reef?"

"YOUR reef, huh? It was really great. Once I got a bit more comfortable with having my face underwater like that, I really enjoyed it out there. I'll bet it's even neater — at least easier — using a snorkel."

"True. Breathing is a much simpler process when you don't have to keep sticking your head up."

"When I first saw you terrorizing that poor turtle, I thought..."

"Now STOP it, Ben. Pacific green sea turtles are one of my favorite animals. I would NEVER bother one of them, and I don't even like you to kid me about it. I swam down under a coral head because I saw a squid in the sand, and I wanted to get a closer view. That's when the turtle came flapping on by. I only followed him."

"All right, all right — I'll stop teasing you. But I want you to know that I was really impressed with your ability to swim. You know, I've got to admit that when you told me this morning that you were *hapa haole*, I didn't realize just how diverse your ancestry was."

"What do you mean by that?"

"I didn't realize that you were part fish!"

19

Saturday, February 9, 1957: 12:45 P. M.

"You're really getting burnt, Ben. Why don't we sit in the shade, and I'll put some baby oil on you."

"How could I refuse an offer like that?"

They only had to drag their beach mats a few feet into the shade of the palms. Ben stretched out on his stomach, and Lani kneeled by his side.

"WOW! Hey, that stuff is really cold."

"How could it be cold? More likely, your *haole* skin is burning hot from overdosing on the sun. You're as red as an *ohia* blossom, and you're going to pay for it tonight!"

130

"Yeah well, whatever. Even so, could you please try not to shock an old man so badly. Do you want me to have a heart attack right here?"

Now Ben..." She squirted more oil into her hand and then began to rub it onto his back. "Not a bad physique for such an 'old man'. How old did you say you were?"

"Either in my somewhere around 50 or else just approaching my teens — it all depends upon what year it is you're counting to."

"Well, a teenager seems a little young for me."

"And isn't early fifty-ish a bit too old for you?"

"IT IS NOT!"

"Okay, Okay — I'm just checking. You're only twenty-six. Don't you realize that I could easily be your father?"

"But you're not." Without any warning, Leilani moved from her kneeling position by his left side and straddled his back, resting her buttocks on his. She increased the pressure her hands exerted on the muscles around his neck and shoulders and escalated the application of baby oil into what had now become a full-blown massage.

"Ooooh. That feels just great." He reached back and used his right hand to trace little circles on Lani's thigh. "This is sure an unexpected pleasure."

"Unexpected pleasures are always better than anticipated ones."

"Says who?"

"Says me! Think about it once. Just consider any event that you can imagine. If you somehow act out that dream in your everyday life, the reality is rarely anywhere near as fulfilling as you figured it would be in your original fantasy."

"Agreed. But how could I explain YOU? You're a fantasy come true."

"Exactly my point. That's the unexpected part. If you'd have spent the past several years creating a Polynesian goddess somewhere deep inside your imagination, the real me would stand no chance at living up to your expectations." She paused only long enough to put more oil into her palm and then onto Ben's back. "That's not to say I am a Polynesian goddess."

"You ARE a Polynesian goddess… but I refuse to debate your other point. I doubt that my imagination could possibly fabricate anyone as desirable as you." He reached farther back, trying to rub her leg.

"Hey, stop trying to contort yourself — you'll ruin your massage."

"But that's not fair, Lani. I'm getting all the pleasure out of this. I want you to feel good too."

"I feel great. Can't you sense the enjoyment I'm getting out of this?"

"But it's my back."

"Ben, I just love…"

"Yeah?"

"Well, I love touching you. It feels so… Oh, I don't know how to say it. It just feels so… so right. I want to rub your back — to feel your skin."

He squeezed her leg. "All right then. Your wish is my command, young lady. By the way, did anyone ever tell you what great legs you have."

"Why, thank you, Ben. I'm glad you like them." She leaned over, quickly kissed his neck, and then continued the massage for several more minutes in silence.

When all the baby oil had been rubbed into his back, Lani again reached for the bottle, but Ben gently grabbed her hand. "Okay lady, now it's my turn."

"To do what?"

"To rub your back a bit."

"You don't have to."

"I want to."

"Okay." She climbed off his back and looked for him to roll over. He didn't.

"Well? What are you waiting for?"

"I'm waiting for a minute."

"Ben... What's wrong?"

"Well, to be perfectly honest with you, it's a little bit embarrassing."

"What's embarrassing?"

"Um... What you do to me."

"You're not making any sense here, Ben."

"Let's just say that you make it hard for me concerning certain parts of my anatomy."

"I make it hard for you?"

As Ben rolled over, the lump in his swimming suit made his erection quite obvious.

"Oh, I see what you mean." She blushed as she looked away. "I'm sorry, Ben."

"Sorry for what — being a beautiful young lady and discovering that I'm a real human being?"

"No, um... Oh, you know..."

"Remember, you were the one asking if I found you provocative. Well... what can I say? Look, why don't you lie down here?"

They switched positions, and Ben straddled her back, keeping nearly all his weight on his knees. As he poured a pool of oil into his open hand, Lani reached back with one hand and undid the hook on the top of her swimming suit.

"You know, I didn't realize that two-piece suits were invented by 1957."

"Don't be silly, Ben. Of course, they were. They've been around here for years."

Ben rubbed the oil into her skin and gently but firmly massaged her entire back.

"It feels so good, Ben. I never get my back rubbed."

"Well, you're having it rubbed today. I'm glad you're enjoying it. Now I see what you meant."

"What I meant?"

"Yeah — about the pleasure the rubber gets."

"Huh?"

"Come on, Lani. In order to have a back rub, you need to have a rub-BER and a rub-BEE, and I'm just saying that I agree with you that the rub-BER receives as much pleasure as the rub-BEE."

"Oh, I see what you mean — ur, what I meant..." They both started to laugh.

Ben continued his massage until all the oil was gone. He spread another portion of the moistener uniformly across her back and began to trace designs on her skin.

"Oh, you tease! Hey, that tickles deep inside."

"Oh, jeez-o-man, I'm sorry. I sure don't want to tease you." He hardly muffled a chuckle at the thought of his little white lie.

"Oh, Ben... You're going to drive me nutty."

"Now, now. Hey, let's play a little game here."

"What sort of game?"

"You try to guess what I'm writing on your back."

"All right."

Ben traced his name out.

"That's easy — it's BEN."

"Right. How about this."

"Um... LEILANI."

"Right again." He rubbed his palm against her skin as if to erase her name. "Let's get a little tougher. I'll tell you what — get this one right, and I'll give you a big kiss." He used his right index finger to draw a big heart shape on her back and wrote inside of it.

"Half of that one isn't too difficult at all."

"Which half?"

"The heart part. I'm positive you drew a big heart."

"Are you absolutely, positively certain?"

"Yes."

"Maybe I drew a pretzel — I am from Philadelphia, you know."

"BEN! Don't be silly. It was a heart."

"Hey, no fair — you must have looked."

"I did not loo... HEY! What are you talking about? How could I have possibly looked at my own back?"

Ben laughed. "Gotcha!"

"Now you ruined my concentration. You have to rewrite the inside part all over again."

"Well... This kind of sounds like cheating to me, but for you, I guess I'll..." He traced the words again.

"Let's see. It's BEN something LEILANI."

"Okay — what's the something part?"

"Do it once more."

He traced it one more time.

"BEN LOVES LEILANI."

"BINGO! You figured it out." He leaned forward and gave her a series of little kisses across the back of her neck and began to move around towards her ear. He gently climbed over her back and lay by her side with his arm draped over her back. "Kiss me, you fool."

She turned her head toward him, and he found her lips with his. She opened a teary eye and looked straight into Ben's soul. "Oh, Ben..."

"Lani, why are you crying?"

She sniffled and let out a sigh. "I don't know. It's just..."

"Just what? I thought you were happy?"

"I am, I am..."

"Tears of joy?"

"Sort of..." She turned her body sideways, and her breasts fell free of the unfastened suit top.

"Lani, you'd better hook yourself up here."

"It's okay, Ben. No one's around this beach."

"What made you cry?"

"BEN LOVES LEILANI."

"I didn't want that to make you cry."

"I know. It's just that... Well... I believe you."

"How can that be bad?"

"It's not bad — not bad at all. But Ben, what are we going to do? I mean, it's just so fast."

"Oh, Leilani. Am I moving too fast for you?"

"Oh god, not at all, Ben. It's just that I'M moving too fast for me... for us. What are we going to do?"

"Come on, honey. Can't we just enjoy the day? Enjoy falling in love?"

"Sure we can, Ben. But it'd be so much easier if I loved you and you loved me, and we just lived happily ever after. But we both know damned well that it's just not that simple. What are you going to do about Emily and your kids and your life back there in the nineteen-nineties?"

"I... I... Oh boy, I just don't have the answers. I don't think anyone does. For goodness sake, we can't solve all the problems of the world in one afternoon."

"Hold me close."

Ben embraced her partially nude body and pulled her as tightly into himself as he could without hurting her. He gave her a long, wet kiss. Again, he could feel his pulsating erection grow, this time against her thigh as it was pressed firmly into his middle. "You're so beautiful."

"You're biased."

"No matter — you're still beautiful. And, I might add, you feel so wonderful to cuddle up close to — to feel your warm skin next to mine." Again, he kissed her. And again...

He lost track of how long they remained tangled together, partly out of the pleasure of feeling her warmth, and partly out of the fear of passing the point of no return. A noisy mynah bird squawked loudly from his perch on a bracket of coconuts overhead, and Ben opened his eyes to locate the commotion. The bird dove out of the tree and glided towards the ocean. Ben followed its flight until his eyes crossed the image of a large Hawaiian man standing near a grove of palms some hundred yards distant. The big man was looking right at them.

Ben made no harsh move and whispered into Lani's ear. "Can you look down the beach without letting on that you're the least bit suspicious of anything?"

"Why are you disturbing our love glow? What are you talking about?"

"I'm sorry, Leilani, but I swear some guy is watching us, and I'm sure I've seen him before. Do you have any idea who he is?"

Lani followed his directions and slowly and quietly turned her head towards the man on the beach. He at once reacted by retreating into the trees and leaving the beach desolate once again.

"Did you see him?"

"Briefly."

"Did he look familiar?"

"Not really. But he sure did seem as though he was in a hurry to duck out of here as soon as he knew we were aware of his presence."

"I'm so sorry I broke our communion together."

"It wasn't your fault, Ben. Could you please hook me up back here?" She had replaced her suit top and pulled her shoulder straps back into place, all the while lying on her stomach so as not to reveal her naked breasts to any unseen person on the now-deserted beach.

20
Saturday, February 9, 1957: 2:20 P. M.

As Ben pulled the apartment door closed behind him, he glanced once more at the street below to see if he could spot any suspicious-looking characters again. He couldn't. He shook his head while thinking of just how easy it was for a serious case of paranoia could develop.

"Are you coming in or are you going to spend the afternoon standing out there on the *lanai?*"

"No, no — I'm just checking."

"Checking? Checking for what?"

"Um... you know — that guy... The, um..."

"Come on, Ben. You have to relax a little bit. For goodness sake, you can't think that the whole world is after you just because one weird guy gawks at us while we're making out on the beach. My god, why are you so apprehensive about every little..." As soon as the words rolled off her tongue, Lani realized just how insensitive she must have seemed. "Oh, I'm sorry, Ben. I just caught myself sounding really dumb. Of course, you're apprehensive. Considering what you've been through over the past couple of days, you have every right to feel that way. And stupid me... I should be trying to soothe your anxieties, not trying to convince you that your feelings don't exist..."

"Hey, it's all right, Lani. You're absolutely right — I shouldn't be so doggone fidgety. To be honest with you, I'm not all that certain the guy at the beach was the same fellow I saw before, anyway. Maybe it's all a coincidence."

"I don't want it to be like this."

"Like this? Like what?"

"Us. I mean, I don't want you to be all messed up about people following you. I don't want you worrying about your Univac — you know, your computer thing. I... I... don't want you thinking about going back to... to... her..."

"Emily?"

Her gaze turned to the floor.

"Oh come on, Lani. Don't be jealous of..."

"I'M NOT JEALOUS! It's just... well..."

"It's okay, Lani."

"It's NOT okay, Ben. In case you haven't figured it out yet, I'm falling madly in love with you — head over heels. I couldn't control it even if I wanted to. And I DON'T WANT TO." Lani brushed a bit of moisture from her eye. "I just want us to be like normal people and not have to worry if someone is following us or checking up on us or... or...."

"Believe me, honey, I WANT the same thing..." He put his hands on her shoulders and looked into her eyes. "...but I'm not so sure it's all that easy. The problem is my past life — which quite confusingly, still lies in the future. Oh god, how did this happen?"

"Hold me, Ben."

He pulled her into his chest and squeezed her tightly. "Leilani, you know the same thing's happening to me — and just as fast, if not even faster."

"Worrying about..."

"No, I don't mean worrying. I'm talking about falling in love. Or more correctly, I should use the past tense — I've already FALLEN in love with you. I never knew it could happen so fast."

She lifted her head from his chest and backed away enough to re-establish eye contact with him. "I never realized it either. What are we going to do?"

"DO? Well, first of all, we're going to dry up those tears of yours."

At first, it was obvious that she was forcing a somewhat happier expression, but it rapidly grew into a genuine smile. "I love you, Ben."

"And I love you, Lani."

"Can we..."

Ben immediately fended off her question with a succession of kisses. When he was certain he had subdued her desire to speak, he backed his head away from her and placed his outstretched index finger to her lips. "Shhhh... Before you go on, you must make me one promise."

She kissed his finger and nodded her head in agreement.

"Promise we're just going to have a great rest-of-the-weekend, and neither one of us will linger on any of the pessimistic aspects of this whole thing."

"Can we..."

He again put his index finger to her lips. "Promise?"

She delicately kissed his index finger as he touched it to her lips. "I promise, Ben."

"Now — can we what?"

"Can we go to eat Chinese food tonight and then maybe see a movie?"

"Well, sure — if that's what you want to do. I guess it's a little early right now."

"Hey, I know... What time is it?" She looked at the clock in the kitchen. "Ah, rats — it's almost two-thirty. It's too late."

"Too late for what?"

"Oh, I thought maybe you'd get a kick out of going over to the Moana Hotel — the Banyan Court. They broadcast the *HAWAII CALLS* radio show back to the States from there every Saturday afternoon — from two to two-thirty, our time. Looks like we just missed the show."

"That would have been fun."

"What the heck — we can go next week."

Ben knew he had reservations to fly back to Pennsylvania the following Saturday, but it would be pointless to bring that up right now. Besides, he knew of no commercial airline that scheduled flights into the future! Furthermore, he was absolutely determined to stick to their mutual promise and not mention anything beyond this weekend. Who knew what this week held in store. Maybe he would still be here next Saturday. Maybe he'd be here for a great many Saturdays... "We'll see what happens, love."

21
Saturday, February 9, 1957: 5:40 P. M.

Ben came out of the bathroom, tucking his colorful Hawaiian print shirt into his khakis.

"Oh boy – now you REALLY look like you're from Philadelphia."

"What exactly is that supposed to mean?"

"Only that you look funny with an aloha shirt that's tucked in. Next thing you know, you'll put on a coat and tie. Don't you know they're supposed to be left out? That's the Island style."

"Even if I don't have a potbelly?"

"Potbelly? Oh, Ben."

"Seriously! I thought the only reason Island folks wear such baggy clothes was to try to hide their figures."

"Well, I'm wearing a muumuu, and you saw a great deal of my body at the beach today. I guess you're trying to tell me that my figure supports your theory." She quickly put on her best pouting expression.

"*Touché!* I guess you really have me there." Ben immediately pulled his shirt out and let it hang freely over his trouser tops. "So, what interesting things are you reading about in the paper there?"

"Not much news. To tell you the truth, I've just been looking over the movie advertisements."

"And?"

"And I think I'd like to go see *Friendly Persuasion* at the *Kuhio* Theater."

"*Friendly Persuasion?* Isn't that an old Pat Boone film?"

"Old? Pat Boone? No, silly! It's a brand-new motion picture, and he sings the title song *Friendly Persuasion*. It's number one on all the radio stations right now."

"So, who's in it?"

"Oh — the movie stars Gary Cooper and Dorothy McGuire."

"I swear Pat Boone was in the picture."

"Ben! It must be a pretty good movie. This is the third straight week it's being held over."

"I don't remember it being that..."

"Aw no — you sound as though you've already seen it. Did you?"

"Honestly, I can't remember. But if I did, I know I haven't seen it for... well, probably for forty-some years. I sure can't remember any of the plot."

"We don't have to go to..."

"No, no... *Friendly Persuasion* it is. Now, where is this Chinese restaurant you've been bragging about?"

"Actually, it works out just nice, since it's not too far from the theater the movie's in."

"Do you want me to call a cab?"

"No. If it's okay with you, let's walk. It's a really nice evening out there." She picked up a letter that had been sitting on the windowsill in the kitchen. "Boy-o-boy! Three days... I don't want to forget to mail this again."

"No doubt a letter to your boyfriend."

"Oh, Ben! It's a letter I wrote to my sister Wednesday night, and I keep forgetting to mail it. Would you please grab a stamp in the lampstand drawer there?" She pointed to the small table right next to where he was standing.

Ben opened the drawer and quickly located a strip of stamps. "My god! Only three cents!"

"Certainly. Now I guess you're going to tell me that postage stamps in the 1990s are going to go up in price. Hey, how high can postage get — certainly not much more than a dime or something!"

He couldn't hold back his laughter. "Yeah, right — a dime! You'd better try the 'or something' part..." He handed her the stamp, and she affixed it to her letter.

"I fail to see the humor in a lousy postage stamp. Do I need my purse?"

"I can't think of any reason other than to make sure we have your apartment key, and I'll happily volunteer to carry that right here in my pocket." He patted his upper thigh.

She removed the key from her pocketbook and handed it to him. "Well then, I guess we're ready to go."

22
Saturday, February 9, 1957: 10:20 P. M.

The two left the movie theater and walked hand and hand down the street. A gentle trade wind kept the evening air fresh and comfortable.

"My arm's dead tired."

"From what?"

"From being wrapped around you for two-and-a-half hours."

"So why didn't you move it?"

"Cause I didn't want you to think I didn't like it there."

"That's silly. I mean, if it hurts you, you should have changed positions."

"For goodness sakes, Lani. I'm only kidding you. Didn't you ever hear that schtick Bill Cosby used to do about the pain men suffer when they take a woman to a movie? According to Cosby, it's much more severe than any woman experiences during childbirth." Ben was laughing at the memory of the famous comedian's routine.

"So who's Bill Crosby?"

"You know, the comedian..."

"You don't mean Bing Crosby, do you?"

"Not Crosby. It's COSBY — Bill Cosby. He was in I SPY and..." Ben just couldn't remember the chronology to Bill Cosby's career, but it was obvious that 1957 was too early for him to be the household name he would eventually become. "I guess I'm a bit ahead of your time yet. Look, forget it. It's not that important."

"Whatever you say, Ben. So, what did you think of the motion picture, anyhow?"

"Actually, it wasn't my kind of movie."

"Oh, come on — I thought it was great. Why didn't you like it?"

"Too schmaltzy..."

"Schmaltzy? What's that supposed to mean?"

"You know, schmaltzy — like mushy, sentimental, corny..."

"So now romance seems corny to you, does it?"

"No, now don't be putting words in my mouth. That's not what I'm saying at all. It's just that, for example, remember that scene where Gary Cooper... Nah, you ain't dragging me into this argument."

"What argument?"

"Exactly my point — there IS no argument. If you say that's the best movie that's ever been produced, then the best movie it is... I can see I'm outnumbered by a majority of one here, so I'm going to shut up while I'm ahead — if anyone in his right mind would call this being ahead..."

"Well, it seems as though a heck of a lot of people must agree with me."

"You can say that again. The theater was really crowded considering this picture has been held over... ah, how many weeks?"

"Three weeks."

"Yeah, so far. Plus, I really like the theme song. Um, Pat Boone..." Ben began to croon the first few bars of the song *Friendly Persuasion*, but the melody as he sang it bore little resemblance to the original version.

"You never told me what a great voice you had."

"I never told you a lot of things." He turned to look at Lani as she quietly tried to suppress a giggle. "You bum! I can see you don't really think I sound as good as Pat Boone!"

"Oh, but it's the thought that counts. I really like you singing love songs to me." She squeezed his hand.

"So, do you want to stop and get ice cream or a soda or something?"

"To tell you the truth, I'm still stuffed with Chinese noodles and fried rice from dinner. And I am really tired. Aren't you?"

"Yeah, now that you mention it."

"Besides, I do have some ice cream in my freezer box at home."

"Then home it is, Leilani."

* * *

The uneventful, twenty-five-minute walk home proved to be quite pleasant and served as a refreshing stimulant to both Ben and Leilani. Ben unlocked the apartment door, pushed it open, and followed her into the living room.

"I can't believe how dead it is in this town, considering that Honolulu is already a fairly large city. They must roll the sidewalks up pretty early even on Saturday nights."

"Yeah, I guess there isn't as much nightlife as you Easterners would expect."

"Yet."

"Yet?"

"It's coming."

"It is?

"You can bet on it."

"I don't gamble. I guess I'll have to take your word for it. But if you ask me, I think it's way too busy around here already."

"Just a matter of perspective, my dear. So now what? Are you tired? Do you want to hit the sack?"

"To tell you the truth, I think that walk really woke me up."

"Yeah, me too. Let's see if there's anything on the late show."

"TV, huh?" Her big eyes nearly began to glow as she beamed a rather mischievous looking grin at him.

"Whoa! What does that expression mean?"

"Well now, wouldn't you like to find out?"

"To tell you the truth, yeah, I would. Maybe we can just sit here and talk about your nasty intentions if you want to."

"TALK — I really had my heart set on..." The same devious smile came across her face again. "Hey, come to think of it, why not? Maybe we can find a good movie for you to help overcome your boredom." Leilani turned on the television and flicked through the few channels that were still on the air. She stepped back once she finally came across an obvious movie. "Let's see what this is." She crossed the room and was seated on the sofa next to Ben.

"Aw, man! Don't tell me — another war picture..."

"We don't have to watch, you know." She walked back over to the television, clicked the set off, and turned on the large table radio sitting on a shelf in the kitchen. She began to sing along with the song as she came back over to Ben. "...love me tender, love me true, never let me go..."

"So now Elvis is spotted hiding out in Hawaii?"

"Huh?"

Ben laughed. "So now who's the crooner around here?"

"Oh, I'm sorry. I can't help it. I just love Elvis."

"You and about every other woman on the planet."

"Well, he's so sexy. I can't believe he's actually going to go into the armed forces."

"Somehow, I think the world will get by."

"Yeah, but they're going to cut all that beautiful hair right off his handsome noggin."

Ben put his open hand over his face. "My, my — the sheer horror of it all!"

"Ben! Are you trying to be sarcastic?"

"Now, whatever would make you think that?"

"You are, you bum." In jest, she began to punch his shoulder with her lightly clenched fists.

"Stop it! Stop it! You're hurting me, you vicious woman, you!" Ben mockingly threw his hands in front of his body to feign defending against her attack, but Lani continued her offensive by gently pounding on his hands.

"You bum! You bum! I'm going to get you for this, you no good, rotten bum!"

"Do you always call your lovers such pleasant names?"

She responded by stepping up her bogus brawl.

"I guess you leave me with no other choice, ma'am." Ben grabbed each of her hands with his own to prevent her from continuing her frontal assault. "I hope you recognize the fact that, even though I'm getting up there in years compared to a mere youngster like yourself, I still have the upper hand here. Now then, do you give up?"

"No, no, a thousand times no! You're a bum for teasing me, and I promise I'll get even with you no matter if it's the last thing I ever..."

Ben quickly released her hands and threw his arms around her back. He embraced her in a bear hug and gently wrestled her down onto the sofa. He quieted her protests in a flurry of kisses. Leilani's playful struggled didn't last long as she quickly gave way to passion. She announced her unconditional surrender returning his tender caresses with her own.

"You feel so good just to hold, so... so right."

"Oh Ben, it feels just as good to me. I love you."

"I love you." He pressed his lips to Lani's forehead and continued with a volley of kisses across her cheeks, down her chin and finally onto her neck. For several minutes, the two lovers cuddled even closer, sharing their warmth and passion. The touch of her soft body against his and the sensation of her delicate hands lightly rubbing his back made him suddenly mindful of the fact that the temperature had grown hotter and hotter, both physically and emotionally. As Lani became more animated in her gyrations and more forceful in grinding her thigh into his midsection, he could sense an overpowering flush of desire surging through his entire being.

The very last vestiges of his rapidly failing intellect set off one last alarm, alerting him to the fact that he was at the point of no return. He was acutely aware of the flood of hormones driving him towards total loss of his self-control. Without any warning, he delicately pushed himself back from Leilani and took a deep breath. "Wait, wait... We've GOT to stop, Leilani... I mean..." He expelled a long stream of air. "Oh Jesus! Look, I'm... I'm so sorry."

"Sorry?"

"Leilani, I'm losing control of myself, here. I'm sorry, but we've got to stop, or I know I'm going to do something I'll really regret later."

"Regret?"

"Yes — regret."

"But... don't you mean... Don't you WANT to make love to me?" A frown raced crossed her face.

"Well... sure I do... I mean, I REALLY WANT to make love to you, but..."

Her frown disappeared just as quickly as it had come. "I feel exactly the same way, Ben."

"Oh, Lani, I love you so much. I just don't want to hurt you."

"How could you hurt me by loving me? I just KNOW you'll be gentle."

"Well sure, but... Oh, come on, Lani — you just CAN'T be this innocent. For god's sake, you're twenty-six years old. I mean, even considering that it's 1957, you simply..."

She interrupted his concern with a very throaty whisper. "Do you really think I'm sexy, Ben?"

He couldn't help but wonder just how authentic her little girl persona was, and yet somehow, he was certain that everything about her was perfectly genuine. "You're not just sexy, Lani. You are the most sensual human being I have ever met. There's something about you that makes me want to have you, to touch you and caress you and hold you in my arms, feeling you pressing close to my body."

She continued to whisper in a sultry tone. "You can hold me closer to you, Ben, cuddle up to me tighter. Would you like that Ben? Is that what you'd like?"

"Aw come on, Lani, you know I would. I'd like that very much, but I'm so afraid that I..."

She placed her fingers lightly over his mouth. "Then put your arms around me again and squeeze me close to you. Feel our bodies next to each other. Feel our bodies touching — becoming one."

Ben exhaled a long, slow rush of air. He knew it was useless to continue to defy his feelings. He was almost conscious of the last bit of caution as it departed from his psyche, marking the emotional passage beyond the point of no return. His reason rapidly gave way to his desire. He willfully did just as she asked, embracing her tightly to him, her head buried in his chest.

"Does this feel good, Ben? Do I make you feel all hot being so close to you?"

"Hot? Oh god, you feel so soft and sexy and... and... yeah — very hot. I love you being cuddled up to me this way."

When she began to gently rub his thigh with her hand, Ben knew for certain that he had lost his intellectual struggle, mentally surrendering all his reason to his aroused passions. He simply had no strength left to resist what he so much desired. "I wish that we could feel even closer."

"Would you like to lie here together naked, to feel our bare skin touch each other? That would feel so wonderful, wouldn't it?"

"Is that what YOU want, Leilani?"

"I do, more than anything I've ever wanted in the whole world."

Silently, the two separated only far enough apart to awkwardly pull off their outer clothes and drop them on the floor. Again they cuddled together, naked flesh pressing against naked flesh. As they explored each other's mouth with their tongues, Ben tenderly cupped one of Lani's breasts with his hand.

"Oh Lani, you're so beautiful, so... so sexy. I love being together like this with you."

She attempted to reach her arm around to her back, but being so cramped on the sofa, she met with very little success. "Will you help me undo it?"

Ben found the hook on her bra and clumsily undid it, letting both of her rather ample breasts fall free. He began to caress and fondle her softness. "Does that feel good?"

"Perfect." She reiterated her answer as she found Ben's hardness with her hand and proceeded to tenderly knead it. "And how about that, Ben? Does that feel good to you? Am I doing it too hard?"

"No, no — it's just perfect, Lani."

She tried to turn to free the arm she was lying on top of, but couldn't seem to get in a comfortable position. "It's so cramped on this sofa. Let's go to my bedroom."

"The bedroom?"

"I want us to make love, Ben. I want to feel you deep inside of me. I want us to be one. Will you make love to me?"

"Oh Lani, yes. There's nothing I'd rather do more..."

Holding his outstretched hand, she led him into her bedroom.

23

Saturday, February 10, 1957: 7:15 A. M.

A beam of sunlight fell squarely on Ben's face. Remaining perfectly motionless, he only opened one eye while trying for all the world to make some sense out of his blurry view. In a matter of just a few seconds, he realized he was in Leilani's bed. Leilani! He quickly rolled over only to find her lying wide awake and looking right at him. Quite startled, he quickly sat up. "Lani! Why are you awake already?"

"Wow — no good morning even? What kind of greeting is that?"

"I'm sorry, honey. I guess I should start with good morning. It's just that..."

She placed her index finger to his lips. "First things first. Good morning, Ben. You know that you don't have to get up right away. There's absolutely no place either one of us has to be today."

Ben wiped the fog from his eyes. "Sorry that I was so startled. I was really in a sound sleep and just woke up totally oblivious to the world."

"So, I noticed."

"You did, huh? How long have you been awake?"

"Oh, I don't know. Maybe a half-hour or so."

"Well, thank god, it's morning, and you're still here."

"Now, what's that supposed to mean? I live here. Where else would I be?"

"Nowhere else. I just meant... Oh, you know — the old 'will she still love me in the morning' routine."

"Ben... You're never getting rid of me that easily." She pushed him back down on the bed and kissed him. "It was wonderful. It was better than I ever imagined it could be."

"It was the BEST, Lani. You are the most beautiful, sexiest woman in the whole world, my love."

"You make me feel so great, so much a woman. I just hope you aren't comparing me to... Well... you know..."

"Comparing? No, I'm not comparing... Hey, come on. I mean, for goodness sake — I wouldn't..." It finally dawned on Ben the subtle message she communicated in her tone. "Oh wow! Are you trying to tell me this was the first time you ever...? I mean, in your whole life, you never...?"

Lani flashed a hurt look at him as she slowly shook her head. "Aw, come on, Ben. I told you that I'm not that kind of girl. It depresses me to think that you would even consider — for one minute, even — that I would have..."

"Oh no, Leilani. It's just that in my time, it doesn't seem as though there are a heck of a lot of twenty-six-year-old virgins left."

Her eyebrows arched in surprise. "I'm not so sure I like YOUR time, Ben. Thank god that 'your time' now is here with me in 1957."

* * *

"Would you like more guava juice?"

"I can get it, but thanks anyway."

"Come on, Ben — why are you so resistant to having me do things for you?"

"I'm not — really. You made breakfast, didn't you?"

"Sure, but you still seem so... Oh, I don't know. You just seem so independent of women... Of me. Are — were — you that way with Emily, too?"

"Oh, I see what you're driving at. I guess the world's changed quite a bit during the past half-century or so. Women have become much more — um... I guess you could say independent. And most guys just don't want to be accused of being male chauvinist pigs anymore."

"Chauvinists? What's a chauvinist?"

"That's like being insensitive to the needs of women. Um... kind of having an attitude problem... ah... like thinking that men are somehow better than women." He spread some passion fruit jam on a piece of toast.

"Well, men sure are different from women. I hope you guys in the future haven't made both sexes exactly the same."

"No — nothing like that. But by the nineties, women have won opportunities to pursue any vocation they want to — even ones you may think are reserved for men."

"Now wait a minute, Ben. You're not trying to tell me that women will be able to work on construction crews or fly airplanes or whatever."

"That, dear Lani, is exactly what I'm trying to tell you. Women can be executives, firefighters, ministers, governors. Believe it or not, one-day women will even run for the Presidency of the United States."

"That's just crazy, Ben. What's wrong with being a wife, a mother?"

"Nothing. Only now — in the future — women will simply have a choice as to if or when they want to do the whole family thing."

"How about babies?"

"How about them?"

"Come on, Ben. You know as much or more about the birds and bees than I do. How's a woman go to work every day when she has a baby at home to take care of?"

"Simple. She just doesn't have a baby until she's ready to."

"Yeah, right! Like my friend, Margaret. She was working as a stewardess for an interisland airline when she married her boyfriend. Naturally, the airline made her give up her stewardess job, but she was able to keep working for them selling tickets. She and Gerry were determined to have her work long enough to save up a little nest egg — you know, like no baby right away."

"Well, I hope they practiced some birth control."

"Birth control? They followed exactly what they were told using the, um... the rhythm method."

"Aw man, the rhythm method!" Ben slapped his forehead with his hand.

"Yeah. And four or five months later, she got... um... you know." Lani's eyes looked down at her half-full cup of tea.

"I know, all right — she got pregnant!"

Leilani's face showed mild shock at Ben's choice of terms.

"Aw, come on, Lani. The term pregnant is not a dirty word. For crying out loud — how human can you get. It's just that the rhythm method is not too reliable a way to prevent having unwanted babies. Besides, who told them how to do it?"

"Their parish priest."

"A priest! Oh boy! That's like asking a blind man for advice on what kind of reading lamp to buy!"

"Ben! I AM Catholic, you know. Don't make fun..."

"I'm not making fun — really... I happen to have been brought up Catholic, too. But that's still not a good reason to get pregnant unless you want to. And don't tell me that it's 1957! That's just as true now as it is in..." Ben's mouth involuntarily dropped wide open as it suddenly dawned on him exactly what he was saying. With a note of serious concern, he spoke in a much lower tone of voice. "Leilani, are you taking the pill?" As soon as the words left his mouth, he knew he had asked a very silly question.

"What pill?"

"The pill! The pill! Please don't tell me that there is no pill yet." As hard as he tried to search his memory, he simply had no recollection of when the birth control pill came into popular use.

"Ben, what in god's name are you talking about? I feel fine — absolutely wonderful, even. Why would I want to take any pills?"

Ben audibly exhaled a stream of air. "Forget about it. Just me getting lost in the future again."

"You are very weird, Ben. First, you're talking about getting... having babies, and then you're talking about taking pills. Maybe I should worry about YOU."

"I'm sorry, honey. It's just that... Hey, what are we going to do today?"

"After I do the dishes?"

"After WE do the dishes."

"I'd like to go to ten o'clock mass. Other than that, the day is open. I just might take you to my secret place."

"Your secret place, huh? And you want to go to mass first?"

"Do you want to come with me?"

"Well, it's been quite a while, but why not?"

24

Saturday, February 10, 1957: 1:15 P. M.

"So, it's only a ten or fifteen-minute walk after we get off the bus, she tells me."

"We can stop here if you want to."

"No, no — I'm only teasing you. This is a beautiful walk."

"You won't be sorry when you see the waterfall."

"It amazes me how close we are to the city, and yet we're in the middle of a tropical rain forest."

"It is secluded."

"Hey, what's that?" Ben pointed towards a huge tree.

"D'ya mean the banyan tree?"

"No, I mean the bird there. He's red and blue and really big."

"Looks like a parrot to me."

"I didn't know you had parrots in Hawaii."

"We don't — not naturally, anyway. But a lot of times, pets get loose and take up residence back up here in the valleys. At least they're never going to freeze to death."

"This is so beautiful, so peaceful. It smells unbelievably fresh and clean. And it even SOUNDS great around here — the songs of all the different birds singing at the same time meld together into one, great symphony of the jungle."

"Now, you see why I like to come up here — to my secret place..."

"And you promise me that there are no snakes here — none at all?"

"I promise."

"Thank god! I'll tell you, it's difficult to believe that such a magnificent Eden has yet to be visited by the serpent."

"Don't tell me there still may be hope for the fallen. You sound as though actually you took the Priest's sermon to heart this morning."

Ben answered with a smile and a chuckle.

"Is the picnic basket getting heavy?"

"It's fine."

"My favorite spot is right around the bend up here."

The path became very narrow, only wide enough to comfortably walk single file. Lani stepped out front and led the way. The walls of the valley had gotten closer and closer together as they walked deeper into the canyon. The foliage was denser and greener than Ben could ever remember seeing in his entire life, and they hadn't seen any real signs of humanity since they had gotten off the bus. Without any warning, Lani took off and ran out of sight around a curve in the trail. Ben was left with only the ever-increasing rumbling and gurgling sounds to announce the proximity of their destination.

"Hey, don't forget me." There was no answer. He continued to follow the trail as the roar of water grew louder and louder. At last, he broke into a small clearing along the side of a gushing stream. A beautiful, three-tiered waterfall cascaded gracefully down into an inviting pool at its base. Leilani had opened a mat and was already lying back and sunning herself on a sizable, level slab of smooth lava rock.

"So, do you want any company?"

"I want YOU." She nearly yelled at the top of her lungs to be heard over the thunder of the falls.

Ben put the picnic basket down, took off his shirt, and sat next to Leilani. "Well, you have me, lady. Now the question is, what are you going to do with me?"

Her face lit up. "Aha! Wouldn't you like to know?" She threw her arms around his neck and kissed him. "So, what do you think of it?"

"What? The kiss?"

"No, dummy. You BETTER have liked the kiss — or else..." She mockingly shook her fist at him. "What I meant was simply what do you think about my special place?"

"Hey, what could anyone think? It's just perfect — like paradise..."

"I don't know why, but there's just something so uplifting about the atmosphere created by a gushing waterfall. I can come here in a totally rotten mood and leave with a positive frame of mind."

"Must be positive ions, if you believe the television commercials."

"Huh?"

"Oh, never mind. I guess it's got something to do with the pristine nature of the air. The spray really must purify the atmosphere. And the roar of the water blanks out all other sounds so well that it actually makes it quiet here."

"Do you like the greenery?"

"Are you kidding? It's so incredibly lush, it's hard to believe."

"Do you want to go for a swim?"

"Is it safe?"

"I'll tell you in a minute." She stood and walked off the flat expanse of lava rock and quickly located a bright green plant with long, slender leaves radiating from the top of a woody stalk. She firmly grabbed the stalk with one hand and pulled a leaf off using her other hand.

"What are you doing?"

"I have to get a *ti* leaf."

"A tea leaf as in T-E-A? ...the kind you drink?"

She nearly shouted to be heard over the rumble of the falls. "No, it's *ti* leaf as in T-I. The Hawaiian people say they give you good luck and possess many mystical powers." She stepped over several large boulders and carried the single leaf over to the deep, dark pool at the base of the falls. Once there, she dropped it into the water.

"What's this, some sort of sacrifice or something?"

"No, no sacrifice, you silly *haole*. Look — the *ti* leaf is floating."

"Big deal!"

She glared at him with an expression of disgust and began to walk back towards him."

"Hey, I'm sorry. I didn't mean to be sacrilegious or anything. For crying out loud, you said you were Catholic. Surely you don't believe this sacrifice nonsense."

"I told you it's NOT a sacrifice. It's supposed to be kind of a test, an indication of whether or not it's safe to swim."

"And?"

"If the leaf floats, it's safe to go in."

"Lani!" Ben's head tilted to one side as a look of disbelief crossed his face.

"Ben, I told you before that Hawaiian blood is as much a part of me as my Christianity upbringing. My *aumakua* has been by my side always."

"But I thought you said he was an owl."

"Mostly, but *aumakua* can take whatever form is needed."

"And now he's a *ti* leaf?" Ben again looked out to see the *ti* leaf bobbing high in the water. "So, I guess we have the gods' permission to go for a dip."

Lani shook her head in faint protest. "My aumakua is watching over you, too, Ben." They both took off their shorts, revealing the swimsuits they wore underneath. Again, Lani took the lead, extending her hand for Ben's. "You really have to be careful on these rocks. They're covered with moss and very slippery."

"Don't worry, I'll be extra..." Ben stumbled, broke his fall with his free hand, and was submerged under a foot-and-a-half of brisk, mountain water.

"Oh, Ben! Are you okay?"

"WHOAAAA! It's like an ICE bath in here!"

"Are you all right?"

He communicated his wellbeing by nodding his head in the affirmative, while greatly exaggerating his shivers.

Being fairly confident that Ben didn't hurt himself, she unhesitatingly stepped off the lava outcrop directly into knee-deep water.

"As long as I don't freeze to death, I'll be just fine. I haven't felt anything this cold since... well, since Philadelphia!"

"Oh, come on! It's not THAT cold — only refreshing! Are you sure you're bones are all in one piece over there?"

"How would I possibly know. This water is numbing me beyond all feeling..."

Lani shook her head and, being convinced that Ben was uninjured, pushed off a rock and swam towards the falls as if to refute his complaint by example. Ben lay in the water, attempting to adjust to its temperature as he watched her use her graceful breaststroke to smoothly swim up alongside the gushing cascade of water.

"Come on out, you big chicken." She had to nearly shout to be heard over the thundering torrent of water.

Boy, Ben thought to himself, does she know how to get a guy's goat — just challenge his manhood. Well, here goes nothing. He took a deep breath and shoved himself in the general direction of Leilani. At least she was right — the longer he stayed in the water, the warmer it seemed to get. He quickly swam the hundred or so yards to the falls, trying his best to mimic her breaststroke. As he got closer to Lani, he could see the big grin on her face.

"Nice stroke!"

"I'm glad you like it..."

"So, is the big *haole* still freezing?"

"Okay, okay. I'll admit that it is feeling warmer — even to a big *haole*!" He grabbed onto the ledge from which she was dangling her feet and pulled himself up into a position next to her. "I guess I should know by now not to doubt you. It really does feel refreshing. It's so nice back here that I'm surprised there's not a crowd of people around. Do you ever see anyone else when you come up to these falls?"

"Never — most locals don't want to walk so far, and the tourists don't even know it's here."

"That amazes me. Hey, what are you staring at?"

"Look." Lani was pointing back out across the pool.

"Aw wow — I'm starting to sound like a broken record, but here we go again... That's incredible..." The sunlight was reflecting off the mist kicked up by the waterfall at just the correct angle to create a beautiful, brilliant rainbow. "Does this happen all the time."

"Usually, yes. Of course, at different times of the year, the position and timing of the rainbow changes. Actually, it even disappears for a month or two sometime during the middle of the summer. I call it Leilani's rainbow."

"I couldn't think of a more beautiful person to have a more beautiful rainbow."

"Why thank you, Ben. You know, it always brings me good luck."

"Like a *ti* leaf?" He smiled broadly.

"Hey, stop making fun. It brought you to me, didn't it?"

Ben decided it best not to even attempt to answer her rhetorical question. "I don't claim to know much about good luck or *ti* leaves or rainbows, but I do know that, having only been in your state a few..."

"I keep telling you that it's NOT a state!"

"Yet..."

"Don't tell me about the future."

"I won't. But please pardon me for the slip anyway, young lady. Now then, as I was saying before I was so rudely interrupted — though I've only been in your..." He intentionally cleared his throat quite loudly. "...TERRITORY for only a few days, I have to say it's the most fantastic place on the whole earth — maybe in all the universe." He cupped his two hands and splashed the falling water over his head. "You know, I've heard stories my whole life about how many people get captured by Hawaii — the land, the people, the spirit... I've heard of people so enchanted with the Islands that they have abandoned homes and jobs — even relationships — just to stay here in Eden. I guess I'm beginning to understand. It's all just so... well, so magnificent."

"And how about me?"

"My dear Leilani — you are the most essential part of MY Hawaii, of MY paradise. There'd be no rainbows, no enchantment, no PARADISE at all without you..."

She leaned her head on his shoulder. "You can be so romantic, Ben — at least when you want to be."

"I think WE'RE romantic together. Actually, this whole thing — you, Hawaii, US — it all almost seems too good to be true. In a way, it sort of scares me..."

"Scares you? What do you mean, Ben?"

"Just that I never knew anything could be so perfect. I never even had a dream as wonderful as this — as wonderful as you, I mean. And sometimes I'm nervous that it will all just blink out and disappear."

Ben's attention was caught by a pure white, Hawaiian tropicbird as it dove from the top of the cliff face down into the valley below, trailing its long, flowing tail feathers behind. He kept searching the dense foliage to see where it had vanished, still somehow convinced that at least an elephant or tiger would soon poke its head out of the jungle.

"So, you're going to stay here, Ben? You're going to stay with me?"

Ben kept his gaze on the foliage. "I... I want to, Leilani. You know I want to."

"What do you mean, you WANT to?"

"I mean..." Ben's face was strained. "Lani look, I don't even know what happened to me yet. How'd I get here? What will I do if I stay? For that matter, the entire question of leaving is probably a moot point. Hell, could I go back to my time in the future even if I wanted to?"

"But I don't want you to be stuck here, stuck with me. I want you to choose to be with me — to WANT to be with me."

"Believe me, I DO choose to be with you and WANT you more than anyone else in the universe. It's just that... that..."

"Why are you so hesitant, Ben?"

"Oh, Lani... Don't forget, I still have to worry about my girls. If I never saw Emily again in my entire life, I know I'd have no problem with that. You know that's true. But I'll always worry about Lisa and

161

Bonnie — they're my kids, my flesh and blood. I mean, I still have a responsibility to see that they..." He turned to look at her and saw that she was looking down into the water. He couldn't be certain if the wetness around her eyes was from the mist or from tears. He softly put his hand on her chin and gently turned her head towards him. He spoke in as quiet a tone as he could to still be heard over the falling water. "Hey Lani, I've meant absolutely everything that I've said to you — everything. Last night our souls touched, and it was as real as real could ever be. You're no fling to me, Lani. I love you more than I've ever loved any other human being. I'm not going to somehow duck out on you."

Her subtle sniffle confirmed her tears. "I don't mean to be selfish, but I want you to stay here with me, to stay here in our own paradise together."

A crashing sound interrupted Lani's words. Despite the constant roar of the pounding waterfall, another loud, quite distinct rumbling echoed through the canyon.

"Did you hear that? What was that?"

Lani pointed about a third of the way up the canyon wall some several hundred yards distant. "Over there — it looks like there's a rock slide. That's not all that unusual back here."

Ben looked up towards an apparently natural ledge cut into the side of the valley from where the slide originated. At first, he could see nothing. He continued to scrutinize the cliffs until his squinting eyes finally revealed the figure of a stout man, now scurrying beneath the jungle canopy, trying to scramble back onto the ledge.

"Can you see that?"

Lani kept staring up the steep bank. "See what?"

"I sure hope I'm wrong, but I think the serpent just entered into our Garden of Eden."

25
Sunday, February 10, 1957: 7:30 P. M.

Ben stood up from the table and patted his stomach. "What did you call that?"

"*Ahi.*"

"*Ahi.* And that's supposed to be a tuna fish of some sort?"

"It's not supposed to be — it is! It's yellowfin tuna. Did you like it?"

"Are you kidding? It was great! You notice how much I left on my plate." He pointed toward his totally bare plate. "I'll get the dishes, honey."

"NO!" She practically shouted at him as she jumped up from the table. "I will, Ben. I'll get them."

"It's no problem, Lani. I do the..."

"I said I WILL DO the dishes." She used an exceedingly firm tone of voice as though she was trying to make a point.

"Jeez-o-man, all right already. Don't blow a gasket. What's the big deal about dishes?"

"No big deal... It's just that I don't like this liberation stuff you're always telling me about. I still want to be a woman."

"Hey Lani, you don't have to prove your womanhood to me — especially not by doing the dishes!"

"Let's just say I WANT to do the dishes. I happen to think a woman SHOULD do the dishes."

"Oh boy! If you only knew..."

She abruptly cut him off. "Knew what?"

"Well, if most women I know ever heard you talk like that, they'd think you were ready for the loony bin! That kind of statement would surely get you in a whole bunch of trouble with your soul sisters of the nineties."

"Soul sisters? You know, you always tell me about the weird, futuristic world that you're from, but please don't forget that I'm a 1957 girl and very happy to be such. I wouldn't want to be a woman in your era, even if you could arrange to have me win *THE $64,000 CHALLENGE*. I'm telling you that I have no desire to burn my bra. You make me nervous with all this talk about..."

"My god! Slow down for just a minute here. Nobody wants you to live in the 1990s. Besides that, $64,000 wouldn't really go too far."

"Well, I'm keeping my bra right where it..."

"For crying out loud — how'd we get from doing dinner dishes to burning bras? You've got it all wrong here, Lani. I'm only talking about sharing chores, not anything else. I just happen to agree with the point of view that women weren't meant to be slaves."

"I don't want to be a slave — only the kind of woman that I want to be."

Ben threw both his hands in the air in a gesture of surrender. "Okay, I give up! If your heart is set on doing the dishes, woe is it for me to ruin your plans." He leaned over towards her and kissed her on the cheek.

"Now that's better, Ben. I can do the dishes while you look at the paper. Um... why don't you see if there's anything good on television tonight."

"The boob tube, huh?"

"Boob tube... Hey, that's pretty good. I never heard that before."

"Believe me, it's not too original." Ben reached down to the table and began to collect all the utensils and stack them onto the dirty dishes.

"Ben, I'm NOT going to say it again — I'LL GET IT!"

"Okay, okay. Cool your jets, lady."

"Jets?"

Ben just shook his head in a non-answer. "Hey, you can suit yourself and wash every last one of them if you want, but at least let me carry them over to the sink."

"MEN!"

"Now, what's THAT supposed to mean?"

"Only that men — at least YOU in particular — can really be pig-headed when..." She caught herself in mid-sentence, and her frown immediately transformed into a grin. "Hey, just listen to us. Isn't it wonderful?"

"Wonderful? What's so wonderful about this crazy conversation? It sounds more like an altercation."

"That's exactly the point! We're arguing. Isn't it just WONDERFUL." She held her two hands together and rolled her eyes in an expression that looked for all the world like that of a dazed teenaged girl madly in love. "It sounds as though we're an old married couple who have been together for years. Oh, I wish we were, Ben. I wish it were true. I wish we had our own place, our own children, our own life." Suddenly, reality reappeared on her face. She placed one hand on his shoulder and traced a line down his arm with a finger of her free hand.

"Someday, Leilani. We WILL have all that... someday..."

"Yeah, someday..." She let out a sigh, turned, and retreated towards the sink.

Ben finished clearing off the table. "Do you have a sponge to clean the table with?"

"Will a washrag do?"

He brushed all the crumbs into his hand and shook them off in the trashcan. After pushing the chairs back into place, Ben picked up the Sunday *ADVERTISER* and took it over to the sofa. After checking the front-page index, he shuffled through several sections until he finally folded open the paper.

"Did you find the entertainment section?

"Yeah, I've got it right... Oh my god! How could I have forgotten?"

"Forgotten what?"

"Forgotten the *G. E. Theater*. It's on Sunday nights."

"The *G. E. Theater*, you said?"

"Yep."

"That's on tonight — every Sunday evening. I don't know when it's on back in the States. Remember, they fly those films out here, and we generally get them a week or so later. I usually like their shows, though. What's it supposed to be about tonight?"

"Um... Tony Curtis stars — it says he plays a bullfighter."

"A bullfighter? Ah, I guess that could be interesting. So why are you oh-my-god-ing Tony Curtis?"

"It's not Tony Curtis. It's Reagan — isn't the *G. E. Theater* hosted by Reagan?"

"Begin? I think it starts at eight o'clock."

He raised his voice. "No, not BEGIN… I said REAGAN — it's hosted by Reagan."

"Sorry. Sure — Ronald Reagan is the MC. Big deal."

"You can say that again."

"What?" She continued to have difficulty hearing him over the stream of running water that was filling the sink.

Again, he spoke up. "I only said you can say that again — big deal, I mean."

"Oh. Well, I only mean that he's just a rather nondescript actor — certainly not my favorite."

"Like Elvis?" Ben laughed.

"You can say that again! Actually, I can't really think of any of Reagan's movies that I really liked that much. He'll most likely never really amount to much."

"Yeah, right!" He muttered mostly to himself, "He'll only be the President of the United States…"

At last, she shut off the water and turned towards him. "I'm sorry, Ben. I just couldn't hear you too well with the water running, but the sink's full now. Did you say something about the President?"

God knows, he didn't want to get into a discourse on Ronald Reagan. "Oh, I just said that the President is on a golfing trip to Florida again."

"What else is new? Old Ike sure likes his golf, doesn't he?"

"Sure does."

* * *

"All done, honey?"

"I am, Ben." She finished drying her hands and neatly hung the dishtowel from its rack. "So, do you really want to watch TV tonight?"

"To be perfectly honest with you, not really. It's such a nice night that we ought to go for a walk."

"I'd like that."

"Hey, what time do you have to go to work tomorrow?"

"Like always — nine o'clock. Regular hours are nine 'til five, but I'll try my best to get home early if I can."

"Do you get Tuesday off?"

"Tuesday? No — why?"

"It's Lincoln's Birthday, isn't it?"

"I don't really know. We don't celebrate that in the Territory."

"That's too bad."

Lani sat next to him and placed her hand on his leg. "Yeah, well... You do know it's Valentine's Day this week, don't you?"

Ben nodded his head

"Will you be my Valentine?"

"Only if you'll be mine."

"Take me — I'm yours." She slumped to her side and literally fell into his arms, kissing him fully.

"Keep that up, and we'll never go for a walk tonight."

She smiled broadly. "Oh yeah — what else did you have in mind?"

"Actually, we could get our after-dinner exercise right in there." Ben used his head and eyes to gesture towards Lani's bedroom.

"No fair! How could I refuse that? I'll tell you what — why don't we go for a walk now and make love when we get home?"

"Sounds like the best of both worlds to me. So, what do you need to do before we go for our walk?"

"Nothing — I'm ready."

"Well then, I guess we're out of here. Let's see if we can spot our unfriendly friend tonight."

"I wish you wouldn't worry so much about that, Ben."

"Not worry! Come on, Lani, how do you know this guy's not some kind of maniac? ...or rapist? How do you know he's not just waiting for... for god knows what!"

"Gee, thanks Ben. You sure make a single girl feel really secure!"

"Now, I don't mean it like that."

"Okay, okay. Let's go, already.

26

Sunday, February 10, 1957: 9:10 P. M.

"I just can't believe how crowded Waikiki is."

"I'm telling you, Leilani, you don't know what crowded is. It's really pretty calm around here."

"Now, don't kid me, Ben. You forget that I work in a hotel. I know when we get crowded and — believe me — THIS is crowded. Even Mister Dority told..."

"Dority? Who's this Dority fellow? It sure sounds like a *haole* name to me."

She smiled. "That's one word you're really getting down pat, huh? Well, he is a *haole* — a really nice *haole*. He's the general manager at the Royal Hawaiian and, in the final analysis, he's my boss. I'm really anxious for you to meet him. He's just a very big-hearted guy — the kind of man who would do anything for you, no questions asked. I've become pretty good friends with both him and his wife. They live in a big, wonderful house tucked away in Manoa Valley, not that far from town."

"All right already! So, you have a few rich friends — big deal!"

"BEN! Stop teasing me! I really like them, even babysit for their kids sometimes. Now, what's wrong with that?"

"Absolutely nothing! But what in god's name does all this — and Mister Dority, for that matter — have to do with Waikiki being so crowded?"

"Oh — yeah. As I was saying before you so rudely interrupted me, Mister Dority told us that there are over seven thousand visitors in town right now! Can you believe it?"

"Seven thousand — ha! If you want crowded, try seven million visitors, Lani..."

"Never!"

"Never? Hey, don't kid yourself, lady. They're going to be coming here sooner or later in hordes you'd probably rather do without."

Lani looked at him with an expression indicating that she wasn't quite certain whether to believe him or not. "Seven million? Really? But that won't happen for probably hundreds of years."

Ben slowly turned his head from side to side. "Well, you just stick around for a few decades. I fear you're in for a big surprise, Leilani."

"Aw, come on — you said seven MILLION, didn't you?"

"Maybe even more..."

She shook her head in disbelief.

"So, who are all those guys hanging around over there?" He tipped his head in the direction of the beach right across the street.

"Oh, they're all beach boys."

"THE Beach Boys?" He chuckled to himself. "Is there going to be a rock concert?"

"A rock concert? What are you talking about now?"

"Ah, nothing. I'm just kidding. I guess it's sort of a futuristic joke."

"You're really weird, Ben."

Ben playfully nodded his head in resigned agreement. "So, what do beach boys do for a living?"

"Anything you can think of that has to do with the beach."

"Like stealing cameras and robbing little old ladies."

"NO, Ben! Why are you so gosh-darned distrusting?" She was visibly upset at his suggestion.

"Hey, sorry. I guess living in the nineties tends to make one assume the worst about groups of guys hanging around street corners. But I'm curious – what DO they do, anyway?"

"They help out visitors. Oh, like they take tourists surfing or outrigger canoeing; they give them directions and information; sometimes they act as guides and just generally try to make any visitor's stay here as pleasant as possible."

"How do they make money?"

"The tourists pay them — tips, mostly. The beach boys are a really valuable commodity — they really spread the aloha spirit around."

"Aha! I knew you'd get back to that aloha spirit again sooner or later. So, all the surfboards and canoes and stuff stuck in those racks are theirs?"

"Mostly. But anyone can park their boards or canoes there if they want."

"Some security — they don't even look locked?"

"Locked? Why would you lock up a surfboard? I mean, where's it going to go?"

"You're serious, aren't you?"

"Ben! You're putting me on again, aren't you? Certainly, I'm serious. Why would you lock up a surfboard?"

"I only meant so that no one would steal them."

"STEAL a surfboard? My god, I can't think of one reason anybody would steal a surfboard. What would they do with it?"

"Leilani! People will steal anything that's not tied down and, for that matter, lots of things that are tied down AND locked up. Who knows why — I guess for drugs, most likely..."

"Drugs?"

"Your absolute innocence never fails to amaze me. No wonder having some guy tail us for the whole weekend does nothing to raise your level of paranoia. Speaking of which..." Ben's eyes were glued across the street on the small band of beach boys.

"Suspicious again?"

"You tell me — is it my imagination that the big guy over there in that god-awful yellow shirt is staring right at us?"

Almost as soon as Lani looked over towards the group, she raised both her hands over her head and began to wave them. "Hey, Kawika! Neva get one job yet?"

"Hey, Lani!" One of the beach boys stepped out of the pack and waved back.

"Come on, Ben. I want you to meet one of my friends."

"Whatever you say."

The two crossed the street and were greeted by a very tall young man of obvious Polynesian lineage.

"Kawika, I want you to meet my friend, Ben Decker. Ben, this is Kawika Pakalana." Ben reached for the big guy's already outstretched arm. He couldn't help but anticipate a painful squeeze as his average-sized hand was engulfed by Kawika's enormous mitt, but to Ben's absolute surprise and delight, the beach boy's touch was amazingly soft and gentle.

"Glad to meet you, Kawika."

"Aloha Ben. You from back in da States?"

"Yes, I am."

"Where 'bout?"

"Philadelphia."

"Oh boy, bra, dat's one cold place to be dis time of ye'a. I spent eighteen months in New Jersey — Fort Dix — in the service, ya know." His expression left Ben with the impression that he wasn't exactly fond of the Garden State. "So, is Leilani showin' you da good time?"

"The best."

"Good, good — she is da best."

"Ah, you're biased, Kawika." She turned to Ben. "Kawika's sister, Lea, and I graduated from Saint Joseph's High School together — over in Hilo."

Ben nodded. "So, you grew up on the Big Island too, Kawika?"

He smiled and smiled broadly. "Da Big Island IS Hawaii, bra..."

Lani continued to cling to Ben's arm. "So, have you heard anything from Lea lately?"

"Not lately. She stay busy back dare with one new *keiki* and all."

Lani looked to Ben, almost as if to interpret. "She and her husband live in Oregon. They just had their third child right before Christmas." She turned to Kawika. "Are you guys still looking for hires this late at night?"

"Nah — no neva make no moe hires tonight. We waitin' for da kine big swell to hit the North Shore. Waves supposed to be to twenty feet. Maybe go surfin' dare tomorrow — moe betta den he'a."

"Well, you guys take care up there and have a good time."

"Sure, sure. Hey, was nice meetin' ya, Ben." He patted him on the shoulder with his big hand.

"Yeah, same here, Kawika."

The smiling Islander turned and walked back towards his group. Two or three other beach boys nodded greetings to Leilani, as she and Ben continued their stroll along the beach.

"Looks like you know half of those guys. No wonder you were so quick to defend them."

"Hey, they're good guys. Stop being so negative, Ben."

"Yeah, okay. So, tell me — what language was Kawika speaking there. I mean, his English was generally good and fairly understandable, but once or twice, he drifted off into something that I found very hard to comprehend."

Lani laughed. "You mean the Pidgin English."

"Pidgin English?"

"Yeah, Pidgin English."

"Isn't that the game — or language — we used to play at as kids? Remember, you'd put the last letter of each word first and pronounce the words that way."

"Ah... I don't think that's..." Suddenly, it dawned on Leilani just what Ben was referring to. "BEN! You dummy, you. That's called pig Latin, and it isn't really a language. This is Pidgin English, and it's a REAL language. Actually, I guess it would technically be called a dialect. Pidgin is a hybrid of many different languages. I'm by no means an authority on its origins, but I know it's a combination of several languages, including English, Hawaiian, Japanese, Portuguese, and Spanish, to name a few. Many locals who get away to the States for a while or deal with tourists a lot have to learn more standard English, but it's always so easy to slip back into the Pidgin dialect."

"Well, I'm sure glad you speak English. Actually, I'm surprised that you don't really even have much of an accent."

"You mean a funny one — like yours?"

"Hey, hey — be nice. Philadelphia English is PROPER English. Really though, I'm surprised you don't speak more... well, Pidgin — like Kawika."

"I can when I want to."

"But, you must have learned to speak..."

"It's the nuns."

"Nuns? What nuns?"

"At Saint Joseph's. I told you I went to a Catholic high school in Hilo. Believe me, the nuns would whack our knuckles if we tried to speak in Pidgin at school."

"I bet you just loved that."

"I love you."

173

"Hey, now it finally sounds as though we're making some time here. Speaking of which, what time do you have to get up in the morning?"

"Usually about six-fifteen or six-thirty. Why, what time is it now?"

Ben glanced at his watch, turned it towards a street light, and then squinted. "Um... looks like about quarter 'til ten. Why? Are we in a hurry to go to sleep?"

"No, not really. I don't know about you, but I'm not the least bit tired."

"So, what's the big deal with the time?"

"I'm anxious to get home to bed."

"But you just said you weren't tired — why the big hurry to get into bed so..."

Lani stopped walking and pulled Ben to her side. She slid both her hands around his back and gave him a passionate kiss, her tongue darting deep in his mouth. Suddenly, Ben pulled back far enough to look in Lani's eyes. "Hey kid, we're in public here."

"Ask me if I care."

"Obviously, you don't. Nonetheless, I think I got the idea. Let's go home."

"I thought you'd never ask."

PART FOUR

"He that will enter into Paradise must come with the right key."

— Thomas Fuller

.

27
Monday, February 11, 1957: 8:05 A. M.

"Yummm... What an *ono* breakfast." Lani could see that Ben had no idea what she was talking about. "*Ono, ono...* that's Hawaii for good... tasty..." She smiled at him. "Do you want another half of a papaya?"

"Yeah, please — they're just delicious."

"You can say that again. I think papayas are my most favorite fruit of all." She grabbed the knife, sliced the oblong fruit lengthwise, and easily scraped all the seeds into the wastebasket. "Is one enough?"

"Oh sure — that's plenty."

"I have more."

"Come on, Lani, I've already had two half papayas and a bowl of cereal. Are you secretly trying to make me fat?"

"I just want you to be satisfied." She ran cold water over the knife to clean its blade.

"Satisfied... My, my, young lady, if you only knew just how satisfied you've made me." He doubted that she heard him over the flow of tap water. Almost at once, she shut the spigot and turned back towards the table.

"So, what are you going to do today?"

"Miss you."

She placed his half papaya on his plate and kissed the top of his head. "You probably say the same thing to all your girlfriends."

"Fat chance of that!"

She sat back at her spot on the opposite side of the table from him. "Oh Ben, I felt just wonderful last night. It was the best."

"For me, too, Leilani. I just can't believe what you do to me, how you make me feel. I mean, I swear you make me act like a kid all over again."

"A kid, huh? I'm certainly not embarrassed to confess to my inexperience, but I can tell you for sure that you performed like a full-fledged, adult male last night!"

"Exactly!"

"Huh?"

"That's exactly what I mean. Lani, I haven't... um... aw... you know..."

"Why are you beating around the bush? Spit it out, Ben — haven't what?"

"Haven't... Well, it's just that I haven't done it three times in one night since I was about twenty years old — merely a still-wet-behind-the-ears college kid. And let me add that it's strictly because of how YOU affect me. You really know how to turn me on. Lani, I'm telling you that you had me in an altered state of consciousness last night."

"I'm not sure I'm following you, but I hope what you're saying is good, no?"

"Oh, it's good all right. It's downright wonderful! You're like some erogenous narcotic. You drive me into a trance-like state — give me a real psychedelic experience, even."

"Psycho-what?"

"Psychedelic. Aw, you know — like Lucy in the sky with diamonds... Like the Beatles... Like LSD and..."

The totally blank expression on her face reminded Ben that there was absolutely no way any of those terms could mean a thing to Lani. Oh wow — here it goes again! It seemed that at some point every morning since he had been thrown back in time to the Islands, he had to once again come to the startling realization that he was, in fact, really living back in 1957. "I'm sorry... I'm only trying to say that what you do to me is literally... well... it's indescribable."

"But I still like to hear you TRY to describe it."

"My dear Leilani, I love you not only for what you are but for what I am when you are with me."

She grabbed his hand under the table and squeezed it. "Oh Ben, that's beautiful. You're so poetic."

"Thanks, honey." As hard as he searched his memory, Ben simply couldn't recall exactly where he had heard those words before, but he was certain no harm would come of it if he silently took credit for them now. They certainly seemed appropriate enough for the situation.

* * *

Lani came out of the bathroom, fluffing her long hair back over her shoulders. "So, my love, are you reading anything interesting there?"

Ben dropped the paper to his lap and looked over towards her. "Yeah, Boeing has started flight testing the seven-o-seven. It won't be long now."

"What's a seven-o-seven?"

"It's an airplane — a jet airplane."

"Oh, like the fighter planes they used in Korea?"

"Well, sort of. They're a lot bigger though AND they're passenger planes."

She brushed some lint off her colorful muumuu. "Passenger planes, huh? I wonder if we'll be getting any of them flying to Hawaii."

"Will you ever!"

She grabbed her purse. "What?"

"Um... I think it's safe to say you'll have a few of them landing out here."

She swallowed the last of her hot tea and placed the cup in the sink. "Aw Ben, I really don't feel like going to work. I want to spend the day with you."

"Come on, love — don't make it any worse than it is. You know you have to go. Besides, we'll have tonight all to ourselves."

"Yeah." She cast a sorrowful glance towards the floor. "Well, at the very least, how about lunch?"

"How about it?"

"You could meet me for lunch. I could probably be ready by about eleven-thirty."

"You've got a date. Where?"

"The beach *lanai* — the same place we ate on Friday."

He got up from the sofa and put his arms around her as she stood in front of him. "I love you, Leilani."

"I love you, Ben." She kissed him one last time and walked to the door. "Use the key on the table when you go out. I'll see you about eleven-thirty."

"Okay. Lani."

She pulled the door shut behind her.

28
Monday, February 11, 1957: 9:15 A. M.

Ben took his time cleaning up the kitchen. At this point, no matter what the reason may be for him somehow turning up here in the nine-fifties, there sure didn't seem to be a lot he could do to change the situation. What the heck — he may as well resign himself to trying his best to relax. Yeah, sure — just relax... Isn't that what his doctor always told him that type A personalities like him needed the most? May as well chalk it up to following doctor's orders! As he headed for the bathroom, it crossed his mind to simply consider this unlikely turn of events as a golden opportunity to enjoy the unexpected vacation he knew he so sorely needed.

Ben quickly finished shaving and then savored an especially long shower. As he toweled himself dry, his thoughts turned to just what he should do on such a beautiful morning. It seemed a real waste to spend any more time inside than he had to. Well, he had always wanted to see the sights of downtown Honolulu, and today seemed to present him with the perfect time to do precisely that. Dressed only in his jockey shorts, Ben stood in front of Lani's mirror running a comb through his rapidly thinning hair. He probably had enough time to check out Iolani Palace before he was to meet Leilani. Then maybe this afternoon, he could catch a bus over to...

BANG! BANG! BANG! His quiet thoughts were loudly interrupted by a commotion at the door.

"Just a minute!" Ben grabbed his shorts and quickly pulled them up and buttoned the waist. Now, who the heck could this be? He assumed all of Lani's friends were well aware that she was at work right now. Ah — maybe it was the mailman or a delivery or something like...

BANG! BANG! BANG! This time whoever was at the door managed to vibrate the entire outer wall of the apartment.

"Hey, all right already! I'm coming, I'm coming!" God, could Lani's friends be that impatient? Whatever happened to that mellow, laid back Hawaiian style that everyone seemed to brag so much about? So much for the aloha spirit.

Ben realized he didn't even have a shirt on, but if his unknown visitor was going to be this impatient, then they'd just better be prepared to put up with a naked chest. He quickly got to the unlocked door, reached for the knob, and began to turn it. To his total astonishment, whoever was on the other side smashed into it with almost enough force to rip it off its hinges!

"HEY! What's the problem here? You're going to tear the door right off its..." Totally off guard, Ben was nearly knocked to the floor as two mountain-sized men rammed the door against the wall and hustled right through the threshold. As one slammed the door shut behind them, the other grabbed Ben by the arms and literally lifted him right off the floor.

"Don't try nothing, buddy — you ain't going nowhere! We even got the street covered!"

Ben's pulse rate must have tripled in a matter of seconds. Surely there was some mistake here! Certainly, they didn't want him! He opened his hands as a signal of compliance. "Hey, no problem... I'm not going to try anything at all. Look, you must have the wrong..."

The man holding him — a muscular Caucasian who simply had to weigh in at a good two-hundred-and-fifty pounds — maintained his firm grasp on Ben. "Shut your mouth, pal!"

Ben felt a surge of panic fill his being. His words came out very feebly. "Well, who... who are you lo... looking for?"

The massive form shook him violently as he shouted his words. "Let's get one thing straight right from the top here. WE ask the questions — YOU give the answers! Now I want to know your name, and I want to know it NOW! And I mean your REAL name, buddy."

Ben tried again. "You MUST have the wrong guy, the wrong apartment. I... I..."

The big guy tightened his grip on his captive to such a degree that Ben's arms screamed at the lack of circulation. "We DON'T make mistakes! Now, this is the last time I going to ask you — what's your name, buddy? Your REAL name?"

"B... Ben D... Decker. Um... Ben. Benjamin N. D... Decker." Ben's tone, no doubt, betrayed his fear as his voice quivered nearly out of control.

"NO, IT'S NOT!" His intimidating tormentor practically yelled at the top of his lungs.

The second intruder spoke up from across the room where he had been hurriedly nosing around, looking as though he were searching for some hidden contraband. "Now, why don't you save us all a lot of trouble and come clean with us right away?" A quick study of the man's features rapidly convinced Ben that this particular guy — a very brawny, darkly complected Polynesian — was the same man he had caught watching him on several occasions. "You know, big Jake there has been known to break a few bones every now and then — strictly by accident, of course!"

"I'm t... telling you I don't want any troub... trouble. But I told you my real name. What do you mean, I'm n... not..."

"I said DON'T give us any of that shit, man! We ain't here to play games with you." The Caucasian once again lifted him into the air by his arms and carried him over to the sofa, tossing him down while never once easing up on his grip. "Unless you'd LIKE to play some games... I mean, we can do this the easy way, or we can do this the hard way. The choice is strictly up to you, pal."

Again, Ben tried desperately to get some inkling as to exactly who these thugs were and what it could be that they wanted. "Okay, okay. I'm not an idiot. I c... can see you mean b... business and I sure as all hell don't want t... to get in your way. Now I'll tell you anything you want me to, but first I g... gotta know who you guys are."

"W R O N G! Nice try though, buddy! Now I told you once and I AIN'T going to tell you again — YOU don't ask NO questions here, man, none at all! Got that?"

Ben helplessly nodded his head.

"Only Kimo and I ask the questions. Ain't that right, Kimo?"

"You got it, Jake."

Jake removed his hands from Ben's shoulders and pretended to gently pat them back into place. "There, there. Now let's try a little different approach. We're actually really friendly fellows — reasonable fellows. Honest. So now, do you want to cooperate with us, or would you rather spend the rest of your life in prison?"

"Prison? Aw, now wait just a minute here. You guys come busting in here, toss me all around the room like some common criminal, threaten me with bodily harm, and then begin to question me without even so much as reading me my Miranda rights. Now, do you honestly expect that I'd ever believe that you were really the authorities after carrying on crazy like this?"

Both men looked at him with expressions of disbelief.

"You know, this still IS a United States Territory, and if you really were cops, you'd have to deal with some simple realities — like the Constitution, for instance. I may be a lot of things, but I'm certainly not stupid!"

Kimo glared at him from across the room. "United States? You're in the Hawaiian Territory, buddy — did you forget? And what the hell's a Miranda right, anyway?"

Oh shit, Ben thought to himself — maybe there IS no such thing as a Miranda right... yet... DAMN IT! It's 1957 — remember. STUPID, STUPID, STUPID! He noticed Jake was reaching somewhere under his belt. Oh god no! Was he going to pull a gun on him? Was he simply going to blow his brains out right here and now? Real cool Ben — piss these guys right off before you even know what they want! But what COULD they want? He didn't even have the Alpha-Max 2000 anymore. Surely they had to know that! Hey — maybe the plane crashed! Maybe he was actually dead already! Maybe this was some sort of sinister version of hell! First, he had his spirits built sky high with the likes of Lani, and then these thugs come in here to tear it all down and scare him to death! Aw shit! Please god — tell me this is all some kind of a terrible dream! Please let me wake up!

He still could see Jake's hand struggling to remove something from what appeared to be his waist pocket. Oh, thank god — it didn't look like a gun. Aha — a wallet! He flipped it open and stuck his ID right in Ben's face. "The name's Jake Baxter, United States Federal Bureau of Investigation. My partner, there is Agent Kimo Paaluhi."

Across the room, Kimo — almost on cue — silently flashed his badge without ever really looking up. The big guy was still frantically searching through all Lani's belongings. Ben was much too unsettled to determine whether or not the identifications were authentic, but for now, he simply had to assume that these guys were for real. "All right, all right — I believe you already."

"Sounds to me like we're finally tuned into the same wavelength. Now, can we start at the top again? I want to warn you that I don't appreciate sounding like a broken record — my patience is wearing real thin. What's your name, buddy? And don't give me any of that Decker shit this time!" Jake slid his wallet back into his pants.

"I don't have any idea why you won't believe me, but I'm telling you the truth. My name's Benjamin N. Decker, and I'm a businessman from Philadelphia, Pennsylvania."

"Yeah, and I'm from the moon..."

"This your stuff in here?" Kimo peered out from Lani's bedroom, holding Ben's flight bag in his big hand. It was blatantly apparent that he had been rifling through it.

"Yeah, but you don't have a warrant to..."

"Says here his name is Decker."

"That's what I'm trying to tell you. I told you I wasn't lying. My name's..."

"Ha! Look at this, Jake. Now we're talking some really fake shit here." He walked over to the sofa and handed several cards and papers to his partner.

"So, you were born on January eleventh of forty-seven, were you? Ha! That's a laugh! Let's see — that makes you... um... almost a teenager, huh Decker?"

"Guess you haven't even started to shave yet, did ya, kid?" Kimo smiled at his own joke.

"Hey, I can explain that stuff." As soon as the words came out of his mouth, Ben wondered just exactly how he could EVER explain any of this to anyone, including himself!

"I think we already know the explanation, pal. Like Kimo said — this baby is as phony as a three-dollar bill! I don't know exactly who the hell you're working for, but — hey, come on here — they surely can do better than this! At least give us a real challenge. For crying out loud, you could..."

Kimo was shaking his head as he interrupted Jake. "But you know, I still don't have any idea how Kealoha is involved in this whole thing. She's so pretty — seems so innocent. How about it, Decker? What are you using the women for? It's a damned shame if she's just some sex toy to you!" The big Polynesian seemed genuinely upset that Ben would treat her badly.

"Hey, no way, man, it's nothing at all like that. I... I just met her. I'm not using her. I'm... I'm totally lost as to what you guys think I'm doing?

His assertion was totally ignored. "Are you a communist, Decker? I mean, we know you've been working for the Commies, but do you really believe in that god damned system of theirs, or are you just doing it for the money?" Jake's tone was filled with self-righteous disgust.

"For the communists? Doing what?"

"Come on, Decker. How about Dobrinokov?"

"Who?"

"You heard me. Boris Dobrinokov."

"Dobrinokov?"

Kimo tossed Ben's bag onto the floor. "Your kind disgusts me, Decker. Selling out your own fucking country..."

"I wouldn't think of..."

"Look, SHUT the fuck up, MAN!" Kimo's voice was raised to such a loud level that Ben was intimidated into silence. "I don't need to hear your bullshit, Decker! For Christ's sake — I photographed you myself while you were making the switch at the airport last week. I know you god damned Reds think you can get away with anything, but it won't work, you know." Kimo vented his frustration by kicking Ben's bag with such force that it chipped some paint from where it hit the cinder block wall.

Ben somehow summoned enough courage — or was it stupidity? — to voice a protest. "Made the switch? This is just incredible! You guys really blew it! You couldn't possibly have ONE lousy picture for the simple reason that I don't have any idea what you're talking about. I never switched ANY bag, and I don't know ANY Dobrinokov. And I sure as hell am not ANY communist!"

"You god damned Commies ain't going to stop us, you know."

"Stop you from what?"

Jake held his hand up to Kimo as if to stop him from talking, but Kimo simply ignored his partner. "From developing the ultimate weapon."

"There IS no ultimate weapon! For Christ's sake, haven't you figured that out yet? So big deal, what are you about ready to test? I imagine right about now is when we start to launch a few of those archaic ICBMs downrange towards Kwajalein Atoll?"

"There you go, Kimo. Sounds like he admits to knowing about the tests."

"I don't admit to knowing about anything that isn't published right here in the *HONOLULU ADVERTISER!*" He grabbed the newspaper and tossed it in the general direction of Jake.

"So, you still won't tell us your name, huh?"

"For the umpteenth time, I told you — it's Benjamin Decker."

"We're going to find out, you know."

"Hey, I give up." Ben threw both his hands over his head as a gesture of surrender. "I have no idea what I can do to prove to you just who I am."

Kimo returned to the couch. Having completed his last search through the apartment, he was now satisfied that he had found all there was to find. "That Decker shit don't wash! We ran a check on you, pal. There is no Benjamin Decker living in Philadelphia — at least certainly not any Benjamin Decker in your age bracket."

"Yeah, isn't it funny — you just seem to have popped up at the airport last week, right out of thin air." Jake snapped his fingers. "Just like that!"

"And just when Dobrinokov happens to drop out of sight! I know we have you pegged, Decker. But it still bothers the hell out of me just how the girl's involved in all this. god, she's so pretty, and her record's as clean as a whistle." Kimo was shaking his head. His tone of voice gave Ben the abhorrent thought that just maybe the oversized creep had more than a business-like interest in Leilani.

"Virgin, even — as far as we could determine, anyway. That is if you haven't gotten to her yet..." Jake's face broke into a snidely grin.

Ben's face flushed bright red with a bitter mix of fear and hatred. "You son of a bitch. Leilani doesn't have a god damned thing to do with any of this — nothing at all! And you'd better leave her out of this or else..."

Jake's twisted smile grew wider. "Or else what?"

Kimo was grinding his clenched fist into his palm. "No, YOU'D better leave her out of this, Decker, you sick fucker, you. It makes me sick just to think of some *haole* scum like you with her. Now I'm telling you — don't try to leave this Island, because you can't get off. Remember, you ain't back in the States now. We've got this rock sealed up as tight as a drum, and I'm warning you not to try testing us." The hulk of a man turned the knob, opened the door, and stepped back out into the morning sun. He glared at Ben as he slowly removed a cigarette from his pocket and, using an old wick-type lighter, lit his smoke.

Jake followed close behind and paused as he stepped through the doorway. "We'll be back to see you, Decker — or whatever your name is. You can bet your ass about that." The door slammed, and Ben was at last alone with his pounding heart.

29

Monday, February 11, 1957: 9:45 A. M.

Ben just sat on the sofa for several minutes, his heart racing at breakneck speed. He finally composed himself enough to stand up, walk over to the kitchen sink, and pour himself a large glass of water. How the hell did this happen? What did he get himself into? How could they possibly have confused him at the airport?

He swallowed a half a glass of water in one gulp and considered his sorry situation. There was simply no way they could think he'd switch... Oh, SHIT! Now he remembered. When he went to grab his bag off the baggage truck, the strange guy with the foreign accent tried to grab his bag. He remembered him pointing to his initials — BND. For

Christ's sake — it's not as though he didn't have enough trouble trying to locate his bags, anyway. He finished his water and set the empty glass down on the drainboard. What was the name of the guy Jake said they were after? Boris... Boris... um... Dobrinokov. Yeah, that was it — Boris Dobrinokov. DAMN! BD! If his middle name started with the letter N — then the Russian had the same god damned initials as Ben's! Talk about lousy luck! Of all the rotten coincidences... No wonder someone had been tailing him — it sure as hell LOOKED bad. All right, so now what?

Ben walked into the bedroom and pulled a shirt over his head. He quickly straightened up the apartment as best as he could, closing all the drawers and picking up whatever Kimo had tossed onto the floor. The small area where the paint had been chipped off the wall didn't appear too serious, but it did offer a sad testimony to the bizarre events that had occurred this morning. He didn't know what he was going to do, but he sure needed some quiet contemplation right now, even before — or if — he told this entire unbelievable tale to Leilani.

After placing a quick phone call to the Royal Hawaiian Hotel to leave a brief cancellation message, Ben locked up the apartment and walked off down the street.

30

Monday, February 11, 1957: 10:50 A. M.

He had no idea what the name of the beach was, but the bus driver certainly was right when he told him how easy it was to find. After a short, ten-minute walk from where he had gotten off the bus, Ben came to a small, empty, gravel parking area perched high on top of a cliff. He momentarily sat and rested on a lava rock wall, looking several hundred feet down onto a picturesque, crescent moon beach below. The bay itself had obviously been formed when one side of a volcanic cinder cone had somehow caved into the sea. The clear, azure-blue water was everywhere dotted with coral heads and reefs, broken by lighter blue areas marking pockets of snow-white sand. A dense grove of coconut palms grew right up to the vegetation line fronting the shore.

Ben took only a minute to catch his breath while enjoying the vista in front of him. He began his descent by hiking along the dirt trail. The path followed a series of switchbacks cut into the inside rim of the extinct volcanic cone, its ocean-facing side long ago eroded away by the perpetual pounding of the sea. A quick survey of the bay below revealed fewer than twenty persons either snorkeling over the reef or scattered about the beach itself. He couldn't help but be amazed by how few people were taking advantage of such an idyllic spot on such a perfect day. In less than ten minutes, he had finally reached the fine sand beach. He removed his sandals but, after nearly singeing his feet while testing the blazing hot sand, put them back on for his stroll down to the water's edge. Once there, he was at last able to wade barefoot through the cool comfort of the swash zone with his sandals tucked under his arm. He walked the entire length of the beach before he turned into the grove of coconuts and sat in a shady spot with his back propped up against a stately palm. From this vantage point, he still had a rather good view of both the beach and the cliff trail. If anyone had been following him, they certainly were doing a great job at remaining invisible.

Ben picked up a good-sized seashell and began to absentmindedly scoop the powdery sand, first from one pile onto another, and then back again. What an emotional roller coaster ride the past several days had offered. Okay — he certainly admitted to his initial skepticism about any back-in-time hypothesis. And yet after his remarkable whirlwind weekend of falling in love with Leilani, he actually felt a growing excitement about the prospects of remaining in this island paradise with her indefinitely.

Hey, wait just one minute here! Wasn't he acting like some teenager who was totally obsessed with his first bout of infatuation? Is that what happened? Love? Had he really fallen in love? Yes. YES! OH GOD, YES! He knew he was more in love with Leilani than he had ever thought was possible — more deeply in love than he ever was with

Emily. Even way back in the early days — oh god, over twenty-five or thirty years ago — it just wasn't the same. This was just so... so special...

But now... Dear Lord, whatever had happened to him this morning? He still didn't know what all the implications were. Apparently, his island paradise had turned into an island hell within a matter of seconds! Though he knew his supposed connection with this Dobrinokov fellow was strictly coincidental, he had absolutely no idea of how he could possibly prove his innocence. For that matter, he had no idea of how he could even prove his own identity — at least not to the point where anyone other than Leilani would believe him!

He picked up another small shell and tossed it towards a neighboring stump. SHIT! It hurt so much to be torn between Leilani and his girls. He could readily give up his career, the Alpha Max 2000, his material possessions... They'd be no loss at all. And Emily? Hell... In many ways, he would actually be relieved to escape from his failed relationship with her so easily. But that most certainly wasn't the case with Lisa and Bonnie. They were his only children, his flesh and blood, the crowning accomplishment of his being. In a world in which all individual purpose seemed so damned remote — so incredibly absurd — the one chance for some ultimate meaning in life could only be found in his two children... wasn't that right?

So, did it come down to a choice between his kids and Lani? If only it all could be that clear cut! Wasn't this entire line of reasoning simply moot? Ben knew that the future — or was it his past? — was totally out of his control. There was no choice to be made, was there? His life was somehow barreling along within a flume of rushing events, being absolutely constrained by a set of boundaries he didn't draw, couldn't see, and would never understand. After all, it wasn't as if time travel was something undertaken at the drop of a hat. Could he ever hope to return to the nineties even if he wanted to?

He squiggled his barefoot again and let it bury itself deeper into the cool, soft sand. The most desirable course may have been the easiest — just continue to live out his existence right here in paradise. But that was BEFORE Jake and Kimo paid him their unexpected visit. And now the FBI was hot on his tail. Holy shit — the FBI!

COMMUNISTS! Didn't these guys know the Wall was down, the Iron Curtain was no more, and the cold war was over? Boy, this whole development surely tended to cast a gigantic shadow over his rainbow. Talk about out-of-character experiences — Ben couldn't even remember the last time he had gotten a parking ticket. And now he even had to be concerned that they would constantly be harassing Leilani. Maybe the least he could do was to get out of the Territory and totally forget about Hawaii, forget about Leilani. At least that would allow her to have a peaceful existence, wouldn't it? No way, man...

Ben's solitude was at once invaded by the sound of rustling leaves. He could feel his heart jump into his throat as he spun around, trying to spot the intruder. A commotion erupted from a patch of thickets as suddenly, two young Hawaiian children jumped out of the overgrown brush in which they were hiding and made a mad, noisy dash into the surf. He let out a long sigh of relief, swallowed the lump in his throat, and again tried to collect himself.

Was this the way it was going to be — forever? He hated the feeling of constantly living on the edge of his anxieties, always wondering if today were the day that some unseen bogeyman was coming to get him. Would he now have to live in fear *ad infinitum*, feeling the intense paranoia of a man who is perpetually on the run? Is that any way to live — always trying to return to the peace he once thought he had found, always trying to get back to paradise? No, no, no... He just KNEW he'd never be happy with a life mired in such apprehension and fear. And he was absolutely certain that Lani wouldn't be happy either. GOD DAMN IT! What kind of warped, sick rule of the universe had he discovered here? Why did it seem that every time a mere mortal had a chance to claim a real paradise on earth, some lousy serpent found a way to rear its ugly head? SHIT! This was no heaven on earth — this was becoming a living hell. And the lure of such an enchanting, elusive paradise only made matters much worse. No, Ben knew he couldn't live under this kind of pressure. And now he knew that he wouldn't. But a chill ran through his spine at the realization that, from this moment forward, he'd always be trying to get back to his tropical paradise...

31

Monday, February 11, 1957: 4:45 P. M.

The door flew open, and Leilani stood in the threshold. She stared in aw at Ben as he sat on the living room sofa. "Thank god! You ARE here!" She dropped her purse, ran over to the couch, and threw her arms around him. "Where were you all day? My god, I must have called here fifty times. I was SO worried about you..."

"I'm so sorry I worried you, my love. I'm okay — honest. I would have talked to you, but when I called the Royal Hawaiian, they said you were really busy, and I didn't want to cause any commotion."

"Oh Ben, please don't EVER do that to me again!"

"I didn't mean to DO anything to..."

"PROMISE ME!"

"Hey, all right already. I promise I promise — honest!" He smiled a halfhearted grin as he raised his right hand in the general direction of the ceiling.

"Now, for god's sake, why didn't we have lunch together? Where did you go all day? Why didn't you even answer my phone calls? Talk to me, Ben. Talk to me..."

"Oh, Lani, I don't even know exactly where to start."

"Try the beginning."

"The beginning, huh? Well, here goes nothing... After you left for work this morning, I cleaned up the breakfast dishes and then went into the bathroom to shave and shower. I was standing in front of the mirror, combing my hair when I heard a banging at the door. I swear the ruckus was loud enough to rock this entire building. Naturally, I went to answer the door, and these two huge thugs barged right into..."

* * *

"Come on, Ben — they simply can't do that."

"Yeah — RIGHT!"

"But..."

"No buts, Leilani. What do you mean, they CAN'T do it? They DID do it! I'm not talking about any kind of fantasies here. I'm telling you exactly what happened."

"It had to be a misunderstanding of some sort... a mistaken identity or something."

"It was no mistake, Lani. They know I don't belong here. I told you that they checked up on my missing history..."

"Oh, Ben... So, where'd you go after they left?"

"I don't really know the name of the place, but it was a beautiful, almost round bay over on the other side of Koko Head somewhere."

"Sounds to me like Hanauma Bay. You sure picked a funny day for sightseeing."

"For crying out loud, Lani — I wasn't sightseeing. I just needed to be alone for a while, to think about how to deal with this whole thing, to figure out what I'm going to do."

"DO! What do you mean by that?"

"Well, obviously, I can't just let these lousy creeps wreck both our lives."

"Ben, you're talking about the FBI! I mean, you're talking about the United States Government!"

Ben silently nodded his head.

"Well, come on! Surely you aren't proposing that we take on the entire..."

"I'm not proposing that WE do anything, Leilani. That's exactly my point — I don't want YOU involved in this whole mess at all."

"I already AM involved, Ben — or have you forgotten? I'm involved with you."

"And now you're also involved with the FBI."

"INVOLVED?"

"Right — I mean because you know me. But as far as I can figure it, that's your only connection. Get rid of me and — POOF! — you've gotten rid of your problem!"

"Rid of my problem..."

"Just like that!" Ben snapped his fingers.

Her mouth hung open, and her eyes immediately turned down towards the floor. "I just can't even believe it."

"Like it or not, you have to believe that..."

Lani's eyes became moist. "You really hurt my feelings, Ben. You're starting to terrify me if..." Her voice quieted to silence.

He gently placed two fingers on her chin and tried to turn her head back up even with his so he could better look into her eyes. "I'm... I'm sorry, Lani. I... I didn't want this to happen. I'm only thinking about you."

Her voice began to quiver. "Why do I get the terrible feeling that our relationship means a whole heck of a lot more to me than it does to you?"

Ben started to shake his head from side to side. "Oh no, no, no, no, Lani. It doesn't at all. It's just that I don't know what to do to get out of this mess."

"What to do? Don't be so ridiculous, Ben. Look, why don't we just go downtown to the FBI office turn yourself into them. You know as well as I do that you're not a communist. This may only be a Territory, but it IS an American Territory. The truth will come out, Ben. We've got to clear this whole thing up and then get on with our lives. You've simply HAVE to give them the chance to figure out that you're for real..."

"For REAL!!! Give me a break, Lani. What are they going to figure out — that I'm a for real, honest-to-god time traveler? That I was really just born a decade or so ago? That I am really an expert on computers with artificial intelligence that haven't even been dreamed about yet?"

"But they just HAVE to understand. The real world doesn't just gob... gobble people up like... like a monster in some awful nightmare." Her big eyes were now filled with tears, the overflow beginning to stream down her pretty face. She wriggled in her position on the sofa in a futile attempt to somehow get comfortable and, maintaining her eye contact with Ben, tightly squeezed his hand between both of hers. She slowly shook her head from side to side. "No, no, no — this CAN'T be happening. Please tell me this isn't happening."

"Oh Leilani — I love you, I LOVE you, I LOVE YOU. Don't you know how MUCH I love you? You have to see, Lani. It's because I love you so much that I HAVE to do something, HAVE to get these goons away from you. I can't just let these guys harass you, too. That's not going to help either one of us at all."

Lani was making no pretenses about it now, loudly crying on Ben's shoulder as he held her close in a seemingly unsuccessful attempt to reassure her. "You're... you're g... going to leave me Ben, aren't you? I can FEEL what you're thinking. You... you're going to lea... leave..."

"God, this is so much harder to do now than it was when I went over it in my mind this afternoon. You have to understand that sometimes the greatest act of love one can make is letting go. It's so damned difficult to know exactly when letting go of the one you love can save them from greater harm that could result from hanging on..." Ben fought back the tears in his own eyes.

"Oh, Ben... No, no, no, Ben..." Again she shook her head from side to side.

"I'm going to get the FBI out of your life, love. I have to get them out..."

"But you're g... going to do that by leave... leaving me..." She sniffled between her words.

"It won't be forever, Lani. I just have to leave long enough to give them a chance to work this whole thing out. After they find this Dobrinokov fellow and all, I'm sure things will calm down."

"Suppose they never find him?"

"Now, now — they will find the guy. Believe me, Lani, they will."

"But where could you possibly go, Ben. You c... can't leave this time... time period, can you?"

"Oh god, I don't think so. I... I haven't really even thought about it."

"But you m... must have. I mean, y... you thought about your kids — you t... told me that. Your k... kids don't even exist yet, Ben..."

"You're right, they don't. But they do exist here." Ben used his index finger to point to his head. "I could never get them out of my mind."

"But even if you could get back to them, what would you do? They're grown up, Ben — almost grown up, anyway. It's not like you'd m... make all that much difference now — not like the d... difference that your being here would make with me."

"Oh sure, I'll make a difference. But regrettably, my fear is that the difference I'll make with you will be negative." Ben felt literally torn in two. He was bitterly aware that Lani was as much a part of his mind as were his two children. Furthermore, he was painfully conscious of the fact that he'd have just as little success trying to forget her as he would in attempting to forget his kids. Dear god, what a quandary. But alas, his decision would most likely be made for him — made by the physical laws of nature. After all, he WAS still an engineer and knew only too well just how little chance he had of leaving 1957. "Oh Lani, don't worry about me somehow getting back into the 1990s again. I'm telling you that time travel is flat out IMPOSSIBLE! For goodness sake, I don't have the slightest idea of just how I could ever do that — to go forward in time. "

"IMPOSSIBLE! Oh come on, Ben — you ARE here for goodness sakes. Just because you don't understand exactly how it happened in the first place doesn't mean it didn't happen — won't happen again..."

"I just... I just don't really know..."

"Then how do you know it won't happen again?"

"Well, I don't — not really..."

"Maybe it's you. Maybe by just getting back on a plane, you will..."

"Lani, Lani, Lani. You can't keep worrying about things over which we have no control. Hey, think about it for a minute — I could have a heart attack this afternoon, and you'd never see me again."

"But that's strictly a chance occurrence. You're PLANNING to get on a plane."

"But I'm not planning to..."

"And then you'll NEVER come back, Ben. I'll N... NEVER see you again — EVER... Oh, Ben..." It seemed as though a threshold had been crossed as she finally broke down totally and began to cry hysterically. He helplessly tried to wipe some of her tears with his handkerchief, but in short order, he gave up and let her have the cloth. As hard as he tried to maintain his composure, Ben couldn't prevent the stream of silent tears that had flowed from his eyes, too. After several minutes, her outward display of grief had subsided to quiet sobs. He inconspicuously cleared away his tears in hopes of not setting Leilani off again. "We'll be together again, Lani."

"I want to believe you, Ben. I really do. But I have a really bad feeling about this whole thing."

"Let's be positive, my love."

She took a deep breath. "When? Do you know when you're going to try?"

Ben stared off into the distance, his gaze fixed on some inanimate object out the window. "Tonight. I have a flight out of Honolulu at ten o'clock."

"TONIGHT! TEN O'CLOCK!" Again the tears overflowed from her eyes. "Oh, Ben..."

"It'll be all right, Lani. You'll see."

"Oh god, how will you ever dodge those FBI guys?"

"Well, actually, I'm sort of counting on you to help me with that."

"Oh Ben, Ben... I'm so afraid we'll never be able to find each other again." The tears continued to stream down her face.

"I promise you, Leilani, with god as my witness — we WILL be together again. It will be just you and me together in our little heaven."

"I... I do believe you, Ben. And I promise I'll wait for you forever if I have to... FOREVER..."

He held her tightly to his chest. "Don't cry, Lani. I'll get back to paradise, and we'll be together at last. You can count on that..."

32
Monday, February 11, 1957: 7:15 P. M.

Ben and Leilani stepped out of the little Chinese restaurant. He made no effort whatsoever to hide his carry-on bag from the view of whoever it was he was sure was watching. They walked briskly as they turned first left at one corner and then right at the next. They continued this helter-skelter, evasive pattern that Ben was certain would appear as though they were trying to lose someone. After several minutes of walking, the couple ducked into a small soda parlor. Ben glanced up at the overhead menu and then stepped up to the counter. "Um... I'll have a small cone of... let's see — ah... make it coffee, please. And the lady will have..." He turned to Lani.

"Ah... Do you have *lilikoi*?"

The young man nodded in the affirmative.

"Then I'll have a small *lilikoi*, thank you."

The counter clerk turned and disappeared into the back of the store. Ben looked inquisitively at Lani. "What in god's name is *lilikoi*?"

"*Lilikoi* — it's passion fruit. Um, I just love it." She licked her lips.

"I want a taste."

"Well..." After a brief, playful hesitation, she nodded her head yes. "I guess so... if you're REAL nice to me..."

Ben didn't follow her attempt to lighten the mood. He concentrated his gaze out of the shop's picture window, visually searching the street for anyone or anything suspicious. His ear-to-ear grin announced that he had caught a fleeting glimpse of exactly what it was he had hoped he would see. He excitedly turned back to Lani and patted her on the shoulder. "All right, Leilani. Thank goodness, it looks like lady luck is on our side tonight."

Her smile had been replaced by a look of deep concern. "So much for sweet nothings…"

"What?"

Her answer belied her irritation. "Oh, never mind. I just don't understand why you would actually WANT someone to be following us."

"Oh, it's not that I want just anyone to be following us, my love. It's WHO is following us that's so important."

"Who IS following us?"

"Let's put it this way — from a distance, it sure looks to me as though Agent Paaluhi is working late tonight."

"Agent Paaluhi?"

"Yeah, the big, local guy who was at your apartment this morning. Kimo…"

"Here you are, sir." The fountain clerk handed the two cones to Ben. "That'll be thirty cents, please."

"Thirty cents?" Ben was amazed at how cheap the ice cream was. No matter what happened tonight, he surely would miss the 1957 prices!

"I'm sorry, sir, but I don't set the prices here. If you have a complaint, you'd have to talk to Mister Baldwin. He just raised all the…"

"Hey, no — no problem. I don't have any complaints. Thirty cents seems quite reasonable to me." He handed Lani her cone and reached into his pocket with his free hand and grabbed two quarters. "Here you go."

* * *

Leilani sat in the window seat, head locked straight ahead and staring at seemingly nothing in particular, her silent, blank expression reflecting her deep meditation. There were only a handful of others on the city bus.

"A penny for your thoughts, ma'am."

"What?" She was seemed startled by his intrusion.

"Whoa! You sure seem to be a million miles away."

"Oh Ben, I'm sorry. I didn't even hear what you said. I guess I was daydreaming."

"Jeez, I guess so. I only said, a penny for your thoughts."

"Pardon me."

"Your thoughts, your thoughts — what are you thinking so hard about?"

"Oh, nothing really."

"Come on, Lani — surely you're thinking about something."

Acting quite out of character, her answer was both gruff and to the point. "I'm sure you know."

Ben was afraid he did. "Please, Lani. We just don't have a lot of time left. I want you to talk to me."

She returned her gaze towards the front of the bus and spoke at a very soft level. "I'm really hurting, Ben. Surely that can't be of any surprise to you. I... I simply can't believe you're just up and leaving me like this. It seems to me that you're..."

"Hey, hey — wait a minute, Lani — we've been through this ten times before and..." She turned to him and spoke in a still quiet but stern tone. "No, Ben! YOU'VE been through this ten times before, but now it's MY turn to speak! So, if you'd please be quiet for a few minutes, I'll have MY say now. It seems to me that YOU are the insensitive one in this whole mess. I mean, how the heck do you expect a girl to feel? Just where do you get off using this incredible story of yours to come barging into town to sweep some young woman off her feet with your sweet talk and to lure her into a whirlwind, weekend romance? Do you tell Emily about these conquests of yours when you get home, or isn't your wife's name really even Emily?"

"Hey, now wait just a sec..."

"Will you tell her just how easily you won my trust? Will you tell her how you won me over to such an extent that you claimed my treasured virginity like it was simply some cheap hunting trophy you could put up on your mantle? And now, on top of all this, you're going to just up and skip town on a lousy moment's notice with no intention of ever being seen or heard from again. You know, someday you just may regret leaving me and giving up..."

"Lani Lani, Lani — will you let me get a word in edgewise?" He held both his hands over his head as a sign of surrender. "It sounds as though you're really upset here. Why can't..."

"Really upset? REALLY UPSET!" Her tone of voice grew progressively more enraged, and she began to speak faster and faster, almost as though she were determined not to let Ben get any word in at all. "You're doggone right that I'm really upset. I have every right in the world to be really upset. I mean REALLY upset! Someday you'd better learn that other people have REAL feelings and you can't just treat them like they're your own personal playthings. I don't care one bit about all this time travel nonsense or all the FBI junk — none of that stuff means anything at all to me, NOTHING AT ALL."

Ben looked up briefly to see if any of the other passengers were listening to Lani's tirade.

"There's only ONE thing that really concerns me, only ONE thing that truly matters at all to me, and one thing is US! And it looks like US — as in WE — are all *pau*, all finished, all over! But damn it, there's still one little problem, and that problem is that I have feelings and my feelings are hurt — and I mean hurt REALLY BADLY!" Tears were once again streaming down her face. "I'm... I'm..."

Ben was emotionally decimated. He was convinced he knew how she felt and yet knew he never had any conscious intention of causing her such grief. Though he feared he'd be ineffectual at trying to ease her pain, he felt compelled to make some sort of an attempt to comfort her. "Oh, Leilani, believe me... I know how you feel..."

"YOU DO NOT KNOW HOW I FEEL! If you did, you would NEVER be on your way to the airport right now!"

"But..."

"I'm so upset, Ben. It's as though my heart has been ripped right out of my chest. There's a huge hole in me, and I feel just awful, just t... terrible. And I'm so mad at you for making me feel this way." Ben shifted his arm behind her and tried to somehow silently make up for his stupid I-know-how-you-feel statement with a reassuring touch. She inadvertently wiped her face on Ben's shoulder and continued. "I'm angry, angry, ANGRY... Maybe you're proud of your cold, analytical way of dealing with problems, Ben. Maybe you really don't care how you affect other people's lives. And just maybe you don't even realize just how insensitive you can be to others. But I'm telling you that I'm sick of your stupid engineering approach to MY feelings, and I don't want to put up with it anymore! Oh, why did I ever even meet you, why did I ever TRUST you, why did I ever LOVE you?" She tried in vain to muffle her outburst.

"Oh, Leilani, I'm so, so sorry. I realize it sounds ridiculously inadequate, but I beg you to forgive me, to understand that I never meant for any of this to happen. You have to believe me. I never once lied to you or tried to mislead."

She looked right at him with her beautiful, tear-filled eyes. "I love you, Ben Decker. I'm hurt, and I'm resentful, and I'm angry, and I'm scared as all hell. And yet, for some crazy reason, I'm STILL madly in love with you — I mean more than you ever COULD know. Oh god, I'm trying so hard to accept the fact that you think you have to go, but I still don't want you to." Her voice was suddenly soft and sensual as if all her pain and anger had been vented — totally drained away and abandoned.

"Lani, I swear that I never lied..."

"I know you didn't. I'm the one who should be sorry, Ben. I... I... didn't mean all those things I just said. But my pain is real enough. I'm just so... so totally crushed to think of you not being here anymore, not coming back again."

"I'm coming back, Lani. I promised you, my love — and I mean it. I'm coming back to paradise, and you and I will be together — forever..."

"I love you, Ben."

"And I love you, Leilani."

HISS! The loud, hissing brakes brought the bus to a lurching halt. The oversized driver turned around in his seat, his voice echoing through the nearly empty vehicle. "You folks in the back wanted to get off at the Honolulu Airport, didn't ya? Well, here we are…"

33
Monday, February 11, 1957: 9:30 P. M.

Ben was fully aware of the fact that Agent Paaluhi was keeping a sharp eye on both of them, but he wasn't nearly as certain as to the big Hawaiian's next course of action. It seemed to Ben that there were only three likely alternatives: Kimo would prevent him from boarding the flight, he would continue to follow him right onto the aircraft, or he would somehow contact agents back in the States to arrange to have them meet the plane upon arrival. Ben had his fingers crossed that the brawny FBI man would choose the third option — it surely would make for an easier night.

"Good evening, ladies and gentlemen. Pan America Airways Flight 100, Super Constellation Sleeper Service to Los Angeles will momentarily be ready for boarding at gate twelve. We ask that all passengers please check to make sure your boarding passes are in order." The loudspeaker crackled off as several persons sitting in the waiting area stood and moved towards the doorway.

Lani stared at Ben as though the executioner standing on the gallows stairs had just called his name. "How are you going to do this, Ben? I still don't see how you can shake whoever this agent guy is who's been on our tail."

"I know how difficult this must be for you, but I have to count on you to help me out here, Lani. You're going to be my diversion."

"Diversion?"

"Exactly. I need you to somehow distract that big, Hawaiian guy over there." His slightest nod in Kimo's direction was nearly imperceptible.

Without thinking, she started to raise her head.

"No, no — don't look right at him. Do you know the guy I pointed out to you when we were waiting to catch the bus yet?"

"Yeah."

"Well, that's him — that's Kimo. He really thinks you're..." Ben shook his head and squeezed her hand. "Aw man, you know I wouldn't ask you to do this if there was any other way, don't you?"

Lani swallowed a lump in her throat and nodded her head.

"In spite of all the commotion stirred up by those two FBI agents in your apartment this morning, it quickly became obvious to me that Kimo thought you were... well... you know."

"Know? No, I don't know..."

"Well, he seemed to speak about you as though you were some sort of Polynesian goddess or something. He really seemed to get both emotional and defensive about you when the other agent — that Jake guy — started to talk, um... kind of... well... kind of harshly about you."

"Harshly? What am I missing here?"

"Hey, look, it doesn't really matter right now. Remember, these guys were really trying to shake me up, and they were saying a lot of things about you just to piss me off."

"Ben, that Kimo guy is huge!"

"But he'll be a pussy cat with you — I know it. If I thought you'd be in any danger, I wouldn't have brought you along with me. Believe me, it's ME he wants." Ben silently prayed to god that his analysis was correct.

"I'm not afraid, Ben. I know I can help you. I WILL help you."

"Okay. Now I know you can get his attention away from me, especially if he really thinks I'm already locked away onboard the plane."

"That's fine, but then what are you going to do?"

"Well, I said I was going to get on board that aircraft right over there." He motioned towards the line of people now starting to move through the doorway and out into the evening air. "But I didn't say I planned on staying there. First of all, we'll make sure I'm about the last person to head for the plane before they're going to lock the doors. Now, after we say our good-byes over by the gate there, I'll start walking out towards the plane. That's when you're going to get creative and somehow make sure..."

* * *

"I love you. Oh god, Ben — please change your mind. Please stay here with me."

"I love you too, Leilani. I'm not saying goodbye. For goodness sake, I'll probably be back here in your arms in a couple of days."

She bravely fought back her tears. "Oh, Ben... I love you... love you SO much. And I'll wait for you, my love. I'll wait for weeks or for years or for decades or for whatever it takes — FOREVER if I have to. I promise..."

Ben couldn't believe how difficult this had all become. "I simply have to prove something to myself here, Leilani. Now, I'm going to turn around and march towards that plane. You know what your job is. Just remember — I love you, you love me, and we'll be together again very soon — in our own paradise. And we can't ever look behind us — only ahead..." With tears in his heart, he embraced her one last time as tightly as he could and kissed her deeply.

A very low-pitched voice crackled over the loudspeaker. "This is the last call for boarding Pan Am Flight 100 Super Constellation Sleeper Service bound for Los Angeles. All ticketed passengers should now be..."

Ben released Leilani from his arms, quickly spun around and handed his pass to the airline representative standing next to the doorway. Like a soldier ready to do his duty, he stepped briskly out onto the tarmac. He never did turn back to see Lani's tears, but he could just barely hear her one last time over the din of the lingering crowd. "I love you, Ben, and I'll be waiting..."

She got as close to the doorway as the ticket agent would allow and watched as Ben walked tenaciously across the tarmac. A million thoughts reeled through her mind. Did the past four days really happen? She was certain that they did. Yet why should she help him? After all, he was leaving her, wasn't he? Why should she even care?

But she did — oh dear, she cared about him so much. She loved him — and she KNEW he loved her too. She loved him more than she ever thought possible. Her heart was immersed in love, the kind of love that wasn't explained by words, wasn't justified by logic, wasn't bounded by reason. And she knew that this love — her love — could never be really genuine without a rock steady, unshakable trust in the other, the kind of unwavering faith that could only be experienced wholly within the soul. This level of trust needed no tangible evidence to verify its existence. This trust was simply sensed deep down inside. Intuitively, profoundly, and deep within her heart, she just KNEW Ben would return again... someday...

As emotionally drained as she felt right now, Lani was fully resolved to call on any reserve needed to ensure Ben's safe escape. She continued to watch as Ben neared the portable stairway that had been rolled up next to the plane. Lani was well aware of the fact that her timing would mean everything to the success or failure of the plan, and she unhesitatingly turned around, easily spotted Agent Paaluhi, and immediately walked straight towards him. He, too, was watching as Ben began to ascend the stairway. Leilani needed no acting talent at all to make sure she filled her eyes with genuine tears and her voice with unfeigned sorrow. "Mister Paaluhi — are you Mister Paaluhi?"

Kimo was taken totally off guard, obviously torn between maintaining his vigil over Ben and dealing with his approaching heartthrob. Lani did all she could to inconspicuously remain in his line of sight towards the plane. "Um, pardon me, ma'am. I believe you have the wrong man." He tried to politely duck around to her side, but she once again subtly maneuvered herself to obstruct his view.

"Aren't you Mister Paaluhi — with the FBI, no?"

"Okay, what's the gag here? Obviously, Decker must have pointed me out to you."

"Well yeah, he did. But that's not why I wanted to talk to you. You have to understand that Benjamin is not guilty of anything at all. He'd never break the law. You've got to believe that. I mean, he's such an upstanding United States Citizen."

"All right, all right. You know who I am, and I know who you are, but I still have a job to do here, Miss Kealoha. Now, if you don't mind, I have to..."

Kimo tried to get by her, but Leilani grabbed his arm and hung on to it for dear life. "Mister Paaluhi — Kimo — you don't mind if I call you Kimo, do you?" Now she really needed to call on all her emotional reserves to overcome her absolute revulsion to the big, intimidating creep. She feigned a smile and flirtingly batted her eyelashes at her totally confused nemesis. "Why don't you call me Lani if you'd like?"

"I told you... I..." Kimo knew he was losing the battle to his emotional self. He made one more half-hearted attempt to sight Ben but again found her in his way. He finally was able to dodge a determined Leilani just long enough to catch a quick peek at the empty boarding stairs being pulled back away from the aircraft. Assuming his target had already boarded the plane, he let out a satisfied sigh of relief at a job well done. "Why no — it's okay to call me Kimo. After all, that's what my name is... Lani..."

* * *

Oh, dear god — this was the most difficult thing he had ever done in his entire life. But Ben KNEW he had to keep walking right across the tarmac and not give in to the overwhelming temptation to look back at Leilani. He knew there would only be one chance. This simply HAD to work. Thank god that there weren't any computer systems in widespread use yet. Ben smiled to himself as he inconspicuously reached into his chest pocket and made sure to switch his boarding pass for the Los Angeles flight to his boarding pass for the flight to

San Francisco. Thank goodness he had enough cash to buy a second ticket to a different city. Of course, the more he thought about it, he wondered if it could possibly be this easy — simply purchase another ticket under an assumed name. Well, he'd soon find out. He hurriedly stepped onto the stairway leading up to the plane, knowing full well that it was very unlikely that anyone not having access to a computer could cross-reference his tickets so quickly. As he neared the attractive stewardess waiting at the top of the entrance, he felt a surge of self-confidence rush through his being. Now, if only Leilani could be — at this very second — successful in her distraction of Agent Paaluhi.

"Good evening, sir. Boarding pass, please."

Ben held his ticket holder wide open.

"I'm terribly sorry, sir. There must be some mistake here. This flight is bound for Los Angeles, and you're heading for..."

"San Francisco, ma'am. I've got to be in San Francisco first thing Wednesday morning."

"Why yes, I can see that from your ticket here. I'm sorry, but you somehow came to the wrong plane. You want Pan American Flight 200 — that's the aircraft right over there. She pointed to another Constellation several hundred yards away. "You'll have to really hurry, but I think you can make it.

Ben had already turned and was barreling down the stairs. He briefly glanced back over his shoulder. "Thanks a lot, ma'am." He immediately leaped off the bottom of the stairway and quickly scurried away, trying to get out of the line of sight from the doorway he had just exited the terminal building. If Lani had succeeded in getting Kimo's attention away from him for even twenty seconds, he knew he'd be home free. Ben continued to nearly run across the poorly lit tarmac, reaching the first step leading up to the San Francisco bound plane in only a minute or so.

"You're going to San Francisco?" The stewardess called down to Ben as she gripped the big latch used to seal the plane's door.

"Yes, I am. Sorry — I somehow got mixed up and nearly boarded the wrong flight." By the time he sprinted to the top of the stairs, he realized that he was getting quite short of breath.

"My, my — you just made it, sir. I was just preparing to secure our doors."

Ben paused at the doorway and handed her his boarding pass. "This IS Flight 200, right?"

"Sure thing, Mister... er..." The flight attendant searched his pass for a name. "Dinghoffer — Mister Dinghoffer. Lucky you got here when you did — we're just about ready to depart for San Francisco." She handed his ticket back to him.

As Ben stepped onto the aircraft, he turned to see the boarding ramp being moved away by a small tractor. He could easily make out the silhouette of distant Diamond Head in the light of a nearly full moon. There was no sign of anyone following him. He could only assume that Leilani had been successful with her distraction.

PART FIVE

*"To be without some of the things you want is an
indispensable part of happiness."*

– Bertrand Russell

34

Tuesday, February 12, 1957: 12:20 A. M.

Ben was used to flying — his position with Penn-Comp Corporation assured that. But tonight, even after being airborne for over two hours already, he still was having a great deal of trouble getting used to the rhythmic, droning sound of the propeller-driven aircraft. He finished reading the last section of the newspaper and folded it neatly back together.

"We'll be serving sandwiches in a few minutes. Here, let me get your seat trays in place." The stewardess reached in from her position in the aisle and unlatched the restraints on both his dinner tray and that of his neighbor. "Would either one of you care for another beer?"

"Yes, thank you — one more here." His seatmate held up his empty cup.

"Please. I'll have another Primo, too." Ben also handed his empty cup to her and smiled. "Have you been flying with Pan Am for long?"

"Oh, about four years now."

"This sure is a nice piece of equipment."

"Yes, the Super Connie... Constellation, that is. We only fly the newest and the best." She spoke with obvious pride in her voice.

"You know, I'm amazed at how big these Constellations are — you know, considering that they're props and all."

Her expression communicated bewilderment at what other form of propulsion a passenger plane could possibly be using. Ben continued, "I mean, of course they use props, but it's still remarkable that anyone can build a civilian plane of such dimensions. Just how many passengers are on board our flight tonight?"

"To tell you the truth, we have a full plane tonight, sir — ninety-two passengers and a crew of five."

"It's incredible that such a massive craft can actually get off the ground."

"So true, but I confess to knowing very little about the workings of an airliner. I agree, though — it amazes me too that such a huge plane can fly at all. They tell me the new jet aircraft they're coming out with will be even bigger if you can possibly believe that."

"WOW... How about that..."

"They'll also be a lot faster — all the way to the West Coast in a little over five hours."

"Now, I'll believe THAT when I see it!" Ben amused himself by playing up to some of this 1950s wonderment.

She smiled her agreement. "I know what you mean. Pan American has several of the new jets on order."

"So I've read."

"I can't wait to fly on one. Look, I'll be back with your snacks and beer in a few minutes." The attractive stewardess continued down the aisle.

Ben had spent most of the trip's first hour apprehensively waiting for some unseen arm of the law to reach out and snatch him. Regrettably, he had grown convinced that having disobeyed the FBI agent's command to remain in the Islands, he was now at least in technical violation of the law. Nonetheless, after the plane had reached cruising altitude and still no adversary had made himself apparent, Ben gradually began to relax and recuperate from his hasty escape. His confidence in the realization that his getaway must have been successful grew to such a point that he was able to doze off for nearly an hour or so. He squirmed in his seat, pulled his folded newspaper from his side, and offered it to the older, Oriental man seated next to him. "Would you care to see the evening paper, sir?"

The gentleman turned his shoulders toward Ben as best as his restrictive position allowed and held up his opened hand. "Oh jeez, no thank you — but I do appreciate the offer." Ben was almost surprised that the gray-haired man spoke in perfect, accent-free English. "That is tonight's *STAR BULLETIN*, isn't it?"

Ben nodded his head. "Yes, it is."

"I couldn't help but notice while you were looking at it. I was able to read most of it at my daughter's house before we left for the airport this evening."

"Oh, you're traveling with family?"

"No — no I'm not. My daughter's back on Oahu. I live with her in Honolulu — the Makiki area, actually. She dropped me off at the airport tonight. I'm going back to visit family in California."

"Hawaii, California... That's really nice — to be surrounded by so much of your family, I mean."

"Nice?" The man's hunched shoulders and opened hands indicated that he didn't necessarily agree with Ben's assessment. "Sometimes I have TOO MUCH family — or maybe too little. I guess it all depends on WHO one defines as family."

"I'm not sure I'm following you."

"I only mean that a man's inherent family is rather arbitrary. If you consider the philosophical level, you'll..." The stranger stopped in mid-sentence. "I'm sorry. Please don't mind me. I'm sure that the last thing you need is to hear the ramblings of an old man."

"No, no — not at all. I've sort of... well, um... should I say I've sort of have been giving a lot of thought to the whole concept of the family myself."

"Well... please feel free to stop me if I bore you too much."

"Don't worry about that."

"I was merely pointing out the random nature of blood relatives. Just consider exactly what value there is in the coincidence of birth."

"Value?"

"Yes — value. Don't you see that all apparent meaning arises from the functions of the mind? Now you may call it the luck of the draw if you want to, but it all really comes down to sheer chance. If you're lucky, you feel emotionally close to your family; if you're not so lucky, maybe you can't stand to be around some of them. Chances are that most people will be sometimes lucky, sometimes unlucky — but the really meaningful relationships are ALWAYS formed between friends."

"You're not saying there is no meaningful relationship possible between family members, are you?"

"Oh no, I'm not saying that at all. But there certainly are no close relationships with family members who are not ALSO your friend..."

"Aha, I see what you mean. That's really a very interesting point of view." Considering that they did not yet even know each other's names, Ben was struck by the depth of the man's brief comments. It was obvious that they reflected a lifetime's worth of experiences. "I guess I never quite thought about it that way before. Ah... by the way, my name's Ben Decker." As soon as he offered his hand to his seatmate, he realized he had inadvertently used his real name rather than the Dinghoffer alias written on his ticket.

"Glad to meet you, Ben. My name's Walter Ito." He firmly took Ben's hand in his. "You know, on these long flights, it's best to share a little conversation with your neighbors — at least I prefer it that way. It sure makes the flight seem to go by faster."

"I agree."

"So, where are you from, Ben?"

"Way back in Pennsylvania — ah, more precisely, Philadelphia."

"That's certainly a long way."

"Yeah — you can say that again. So, have you lived in Hawaii your whole life?"

"Yes. Well, more correctly, I've spent a large part of my life in the Islands, but I did live in California for several years. I'm *nisei*." He noticed the blank look on Ben's face. "Um... sorry — that simply means I'm a second-generation Japanese-American. Actually, I'm about as old a *nisei* as you could find today." He chuckled quietly. "My father was in the first group of Japanese who came to Hawaii in the early 1880s to work on the plantations — sugar cane."

"How about that. That must make your children third-generation — just the same as I am. My grandparents came to America from Europe — Germany and Italy — but nonetheless, we were all immigrants." Ben used his hand to draw an imaginary circle including both Walter and himself. "I'm curious as to what you meant about being lucky with family. Family is family, isn't it?"

"Well naturally everyone's entitled to their own opinion, but to me, no — all family is NOT family. Stop and think about it for a minute. All family members are human beings, and I believe that all human beings are individuals, are unique. Now, if you buy that uniqueness argument, then who's to say that you'll like all family members the same? Actually, who's to say you even have to LIKE some family members at all?"

"I guess I know what you mean there."

"The REAL family consists of those who are family in the mind. Take me, for example — the closest relationship I have had in my sixty-six years has been with someone to whom I was not related at all."

"Now that's interesting, Walter. Ah... if you don't mind my asking, who is that?"

"Kazuko, she's my bride."

"Of course — I should have known. And you still call her your bride after many years. You must love her dearly."

Walter's head dipped just barely enough to be noticed.

"Is she in California, now?"

"Well yes, in a matter of speaking, she is. At least, her ashes are."

"Aw boy — I'm sorry, Walter." Ben felt genuine remorse for pressing the point.

"No need. I mean, it's been nearly fifteen years now. Eventually, we'll be together again — I KNOW that."

"I admire your strong faith."

"You call it faith — I call it knowledge. Over the years, I have become convinced that we are all a part of the same whole. Believe me, I haven't always felt this way. It has taken me much time to arrive in a peaceful state of mind — to finally get over the bitterness at things that I cannot change. Bitterness is an extremely counterproductive fire to have burning inside, you know. It can quickly consume the very soul."

"Bitterness? I... I fear I'm getting too personal here, but why bitter? I mean, I've only known you for a few minutes, but you seem to be such a gentle person, one who takes great pains to see the other's point of view."

"Oh, I am very human... in fact, I'm TOO human at times." Walter's eyes somehow disclosed profound pain.

Ben couldn't help but think he had inadvertently arrived at the threshold of an emotional territory at which he had no business being. He quickly groped for a diplomatic way to give Walter an easy out from such a painful disclosure. "Hey Walter, we're all human."

"Sure... we are all human, we all feel pain, and we all feel grief. But simply recognizing that fact doesn't make the pain go away..." The old man shifted uncomfortably in his seat. "...nor understanding, nor avoidance, nor denial, nor compensation — none of these things can make the pain go away — certainly not THAT kind of pain, anyway. Only a good amount of time and an acceptance that the pain must hurt deep inside. It's almost as though it must work its way out of you. No, I certainly don't pretend to speak for everyone, but for me, I have to relive the pain and just let it run its course to get it out of me."

Ben understood that Walter wanted to talk, and maybe a stranger could be the perfect listener. He put his open hands up in front of his shoulders as if to let his new friend know that it was okay to stop right here. "Obviously, I can see that whatever was the cause of your wife's passing has caused you a great deal of anguish, but you don't have to talk about it." He felt foolish for stating the obvious but sensed he needed to allow him one more chance to slip off the hook.

But Walter didn't want to avoid any hooks. "Surely you can see that I'm an old man, Ben. When you get to be my age, you talk about what you want to talk about." Walter took a deep breath of air. "Oh, it seems so very long ago. Kazuko was the most beautiful girl in all the Territory — in all the world, as far as I was concerned. We had a very good life in Honolulu, but the promise of California seemed even better. You have to understand that the promise of the States offered opportunity, offered hope. The country was just working its way back from the Depression. It was about then that my Dad retired from the sugar plantation. I say retired, but in reality, he just was no longer physically able to stay in the fields, and nobody wants to pay a sickly old man who can no longer swing his machete. Anyway, we soon moved the whole family to California."

"You worked on the plantation, too?"

"No way — I worked as a fisherman. I always knew I'd feel too trapped working on the plantation. Nonetheless, it was MY decision to move — to make a better life for us, for the kids. At least that's what I thought." He softly tapped his clenched fist to his heart several times. "And after a few years, our financial lot in life did improve somewhat — just using income as a yardstick. But it didn't matter at all because, in the long run, I lost my Kazuko..."

At this point, Ben knew he had somehow won the role of confidant, and he thought the very least he could do was to try to comfort the old man by giving him his total attention. "How, Walter? What caused her to... um... why'd she die?"

He remained quite calm, first exhaled quite loudly, and then spoke in a soft, sorrowful tone. "The direct cause of her... her death was — well, the short of it was a cold. She caught a cold, and that developed into pneumonia and — it's a downhill spiral from there, and you can figure the rest. It only took ten days. She was perfectly healthy on a Monday, and Thursday a week later, she was... gone..." He hung his head.

"I'm... I'm sorry, Walter." Ben couldn't help but wonder what it was about the people he had met during the past several days. Except the two FBI agents, the Territorial people he had come to know were all so sincere, so open, so trusting. He couldn't help but think of Leilani attributing the warmth of the Hawaiian people to the aloha spirit.

"Thank you — it's really okay. I've spent many years getting to a point where I've finally grown to accept it. That primary pain and initial suffering are gone now, but naturally, I will always have a sadness — a hole — in my heart. In a way, talking about it has been — continues to be, for that matter — quite therapeutic for me."

"That's good, Walter. I guess sometimes it helps to talk. Anyway, couldn't the doctors help her?" Ben put four fingers to his forehead. "Or... ah... was that it? You couldn't afford a doctor?"

"Oh no... at least, not exactly. We could have afforded a doctor a year earlier. As I said, I was a fisherman — first for a company in Hawaii and then on my own in California. Actually, I had gotten to a point where my business was doing quite well financially. That is everything WAS going well until they took my boat and equipment and house..." He breathed deeply. "They took everything — that is of course except for one grocery bag for each of us... when..."

"My god, Walter! Who would have done such a thing?"

The old man looked at him with such soft, gentle eyes. "You certainly must be old enough to remember. Do you really not know?"

"Know? How would I know? I'm... I'm sorry..."

"Surely you... Just look at me. What is the first thing you notice, the first thing anyone would notice."

"Well, it's obvious that you're a senior citizen."

"A what?"

"A..." Ben quickly caught himself. "Well, ah... ah... an older man, gray hair, gentle, full of wisdom..."

"Come on, Ben — surely you don't see many of my kind in Philadelphia. Look at my eyes..."

"Your kind? Ah... you mean that you're Asian..."

"Of course! I'm Japanese."

It suddenly dawned on Ben just where Walter was going with this. "And the United States Government confiscated all your possessions..."

"They most certainly did, very soon after Pearl Harbor was bombed. The craziest thing about it is that my twin brother worked in the Pearl Harbor Naval Yard and was killed in the attack. No matter — all our possessions were confiscated, and we were relocated at an internment camp out in the barren desert. Believe me, it got quite cold there at night, and the accommodations certainly weren't the best. That's where my Kazuko..." Walter swallowed hard. "Kazuko caught her cold..."

"An internment camp? How awful! And all because... simply because you were of Japanese ancestry?"

Walter softly nodded his head.

"You seem so... so resigned to all this, so accepting. How can you be so... so..."

"Believe me, I haven't always been so... as you say, accepting... But what else could I be... now?"

"Why? Are you a Buddhist, Walter?"

"Ha — my Buddhist friends would be entertained by your question. My dad was Buddhist, and my mother was a Christian — a Baptist. As kids, we had access to both doctrines, but we were indoctrinated to neither. In many ways, I regret that my personality is not strong enough to be a good Buddhist. I have been quite unsuccessful in all attempts to free myself of earthly possessions and earthly egos. I'm sorry to say, I don't think I would be much of a model to Buddha."

"You sure seem to me to be an extremely strong individual, Walter. At least now you can live out your retired years with your children — or your daughter. At least you still have someone."

"Ha! Yes, I guess you could say that I have SOMEONE. I certainly don't have the resources to live on my own. And thank god I still have my health. But my children pass me around like I have some plague, always arguing why the others should have me for the longer time period."

"God... How awful... I... I..."

"Believe me, I hate to say that. That's what I meant at the start of our conversation when I said that sometimes you're not so lucky with family. Oh, I guess it's understandable why my kids are that way, considering the time we spent in the camp and all. But as I said, mere understanding doesn't necessarily alleviate, or even lessen, the pain."

"But why, Walter? Why do your kids... ah... not want to... ah... you know what I mean?"

"Oh sure, I know exactly what you mean. My kids try to get rid of me because I'm Japanese."

"Now wait a minute here — that's silly. I'm taking for granted that Kazuko was Japanese, too. Wasn't she?"

"Yes — also *nisei.*"

"Well, for Christ's sake! Obviously, they are Japanese by ancestry, too — they HAVE to be. I... I'm not following you at all here, Walter."

"Japanese by birth? Naturally! Ah, but don't tell them that. They are American. My youngest daughter had her eyes FIXED. That's what she calls it — FIXED! Can you believe that? Some newfangled plastic surgery — I believe that's what they call it. You see, I've always been proud of my cultural heritage, and yet I have disagreed violently with the politics of the Japanese Government of Hirohito. No matter! To most Americans — and sadly, even to my own children — there is no difference between Japanese culture and Japanese politics."

"But my ancestors were from BOTH Germany and Italy — both enemies of the United States during World War Two, but no one holds that against me."

"You are lucky you don't know — some still DO hold you responsible, believe me. But you have another factor that saves you from recognition, from being an easy target."

"What's that, Walter?"

"Your eyes are not slanted..."

"I'm sorry I took so long. Here, let me give you your beers." The two men had been so engrossed in conversation that they never noticed that the stewardess had returned with a tray of sandwiches and drinks. She placed a cup of beer in front of each. "Now, you have a choice between either ham and cheese or turkey…"

35
Tuesday, February 12, 1957: 4:15 A. M.

Both Ben and Walter continued their conversation for quite a while until sleep finally claimed the older man. Ben tried to take another nap but, after several attempts proved totally unsuccessful, he took a walk down the aisle and was completely surprised to find that the old, classic airliner even had a small lounge set up in the back of the cabin. On the way back to his seat, the plane encountered some bumpy air. Ben was immediately convinced that this was finally going to be it — his miraculous return through time to the 1990s was at hand. But alas, the turbulence quickly passed, and Ben still found himself in the same 1957 Constellation. When he finally did get back to his place, he found Walter wide awake and trying to rub the kinks out of his neck.

"Never could sleep too well in these confounded machines. Now I'll have sore muscles for a week."

"Believe me, I know what you mean. I don't know why Pan Am advertises this as Sleeperette Service."

"Oh that. I think they may have some more comfortable recliner seats in first-class — they go back far enough to allow you to stretch out. Of course, who could afford such a luxury?"

"Yeah, that's for sure."

Ben fastened his belt across his lap. "So, it sounds like you have mixed feelings about flying back to California, huh Walter?"

"Not really, there are no mixed feelings about it — I simply hate it. But, as I told you earlier, I don't really have much say in the matter anymore. Someday I'll reach a point where I just take a little walk… maybe… maybe into the sea."

"The sea? Now, why would... Nah, you mean... Aw... come on, Walter — you don't mean suicide, do you?"

"There comes a time..."

"But they're your kids. My god, you've sacrificed your life for them."

"The worst thing I ever did, really..."

"What the... You mean your kids?"

"Not exactly. I really mean going to California in the first place. You know, I've always believed in a philosophy of never looking back, but I still get trapped into thinking that if I could just change one thing — one stupid mistake in my entire life — it would be that I would have never left Hawaii back in the thirties..."

Ben couldn't help but be captured by the old man's use of the same never-look-back phrase he had used with Leilani. "Well, that's sure understandable in light of what happened."

"Oh, it is, and it isn't. I know you're thinking about the internment, and you're right in a way — that was a big part of the problem. But it was more than that."

"More? In what way?"

"When we left Hawaii, in many ways, I never had a chance to see Kazuko anymore. You know, the dream was to earn more money so that Kazuko and the kids could have more things, more opportunities. But too late I learned that THINGS aren't opportunities and OPPORTUNITIES aren't happiness. Once I started my own business, the responsibilities were tremendous and the demand on time enormous. Oh sure, I made a lot more money than I did in Hawaii, but proportionately, we had to spend even more than that. It seemed we could never catch up. In the long run, I finally learned that we hadn't gained a thing. Actually, considering the colder weather, not having lifelong friends nearby, and the difference in attitude expressed towards us Japanese folks back in the States, I became convinced our lives were not even AS rich, not AS happy as they were in the Islands. I used to have a reoccurring nightmare about a hungry snake, always curling around chasing its tail. Eventually, the snake reached his goal, caught his own tail, and then swallowed himself and ending his existence. Eventually, I found out that I was that snake, but I realized it too late. We never had the time, the money or the opportunity to go back."

"Yeah, but come on, Walter. You certainly know better than I do that life just doesn't work that way. Now you must admit that if you never tried to make a go of it on your own on the West Coast, right now you'd probably be sitting in Hawaii, forever wondering what if... But isn't that the problem with second-guessing? You're always condemned to wondering what if..."

"Oh, I guess you're right — to a point. It's the same old story that if only we knew as kids what we have learned as adults... If only there were some way to learn the real value of what we have without losing it. But in my sixty-six years, I never have discovered such a secret. Of course, there is one major difference in my case. I KNEW what I had in Kazuko, and yet I let it slip away despite knowing."

"But you still had to try to better yourself for your kids — make sure they made out all right. Isn't that what they say life's all about..."

"THEY?"

"Yeah — you know..."

"You don't see it, do you, Ben? That was my biggest mistake. Needs and wants, needs and wants — the mark of parenthood is distinguishing between the two. Once you have fulfilled all your children's needs, it's merely an illusion to think you can also fulfill their wants. Wants are personal — they come from within... therefore, they can only be satisfied from within. A parent can NEVER satisfy all their child's desires. Trying to fulfill another's wants only results in GREATER yearning. It's a never-ending cycle. That brings to mind the old Japanese fable of the lady who had several mice in her house, and they caused her quite a bother. To alleviate the problem, she promised to give the little rodents all they could ever possibly want to eat. Well, I don't have to tell you where that led. The more she tried to satisfy them, the more of them there were to be satisfied. No, I'm afraid that trying to fulfill your children's material wants is just as impossible — the more you give, the more they want."

"So, what are you saying here, Walter — we shouldn't give anything at all to your children? I think I must respectfully disagree."

"Well no, that's not at all what I'm trying to say. On the contrary, my point is that it's your duty to see that all the NEEDS of your offspring are fulfilled as best as you can satisfy them. But desires..." The old man slowly shook his head from side to side. "Once your children are born, it's really only possible to provide them with two things: you can give them the basic physical needs for survival — food, clothing, and shelter, and you can nurture them with the basic emotional requirement for growth and well-being — love. Oh, I realize that is an oversimplification of a generation-long commitment, but I know for a fact that the worst thing I ever did for both myself and my family was moving away from Hawaii — leaving our paradise to make more money. Security for the kids, I thought. Well, nobody at all benefited from that decision... absolutely nobody at all..."

"Okay, I can go along with that — money's not all it's cracked up to be. But when you're talking about this need/want dichotomy, how can you ever determine the difference between a need and a want? It seems to me that it makes more sense to err on the side of wants so as not to see you kid go without something."

"Now come on, Ben. That's taking — oh, how do the kids say it? — the chicken's way out! You can't be chicken. As a parent, you MUST decide. My kids were brought up through the Depression, and yet none of them starved. It's better to be lean and industrious than to be fat and lazy."

Ben unconsciously mumbled to himself. "I don't know if our consumeristic America would agree with that..."

"Pardon me?"

"Oh, no, no... Excuse me, please. I'm just babbling to myself here, trying to digest what you've said."

"Well, while you're digesting, would you excuse me for a moment while I take a little walk to the restroom?"

* * *

Ben just laid back in his seat, the cushion reclined as far back as the mechanism would allow. He didn't really know if he bought the old man's whole argument about needs versus wants, but it sure did make him remember just why HE was trying to go back, trying to recall what his logic had been. It certainly wasn't for Emily's sake. He was certain that their relationship had ended long ago. But now he felt an urgency to reevaluate his need — or was it a desire? — to see his children again. If he considered the philosophy that Walter had just expressed, all their physical needs would be met well into the future. Even the tuition for a college education was assured if that's what they wanted. He was secure in the fact that if he never turned up in the nineties again, surely they'd have an ample supply of funds — maybe even quite a bit more than ample, depending upon what happened with his life insurance money and all. Of course, would he be considered dead? Missing? Did it even matter? If he never got back to his own time, it'd be a totally moot point, since he'd never know — at least not for another thirty-five years or so. And his business? Thank god he'd made enough money in his life to realize that that's all it was — only money. Nah — there was no sweat involved as far as Penn-Comp was concerned. They'd get along just fine without him. Oh, old Bill Katzenbach would probably panic at first, but he'd get over it in short order...

Ah, but now how about Leilani? Was she for real? Oh god, their relationship had developed so quickly, so deeply — it was simply difficult to be certain that it wasn't all a dream. Was that it — was Leilani merely some heavenly dream? After all, the human mind was an amazingly inventive device. Maybe she was only some delightful mental construct, thrown at him by his emotionally spent psyche in some warped attempt at having him forget Emily. After all, he had left her — possibly to never again see her — and he didn't have one lousy snapshot of her or even a perfumed letter penned in her own handwriting. In terms of any tangible proof of her existence, there was absolutely none to be found. But Ben KNEW she was for real, KNEW their relationship was for real. But was it now over?

Oh god, no! It couldn't be — could it? Ben shifted uncomfortably in his seat. The more he considered just what he was doing, the more he was beginning to second-guess himself. Don't look back! Yeah sure, in a rat's behind! Besides, who says don't look back, anyway? Walter talked of his mistaken decision to go to California because he knew what he had with Kazuko in Hawaii. Didn't Ben KNOW what he had with Leilani in Hawaii? Didn't he KNOW exactly what he wanted? ...KNOW exactly WHO he wanted? Oh, shit — those nagging doubts were growing bigger and bigger. Doubts? Oh sure, he wanted to somehow check on Lisa and Bonnie — whatever that meant. But now he knew he HAD to be with Leilani, would NEVER be happy without her. He could sense that in his gut.

But come on now. After all, he didn't decide to leave just for the fun of it. Let's not forget little details like the FBI. It wasn't as though they had been totally understanding and congenial with him this morning. Ah, but was running away going to solve the problem. Hell, Kimo would probably have someone meet this San Francisco flight just to play it safe. Maybe he should have told them the truth. The truth! Yeah, right! Just let old FBI Director J. Edgar Hoover know that a few of his agents had come across a genuine time traveler out in the Hawaiian Territory. But eventually, couldn't he have convinced them that he really was being honest? Couldn't he have somehow proved that he wasn't any communist? So what if it took a few weeks, a few months — could it maybe have taken a few years? Even then, it's only time he was talking about here. TIME! HA, HA... What a cruel joke... In the past week or so, he surely had discovered just how relative time could be, hadn't he?

Ben looked out the window. Flying in the same direction as the earth's rotation, the sunrise surely came early. The warm, pinkish glow that lit the wing confirmed that the two big propeller engines on his side continued to whine their way across the Northern Pacific. For crying out loud, he hadn't gone forward in time, so this entire mental conversation with himself was most likely meaningless anyway. He had no idea why he thought he was somehow going to find himself back in the nineties. Scientifically, it didn't make one bit of sense. Of course, going back in time had made no sense either... Well, okay self — let's make a deal. HA, HA! A smile came over his face. He thought of his friend David — the hotshot Philadelphia psychiatrist. What would old David say if he could somehow listen in on Ben's seemingly schizophrenic conversation with himself? The good doctor surely would have Ben committed after hearing his left hemisphere talk deals with and make promises to his right hemisphere, with only his corpus callosum there as a referee.

Well, straight jacket or not, here's the deal: Ben would get this crazy thought of checking up on his daughters out of his system by continuing his flight all the way to the East Coast. As long as he didn't wind up traveling through time again — and he was now certain he wouldn't — he'd merely turn around and fly back. He'd take no chance of running into his folks, or — horror of horrors — running into himself as a child! He wouldn't even call Leilani — he'd just jump on a plane, fly back to Hawaii and surprise her. Then he'd turn himself in at the FBI office, deal with any consequences there, and live happily ever after, hallelujah and amen. Hell, if they needed to, they could move to Tahiti or Fiji or some other Pacific paradise. As long as he and Leilani would be together again, they'd make their own paradise.

He mentally shook hands with himself and consummated the deal. As he continued to stare out the window, he became quite hypnotized by the throbbing roar of the engines. He was amazed at just how effective the loud props were at screening out the rest of the world. He never was even aware of the fact that Walter had returned and buckled himself back into his seat. In no time at all, Ben had fallen into a deep, restful sleep.

36

Tuesday, February 12, 1957: 10:10 A. M.

"Mister Dinghoffer... Mister Dinghoffer..."

Dinghoffer? It took Ben a moment to recall that he had borrowed the Wisconsin dairy's name to use as his alias. God, how did she remember that all night after only seeing his ticket one time? He opened one eye, suddenly sat straight up, and stared at the smiling stewardess. "Jeez-o-man! What time is it?"

"It's after ten o'clock in the morning, California time. You've been sleeping for quite a while, Mister Dinghoffer. I'm sorry — I didn't want to wake you, but we are preparing to land, and I have to remind you to put your seat in the upright position. We'll be arriving in San Francisco in a very short time."

"Ah... Thank you." Ben wiped his eyes and stretched as much as his confined space would allow.

"Dinghoffer, huh? And here I thought your name was Decker." Walter scratched his head and smiled a crooked grin. "You were really out cold there, Ben. I sure wish I could sleep like that when I'm on a plane."

Knowing he only had a few minutes left with the old man, Ben thought it best to simply ignore the contradiction of last names. "Jeez — I can hardly believe it myself."

Walter's expression was very concerned. "You know, it's really none of my business, but I'll say it anyway. You can lie to the whole world, but you can never lie to yourself. NEVER..."

God knows Ben couldn't agree more, but there was no way he could tell the whole story to the old man now. He looked back out the window and, sure enough, a sizable city lay below. From the looks of the large suspension bridge spanning a narrowing of a bay, it certainly looked like San Francisco — complete with her Golden Gate. But if it really were the Bay Area, every outward appearance certainly indicated that it was a decades-old San Francisco, a 1950s San Francisco. There simply weren't enough buildings down there — especially of the taller variety — for it to be in the 1990s. Aha, Ben thought — that confirms it! As the plane banked down across the bay, he couldn't sight Candlestick Park where he KNEW it had to be. Having been an avid follower of pro sports for most of his life, he had grown accustomed to familiarizing himself with various sports stadiums throughout the country. Candlestick Park wasn't — won't? — be built until the early 1960s. Hell — did they move in 1957 or 1958? The more he thought about it, he seemed to recall that this was the year the baseball Giants were to move from New York City...

37
Tuesday, February 12, 1957: 11:15 A. M.

Ben was surprised at the long line of people waiting to purchase tickets. He could never remember Lincoln's Birthday being that big of a deal, but maybe some airline employees had the holiday off. He had been unable to spot any tail since he had gotten off the Hawaii flight. Maybe the FBI simply wasn't that interested in him. Thank goodness he hadn't stood in the Pan American line just to find out they don't fly to Philly from here. Hopefully, he'd have more luck finding a last-minute ticket on a TWA flight to Philadelphia.

"May I help you, sir?"

"I sure hope so. Do you have anything open to Philadelphia today?"

"Um... Let me see..." Her hands began to skillfully flip through reams of paper. Paging through a master list of airline schedules? Ben couldn't help but think that it sure was such an archaic method to book a reservation. Of course, what could he expect? This was the current, 1957 state-of-the-art technology — if one could call it technology. The ticket agent held one finger on a line of small print and used her free hand to pick up a phone and dial, the receiver propped between her shoulder and ear.

As Ben turned to survey the crowded, noisy terminal area, he couldn't shake the feeling that he was merely playing a part in some old black and white movie. The old-fashioned dress and hair and baggage especially fascinated him, as did the dated style of absolutely everything surrounding him. And he was acutely aware of the fact that seemingly everyone had a cigarette dangling from his or her mouth.

"I'm sorry, but we can't get you to Philadelphia today. Both of our flights have morning departures, and the second one is just leaving the gate now. We do have openings on either one tomorrow if..."

"How about other airports — maybe you could get me back to Kennedy this afternoon?"

"Kennedy? I'm sorry, but I'm not familiar with a Kennedy..."

Ben softly patted his head with his open hand. How stupid of him — of course, she had never heard of Kennedy Airport. "I'm sorry. My appointment is with a Kennedy. I guess after flying all night, I'm kind of punch drunk — I don't even know what I'm saying. I was trying to ask if you have any flights to New York City, maybe Idlewild Airport. I have to see a business associate early tomorrow morning."

"Aha! Now I think you'll be in luck going to Idlewild. We have a lot more flights scheduled to New York, some later in the afternoon." She again retreated into her stacks of papers. In a matter of a few minutes, she was writing out a ticket for him.

* * *

He was still intrigued by the experience of the Trans World Airlines Lockheed Constellation. The constant drone of the engines was nearly imperceptible after several hours of flight. Ever since he boarded the plane, Ben felt as excited as a little kid taking his first ride in an airplane. He vividly remembered gluing together a plastic model kit of a Constellation as a kid — complete with its three, distinguishing vertical fins on the tail — just as clearly as if it were yesterday. The kit was a birthday present during the fifth or sixth grade. He even recalled finishing it with red and white TWA decals. In his wildest dreams, he never thought he could possibly fly in one, but here he was, nearly completing a transcontinental trip in a classic Connie.

Ben had just returned from the lavatory and re-buckled himself into his seat. The winter night was brightly lit by a nearly full moon. He peered out the window as the dark farmland of Pennsylvania was quickly giving way to the street-lit suburban sprawl of Northern New Jersey. Though he didn't know any exact numbers, it was nonetheless blatantly obvious that a whole lot of Americans lived in the Northeast, even back here during the fifties. Of course, the more he mulled it over, the more he seemed to recall that these industrial belt cities had a greater population before the 'white flight' years of the Sixties and Seventies.

His contemplation of such an inconsequential piece of demographic trivia was quickly supplanted by the personal dilemma still facing him. He felt as helpless as a dandelion seed at the mercy of a stiff wind. Like it or not, unless something dramatic happened very quickly, his decision about returning to the future had apparently been made for him. A quiet grin invaded his face as he considered the fact that he had probably made at least a half a dozen trips to airliner restrooms during the past twenty-four hours, but still, no serious turbulence resulted in any bumped heads or time travel. He could smile as much as he wanted — it was obvious that he would have no choice but to live out his life from 1957 forward.

So, it was 1957 onward, huh? He felt... how did he feel? He experienced some strange combination of uneasy, restless relief. Would history be the same? Had he really traveled back in time, or was this some sort of parallel universe? Being an electrical engineer, he had studied enough physics during his life to realize that some of the more esoteric theories in quantum mechanics predicted such things as alternate realities, but he'd most certainly be the first to admit to having a lack of any real expertise in these matters. Were there really an infinite number of parallel universes? Was it possible for an individual like him to somehow travel between two of them? Did anyone know the answers to these kinds of questions? Well, it certainly wasn't Ben Decker!

As regrettable as it may be, he was painfully aware of the fact that he possessed only enough information in these areas to be dangerous. God forbid! Would known events begin to repeat themselves? Ben's imagination lingered intensely on that consideration. How totally absurd — he could possibly be the only human being alive who would remember TWO TOTALLY DIFFERENT THINGS he was doing the EXACT instant that President Kennedy was shot! Oh my god! How utterly preposterous! He had no idea why his brain even speculated on such a morbid idea, but for some reason, he simply couldn't shake the thought from his mind.

"Ladies and gentlemen, please do not be alarmed at the noise you are hearing. It is only the normal sound of the landing gear being lowered and locked into place in preparation for our arrival at New York Idlewild. I ask that you be sure all seats are upright and that your safety belts are..."

Ben again turned toward the window. His view from the left side of the plane was spectacular. He hypothesized that it was a very cold night in New York City because the air was extremely clear and the visibility was excellent. He was certain the bright glow had to be the lights of Manhattan in the distance. Almost directly below, he could see the majestic beauty of the Statue of Liberty, lit up just as proudly as she ever could be. As they continued to decrease in altitude and speed, Ben could make out the easily identifiable Brooklyn Bridge. But sure enough, as he visually searched between the two famous landmarks, the twin towers of the World Trade Center were simply nowhere to be found. Of course, how could they be — they hadn't even been designed yet!

* * *

So, this was Idlewild before it was renamed JFK? Ben sat on an incredibly uncomfortable bench, but considering just how weary and exhausted he felt, he still thought he might drift off to sleep. He surely had enough money to get a room if he wanted, but he knew he didn't belong in New York City. No, he had to go back to Hawaii —

WANTED to go back to Leilani. Thank god it turned out this way, after all. Stosh's face appeared in his mind's eye, telling Ben just what a loyal person he had always been. Well, you're damned right he was loyal! And he was mighty proud of it, too! But the more he reflected back on his conversation with Walter Ito, the more convinced he had become that Lisa and Bonnie would be just fine. Hey, what the heck — he'd miss them and they'd miss him. For crying out loud, they were all red-blooded human beings! But in the long haul, he was positive that they'd make out just fine. Was he rationalizing or being realistic? Considering the lack of options at hand, did it even matter?

Nah — case closed! The sooner he went back to paradise, the better everything would be. Of course, it could be a fascinating experiment to simply catch a train down to Philly and go back into his old neighborhood. Would everything be the same? Could he somehow actually determine whether he had traveled through time or if he had somehow arrived in a completely different universe? Most likely not. And yet he had to admit that his scientific curiosity had been piqued. It would only take him a day or two.

For god's sake — what was he thinking about here? He knew damned well that he'd better leave well enough alone. Just suppose for one instance that he unexpectedly ran into his folks or — worse yet — himself! Who could predict the outcome? He couldn't help but recall an old science fiction story he had read a long time ago in which the lead character had somehow traveled back in time. Quite inadvertently, this person caused one event to be played out differently. One alteration of facts led to another, then to another. The transformation of events propagated itself through history like a row of falling dominoes. Before the story's protagonist knew it, he was trapped in some irresolvable time paradox. Try as he did, Ben couldn't quite remember exactly what happened, but it had something to do with the man accidentally killing his own mother before she had given birth to him — very weird stuff. Whatever the detail may have been, the plot's paradoxical climax resulted in the entire history of the universe to be totally, hopelessly changed.

Hey, no thanks! Ben felt no desire to rewrite any history. He already had to consider Leilani, two daughters, a wife, his partner, the FBI... No way, Jose! The very last responsibility Ben needed to carry on his shoulders was the burden of an entire universe!

He mustered his strength and stood up to search for the Pan American counter. Hotel? No need... If he tried to sleep as best as he could on the plane, maybe he'd still get back to Hawaii in time to make Leilani his Valentine.

38

Thursday, February 14, 1957: 11:30 A. M.

Ben had been flying for the better part of three days. At least lady luck had been on his side in not arranging for him to befriend anymore of his fellow passengers. He was simply too physically burnt out from all the traveling and too emotionally spent from this entire fiasco to be sidetracked in any sort of meaningful conversation. Most likely, he wouldn't have met with much success at striking up new relationships anyway — the lack of a shower for sixty-plus hours had most certainly helped him ward off any potential companions. One can only try to freshen up so many times in public restrooms until the law of diminishing returns sets in. And sleep — he had tried to sleep as best as he could, but the human anatomy can only take so many plane seats and airport benches. He had been fortunate on this flight out of Los Angeles since no one was seated next to him. At least the extra space gave him a little more room to sprawl out a bit.

His forehead leaned against the Constellation's window, as he stared blankly at the spotty clouds drifting over the vast ocean below. How many miles had he flown in two-and-a-half days? Ten thousand? Twelve thousand? Considering how long it took for prop-driven planes to fly from Honolulu to New York to Honolulu again, he was positive he could have flown around the world a few times in any modern commercial jet. Well, depending on how the FBI decided to treat him after his return, Ben swore it would be a long time until he'd voluntarily get onto an airplane again — especially a noisy propeller model!

"Ladies and gentlemen, we will be preparing for arrival in Honolulu shortly. Would all passengers..."

He nearly thought he was going to scream! Ben simply could not bear to hear this spiel one more time. He unhooked his seatbelt. It seemed funny to him right now, but it had almost become a ritual after all his years of flying — he'd better make one last trip to the restroom before they landed. He stood and waited as two stewardesses moved down the aisle, picking up wrappers, cups, and napkins. He was again amazed at the size of this pre-jet age airliner. It was by no means a jumbo jet, but then again, this WAS 1957. At last, he was able to make his way down the aisle and take his place in a short line waiting to use the lavatory. Surveying the mix of people around him proved fascinating. The milieu of colors and cultures were quite evident. He thought the mixes of Polynesian blood were so unique, so beautiful. What term did Lani use? *Hapa haole?* God knows he couldn't wait to get back to THAT *hapa haole!* Now he and Leilani would live out the rest of their lives — TOGETHER.

He felt a bump of air turbulence as the intercom briefly hissed to life. There were a few seconds of barely audible static, and then just as quickly, the speakers went silent again. Finally, the crackle returned as a female voice spoke her practiced message. "The captain has turned on the seat belt sign. Would all passengers please return to their seats at this time and prepare for arrival." An attendant stooping down and cleaning up food trays next to Ben looked up at him. "Oh, go ahead. You're the last one in line there. You still have a little time, but you'd better hurry."

"Thanks. I'll only be a minute." Ben heard the latch on the lavatory door begin to open. Suddenly he was struck by an overwhelming sense of *déjà vu.* God knows he felt as though he had been exactly in this precise situation before, only somehow it was different. He felt almost stunned at the uncanny feeling, and for a minute, he had totally lost track of just why it was he was standing in the back of this antique plane.

"...sorry, but you'll have to hurry, sir. We'll be landing in about ten minutes, and you have to get back to your seat. The captain is expecting some rather bumpy flying up ahead. Do you need any help? Are you all right, sir?"

The trance was snapped. He looked over at the stewardess, and, just as he considered his response, he heard a loud bang. The plane began a wild, rhythmic vibration. Ben grabbed for the bulkhead to steady himself, but almost immediately, the plane dropped and rolled to one side. He had been shaken by air pockets before, but never as severe as this one — except... He struggled with his foggy memory to recall another time, another flight... ZAP! *Déjà vu!* Oh god, no! This wasn't all happening one more time — and even in the exact same way...

The plane once again shook fiercely, eliciting several cries of panic from a disbelieving load of fellow passengers. Sure — he remembered perfectly. He was on the United flight to his Hawaiian convention when... The whole craft shuddered hard once again. He tried to recall more detail of that previous flight, but the circumstances simply wouldn't allow it. The Constellation pitched forward and rolled savagely back to the other side, violently tossing its passengers about. Aw damn, he thought, talk about being shoved into a nightmare without any warning. Please tell me the whole god damned plane isn't going down! Aw shit! Where's a seatbelt when you need one? He sensed that he was lurching out of control toward the corner of the bulkhead wall, but there was absolutely nothing he could do to prevent the impact. He automatically threw his hands in front of his face trying to soften the blow. But he somehow knew that his effort was totally in vain...

* * *

"Mister Decker, are you okay? Mister Decker?" He moved his head slowly back and forth as though he were trying out each muscle in his neck all over again. "Are you all right? We must have just hit a pretty nasty bump, and you really banged your head here — I'm sure you're going to be all right." The woman was rubbing his head where he had hit it against the corner of the bulkhead.

Ben opened his eyes to see the flight attendant, down on one knee and looking at him with an expression of deep concern. He didn't recognize her face at all. "What... What happened?"

"Turbulence — it must have been severe air turbulence. Here, let me help you get back to your seat." She grabbed him under one arm and helped him to his feet. She quickly, but surely, led him back up the aisle.

Ben's rapidly growing bump hurt like the dickens, but he somehow sensed that other than a headache, he'd come through the whole event in pretty good physical shape. As the two made their way up the aisle, he quickly became conscious of many heads turning and staring at him. He was amazed at the incredible number of people, more people than he had remembered on the... MY GOD! There simply weren't this many people on the plane before he had bumped his head — no way! There seemed to be literally hundreds of people on this plane. HUNDREDS! HOLY SHIT! He was back on a jumbo jet again. A JUMBO JET! Oh no — that could mean only one thing...

The flight attendant helped him into his seat. "Please fasten your belt, Mister... um...

"Decker, Ben Decker..."

"Yes, Mister Decker. We don't know if there's going to be more bumpy air up ahead. Besides, we'll be landing in Honolulu in less than an hour."

Ben couldn't help but wonder just how accurately he had retraced his journey into the future. "Where are the Penroses?"

"Who, sir?"

"The Penroses — the older couple sitting next to me here."

"Why I'm sorry, but I'm not familiar with that name. Maybe you're a little disoriented, confused. Both of these seats have been vacant ever since we left Chicago. Look, if you want, I'll get you a few aspirins."

"Yeah, that would be great, thank you."

Ben quickly tried to sum up his situation. *Déjà vu*, huh? Well, not exactly... He was certainly on a jumbo jet — a United one at that. But now he had a different stewardess then the last time, and there was no trace of his former seatmates, Martin and Betty Jo Penrose. He reached for his flight bag tucked under the seat in front of him. In a split second, he located the Alpha-Max 2000. Damn! Well, that settles THAT! If there was any lingering doubt about his actually traveling in time, the reappearance of the Alpha-Max 2000 certainly confirmed it once and for all. It was pretty obvious that he had once again somehow jumped through time. And yet from the looks of it, he certainly had not retraced his journey with any great degree of precision. Could the entire affair have merely been a dream?

The flight attendant quickly returned with two white pills in a small container and a plastic glass filled with water. "Here you are, Mister Decker. You know, I could easily have the captain radio ahead to have an emergency medical team meet us upon arrival on Oahu."

As Ben downed the aspirins and swallowed the entire glass of water, he held his open hand up in front of himself. "Gee, ah... no thanks — I really appreciate your concern, but I'm sure I'm all right. I'll just rest myself here and give the aspirin a chance to work."

"Whatever you say, Mister Decker. I'll leave you in peace, and we'll see if your headache goes away by the time we arrive at Honolulu International. If not, let me know." She patted his shoulder. "I'm going to have to fill out an incident report anyway — FAA regulations, you know." She smiled and walked away.

Ben leaned back and closed his eyes. If he were lucky, maybe he could shake this awful headache by the time they landed. But somehow, he felt a foreboding fear growing deep inside that kept telling him that he'd still suffer... forever...

PART SIX

*"Ever has it been that love knows not its own
depth until the hour of separation."*

– Kahlil Gibran

39
Sunday, February 14, 1999: 3:40 P. M

The big jumbo jet had come to rest, and several of the jetway tubes linking its exit doors directly with the terminal building were already in place. Ah yes — modern technology thought Ben as he walked through the air-conditioned tunnel. He was disappointed by the realization that this little bit of modernization surely must leave a first-time visitor with a much less powerful initial impression of the Islands. As contrasted to the distinctive blast of warm, humid, flower-scented air that captivated all who disembarked from a 1950s propeller-driven plane, this bland, jet-age, skyway greeting was totally indistinguishable from that at any other state-of-the-art airport in Chicago or New York, Los Angeles or London.

By the time he reached the end of the tube and entered the terminal building proper, his mood was somewhat lifted by the sweet, tropical fragrances he had missed in the jetway. The first hint of plumeria amplified his already obsessive thoughts of Lani. He quickly made his way through a sea of lei-bedecked people and exited from the air-conditioned building. A stiff trade wind filled his lungs with a rush of invigorating air. Being confined within planes and at airports for nearly three days did little to boost one's spirits in the best of circumstances. Having left his accidental paradise made matters even worse. He tried to recall how Walter Ito said it — if only there were some way to learn the real value of what we have without first losing it...

A *wiki wiki* tram pulling several air-conditioned cars quietly came to a stop in front of Ben, and all its doors hissed open. "Main terminal building, ticket counters, baggage areas, Neighbor Island terminal — watch your step, please."

No thank you, Ben thought to himself. He'd been sitting for what seemed to be forever, and he'd be more than happy to take a leisurely walk with the brisk breeze at his back. He adjusted his grip on his flight bag and began to hike along the rampway towards the central hub. As he glanced to his right, the obstructed sight of a city growing sadly out of control overwhelmed him. The once pristine view of Diamond Head was now violated by a cluttered sprawl of glass and concrete. And now — after relishing in several dozen breaths of what should be fresh air — he was saddened by an ugly blast of vehicular exhaust. No doubt that the world had changed drastically in the past forty years or so, and in Ben's mind, much of the change was definitely not for the better.

He kept walking at a lively pace, for some reason displaying much more zest then his physical or mental state should have allowed. The entire air terminal complex seemed completely unrecognizable from the little airport he had arrived at just last Thursday — more than forty years ago! He knew from his frequent travels through here while servicing their Asiatic accounts that the Fiftieth State had become the vacation destination for millions of people every year, and, to his chagrin, it appeared that all those people were congregating at Honolulu International right now. After passing several departure and arrival gates, he finally walked through the entrance into the main terminal structure. He was at once greeted by a clamorous madhouse of activity.

There was a flurry of humanity everywhere! Hard as he tried, he simply could not get over how busy Honolulu International had become during the past several decades. He was dazzled by the multitudes of people who were hustling and bustling about to an endless array of check-in counters, lei stands, car rental booths, flower shops, agricultural inspection stations, ticket counters, baggage claim areas, snack carts, pineapple stands, taverns, tourist information centers, restaurants, insurance booths, gift shops, and newsstands. He imagined this is what it would be like to be an ant in a giant colony whose members were all trying to run in different directions at the exact same time. He knew his baggage couldn't be on this flight since he had left it all at Leilani's 1957 apartment. Most likely, his best course of action was to escape from all this chaos as quickly as possible. But where would he go?

Ben located a bank of public pay phones and immediately made a beeline to the first one he spotted that was not in use. He quickly opened a dog-eared copy of the yellow pages to the section listing hotels, felt in his pants pocket for change, and fished out a shiny, new quarter. He reflexively reached for the slot in which to deposit the toll. On a whim, he pulled the coin back and held it up to his eye to inspect the date. Aha — a brand new, 1956 quarter! It seemed almost a shame to throw it away on a phone call. God only knew what real silver coins were worth nowadays! Oh well, there was certainly no time to try to find change right now amid all this confusion. He reluctantly deposited the coin and dialed the number.

"Aloha. This is the Hilton Hawaiian Village. May I help you?"

"Ah... yes, you may. My name is Ben Decker. I had a reservation for a room in your Rainbow Tower last week and was wondering if I could still..."

40

Sunday, February 14, 1999: 5:25 P. M.

Ben hardly could have expected the Hilton Hawaiian Village to keep his room vacant for an entire week at any time of year. It was even more understandable considering that February was the busiest peak of the tourist season in Waikiki. But seventy-five minutes on the lousy phone to locate a shabby, second-rate hotel room seemed ridiculous. And now, as he drove by looking for a place to park, his first impressions of the place told him it was a real dump. Oh well — beggars can't be choosers! At least he was thankful that his missing credit cards had miraculously turned up in his wallet, just exactly where they were supposed to be. Just imagine trying to rent an automobile nowadays without having a major credit card! He pulled the little, leased compact into a parking garage several hundred feet farther down the street and spent several frustrating minutes attempting to find an open space. He automatically flipped the latch to the locked position as he slid out of the car. As Ben stepped away from the rental, he nearly laughed at his realization of his instinctive attempt to guard against crime. Here he stood with his flight bag in his hand — as far as he was concerned, this was the sum total of all his earthly possessions. He had absolutely nothing else of his in the car, nothing else anywhere. Nonetheless, he was a creature of habit, and this modern-day world required that one habitually lock his vehicle — another sad-but-true commentary on his times.

He patted his pants to make sure he had his keys, and he slipped the parking stub in his shirt pocket. Ben stepped out onto the sidewalk and headed directly for the hotel. The building itself was located a few blocks back from the beachfront and seemed to be in the shabbier part of Waikiki. The structure itself was only three stories high and presented a very old, rundown appearance. All in all, it was quite out of place in a Waikiki that had sprouted new, twenty and thirty-story buildings on almost every block. He was convinced that the worth of the land greatly exceeded the value of the dilapidated building and that sooner or later, some fat cat developer would make an offer that would simply be too good to refuse. Well, that certainly wasn't Ben's problem. At least with a little bit of luck, he could grab a few hours of sleep, a clean shave, and a hot shower. Ben knew he was running dangerously close to empty and was in dire need of some rest before he could give serious consideration to any plan of action. After all, since yesterday the world had somehow waited for him for forty-some years! As preposterous as that sounded, what harm could a few more hours possibly do?

"Hey, big guy — are you looking for a good time?" A young woman who couldn't have been a day older than his college-aged daughter came out of nowhere to grab at Ben's hand. She was wearing a skin-tight, low cut red top that flaunted the little cleavage she had, bright red high heels that added a good six inches to her height, and a black leather skirt that was short enough to be mistaken for a wide belt. Her makeup was caked on so thickly that Ben could not decide if she really had the potential to be attractive or not. "Come on, honey — why don't you show me how big you are? I mean, I'll do anything you want — ANYTHING..." She ran her tongue over her upper lip.

"Oh god — um... not really. Ah... I mean, I really can't — not tonight." His words revealed a more uncomfortable, nervous response than he would have predicted for himself.

"You won't be disappointed... Promise..." She batted her exaggerated eyelashes and tried her best to flash a practiced, seductive pout.

"No, I'm... I'm sure I wouldn't be. But I already have a, um... a date and have to g... get going right now. Um... sorry..."

The young woman answered by turning her back and calmly moving on in a conspicuous search for other potential customers. Wasn't it too early for a lady of the night to be out looking for a mark before it had even gotten dark? Ben couldn't help but be both saddened and disturbed by the apparent ease with which she nonchalantly accepted his rejection. Oh well, at least he couldn't justifiably blame prostitution on the nineties. Wasn't it the Bible that called it the world's oldest profession? Ben slowly shook his head, turned away from the street, and quickly entered the shabby hotel.

* * *

Sadly enough, the musty room was just as bad as he expected. He dropped his bag on the bed and plopped himself down next to it. Oh god! Every bone and muscle in his body was screaming from the horrible torture inflicted upon each by nearly three solid days of constant travel. He opened the bag and took a quick inventory — a change of clothes, his toilet bag, his computer, and... a newspaper. He folded the paper open. Well now, how about that! He silently read the masthead — *THE HONOLULU STAR BULLETIN* dated Tuesday,

247

February 12, 1957. And it was in pristine condition without the slightest bit of yellowing. He shoved it back into his bag — may as well save it for posterity's sake. He snapped open the Alpha-Max 2000, and the processor immediately came to life.

"You have one hundred and seven-eight messages, thirty-seven marked personal and urgent. Would you like me to read them to you, Mister Decker?"

Aha — the battery still had enough juice to power her up. "Ah, no wait a minute, Alpha." Son of a gun! Everything appeared to be in perfect order, precisely the same way he had left it before this entire fiasco began. How utterly absurd! No doubt they were looking for him all over Honolulu. He wondered how long it would be until they tracked him down through the charge card he used to rent the vehicle. For over a minute, Ben considered going through his messages. What had he done? He didn't WANT to be back in the present, didn't WANT to respond to all his correspondence. He closed the cover of the Alpha-Max 2000 and set it on the bed.

He stood, slipped his shirt over his head, and then stepped out of his trousers. As he placed his wallet on the nightstand, Ben shook his head in bewilderment. He didn't pretend to have the slightest idea of just what had taken place for these past seven days. Even worse, it boggled his mind to find that both his computer and wallet — including all his reappearing credit cards — once again exactly the way they had been last Thursday morning back in Philadelphia. He stared at the computer, wondering just where it had been for the past week. For that matter, he knew it was possible to send out a tracer signal, ping his unit, and locate it through simple triangulation. Why didn't Katzenbach put out a tracer on it once he knew he was missing? Was it possible that they too had been suspended or lost in some bizarre time warp? He bent over and jabbed his finger at a switch that deactivated the Alpha-Max 2000's radio connection to the Internet. There was no sense in being found sooner than he had to be. He slipped the computer back into his bag.

Once stripped down to only his underpants, Ben grabbed his shaving kit and headed for the bathroom. When he flipped on the overhead light in the bath, he saw several shadows scurry across the floor and quickly disappear behind the toilet and under the sink. Lizards? Roaches? Worse? No way man! He flat out refused to investigate. In the condition he was in, he was certain that he'd be much better off not knowing what shared the room with him. He placed his toilet bag on the vanity and unzipped it. He could remember a few times in his life that he had looked forward more to getting cleaned up.

The shower and shave made him feel a thousand percent better, both physically and psychologically. The refreshing combination had relaxed him to such a point where he knew he was going to soon lose consciousness whether he liked it or not. He liked it.

He turned down the covers and climbed into the bed. Ah! It felt wonderful to finally enjoy the luxury of stretching out on a REAL bed. Tonight he was fatigued to the point that it didn't even matter what a second rate, rundown hotel this place was. He swore he never wanted to try to sleep on another plane for as long as he lived. As he rolled onto his side, he fluffed up the pillow and was at once disgusted by the odor of mildew that permeated it. Yuck! Was this really the last room left anywhere in Waikiki? If he only had enough energy, he would have tried to find another room, but he was so damned tired that he couldn't even...

41

Monday, February 15, 1999: 5:00 A. M.

Ben awoke with the overpowering stench of mildew entrenched in his nose. He sat up and tested his eyes, blinking them while quickly surveying the dingy room. Oh wow! He hadn't even turned the lights out before he had fainted nearly... nearly... He leaned over and groped around the small nightstand for his watch. Eleven hours! He seemed to remember reading that you can never make up for lost sleep. Oh well... He certainly had given it a good try.

He swung his legs over the side of the bed and attempted to consciously will himself into an alert state of mind. It only took him a minute or two to concede defeat! After all, an addiction is an addiction. He simply had to face the fact that he was in serious need of some caffeine to roust his sluggish cerebrum — most preferably in the form of an aromatic, hot cup of coffee. And then? Should he look in on the ending of his missed convention? Or should he immediately try to track down Leilani? Hey, that's not even a serious choice — to hell with the convention! He amazed even himself at just how rapidly his concern for the modern-day world was fading. The urgency of trying to sell the Alpha-Max 2000 seemed to pale when compared to finding Leilani. He stood up and took a deep breath. Ugh! The heavy smell of mildew reminded him of the necessity for getting out of this dump — the sooner, the better. Right now, that had to be his number one priority.

* * *

Ben sat at the counter in the little coffee shop right across the street from Waikiki Beach. Sadly enough, from this vantage point, there was little indication that any ocean was nearby. The big picture window faced directly towards the spot where he stood with Leilani just the other night while speaking with her beach boyfriend. His mind whirled at the thought of the reality that that night occurred a good forty years ago! He couldn't help but be appalled at what happened to that beautiful stretch of sand. Now there was a police substation sitting right where the surfboard racks had been. Regretfully, it was almost impossible to get an unobstructed view of the ocean from anywhere on this side of the street, nearly every line of sight being screened out by a nearly solid wall of high rises and condominiums. Only several tall coconut palms and the bright aloha apparel worn by many early rises offered any confirmation of his mid-Pacific location.

Ben sipped his much-welcomed coffee. He felt old — a heck of a lot older than anyone should have felt after spending his nearly five decades on this earth. Holy shit! A sudden thought rattled his composure. Was he really making a wild assumption in thinking that this still was the same earth? Reflecting on what had occurred, it was blatantly obvious to him that his perspective was quite different from that of anyone else. Oh sure, many folks grumbled about how their own little paradise may have changed dramatically throughout their lifetime. At least they had seventy or eighty years over which to absorb the shock and to slowly grow used to all the transitions. But here Ben sat, totally blown away by the shocking sight of four-plus decades of helter-skelter growth less than five days after he had been living there! The jolt was simply unbelievable. Of course, now that he considered it, just what would Leilani be like after forty-some years? He felt a chill rush down his spine. Did she ever marry? He could hardly have expected her to wait for half a lifetime! Did she still live in Honolulu? Oh god! She'd have to be — he unconsciously added up the years on his fingers — well into her sixties. For that matter — was she even alive anymore?

He spread a healthy portion of jam onto his toast. The word on the label — *lilikoi* — jumped out and caught his eye. He could hear Leilani explaining that Hawaiians always pronounced the letter I with a long E sound. LEE-LEE-KOI. As he sounded the syllables in his mind, he could feel his eyes beginning to get moist. *Lilikoi* — the local word for passion fruit. Wasn't that Lani's favorite? Her tear-streaked face filled his mind's eye, and he could hear her melodic voice. "I love you and will wait for you — FOREVER... I PROMISE..." God only knew why she would have done that — for him, no less. It was stupid to think she actually would have. And yet somehow, Ben almost feared that that was exactly what she had done.

He couldn't help but reminisce while he finished up his toast and coffee. A quick glance at his watch told him that Honolulu had to be pretty much awake by now. He had a lot of tracking down to do before the weekend got in his way. He pulled some bills from his wallet and tucked them under his empty plate. Ben spun around on his stool and exited the little coffee shop. As he stepped out onto the sidewalk, a warm ocean breeze coming in from the south portended that an unseasonably warm day was in store, even for Hawaii.

42

Monday, February 15, 1999: 8:10 A. M.

Ben was amazed; even though it was immersed in a turbulent sea of growth and change, the Royal Hawaiian Hotel somehow maintained its old charm miraculously well. Naturally, there were some minor "improvements" that Ben's discerning eye could identify — modern electrical wiring, upgraded air conditioning, and a new computer system in use at the front desk. An adjoining, high rise addition had even been built on what had previously been an open, grassy area by the beach. But the old "Pink Palace" itself remained quite unspoiled — a welcomed throwback to yesteryear.

Luckily, Ben didn't have to wait too long. The cute front desk clerk returned from the office that was hidden away behind a bank of mailboxes. "No, Mister Decker, I'm afraid nobody around here seems to remember anyone by that name — at least no one who worked here at the Royal. You have to understand that Kealoha is a rather common surname here in the Islands."

"Sure, I understand. How about this Mister Dority fellow? Did anyone remember him?"

"Well, certainly he was the general manager here way back then. But you know, it's been such a long time."

"Yeah, I know." Ben felt foolish. The young lady was at most only in her mid-twenties. He was fully cognizant of the fact that there was no way that she could even have been dreamed about forty-some years ago.

"...but my friend, Billy, says that if anyone at all would recall him, it'd be Myra Pakele."

"Myra Pakele?"

"Yes, Myra works in our personnel department — been with the Royal for over forty years." The woman tactfully covered a giggle with her open hand. "I guess I should be more careful at giving away her age."

Ben returned the lighthearted smile. "I promise I won't tell. Do you think I could possibly speak with her?"

"Oh, sure. But I don't think she's in yet. The gang in personnel doesn't usually get in until around nine o'clock. Here, just a second." The desk clerk looked at her watch as she picked up a telephone and punched at the buttons on its face. "Good morning. Do you know if Myra came in yet? Would you mind checking? Oh sure, I'll wait."

Ben turned around and, leaning on the counter with one elbow, scanned his surroundings. It was downright uncanny how little had changed at the Royal. He was certain that many of the stylish trappings could not possibly still be the originals — the wall and floor coverings, the upholstery, the fresh paint, and so forth. But no matter how they did it, the refurbishment surely seemed authentic enough and was identical to the decor — and the ambiance — that existed here back in the fifties. From the looks of the busy lobby area, the Royal Hawaiian once again had a full house. He wondered just how many Februarys the old hotel had seen more visitors then she knew what to do with.

"You're in luck, Mister Decker." Ben spun around face to face with the pretty desk clerk. "Myra evidently came in an hour early today and is willing to speak with you right now, if you want."

"Hey, that's great."

"The personnel office is right over there, around the other side of that archway." She pointed across the lobby towards a series of little gift shops. "Just go around to the other side there, and you can't miss it."

"Believe me, I can't tell you how much I appreciate your help. Thanks again."

"No problem. I hope you are successful in your search. Aloha."

Ben only needed to walk a few hundred feet and had no trouble at all finding the personnel office. As soon as he entered the glass door, a heavyset, older lady practically fell over her desk as she jumped up to greet him.

"You're Mister... um... You're the gentleman asking about some of our old-timers, are you?"

"Why yes, I am, ma'am. My name is Decker — Ben Decker. And I assume that you are Miss Pakele."

"Ah, yes — Myra, please. You make me feel like an old lady with that Mrs. stuff." The perky woman was dressed in a flowing, red print muumuu that did a marvelous job at hiding the consequences of a lifetime's worth of too much pork and poi. Ben estimated she had to be nearing retirement age. "So, what can I do for you? One of our girls at the front desk said you were trying to find someone."

"Exactly. A former employee of the Royal Hawaiian, ah... her name is Leilani Kealoha. Do you, by any chance, remember her? I realize it's been forty or more years since..."

The older lady held her open hand up as if to say enough. "Such a beautiful young lady. Oh, I remember Lani Kealoha, all right. We both started working here pretty much at the same time. Just a wonderful person — fun to be with — but right before she left here, she had such a tough time of it."

"A tough time? Why do you say that?"

"Well, it seems she had a boyfriend — or a lover." The woman lowered the volume of her voice and partially covered her mouth with her hand as if she were trying to hide some scandal from unseen snoops. "But the lover just... Hey, now wait a minute here. Is she in some kind of trouble or something? Why do you want her? I haven't seen Leilani for..."

"No, no, no — it's nothing like that. I work for a... Let's just say I work for a gentleman who would like to reestablish contact with her. Believe me, she'd be more than happy to hear from him again."

"Aha! So, you must be a private investigator. Maybe a real PI even — like Magnum?"

"Well, I'm..." Before Ben could get another word out of his mouth, her slowly nodding head announced that she had sized him up and — at least within her own mind — had confirmed his authenticity as some TV detective.

"It was such a shame. She was an excellent employee — couldn't ask for more. Like I said, we both started working here around the same time... not in the same department, mind you." Myra grabbed two paper cups and began to fill them with coffee. "I can't remember exactly when it happened, but sometime back in the fifties, she must have really fallen deeply in love with some older fellow — I think he was a *haole* guy from back East somewhere. Well, for some reason, he had to leave on the spur of the moment." She handed Ben a steaming cup of coffee. "I guess I should have asked you if you wanted any."

"Sure, why not. Thanks a lot."

"Anyway, I remember hearing rumors at the time — about the guy, I mean."

"Rumors? What kind of rumors?"

"Well, you remember all the Red scares in those days, don't you?" She smiled when it at once dawned on her that Ben had to be fifteen or so years her junior. "Of course you don't — you're probably too young. But believe me, they were looking for communist sympathizers under every bed. Anyway, I guess that the guy turned out to be a communist spy or something. Whatever the case was, one day he just up and disappeared."

"But how about Leilani. Do you have any idea what happened to her?"

"All I know is that she seemed crushed by the whole affair. She only stayed here a very short while after that — maybe three or four weeks. It surprised us all — she had such a career ahead of her here at the Royal. I remember talking to her the day she came in here to fill out her termination papers — even way back then, you still couldn't escape all the paperwork." A fleeting smile crossed the big woman's face. "Oh boy, now that brings back a lot of memories... I was only a clerk then, you know."

Ben politely nodded his head.

She took a gulp of her coffee. "Yeah, lots of memories, all right. Certainly was a long time ago."

"That's for sure." Ben smiled and gestured agreement in an attempt to nudge her on with the rest of the story.

"Well, she did talk to me some that morning. The poor girl was so sad. I'll always remember her that day because she simply couldn't stop crying. Oh, I don't mean she was loud or anything — just constantly sobbing big, silent tears. Every time I thought she had gotten herself under control, I'd see more tears start to come. Nonetheless, she told me she had promised this gentleman she would wait for him, but it seemed that he was either going to be back in a week or two or else not for a long, long time. I asked her how that was even possible, but she just wasn't willing to go into any detail. Hey, it wasn't any of my business or anything, but it just seemed so strange to me."

"Strange?"

"Well yeah, only because she insisted on such contradictory alternatives — he'd either be back in a few weeks or else half a lifetime. There didn't seem to be anything at all in between. I figured the guy had to be some commie spy or something — maybe on the run, maybe in prison for a long time... who knows?"

"That does sound rather strange. Do you have any idea where she was going? Maybe where she'd be now?"

"Goodness, not really. I think she had grown up on one of the Neighbor Islands, maybe the Big Island. Nah — maybe it was Maui... Ah... I'm sorry. I'm just not sure of either where she was from or where she went. But I'll always, always remember those big, brown eyes — she was such a beautiful woman, you know. Yeah, whoever that jerk was, he certainly was a fool to leave such a beautiful, kindhearted woman behind."

"It sure sounds that way."

"I always figured he was a fraud."

"Why a fraud?"

"Well, think about it. If he actually loved her and wasn't just taking advantage of her, he'd have taken Lani along somehow even though the government was chasing after him. Yeah — if he REALLY cared for her, he would have found a way to stay with her."

The woman's words rattled Ben's conscience. Oh god, if it had only been that simple. "You never know, I guess..."

"But like I said — I never could understand the mystery of why he had to either be back in a few weeks or such a long time later. Though Leilani kept her secret private, I still remember feeling there was a kind of spooky air about the entire episode. Of course, I haven't thought about her for years, but... Hmmm..." Myra suddenly hesitated as she grabbed her chin with her hand. "Hey, ah... this guy you work for wouldn't be the man who broke her heart, would he?"

"No, no — that's certainly not the case. Actually, I'm sure of that for the simple reason that he's the wrong age — too young."

"Hmmm..." She considered his logic and then quickly seemed to accept his explanation.

"Tell me, Myra — surely you would remember a Mister Dority, wouldn't you?"

"Naturally. He was our general manager for years and years. And on top of that, he was a really nice man, a gentleman. ...always cared about the employees."

"Was? Do you have any idea where he is? Or, for that matter, is he still alive?"

"Still alive! Ha!" A big smile crossed her face. "God knows, Duke Dority will outlive us all. He's eighty-something going on eighteen!"

"Duke, huh?"

"Yeah — Duke. You know now that I think about it, though, I have no idea why people call him Duke. His real first name is William."

"And he still lives in the Islands?"

"Oh sure. He has a beautiful place somewhere back up in Manoa Valley — way up past the University, even. He and his wife still come to the company Christmas party every year. They are both in their eighties now, but they seem to keep really active. They raise some fancy breed of dogs back up there. If you have a minute, I could get you their address."

"That would be just great. I can't tell you what a big help you've been."

"Oh, it's no problem — no problem at all. If you ever do find Leilani, tell her Myra still remembers her. You know we were about the same age. I'm curious as all heck to know just what she's doing nowadays."

"If I find her, I promise I'll relay the message."

"I'd like that. Here, let me find that address." Myra grabbed a big Rolodex from a nearby desk and quickly began to finger her way through it.

43

Monday, February 15, 1999: 11:25 A. M.

Ben unconsciously patted his carry-on bag, checking on the Alpha-Max 2000. He walked at a brisk pace back towards the car. As he rounded the corner onto the street on which he had parked, he feared seeing police officers lying in wait for him. There was no doubt that someone had contacted the police about his disappearance by now — his wife, his partner, his daughters... It had to be an easy matter tracking his credit card, and he did use it to rent the car. He looked up and down the street before he unlocked the rental, but there was no one suspicious anywhere in sight.

The brief conversation with Myra had Ben doing what he swore he'd never do — second-guessing. For the entire drive to Duke Dority's house, his divided psyche kept him in constant torment. Over and over again, he'd first see the image of a twenty-six-year-old, teary-eyed Leilani begging him to stay, and then he sees a disgusted Myra saying, "Yeah, whoever that jerk was, he sure was a fool to leave such a beautiful, kindhearted woman behind." Oh god, maybe Myra was right. Maybe he SHOULD have taken Leilani with him — or never left in the first place. Oh shit! How did this ever happen? And why?

HA! Don't ever look back? Yeah, right! That advice made so much more sense in 1957 than it did right now.

He turned his rental car onto Keaw Street and followed along as it winded its way into a smaller branch valley. Thick, tropical foliage threatened to overgrow the road, and colorful birds darted playfully from tree to tree. The farther in he drove, the more isolated the valley became. It finally dawned on him that this had to be very near to the waterfall that marked Leilani's secret place. Thank god that at least the out of control development hadn't spread back up here... yet... He slowed the car as he neared a rather modest, two-story home. The dwelling was quite meticulously kept, and the fresh brilliance of its white clapboard siding and green tin roof attested to a recent coat of paint. On two sides dense, jungle-like vegetation isolated the structure from any neighbors, with a nearly vertical canyon wall bordering the back of the property. He pulled his car to the side of the now narrow road and checked the neatly lettered mailbox — W. DORITY.

Ben set his parking brake and climbed out of the little import. Oh wow! Just look at this place! The spectacular setting impressed Ben — not opulent, just cozy. It was an idyllic location in which to spend one's retirement years. A vociferous symphony of bird calls and songs emanated from a countless variety of birds, greeting the visitor as he slowly approached the front gate.

"Mister Dority! Mister Dority!"

"Woof! Woof! Woof!" Ben knew a canine commotion headed his way, but he couldn't yet identify the source of the barks. He was certain there were at least several dogs — their low-pitched tones indicating giants — but he didn't know if they were pit bulls or mastiffs. Ben's uncontrolled anxiety caused his heart to climb seemingly all the way to the back of his throat. He braced himself just in time to witness half-a-dozen droopy-eyed basset hounds round a row of hibiscus. A smile crept over his face as he breathed a sigh of relief. The pack of wrinkled pups came tripping and tumbling, ears over tails, yelping their way right up to the front gate. Was THIS the FANCY breed Myra had referred to?

"Hi, guys." Though Ben felt much more secure at the welcomed appearance of such usually friendly hunting dogs, he still didn't risk an unauthorized pet without Mister Dority being present.

"Can I help you, young man?" A little, old lady peered out from a small garden, armed only with a pair of clippers and several long-stemmed roses.

"Yes, please. I'd like to see Mister Dority if he has a few minutes."

"You're not one of those Jehovah people, are you?"

"Oh goodness no — ah... it's nothing at all like that."

Unexpectedly, a rather tall man materialized from behind the same row of bright red hibiscus. As he neared the gate, his younger-than-expected appearance surprised Ben. "What can I do for you?"

"Mister Dority?"

"That's me." He placed one hand on the gate, while he stroked one of his dogs with the other.

"So, you raise basset hounds, do you?"

"We sure do." He looked down at the low slung, pathetic looking creatures and — holding one opened hand up — spoke in a stern voice. "STAY!" The older man opened the gate. Even though every tail kept wagging and the boisterous cries of excitement continued, each of the hound dogs sat more-or-less upright and remained pretty much in place. "You don't have to fear these fellows."

Ben stepped into the yard. "Oh, I figured that, Mister Dority. I understand that bassets are a very friendly breed."

"Well that they are — you're just not going to find a more mildly tempered dog. They're not the easiest breed to train, but they make up for brains with their temperament. I've got a bitch coming into heat — sometime in April. Just how many puppies are you interested in, Mister... ah... Mister?" He offered his hand in greeting.

"Decker — my name's Ben Decker." Ben grasped his hand.

"Welcome to our little paradise, Ben. This here's my wife, Rebecca." The smiling lady nodded her head and went back to finish whatever it was that she had been doing with her roses.

"Actually, the purpose of my visit really doesn't concern the dogs, Mister Dority. If it's okay with you, I need to get some information."

"Information, huh? Why don't we go sit in the shade over there? These *kona* winds are really bringing in some muggy air for this time of year." Mister Dority produced a red handkerchief from his hip pocket and proceeded to mop his brow. As he turned to lead the way to the shade, he released his dogs with a slap of his hands. They all immediately surrounded Ben, their big noses working overtime trying to identify his scent. "If they bother you, just let me know."

"Oh, I'm sure they'll be just fine."

"So, what brings you up here to our home, Ben? Um... you don't mind if I call you Ben, do you?"

"No, not at all."

"What kind of information could an old man have that you'd be interested in?" He sat on a dried-out stump and extended his hand in the direction of a large, flat lava rock that he obviously left under the tree just for sitting.

Ben rested himself on the natural bench. He shook his head, restraining himself from laughter while watching the pack of sad-looking dogs make a spectacle of themselves. The docile, long-eared pups simply had way too much skin for their low-slung bodies. The band of wrinkled bassets, totally exhausted from their two minutes of excitement, all flopped down in the shady grass and piled themselves on top of one another and up against Mister Dority's legs. "To tell you the truth, Mister Dority, I was hoping you would remember an old employee of yours."

Dority ignored Ben's words in favor of doing a bit of exploring on his own. "You know, we're pretty informal here in the Islands. I take it you're from the Mainland somewhere. From the sound of your accent, I'd say you're from someplace in the Northeast — New Jersey or Pennsylvania."

Ben nodded his head. "Hey, that's pretty good."

"Where bouts?"

"You're right on with Pennsylvania — it's Philadelphia, actually."

"That's a long way off, Ben. Anyway, like I was saying — we're used to being pretty informal here. I feel more comfortable if you don't mind using my first name."

Ben nodded in the affirmative.

"It's Duke. Actually, it's William, but everyone calls me Duke. I figure there's no point in changing it after eighty-two years." He smiled a warm grin that reached clearly from one ear to the other.

"Then, Duke it is."

"Now then, what kind of information are we talking about here?"

"Well Duke, like I said, I'm looking for someone — someone who used to be one of your employees at the Royal Hawaiian Hotel. The trouble is, she worked there a long time ago."

"That's all right. I've got a hell of a memory, Ben, just like an elephant's. Some folks think my memory is TOO good." He tilted his head in the general direction of where Rebecca had been cutting flowers, though she was now no longer anywhere to be seen.

"I think the person I'm looking for left the Royal way back in about fifty-seven or so."

"1957, huh? You know I swear that the older I get, the better I remember the old days. So help me, 1957 seems just like last week to me. Exactly who is it you're looking for?" He dropped his hand and scratched one of his hound dog's heads.

He couldn't help but think it strangely coincidental for Dority to refer to 1957 as seeming just last week. To Ben, it actually WAS last week. "Her name was... er... is Leilani Kealoha, and she worked in your public relations..."

The old man's expression immediately turned grim, and his jovial timbre was replaced by a deeper, more serious tone. "Who are you?"

"I told you — my... my name's Ben Decker."

"What business do you have asking about Leilani?"

"I'm trying to locate her for ah... a fr... friend." Ben suddenly felt quite uneasy and feared Duke had some reason not to talk about Lani.

"Not good enough. Who are you working for?"

Oh shit! It now crossed his mind that Dority wasn't going to give him any information at all. But he simply had to find Leilani somehow. From out of nowhere, Ben felt a surge of courage and determination flush into his being. He spoke forcefully and with renewed confidence. "Um... quite frankly, I'm not really at liberty to give you any details. But let's just say I'm working for some of her relatives on the West Coast. It involves a great deal of insurance money. Ah... an inheritance of sorts."

"Insurance money? Inheritance? You're trying to tell me her older sister somehow came into money?" Duke's head moved slowly side to side as if to indicate his disbelief.

"I'm sorry, Duke, but I've already told you more than I should have. Believe me, she'll thank you when I finally do find her."

Duke sat quietly, obviously mulling Ben's words over in his mind. As if by some magical command, Rebecca walked up to the two men carrying a tray with a full, sweating pitcher and three tall tumblers. "Could I interest you fellows in a glass of iced tea? I just now brewed it?"

They both nodded their approval. Duke quickly stood and disappeared around a tree. Just as quickly he returned, pocket knife in hand, neatly slicing a freshly picked lemon. As Rebecca filled each glass, Duke ritualistically hooked a slice of the citrus onto the top of each glass. Though Leilani's old boss kept perfectly quiet, Ben sensed that he surely knew something about her whereabouts. But he was much less certain that the octogenarian had any intention at all of ever sharing it with him.

Rebecca seated herself on a lawn chair next to her husband. Duke consumed a third of the glass of tea in one swallow and then dropped the lemon slice in, swishing it all around his drink. "You know, Ben, I hate to tell you this, but that insurance malarkey just doesn't wash at all with me."

As the old man very consciously continued to oscillate his glass, his silent pause became nearly deafening to Ben's ears. He felt that he simply had to say something — ANYTHING — to fill the verbal void, to nudge old man Dority into revealing whatever it was that he knew about Leilani. Ben was scared to death that this could be his last chance at finding a lead, but it seemed that the harder he tried to speak, the less chance there was of anything intelligent coming out of his mouth. Finally, Duke shifted himself on the stump, almost as if to indicate that he had somehow read Ben's mind in great enough detail to proceed.

"I've always been a straight shooter, Ben, and I always like to deal with straight shooters." Dority looked at Decker and captured his eyes with his own. "Quite honestly, my head keeps whispering to me that you sure as hell don't represent any sort of insurance agency. Yet for some unknown reason, my heart is simultaneously shouting out to me that you have your reasons for not revealing yourself — that you're right this minute enduring a great amount of personal pain."

Again, Dority paused. Ben wanted to answer — to tell him everything — but he couldn't. The best he could manage was a nearly imperceptible nodding of his head.

"I've done quite well for eighty-two years acting on my intuition when I've needed to, and right now, my intuition tells me that I can somehow help Leilani by helping you." The tricolor hound he had been petting rolled over onto his back and let out a loud groan.

"I appreciate your sensitivity, Duke. I wish I could be more open with you, but I can't. And yet you have to believe me, I only want to do what's right for Leilani myself."

"Leilani was one of my best employees. Actually, she was much more than that. I guess you could say she became our close personal friend — later on almost like a daughter — though much of that happened after she left the Royal Hawaiian. She was really bright and had a hell of a lot of common sense. I'm convinced she probably could have done almost anything she wanted to do with her life despite the times in which she grew up. I'm not exactly sure how she befriended Rebecca and me, but — like I said — we got to know her better than you'd ever expect to get to know an employee. I guess our friendship really began to bloom once she started to come over to the house and babysit for the kids.

"Anyway, several weeks before she finally quit her job, she met an older man — a Caucasian fellow from somewhere back on the East

Coast. To tell you the truth, I think she said he was from your hometown — Philadelphia — but she never once mentioned his name." The old man stared right through Ben as though he possessed some supernatural, x-ray vision. "You know, Lani was a very special girl. She never had a lot of boyfriends. I can still remember the day she excitedly gave me the good news — I mean, she had fallen head over heels for this guy..."

Rebecca leaned forward and continued, "...and I might emphasize my husband's point that she really wasn't the kind of girl who was prone to infatuation. Lani was really quite shy and self-conscious of men courting her. Like Duke said, she didn't exactly date a lot — honestly, she hardly dated at all." She let out a sigh and sipped her drink. "Truth be told, a love-at-first-sight relationship seemed totally out of character for Leilani."

Duke reluctantly agreed with her. "Anyway, she was totally taken in by this chap, right to the point where she seemed to be walking with her head in the clouds, simply swept right off her feet. I tried to warn her, but it just didn't matter, if you know what I mean."

Ben's slowly nodded, knowing full well he was the man she had met.

"Well, wouldn't you know, in a very short while — oh, I don't remember exactly if it had been one week or two — Leilani came dragging into work one morning with a face a mile long. She never told either one of us precisely what happened, and it certainly wasn't the sort of thing you'd want to press her about. But one way or the other, her... well, er... her boyfriend — if you could call a guy who'd do THAT to her a friend — he just up and left for no good reason. She never was too clear about it and never spoke of any details, but she was convinced he'd be back very soon — in a matter of a few weeks or so. Needless to say, when he didn't show up, she was totally heartbroken. Then on top of all that, she had... well..." Duke looked down at one of his dog's and stroked its long ear. "Let's just say she had a problem of sorts, and she needed a little help."

"A problem? What kind of problem are you talking about?"

Duke again looked Ben up and down as though he were still trying to size him up. "Look, maybe we already told you too much. Let's just leave it at that — she had a really tough time after this guy took off. Soon after, she resigned from her position at the Royal. Though she never asked for a thing, we lent her a small amount of money to get her through some tough times. True to character, Leilani was incredibly grateful."

"I'm sorry, Duke, but I'm just not following all this talk about her problem and tough times and all."

"Well, some things just aren't any of my business to talk about." Dority's tone left no doubt that he refused to go any further. "When you find her — IF you find her — I'll leave it to Lani to reveal as much of her story to you as she cares to. But I will tell you this much — she did move back over to the Big Island — somewhere on the Hilo side. I know she was there in the mid-Seventies yet, but regrettably, she just up and disappeared. Yet sure enough, she paid us back the money she borrowed..."

"...every single penny of it." Again, Rebecca interjected. "She wrote to us steady like for years — always stayed in touch. And then with no notice at all — nothing."

Ben was leaning forward on the big lava slab. "You mean she never gave you any indication of where she was going?"

"Well..."

"Ah..." Duke immediately cut off whatever attempt his wife was going to make at an answer. He shot an instantaneous glare at her that left no doubt as to the unwelcome nature of her comment. But just as quickly, his dire scowl was replaced by a more neutral expression. "None at all. For that matter, the last time Rebecca and I were over on the Big Island — when was that, Rebecca?"

"Early Eighties, I reckon. Um... eighty-three, eighty-four maybe..."

"Okay — the early Eighties. We tried looking her up, but no one could tell us just where she had gone. Naturally, we were quite concerned, but hey — what are you going to do?" He held both hands out as if heaven might somehow give him an answer. "Her disappearance has been a real mystery to me." The old man avoided any eye contact with Ben, instead fixing his gaze on the bassets piled up at his feet.

Ben wanted to believe him, but his intuition kept shouting out that Duke knew so much more than he cared to admit...

"I think that fellow came back." Rebecca quickly squeezed her statement in, finished her tea, and carefully placed the empty glass on the tray.

"Fellow? What fellow? Do you mean..." Duke placed his hand on her knee, obviously confused by her comment. "What are you talking about, dear?"

"You don't know the whole story, Duke. We used to talk like... well, like girls talk. She promised the gentleman she'd wait for him, and he assured her he would be back. She believed him with all her heart — I KNOW that."

"You KNOW that, Mrs. Dority?" Ben was intrigued by her assuredness.

"Well, I certainly believe that SHE knew it. She never doubted that man for one minute. But it was a very strange situation, to say the least."

Ben was leaning forward now. "Why do you say that?"

Rebecca looked to her husband, almost as if she needed his permission to continue. He barely changed his expression even a little bit, but she read him loud and clear. "Like I said, it was really mysterious. She knew he'd either be back in a few weeks or not for several decades —there was no middle ground. Yet Lani swore she'd wait either way. I never could understand it. It was simply crazy — either right away or decades later." She nodded her head as she repeated the alternatives, almost trying to convince herself that they made sense. "But no matter what the case, she vowed that she'd still be waiting for him whenever he returned."

"You never told me this part, Rebecca." Duke almost sounded hurt.

"You never asked. I think the gentleman came back — that's my theory. As a matter of fact, that's probably where she is now — with him."

Ben only wished she had been correct. "Well, hopefully, we'll see about that, Mrs. Dority. No matter what, I guess I'd better start looking in Hilo." He held out his empty glass, and Rebecca took it from his hand. As he stood, a pack of basset hounds again surrounded him, one perky pup jumping up to his waist.

"DOWN, Sylvester!" Duke Dority's command was begrudgingly obeyed, as Sylvester dropped his front paws to the ground and whimpered away to the back of the pack.

"I can't thank you both enough — from the bottom of my heart. You've been more than helpful to me. I'll certainly let you know when I finally find her. I promise."

44
Monday, February 15, 1999: 3:10 P. M.

When he dropped the rental off back at the airport, Ben was almost surprised no one ever mentioned that people were looking for him. Nevertheless, he paid for his interisland tickets with cash.

The view offered by the Orchid Island Airlines 737 was simply spectacular as he peered at the pure white twin peaks of Mauna Kea and Mauna Loa. He never doubted Leilani, but the sight of the two mountain peaks confirmed her claim — snow in Hawaii! Still, Ben could hardly believe he was back on a plane again so soon. Luckily, the quick hop over to the Big Island was scheduled to take less than forty-five minutes or so. With any luck, he could find a better lead or — hope on hope — maybe even find Leilani.

"Are you just visiting Hilo?" A pretty, middle-aged woman seated next to him seemed genuinely curious.

"Yes... Why, yes I am. Um... it's my first time here, actually."

"You'll love it. It's not at all hectic the way Honolulu is." The woman, though a blond Caucasian, gave every indication that she was a longtime resident of the Big Island and quite proud of it.

"So, you live in Hilo, do you?"

"Sure do — just outside, really, in Waiākea. My husband and I moved here from back east over twenty years ago now, and we'd never think of leaving. It's just a great place to live."

"Back east, huh? Where about?"

"Providence — Providence, Rhode Island."

"How about that. I'm from Philadelphia. Do you get over to Honolulu that often?"

"No more than I have to. I was only there overnight — on a shopping trip. A couple of times a year, I go over to visit my friend. She lives in Pearl City. We get to do some shopping and maybe see a show or two. Ian usually stays at home — someone has to earn a paycheck, you know." She flashed a mischievous smile. "I guess I really ought to introduce myself. My name's Angela, but everyone calls me Angie."

"Glad to meet you, Angie. I'm Ben Decker."

She nodded. "So, are you here on holiday?"

"Well, not exactly. I'm trying to locate an old friend."

"That's nice. Does he live right in Hilo?"

"Quite frankly, I'm really not certain — and, he is she."

"Pardon."

"She's a woman — the individual I'm looking for is female."

"Oh, I see. Just who is it you're looking for? My husband's in real estate, and we get to meet a lot of people. Besides that, Hilo is NOT a big city. Maybe by chance, we know your friend."

Right! What are the chances of being that fortunate, Ben thought to himself? But what the heck, you never know. "Her name's Leilani Kealoha. Ring any bells?"

"Kealoha, huh? You know that in Hawaii, that's about as common as Smith is back on the Mainland."

"Regrettably, that's what I hear."

"There is a Kealoha family in our parish, though."

"Oh yeah? And what parish is that?"

"Saint Joseph's — it's the Roman Catholic parish right in Hilo Town."

Ben's interest suddenly perked up. "Do you know any of them?"

"Well, I know the name, but I don't know any of them personally. I guess the family has always been quite active at the school — Saint Joseph High School, that is. Ian and I don't have any children, so we haven't been too involved with the school ourselves. I do know that one of the Kealoha women is a Eucharistic Minister at the Saturday evening Mass we generally attend. But again, I don't know her other than to say hi to."

"Tell me, is it hard to get around town?"

"Hard?" The woman snickered at the thought.

"Yeah, ah, you know, is it difficult finding things?"

"Oh goodness, no. Like I said, Hilo is not at all too big. Are you renting a car?"

"Yes, I am."

"No problem then. They'll give you a good map. You'll have no problem finding any place you need to."

Ben anxiously sensed the plane dropping into a rather steep descent. He directed his view out the window and could see a multitude of gushing, white waterfalls cutting unexpected gashes through the bright green fields below. In many spots, what looked like crops were interrupted by large expanses of trees, all neatly planted in perfect rows. "Do you have any idea what the orchards are?"

"Oh sure. They're macnuts — um... macadamia nuts."

"How about that. I didn't realize they were growing so many of them over here now."

"Every year, more and more of the cane fields are being planted with macnuts — I guess they earn a lot more money per acre than sugar does — or I guess I should say than sugar did. What with the cheap imports and all, there's really no commercial sugar left on the Big Island anymore."

A muffled bang, bang, announced the landing gear being lowered into place. Ben could see spotted subdivisions give way to a small city wrapped tightly around the perimeter of a splendidly blue bay. A crescent moon, black sand beach separated the town from the ocean. "Now that's just beautiful! I guess it must be Hilo."

"You guess exactly right. It's the world's most delightful little city. Ian and I live right up there." She pointed past Ben and out the window.

He looked in the direction she indicated, but from a quickly moving jet coming in at a mere thousand feet or so, he had absolutely no idea of just where she was pointing. Nonetheless, he tried his best to be polite despite his uncertainty. "Aw yeah — it looks just lovely up that way."

45

Monday, February 15, 1999: 4:25 P. M.

Ben was still paranoid about renting the car using his credit card, but he simply had no choice, no matter what was going to happen. His more immediate problem was where could he possibly begin to look for Leilani in a strange city in which he didn't know one single soul? No, he couldn't even stretch the point to include the lady he had met on the flight over — after all, she had never even indicated her last name. Oh well, he had heard the Kealoha name mentioned often enough in connection with Saint Joseph's School, so at least that made sense as a likely starting point. His only fear was that this late on a Friday afternoon, he'd stand no chance at still finding anyone there.

* * *

The car rental map did prove quite easy to read. It was only a five-minute drive from the airport to the downtown location of the little Catholic school. He parked in a small traffic circle out in front and glanced at the entrance. Today just might be his lucky day — the doors were still wide open. He got out of his car and walked through the main entrance into a long hallway. From the looks of all the banners hanging on the walls, there had to be a big basketball game to be played sometime over the weekend.

"Can I help you?" A rather disheveled looking man with a peppered beard and unkempt hair stood juggling an armful of papers. Ben assumed he was probably a teacher.

"I think so. Could you tell me where the principal's office is?"

"Sure thing. It's right there." Since he had no free hand with which to point, the middle-aged man merely looked over the top of his glasses at an open door. "But I wouldn't guarantee that Sister's in there right now. It's a holiday, and there's no school today so she could be off wandering."

"Thanks a lot. Hopefully, I'll find her."

"No problem."

Ben walked over to the open door and entered. His first look at the little high school's office was like being in a time machine, causing his mind to whirl with an array of vivid memories of his youth. Having had two teenage daughters and a teacher for a wife, he had been no stranger to the inside of a school building. But the modern, sterile design that characterized the architecture of Grovesnor High School didn't in any way stimulate the nostalgic images that this old school certainly did. From the old-fashioned regulator clock on the wall to the nearly antique ditto machine in the corner, this setting was a definite throwback to the 1940s. Ben couldn't help but think that it must have looked precisely like this when Leilani was a student here. He scanned the room and quickly ascertained that it was vacant. He walked up to the counter and glanced towards a half-opened door labeled PRINCIPAL'S OFFICE, SISTER VALERIE, OSF. He leaned over the counter to see if anyone could be detected in the office. "Hello. Is anybody here?"

The door swung fully open, revealing a little old lady wearing a black skirt, a light blue blouse, and a nun's veil on her head. "Good afternoon. Can I help you?" The sister beamed the kind of radiant smile that could only be found on the face of a religious person.

"I hope so, Sister. My name's Ben Decker, and I'm here in search of some information."

"Well, I don't know that I can help you any, but why don't you come right in here and have a seat." She walked back into her office as Ben followed. Now that he was finally standing right by her side, he was absolutely amazed at her height — or lack of it. He was convinced that, at best, she couldn't have stood more than four-and-a-half feet tall. "I'm really glad I caught you in so late on a Friday, Sister."

"If it wasn't for the game tonight, I doubt you would have — not on a Friday, anyway. You realize that sisters like a little time off, too!" She pulled her chair out from behind her desk. The more Ben looked at her, the more he became certain that she had at least some Asian blood in her ancestry. "The boys are playing in the Big Island Championships at the Civic Center this evening. Of course, I wouldn't miss the game for anything. I've even made a little wager with Donald Sasaki — he's the principal over at Hilo High. Well, I bet him that our boys will win by five or more tonight." Between the naughty little smirk that came over her face and the marvelous twinkle that appeared in her eye, the seemingly friendly nun immediately won Ben's heart. "Sit down... Please..." She held her hand out towards the chair across the desk from her.

"This seems to be a great, little school you have here, Sister Valerie. I assume you are she."

"I am. I'm Sister Valerie Fernandez. And thank you for your kind words about our school — we really think we're doing something right around here. We only have two-hundred-and-fifty students enrolled, but thirty-nine out of forty-three seniors went on to college last year." He could see the pride in her boasting about her graduates.

"Well, congratulations — that's just a remarkable achievement."

She bowed her head towards him. "So, Mister... um..."

"Decker, Sister — Ben Decker."

"So, Mister Decker, what kind of information are you looking for?" She moved a stack of papers from the middle of her neatly kept desk into a file marked OUT.

"I'm looking for an old friend — someone I lost contact with years ago."

"I don't see how I could help you, Mister Decker."

"It's only that she is a graduate of your high school."

"Oh, well, I may know her — or her family. When was she graduated?"

"Oh gosh — way back in the early fifties."

"Oh, gee — I'm afraid I wasn't here at Saint Joseph's until 1960."

"Well, maybe you know the name anyway — Leilani Kealoha."

"We have a lot of Kealohas here at Saint Joseph's, Mister Decker. But I'm not sure I can just release that kind of information to... to anyone."

"Aw, come on, Sister. We were very close friends and..."

"...and you lost contact. Usually, CLOSE friends stay in contact, Mister Decker."

"It's a really long story, Sister. To be honest with you, there's very little of it I could tell you."

The nun sat for nearly a minute in total silence. Ben couldn't help but be frustrated at his continued inability to be honest with those from whom he sought help. Yet there was no way he could tell the whole story, could he? Finally, he broke the silence. "Maybe if you could just tell me where I could contact someone in the family. Anyone related to her would give me a start."

She leaned forward in her chair. "But you have to understand. Nowadays, we have to be cognizant of all the legal responsibilities involved with divulging information. I mean, I certainly don't much like the direction the world has taken lately, but my position dictates that I have to be concerned enough here to abide by the rules.

Goodness knows, with lawsuits and all..." She didn't seem the least bit nervous, and yet she still kept fidgeting with her Rolodex.

"Well naturally, I can understand that. Do you think... um... maybe you could at least tell me if her family is still even in the parish?"

"I'm very sorry, Mister Decker. Maybe Father Bill could help you with that. I would simply be out of place to do such a thing. If only I..."

A voice intruded. "Oh, Sister Valerie, I need to... Oh my, pardon me, Sister. I didn't know you had anyone in here." Another nun dressed in a full habit stood in the principal's doorway looking at Ben. "I'll come back a..."

"No, no, Sister, it's all right. I'll see to that matter right now. Please excuse me, Mister Decker. I'll be back in one moment." The little nun stood and – quite nonchalantly – turned her phone file so that it was open and facing directly towards Ben. She quickly walked to the door, and the two nuns hurried away.

At first, Ben didn't realize exactly what had happened, but he quickly thought it funny that she had turned her Rolodex right towards him. He glanced at the open leaf and read: MALIA KEALOHA. Now, this simply had to be more than a coincidence. He quickly jotted down the address. He had no sooner slipped the paper into his shirt pocket than Sister Valerie came back into the office and returned to her seat.

"I'm sorry for the interruption, Mister Decker. I'm not sure that I can be of further assistance to you. I wish I could have been more helpful."

"Sister, you've been of immense help. Good luck with your wager tonight. I hope the Saints do..."

"The Saints?"

"Isn't that your mascot? The Saints, I mean..."

"Oh no. We're the Cardinals, Mister Decker."

"I see. The bishop kind?"

"Kind?"

"Of cardinal, I mean."

She tactfully covered a snicker with her open hand. "Oh no — the bird kind."

"Jeez, I'm sorry. In any case, let me wish the Cardinals all the luck in the world tonight." He turned and quickly moved back to the door.

"Surely, you know that we can do better than that."

Ben scratched his head. "Better than that? How's that, Sister?"

"We get our help from OUT OF this world — from heaven to be precise." She sat back in her chair and smiled, again revealing that angelic twinkle.

Ben walked briskly out the front door and climbed into his car. He was totally befuddled at just why Sister Valerie was so purposeful in making sure that he found the address. It was intentional — wasn't it? He pulled the piece of paper from his pocket and looked at the street map he had folded open on the front seat. He quickly located Keaukaha. That section of town — like everything else in Hilo — appeared very close by and quite easy to find. He started the engine and stared absentmindedly out the windshield. He knew that he needed to quickly think about what he was going to say. He shook his head side-to-side – first, Sister Valerie says she can't help him, and then she gives him an address. He put the car in gear and pulled out of the drive. He still felt utter bewilderment. Why was the good Sister so helpful? There had to be a thousand cards in that Rolodex. Ben let out a sigh. He was absolutely convinced it could have never flipped open to just the right entry by accident... Could it?

46

Monday, February 15, 1999: 5:05 P. M.

He drove along the ocean, delighting in a sky filled with big, fluffy trade wind clouds. The late afternoon sun rapidly painted the fair-weather cumulus a bright fluorescent orange. This coastal section of Hilo appeared quite old and, from the looks of the kids he saw playing at several beach parks he passed, was predominantly populated by folks with Hawaiian and mixed-Hawaiian bloodlines. The shoreline displayed a rugged character and was remarkably different from what he had become used to seeing in the Islands — or at least in Honolulu. A haphazard scattering of black and green sand broke up the jagged lava flows as they spilled into the sea. The small pockets of sand formed a myriad of little swimming holes, and every last one seemed to be occupied by a lone fisherman or a few snorkelers. Stands of coconut palms and ironwood trees added a verdant hue to the landscape. In more dense areas of growth, many trees showed signs of fighting for their very lives, constantly in competition with the tangles of giant philodendrons that wound their way towards the sun using any available trunk space for support.

Ben slowed the car and double-checked the address. Yep, this had to be the place. He pulled his rental off the road in front of a rather large, quite rundown old house. Sadly, the property seemed to be losing its battle with the out-of-control jungle that completely surrounded it. He slid out of the car and eyeballed the place. The dwelling itself gave him the distinct impression that it had somehow sprawled and overflowed its space to a much greater extent than its original designer ever intended. If his initial assessment was correct, the central structure was barely visible through the numerous additions and extensions built onto it over its long history. The paint peeled badly, large areas of dry rot marred much of the wood, and the corrugated roof rusted nearly everywhere.

There was no front sidewalk at all. Ben followed a well-beaten, dirt path that led up to what passed for a small front porch. As he stepped up onto the old, rickety stoop, he marveled at another representative of the apparently never-ending supply of philodendrons overgrowing this entire part of Hilo. This particularly rambling plant poked several of its two-foot-long leaves right through one of the shack's open front windows. The incredibly vigorous specimen so enticed him that he felt an urgent need to reach out and touch its three-inch thick, woody vine. Ben ran his hand over the smooth texture of the monstrous philodendron's stem. He nearly laughed, conjuring up an image of this vine's poor, feeble relative struggling for mere survival in his upstairs bathroom in Pennsylvania. It was difficult to believe that his frail, sickly houseplant was of the exact same species.

"What do ya want?" The slow speaking, gruff voice didn't sound the least bit friendly.

Somewhat startled, Decker wheeled around to try to locate the voice. At once, he spotted a rather large, young *haole* standing next to the porch. Ben felt somewhat surprised to see the brawny looking Caucasian right here in the middle of such an overwhelmingly Hawaiian community. The burly young man effortlessly held what had to be a sixty-pound bunch of bananas in one of his big hands and, to Ben's chagrin, menacingly wielded a two-foot-long machete in the other. His rather grim expression seemed to telegraph a less than tolerant disposition towards visitors. Decker couldn't help but think that maybe his luck had just run out. "Ah... gee... I was just admiring this philodendron." As soon as the words came out of his mouth, Ben immediately realized just how stupid he must have sounded. After all, he WAS trespassing.

"I said, what do ya want? You're standing on PRIVATE property, you know!" The rapidity with which the big guy's voice grew loud indicated his impatience.

"I'm looking for the Kealoha residence." Oh Shit! Okay already — evidentially he had found the wrong house — or the wrong Kealohas...

"This is the LAST time I'm going to ask you — what do ya want here?"

Few times in his life did Ben feel more unwelcome. "I'm trying to locate an old friend of mine — Malia Kealoha. I was led to believe that maybe she lived..."

"How would you know her?" The man lowered his voice somewhat, but still sounded quite irritated. He dropped the heavy bunch of bananas on the ground and slid his machete between two loose porch boards.

"To be perfectly honest with you, I don't know Malia, but I'm looking for a relative of hers — Leilani Kealoha." Ben knew damned well he had no idea at all if Malia was really a relative of Leilani's. At least it seemed a reasonable assumption, and, being put on the spot, he could think of no other way to justify his visit.

"So now you're looking for Leilani. Hey, come on already, bro! Just who the hell are you, anyway?"

"My name's Decker — Ben Decker. I'm really sorry to interrupt you like this." He offered his hand, but the big guy simply kept his arms crossed, never making any sign at all that he even considered shaking Ben's hand.

"I said, what do you want with Leilani?"

"She's an old friend of mine. Actually, we were very good friends."

"Friends?" The man's tone suddenly seemed to shift into neutral, as though Ben had placed his hand on some magical key, but hadn't yet managed to yet open the lock.

"Yeah. We were best of friends once — but that was a long time ago."

"You were, huh? Where'd you meet her?"

Ben got the impression that he was being sized up and evaluated by his reluctant host. God only knew what would happen if he failed the test. He wanted for all the world to be fully honest, but just how far could he really go and still be believed? "We met in Honolulu — many years ago. She used to work in customer relations at the Royal Hawaiian Hotel."

BINGO! Ben must have finally said the magical words. The big guy's stern face finally thawed as he broke into a smile and extended his massive hand towards Ben. "How about that. You knew my mom way back when."

MOM! Did this big, white fellow just say mom? Now wait a minute here — this was supposed to be Leilani's son? Nah! No way! Ben couldn't believe it. How could the big Caucasian possibly be Leilani's son? He certainly didn't look as though he had one single cell of Hawaiian blood in him. "Ah... um..." Ben didn't know if his face showed surprise, but his inability to speak certainly must have communicated his shock. His mouth mostly just hung agape.

"Hey... Oh boy — don't you look surprised? My name's Lopaka Kealoha. Ah... actually, Bob's just fine."

"I'm... I'm really sorry. I'm... I'm just sort of surprised that... that..."

"That I'm a *haole*?"

"Well... yeah, to tell you the truth. It's been so long since Leilani and I have been in touch. I have to admit that I didn't even know she married."

"Married?"

"Yeah. Well, I assume your father's a *haole*."

"Well he was, but... You see, you're making some pretty invalid assumptions here. I guess Malia's father was a *haole* — mom never really talked about him to us too much. But as for me, I'm her *hanai* son."

"*Hanai*? I'm sorry, but..."

"Naturally — how would you know." Lopaka wiped a bead of perspiration from his brow. "*Hanai* simply means I'm... well, I guess you could say I'm kind of her adopted child. Both of my biological parents were *haoles*, but my Dad died in Nam — back in '64 — and my real mother died not long after that. Leilani used to work over at Saint Joseph's — it's a high school here in town. The whole family's been active in the Parish — especially in the school. Anyway, I was just sort of taken in by them all. Eventually, Leilani made it legal — at least I became her foster child. Well, I've been here ever since."

"You mentioned your whole family? Just how big is your family? I mean, how many brothers and sisters do you have?"

"Actually, by blood — none. Malia is Leilani's real child — her only child — and to me, she was always my real sister. But my aunties and uncles all live here, too. You know, Hawaiians call it *ohana* or family — it's just one big, happy, extended family."

"Well, I'll be... I'm really sorry I scared you there. I didn't mean to come barging in like this, but I was just about to knock when you sort of popped out on me."

Lopaka put his open hand up. "Nah — you don't need to be sorry. If you're a friend of my mom's, you're a friend to us all. Our house is your house. I'm the one who should apologize for such a lousy how-do-you-do. It's just that you never know about some of the crazy people who come over here from the beach. A lot of times, we get these weirdo Jesus freaks pushing some crackpot religion. And of course, once in a while we find some overly eager tourist stomping around the yard trying to photograph a mongoose or a banana tree or a gecko. Hey, you name it, and tourists photograph it. Sadly enough, many times they have no respect whatsoever for anybody's private property. Sorry, but I have to admit that's what I thought you were up to." He dropped his head down momentarily. "You know, I don't think anyone's around right now, excepting maybe *Kuku Wahine*."

Ben's expression told the young man he didn't understand.

"There I go again. *Kuku Wahine's* my grandma, but she's pretty much deaf anymore. You know, I'd really like to hear about back when you knew mom. If you're not in a big hurry, maybe you'd have a Primo with me."

"A Primo? Beer?"

"Yeah — a beer."

"Why ah... Hey sure, why not?"

47

Monday, February 15, 1999: 5:50 P. M.

It was a clear evening and – except for a few scattered cumulus clouds – both Mauna Kea and Mauna Loa were easily visible from Hilo. Ben was in aw of the two three-mile-high mountains, their dark silhouettes back-lit by an unseen sun. Lopaka came bounding back out of the old shack with two cans of Primo in his hands.

"Ya mind drinking from the can?"

"No, not at all."

He popped both cans and handed one to Ben. He sat on the stoop next to his visitor and swallowed a mouthful of cold beer. "*Pau hana* – the workday is done! Holiday afternoons must be the same all over the world — at least, as long as you don't have to work today." He briefly laughed.

"So, where do you work, Bob?"

"The docks — in town. We load and unload freight containers... from barges, mostly. It can be hard work, but the money's pretty good — maritime union, you know..."

Ben was dying to find out all he could about Leilani but thought it best to first share some small talk with the young man in hopes of winning his confidence. "You been with them long?" Ben sipped on his Primo.

"Oh, I guess about fifteen years now."

"God, you don't look that old. I don't mean that the way it sounds."

"Yeah, I know. But I'm old enough..." Bob grinned. "I hear that a lot, though… about looking young. Sure used to make it tough when I wanted to buy a six-pack. I was born back in fifty-nine. My age always worked out so well with Malia. I mean, she was my older sister, but we were so close in age."

"So how old's Malia?" Ben was almost afraid to ask. Did Leilani find another lover so soon after he had left?

"Well, let's see. She must have been born in... um..." He mumbled a string of inaudible numbers to himself. "She had to be born in fifty-seven. I'm pretty sure of that because she was just forty the other year... two years at most.".

Holy shit! Ben knew he didn't need his calculator to start drawing some startling conclusions. He tried very hard to maintain his composure. "Fifty-seven, huh?"

"Yeah — you know, to be perfectly honest with you, I never was one for dates and such. But Father Bill — he's our Parish priest — anyway, he was over at the house that Sunday she had her fortieth birthday. I remember because he was kidding her about closing in on forty or being forty — whatever."

"When… what time of year was that?"

"Her birthday?" He took another gulp of beer.

"Yeah, her birthday — Malia's birthday…"

Bob shook his head. "Ah, damn. I told you I'm not too good at dates. It's sometime before Thanksgiving, though… November twelfth, thirteenth, something like that. Why do you ask?"

Oh my god! Ben couldn't believe his ears! Could Malia be his… HOLY SHIT! He couldn't worry about that right now. Ben made a conscious effort to continue his conversation with Bob. "Oh jeez, I'm just curious. It seems hard to believe Leilani could have a daughter that age already. Speaking of which, just where IS your mom?"

"Good question." Bob paused for a moment and stared blankly across the street at seemingly nothing in particular. "It's been a mystery to the whole family. She just disappeared one day several years back. The police think there was foul play, but nothing was ever found."

"Nothing? Why'd the police suspect violence then?"

"I guess just because it was so unlike her to go away without telling anyone. Mom was a real homebody. I mean, other than working at the school… she was a secretary there, you know… and going to church, she spent almost all her time right here. For crying out loud, she didn't even go out on dates or anything. As a kid, that didn't seem too strange to me, but now that I'm an adult, I've often wondered why she was so… well, so doggone celibate!"

Ben wondered just how much Bob could know. "How about Malia's Dad? Did he die or what?"

"Don't know?"

"Well, do you — or maybe Malia — still hear from him or…"

"Never knew him. Neither did Malia, for that matter. Actually, I guess there was always a lot of mystery involved with exactly who he was." Bob crumbled his empty can and tossed it into a half-full barrel of aluminum cans sitting next to the porch. He scratched his ear and looked for all the world as though he had quickly withdrawn into deep thought. He was quiet for nearly a full minute. The silence was finally shattered by the squawks from a flock of playful mynah birds in the front yard. "You know, I'm not so sure I should be telling you all this. I mean, I don't really even know who the hell you are."

"I told you who I am, Bob. Your mother and I were very good friends."

"Yeah, well I don't think that's good enough. Where are ya from?"

"Pennsylvania. I'm from Philadelphia."

"I don't believe my mom ever traveled that far back east. How would you have known her?"

Though Ben knew he'd been over this part before, he thought it best to go along with Bob's reservations. "Well, like I said, I met her over on Oahu back in the fifties — when she worked for the Royal Hawaiian Hotel."

"Yeah, yeah... And you just disappeared for forty-some years. Actually, the more I think about it, aren't you too young to have known my mom back then?

Ben lied. "I'm fifty-nine."

"You don't look it."

"How about that — I guess that makes us even."

"Pardon me?"

"Not looking that old — that's just what I told YOU a few minutes ago!" Ben knew he was on the hot seat and could only hope he'd pass muster.

"Yeah... I guess I can buy your age, but how'd you wind up finding us over here?"

"Well naturally, I knew your mom grew up here. And a mutual friend of ours over in Honolulu — Mister Dority, Duke Dority — told me that the last he knew, your mom was living back here in Hilo somewhere. He told me about how he had helped your mom out with some financial support, and about how she simply vanished several years back, but he really didn't know about any details. That's exactly what brought me over here, hoping I'd meet Malia and be able to get some leads from her."

"So, you know Uncle Duke, huh?"

Ben again sensed he had the good fortune to open another door by sheer, dumb luck. "Oh yeah. Very well, to tell you the truth. He was a mentor of mine years ago — when he managed the Royal Hawaiian. You know, we'd all like to find your mom, and I was kind of volunteered to do the looking."

"All right! Now that sounds pretty legitimate to me, especially as long as Uncle Duke is involved. But I don't really know what I can tell you. After mom disappeared — oh, maybe ten years ago or so — Malia really hunted for her. I remember one summer that she used up all her vacation time and half of her savings to go on a search — to Oahu, to California... God only knows all the places she went to — you'd have to talk to her about that. But I do know she dug up a lot of interesting hearsay about her father. Only trouble is, she never told me much about it."

"That's too bad."

"Remember — he was no relative of mine."

"Okay, I can certainly understand that. Is Malia still living here?"

"Oh sure. She works in civil service — um... she's a clerk in the State Offices Building downtown. She won't be home until late tonight, though, because of the game."

"What game?"

"The Cardinals are playing in the tournament tonight, and she's the cheerleader advisor. The whole family is a pushover for these volunteer positions, you know. Damned Catholic schools don't have jack shit to pay with. I guess they saw the Kealoha Family comin'..." He laughed.

"I'd really like to talk to her."

"Well, I imagine you could either see her later tonight or stop back tomorrow morning?"

Ben hesitated. The game! After Sister Valerie, he should have known as much. He was still exhausted from all the flying, but he didn't want to blow his opportunity. "Well..."

"Care for another Primo?"

"Ah... Nah — I guess not... not really. I've got to admit that I'm just dead tired. I did a whole lot of traveling this past week. I will try to get to see Malia tomorrow morning. I think I'll just drive back to my hotel and turn in early tonight."

"Where are you staying?"

"The Hilo Hawaiian — right in town."

"Hey, that's pretty nice now that they redid the whole place."

"Yeah. Ah... if you don't mind, I'd appreciate it if you'd tell Malia I'll call her first thing in the morning."

"Sure thing — but I wouldn't call much before eleven, though. She sure likes to sleep in on weekends. And she can be a real bear when someone wakes her up."

"Thanks for the tip."

48

Tuesday, February 16, 1999: 8:15 A. M.

Ben was certain he could get used to this summer-in-February climate. He sat on the *lanai* reading the morning newspaper for the past hour or so, sipping the better part of the pot coffee that room service had delivered. He looked out over a placid Hilo Bay. The quaint little city started with an open, green park along the black sand bayfront and continued to climb right up to the gentle slopes of the giant shield volcano, displaying a variety of well kept, picturesque dwellings. He was surprised by how alive the bay was for a Tuesday morning with scores of sleek, colorful outrigger canoes running their practice courses through the turquoise water. In the distance, the pure white snowcaps of Mauna Loa and Mauna Kea loomed larger than life over Hilo, offering a drastically frigid contrast to the warm, tropical setting down here at sea level. A loud bird call cut through the idyllic setting and swept his eyes across the hotel lawn to find the source of the clatter. Perched on a fence line between a row of hibiscus and the edge of a black sand beach, Ben recognized a Hawaiian owl, *pueo* Leilani called it. Oh man... was that last week or forty-some years ago... *Pueo...* Alpha-Max 2000

The ring of his telephone jolted his thoughts of Leilani and tore his attention away from the tropical vista out from his *lanai*. For the life of him, Ben couldn't imagine who would be calling him here. For that matter, who even knew he was on this Island? As he walked to answer the phone, he was struck with a flash of terror that Emily or Katzenbach had finally found him. He could only hope that it was the front desk calling to check on something.

"Hello."

"Good morning, Mister Decker." There was a momentary lapse as the caller did not identify herself.

"Good morning. Ah... to whom am I speaking, please?"

"Ah... this is Malia Kealoha, Mister Decker. My brother told me you were staying at the Hilo Hawaiian."

"What a surprise! It's so good to hear from you, Malia. Your brother told me not to call you until after eleven. I wasn't expecting you'd be awake so early."

"Well, he told me about your visit last night, and I wanted to call you right then and there. Of course, I knew you'd be sleeping, so I waited until now. I understand that you were friends with my mother."

"That's right, Malia."

She let out a sigh. "I'm so anxious to talk to you about her. Do you know, I could hardly sleep at all last night!"

"Listen, why don't we have breakfast together. I could drive over to your place and pick you up whenever — right away if you want."

"You don't have to do that, Mister Decker."

"I really don't mind. You have to eat, anyway. So why don't we just..."

"No... you don't understand. I already ate breakfast and, besides that, I'm right downstairs here in the lobby."

"You're right here at the Hilo Hawaiian? Right now?"

"Yes, I am — near the front desk."

"Oh, jeez! Look, don't go anywhere. I'll be down in a minute."

Ben nearly threw the receiver, almost missing its cradle entirely. He took off his tee-shirt and slipped into a brand-new pullover he had purchased last evening in one of the hotel's little shops. In no time at all, he was out of his room and entering the elevator. He pressed L for the lobby. The polished metal doors hissed shut, and the elevator began its descent. Ben's expectations climbed in precisely the opposite direction. He couldn't help but remember another elevator journey he had made back at the Royal Hawaiian Hotel. But dear god, was that only one week ago or was it really over forty years in the past? The fraction of a minute trip seemed to take forever. His gut told him that no matter what Malia turned out to be like, Leilani just had to be close at hand.

He looked at his reflection in the shiny door. Now he remembered quite vividly how the door had opened at the Royal Hawaiian revealing Leilani standing there in all her radiant beauty. He wanted to will it to happen again — the exact same way. But my god, he wasn't talking about Leilani here. Malia was a stranger. A forty-year-old unknown woman who simply HAD to be... his daughter. Oh, dear Jesus! His emotions were a jumble of utter confusion. All the wishing in the universe wouldn't make Malia be Leilani. But maybe she could help him find her. The elevator's bell chimed, and the doors began to open. He concentrated on his reflected image in the metal doors as it was quickly replaced by — an empty hallway. Disappointment! He let out a sigh of failed relief.

Ben headed quickly down the marble-floored hall and past a series of decorative fountains. As he entered the lobby, he paused in an attempt to locate his visitor. Except for a lone clerk immersed in a telephone conversation, no one else was apparent anywhere near the front desk. He scanned the lobby area until his gaze reached the large, semicircular terrace that extended away from the main entrance of the seaside hotel and out over the rugged lava coastline fronting Hilo Bay. The silhouette of a longhaired woman sitting with her back to his line of sight caught his attention. He noticed that she apparently wrestled with something in her purse. He knew that simply had to be Malia.

Ben's stomach felt slightly queasy as he walked towards the stranger. He was somewhat amazed that there were absolutely no other people taking advantage of such a gorgeous morning on the sun-drenched, open-sided verandah. As he neared the woman, a gentle trade wind whisked the scent of a fragrant plumeria through the open doors. A panicky group of boisterous mynahs made a spectacle of themselves as the entire flock frenziedly ascended from the nearby lawn up into a majestic coconut palm that was somehow thriving on a lifeless slab of lava.

"Malia? Malia Kealoha?"

The woman turned around, and her gaze nearly knocked Ben to the floor. Her eyes — such beautiful eyes — looked right through him. "Mister Decker, I presume."

Déjà vu? No, it certainly wasn't *déjà vu!* Ben didn't THINK he had seen this woman before — he KNEW he had seen her. And he knew exactly WHERE he had seen her before. He couldn't have forgotten her radiant beauty even if he had wanted to, and he most certainly didn't want to forget. This was the beautiful Island woman that had captured his soul just before he was knocked unconscious on the plane last week — immediately before his jolt through time. Of course, did he really see her then, or had it been some crazy psychic vision? He surely didn't know – maybe he'd never know – but he knew he couldn't deal with that question right now. There were things of much greater consequence on his mind. "Ah... why yes — Ben Decker..."

"Good morning. Welcome to the Big Island."

Ben, quite unable to get any words out, merely nodded his head. He nearly tripped on the rug as he mindlessly stepped around the wicker sofa on which she was seated and stood trance-like, staring right into her eyes. She was simply beautiful — and uncomfortably familiar. How uncanny! Now it was incredibly obvious that she had to be Leilani's daughter — HIS daughter — but the notion never once crossed his mind before last evening. He felt overly self-conscious, aware of the fact that his brain was very sluggish. He was positive that he was now affected by the same hypnotic spell she had somehow cast over him on the airliner — if she really had been on board. His words stumbled nervously from his lips. "S... so nice to m... meet you, Malia. That's such, ah... a beautiful name..."

"Why, thank you, Mister Decker." She continued to involuntary paralyze him with her eyes, while Ben's silent thoughts begged to be released from her hold. "Well, ah... Why don't you sit down?" She gestured towards the vacant chair. "The sun won't get your eyes there."

"Ah... sun... um, ah... of course." Ben was relieved to be seated at last, since he was sure his weakening knees would have shortly given out. "It's... it's so n... nice to finally meet you, Malia." He was embarrassed at his realization that he was simply a nervous wreck, and he wished he could somehow overcome his anxiety. When compared to him, Malia was incredibly composed.

"I'm glad you could get over to Hilo, Mister Decker. Lopaka — er, my brother — tells me you're looking for my mother."

"Y... yes, I am."

"I wish you'd relax, Mister Decker. You're in Hawaii now — the Big Island, no less. I promise that I won't bite." Her smile was exactly that of Leilani's, and Ben could sense the unwelcome renewal of his heart's pain over her loss.

"I... I just don't know what's wrong with me, what's come over me. I'm... I'm sure it's not your fault. You... you just look so familiar."

"Well, I look a lot like my mom and seeing as how you knew her so..."

"No, no — I mean..." Ben felt silly asking but knew he would be restless until he did. "...like I've seen you before... maybe on my flight from the Mainland last week. Were you by any chance..." He didn't want to tell her that her face had become a recurring focus in his dreams the past several nights.

"No, you must be mistaken. I have been back to the Mainland for... well, it's been several years now."

Ben shook his head. Can spirits just appear out of nowhere? Did he have a vision of some sort just before the accident? It seemed impossible to EVER mistake Malia's eyes. "It's difficult to believe I could mistake someone as... as beautiful as you."

She self-consciously batted her eyes. "You're too kind, Mister Decker."

"You know, I feel a lot more comfortable if you called me Ben. Ah...if that's okay with you..."

"Oh sure... Ben... So how long have you been looking for my mom?"

"Quite honestly — for many more years than I care to admit."

The attractive young lady repositioned her shapely legs and adjusted the red, printed sundress she was wearing. "Where have you tried looking?"

"Well, to tell you the truth, I've flown across the country and back, but haven't met with any success. I talked with Duke Dority over in Honolulu, and he seemed to think just maybe she'd be here on the Big Island."

"He did, did he?" Ben couldn't help but hear in her tone of voice that she was well aware of the fact that Duke Dority didn't really believe Leilani would be here in Hilo.

"Well, he didn't say she WAS here, only that this was the last place in which he knew she had lived."

"So, Uncle Duke had no idea where she went from here, huh?" Again, her nonverbal cues told him that both she and Duke knew a whole heck of a lot more than either one was willing to admit — at least up until this point. Well, maybe if he was ever going to locate Leilani, now was the time to give away some of his secrets and play his gambit.

"You found her, Malia, didn't you?"

The young woman sat with one leg crossed over her knee, her leg now nervously bouncing up and down. She kept studying him with her breathtaking eyes. "I can't believe Uncle Duke told you THAT."

"HE didn't. But YOU are. Just look at yourself — you're telling me that right now by the way you're fidgeting, the way you're reacting to my question, Malia."

"I didn't say that — or imply it, even." She shuffled her position and sat up straighter. He could feel her somehow making a conscious effort to stop her nervous leg from bobbing up and down.

"Do you mind telling me where you looked for your mom?" Ben was suddenly aware of the fact that her original confidence in being able to control the situation had dissipated. Maybe now he could finally take a stab at getting to the crux of the matter.

"Not that fast. You tell ME about my mom — how you met her, how long you knew her..."

Okay, so he had to pass her test first. "Oh, it was so, so long ago. She worked at the Royal Hawaiian in Honolulu. I was a tourist staying there — that's how we met."

"And?"

"And, she was just so helpful to me. She went out of her way to make a young guy more comfortable being five thousand miles away from home. I guess you could say she sort of touched my heart." A smile rushed onto his face. "Leilani always called it the aloha spirit. But I was never fooled — it was Leilani's spirit that captured me. She was a really wonderful woman, Malia."

"Go on..."

Ben hesitated as he glanced out over Hilo Bay. He had no idea just how honest, how thorough, he could be with Malia — or SHOULD be with Malia, for that matter. After all, did it really make any sense to go into all the sordid details right here and now? Should he tell exactly how he took her mother's virginity and broke her heart? How he made her spend a lifetime waiting for him to return? Could he honestly tell Malia that he was certain he was actually her... her... NO! He simply had to get a hold of himself. It was too late for all that now. He had to be content to meet Malia and to see if she could, in some way, help him return to Leilani. Now was not the time to revel in the sorrow of his past...

"...all right? Ben, are you all right?"

He rolled his head as if to clear it.

"My goodness, where'd YOU go?"

"Aw jeez, I'm sorry. I guess I sort of got carried away in my thoughts. Um... your mom somehow can do that to me."

"Yeah — I can get lost in thoughts about her, too. So what else can you tell me about your relationship with her?"

"Well, not a lot, really. We were just... friends."

"Don't patronize me, Ben." Her tone reflected a certain degree of anger. "I find it quite difficult to believe that you could simply meet someone while you're on vacation, know them only briefly on a strictly superficial, platonic level, and then — some forty years later — travel all over god knows where trying to find that same person. Think about it for a second — it just doesn't make any sense at all."

Ben held both his hands open in front of him. "Well..."

"So now here you are in Hilo, looking for this elderly woman. And miraculously, you still look about the same age you were when you met her. That's about it, isn't it? Did I sum the story up pretty well?"

"Um... But listen, ah..."

"Well excuse me, but I can't be buying any of these ifs, ands, or buts. Face up to it — that's exactly what you're trying to tell me here. I AM right, aren't I?"

He expelled a long, loud breath of air. "It's just not exactly the way it seems."

"You loved her, Ben, didn't you? Tell me you loved her!"

He again took a deep breath. "I did — more than I ever loved another human being — or ever COULD love another human, for that matter."

"My mom felt the same way, you know. She'd have done anything for you — anything at all. She'd have given her life for you. Hell, the way it turned out, she gave a lifetime to you."

Ben was suddenly aware of the fact that Malia knew a lot more than he had suspected. "Leilani told you this?"

"She did."

"What else did she tell you?"

"Everything."

"Everything? She couldn't have told you everything..."

"Oh yes, she could have — and did! We were really close. I was the only thing she had left."

"What do you mean, left? I'm not following you, Malia."

"She said you left her, Ben, without even leaving a picture of yourself for her to remember you by. She always told me that the only thing she had of yours was... well..."

"Was what, Malia?"

"The only thing she had of yours was ME." She firmly pounded her chest with her closed fist. One big tear had grown in the corner of her eye to such a size that it now flooded down her cheek. "She shared almost everything she could with me, in hopes that it would somehow eventually get back to you. She KNEW you'd be back — right down to the year and month. She waited and waited for today to come — so patiently, and without ever complaining — for nearly forty years she waited. When Lopaka told me you were at the house yesterday, I wasn't at all surprised. I knew EXACTLY who you were. You see, I've waited for you most of my life, too. And at last, you have returned."

"Oh god... Where's Leilani? You have to tell me where she is, Malia."

She held up her hand to indicate she'd get to it in her own time. "You know, Uncle Duke was so good to mom. After you left, mom needed the time to bring me into this world — the right way, she always told me later. Uncle Duke helped her out. He helped a whole lot! He gave her a great deal of money, you know?"

"Kind of... He did mention to me that he had lent Leilani some money. And he told me that she paid it all back, too."

Malia rolled her eyes briefly skyward. "Yeah, RIGHT! Maybe with love, respect, and friendship, but certainly not with cash. For god's sake, where's a parochial school secretary who works for practically peanuts get that kind of money to pay him back with? Nah, believe me — he supported the two of us for many years. There were always the monthly checks, the tuition payments, the medical bills — right up until..." She looked away and focused her sight somewhere out in the middle of the blue Pacific, her stunning eyes remaining quite wet with emotion.

"Until?"

Malia sat motionlessly, her tears nearly held in check, and yet still evident enough to occasionally initiate a single drop that would unobtrusively wind its way down her cheek.

"Can you tell me where you saw your mom last, Malia?"

"Minnesota."

"My god! Why would she ever move there? She loved the warm weather, the warm water, and the island spirit. Why move to Minnesota?"

"She didn't exactly move there."

"Well, why'd she go there then?"

Again, Malia remained silent for the better part of a minute. Finally, she let out a sigh and answered. "Uncle Duke thought it was best. He had some friends there — said they owed him a favor or two."

"A favor or two — what kind of friends was he talking about?"

"Doctors. He knew several doctors there — oncologist, I think he called them. They all did research at the Mayo Clinic there."

"The Mayo Clinic... Oh god!" Ben dropped his face down and covered it with his hands.

The two of them remained motionless, totally oblivious to any of the outside world. Finally, though still keeping his face buried in his hands, Ben broke the respite with a scarcely understandable mumble. "What was it?"

"She had a rare form of cancer — I guess it was a type of leukemia. The doctors here in Hilo never even figured out that anything was wrong. They kept telling her it was all in her head, psychosomatic. At least at Queens Hospital — over in Honolulu — the doctors made the correct diagnoses, but they were totally helpless to offer any real treatment."

Ben raised his head enough to look at Malia. In a hoarse, almost inaudible voice, he could only manage one word. "She's..."

Malia slowly nodded her head yes.

They both sat in total silence for several minutes. Ben concentrated on the halo of puffy, white clouds that were beginning to congregate around the snowy summit of Mauna Kea. He felt as though he had been running and running and running forever, always trying to capture a prize dangling out in front of him. And now, when at last he had his elusive goal in sight, some sadistic force of evil simply yanked it away from him. He felt as though his emotion had been totally spent, and yet he hadn't even begun to mourn. Finally, he mustered up enough energy and will to stand and walk over to the railing surrounding the terrace. He leaned silently on the cold metal, his head hanging over its side, watching the surf pound into the lava rocks below. Suddenly he was aware of Malia's presence next to him.

She whispered in a quiet, raspy tone. "I'm sorry..." She stood next to him with her hands also holding onto the cast-iron rail.

Ben placed his hand over hers and squeezed. He could sense both sorrow and love flowing through their touch as though these emotions were a tangible fluid pulsing through one's veins. "I'm the one who's sorry, Malia. After all, she was your mother."

Malia just shook her head from side to side.

"How long ago did it happen?"

"Back in 1989 — during the spring and summer. It was so... so fast. She only missed a few days of work in May, and she was... was gone by August..."

"Who knows about this?"

"No one, really. Myself, Duke, naturally the doctors — that's about it. She requested that we didn't tell anybody. She didn't want anyone to mourn, to feel sorrow. That's how she was, always worried about everyone else being okay. She said she'd get her reward in paradise.

And you know something, I'm convinced that she really believed it, too."

"But didn't she realize that all those people close to her would worry anyway — worry about whatever it was that happened to her. Take your brother, for example — he thinks she probably met with foul play."

Malia shook her head. "Yeah, but he doesn't KNOW what happened. Believe me — whether you agree or not — mom fully understood exactly what she was doing. She believed it was better for everyone else to live with hope — the hope that one day they'd see her again."

"I... I don't understand."

"Oh, come on..." She wiped her eyes and brushed her long hair back over her shoulders in a manner so reminiscent of Leilani. "She spent over thirty years living with hope — FULL of hope that one day the two of you would once again be together. I can't even tell you how strong her belief in that was. She used to tell me that she didn't just believe her Ben would come back — she told me she KNEW you'd return. We'll be together again — together in paradise... She always used to tell me that..."

Ben's eyes had once again refilled with tears. "Please don't hate me, Malia."

She turned to him and hugged him tightly. "Hate you? Oh god, no. I've waited so long for you to complete your journey. You know, I've missed you, too." She sniffled on his shoulder. "And I love you — dad..."

PART SEVEN

"Even paradise could become a prison if one had enough time to take notice of the walls."

— Morgan Rhodes

49
Tuesday, February 16, 1999: 2:25 P. M.

The Orchard Island Air jet completed its takeoff and climbed at what seemed to be an incredibly steep angle. The mid-afternoon interisland flight was only about two-thirds full, with many of the passengers apparently members of a Japanese tour group. Having been fortunate enough to find an unoccupied row, Ben pulled his flight bag from where it was stowed on the floor during departure and placed it on the vacant seat next to him. He carefully pulled the old, 1957 *HONOLULU STAR BULLETIN* from his bag and gently placed it on his lap. He quite delicately ran his fingers over its pages — in a strange way, almost fondling it — as though it were the only memento he would ever have to remind him of his glorious days with Leilani. In fact, aside from the few old coins he still had in his bag, it was his ONLY material remembrance of her — just one lousy newspaper! Ben fought back the tears he knew were desperate for release. He only hoped he could hold them off long enough to find seclusion.

He leaned over and blankly peered out the window at a rapidly fading Hilo, let out a gasp of air, and tried to swallow the developing lump in his throat. Oh god! No matter how hard he tried, he was absolutely certain he could never get over the thought of Leilani waiting — willingly giving up what proved to be an entire lifetime — in a futile attempt to be with him again. How many times during the last few days had he honestly felt as though it was four decades since he last saw her? It surely SEEMED that way to him. But for Leilani, it REALLY WAS forty-plus years until he returned! But sadly enough, she just didn't have the whole four decades to spend on the wait.

He could see her face, watch her running playfully into the surf. She was so young, so full of life, so full of spirit. And like a captured bird forced to spend the rest of its life in a cage, she was trapped by a quirk in time into waiting — waiting for a lover who simply had not even the slightest chance of returning in time. Oh, what pain she must have felt, what agony she must have experienced! And yet Ben was absolutely certain she would have kept it all inside, never sharing it with anyone at all — not even with Malia. And she guarded her secret for how many years, living with the hope that she could hang onto her sanity — her very life — until the passage of time allowed Ben to return to her world. Oh god, don't let me cry out loud — at least not just yet...

"Would you..."

Ben nearly jumped out of his seat despite his tightened safety restraint.

"I'm so sorry, sir." The young flight attendant was as surprised as Ben concerning his unexpected reaction. She leaned into his vacant row and gently placed a reassuring hand on his shoulder. "I didn't mean to startle you."

"Please forgive ME. I'm the one who was overreacting a bit. I guess I was just so lost in thought. I'm... I'm so sorry for unnerving you like that."

She smiled. "I simply wanted to ask if you cared for a drink? We have complimentary fruit punch or soft drinks. We also serve beer, wine, or mixed drinks, but we do charge for alcoholic beverages."

"Um... no, no — I'm all right, thank you."

"That's just fine. If you need anything at all, please let me know. It won't be long until we are in Honolulu. So sorry again for the bother."

Ben held his open hand up. "You were no bother. I'll be less jumpy the next time you go by — I promise."

She turned and walked on down the aisle. Oh boy — promise, huh? He couldn't help but recall the last time he had promised anyone anything. He could see the image of Leilani, bravely holding back her tears as best as she could, listening to him as he promised her he would return to be with her. Yeah, sure! He kept his promise all right — only he was nearly a decade too late... In rapid succession, Ben felt first wetness in his eyes, then a welling up of tears, and finally a full-blown crying jag screaming at his psyche to let it out. Please, please, please, dear god — not right here, not in front of a plane full of people. He simply had to hold himself together long enough until he got... got... Until he got where?

Ben used the crumpled-up Kleenex he had tucked into his shirt pocket to mop up his tears. He had been in such a hurry to catch the first available flight out of Hilo that it never even dawned on him just where it was he was hurrying TO. So now what? Go back to Philly? Back to his wife? For goodness sake, he still had his OTHER kids, his job, the Alpha-Max 2000... But god — go back and live with Emily? Nah — no way. Not now anyway. He knew that relationship was over — for good! Actually, it had been over for... for... Oh wow! What a weird thought — what a REALLY weird thought! Now that he considered his life in this way, he had to admit that his relationship with Emily Harris had been over since 1957, from the very second he met Leilani. Of course, that presented a small problem in the scheme of things, since 1957 was fully a decade before he ever even met Emily. So, who was he to thank for these sweet paradoxes of time travel? The airline company? Albert Einstein? God above?

The plane finished its banked turn and leveled off at cruise altitude. He could now make out only the carpet vegetation below, growing right up to the rugged lava cliffs that met the restless sea. The jet was angling out away from the island. Soon he'd be back in Honolulu — only as far as he was concerned, he'd be there forty years too late...

Only if... ONLY IF... the saddest words known to all humanity! Ben couldn't stop second-guessing what would have happened if he had stayed. Hell — wasn't that pretty simple? He and Leilani would have married, raised a family, and lived happily ever after. Uncle Duke wouldn't have had to support her — Ben would have. For goodness sake, he could have easily caught on as a technician in some little television repair shop. Sure, he'd have made a lot less money than he did with Penn-Comp, but that was no big deal. After all, he and Leilani just wouldn't have needed that much income. It would have been a simple life, but a good life. Heck, worse things could happen — DID happen! For all he knew, maybe he could have used his electrical engineering background to anonymously point the world in the direction of the microchip revolution a little bit sooner than it had done so on its own. Would that have resulted in more problems, more time paradoxes? Big deal! That certainly wasn't anything for him to concern himself with now, because he DIDN'T stay. DAMN IT!

So here he was, stuck in a world he didn't want to be in, isolated from the one he dearly loved by the impenetrable barrier of time. He was stranded in an era in which he supposedly belonged, and yet he knew he didn't. Well, whether he liked it or not, it looked as though he was undeniably facing life today, and he had better somehow decide exactly how he was best going to deal with it. It made sense to stay in Hawaii for a time — at least long enough to figure out exactly where he was headed.

Oh shit! He couldn't do that. He was expected back in Philly tomorrow night. That's all he needed to do to add to his already impressive record of sleaziness — the abandonment of his wife and children! Hell, he could be certain his partner was already well aware of the fact that he never made his scheduled presentation at the convention. For all Ben knew, the authorities were right this very minute looking for him. Yeah, they'd most likely expect foul play — some sinister plot arranged to rip off the Alpha-Max 2000. After all, isn't that what Ben himself thought originally? Well, it sure would be easy to run the Decker name through all the hotel registers in Hawaii. Amazing what a little computer technology could do — like kick out his registration form at the Hilo Hawaii on the Big Island. Even the rental cars he had used would be an easy means of tracing him. And god, his credit cards had most likely left a paper trail that was miles long by now. No way, man! There was just no way in hell he could stay in Hawaii — not now.

Ben was again aware of the vintage newspaper sitting on his lap. He had to remind himself of just why he decided to leave Leilani in the first place. It wasn't as though he WANTED to leave her! After all, the FBI surely had become the snake in his Eden, the storm clouds in his sun-filled paradise. That WAS the way it was, wasn't it? Or was it simply a pathetic excuse? He shook his head at the realization of how that invincible mechanism we call history just keeps churning right along under its own, massive momentum, grinding up mere mortals as if they were only so much fodder. Did any individual really have reign over their own destiny? Ben had certainly been brought up to believe strongly in a free and personal volition. After all, he had spent his entire adult life working diligently, striving to do his best, always honoring every legitimate authority. When he considered all those years of study in college and graduate school, the weekends and nights working overtime, the sacrifices he unselfishly made for Emily and the kids — no, there was hardly any room to argue. Ben had no doubt paid his dues to the gods of self-control. And yet amazingly, despite his nearly religious reverence to the establishment, here he was, a man hunted by the authorities in two different decades.

"Good afternoon, ladies and gentlemen. You will notice that Captain Chan has turned off the seat belt sign, but we advise you to still keep it fastened at all times unless you need to leave your seat. Our flight plan to Honolulu today will have us arriving in another half an hour. For those of you on the right side of the aircraft, we will shortly be passing the Island of Maui, known to Hawaiians as the Valley Isle. Just now coming into view is the summit of Haleakala, which reaches an altitude of..."

Ben leaned his forehead on the window and, identifying the growing point of land in the distance as Maui, willed his ears closed to the woman's voice filling the cabin through the intercom. He just couldn't bear hearing the trivial banter spoken expressly for the sake of the many joyful tourists who comprised a good portion of passengers on these interisland flights. He felt no joy; didn't WANT to feel joy; never again would feel joy — EVER! He was masochistically content to wallow in his own self-pity, shutting out the rest of the world for... for how long? He didn't know and — right now at least — he honestly didn't care. Life itself made no sense now. Maybe it was true that time could heal a broken heart — for most. But he was painfully aware of the fact that those rules simply couldn't apply to him. After all, it was time itself that had broken his heart — and had taken Leilani's life.

Is this what grief was? Was this part of an early stage in the process of mourning? It most certainly had to be. As hard as he tried, he simply couldn't get her image out of his mind — or her voice, or her smile, or her laugh... His mind seemed to be of a single purpose — to somehow remember every single facet of her life, of their relationship.

A strong fragrance of plumeria filled his nose. Oh god — that so reminded him of Lani, the vision of her tucking the yellow-white bloom behind her ear filled his inner eye. Ben felt a gentle touch on his shoulder again. Go away, he thought. He kept his face glued to the window and merely gestured with his open palm that he didn't want anything. Why couldn't the attendant simply leave him alone — alone to lick his wounds, to feel sorry for himself and...

"Ben."

He was at once aware that someone had taken the seat next to him. Now why in the world would a stewardess... Hey, how did she know his name?

"Ben."

And the voice — the voice was so familiar, was so... He quickly spun his body as best as the confining safety belt would allow. He was at once astonished, his mouth hanging open as if he saw a ghost! "Lei... Leilani. IT CAN'T BE... How did you..."

She silenced his question by placing one of her fingers to his lips. "Does it really matter how? I'm here, Ben — I'm really here!" She leaned over the armrest and kissed him. Ben at once surrendered and, feeling her warmth and love pulse into his heart, returned her kiss totally oblivious to all who might witness. After an embrace that seemed to span the entire four-plus decades they were apart, Leilani pulled back and gazed deeply into Ben's eyes. "I promised you I would wait — that we'd be together again... Forever this time..."

"I'm so sorry, so terribly sorry it took me this long, Lani. Oh god, I just... just couldn't get back."

Her eyes were just as warm and radiant as he remembered them. In fact, as he delighted in the sight of her face, he had to reach out and touch her in disbelief — running his fingers over her soft skin and through her long hair, drinking in the sweet smell of her plumeria lei. It was almost as though he needed to confirm her existence, to prove to himself that she was REALLY real. He let out a deep sigh of relief, of delight — indeed she was genuine! Thank you, god! Again, he could feel tears welling up inside, but these tears were different — these were tears of joy, tears of ecstasy.

He pulled her closer to his side and again embraced her in a sensuous kiss. His mind continued to reel in a whirlwind of confusion. How could she have returned? She looked EXACTLY the same as she did the last time he had seen her in 1957. Surely, she had to age through so many years. But she hadn't... Could she somehow have discovered how to travel through time? He relished in the soft touch of her hands as they ran so gently, so lovingly, up and down his back. Oh yes, Leilani was real all right — just as certain, as indisputable as the love he had in his heart for her. There'd be time enough later for his questions, for his curiosity. But finally, it was time for his intellect to give way to his emotion — to FEEL instead of THINK.

"Oh, Ben — if you only knew... I've waited for you for so long. I love you so much, Ben. I love you more than anything in the whole universe..."

"And I love you, Leilani. Oh god, I love you. At last, our promise is fulfilled — we're finally together. And this time, it will be forever..."

The surge of passion pulsing through their veins was so strong that neither one was even slightly conscious of the jolt that shook the aircraft as that first, small piece of the fuselage peeled away. They pressed their lips tighter together as almost the entire roof of the plane tore open. And they merely increased the strength of their tight embrace when a section of the bulkhead was shredded by decompression, and a horrifying rush of cold air slammed their seats with a shower of shredded aluminum. By the time their brave captain had struggled to regain some control of the craft and fought to valiantly pilot the severely crippled plane to an emergency landing, neither Leilani nor Ben was any longer part of this world.

50
Tuesday, February 16, 1999: 4:55 P. M.

"So, you're sure that's it?" Sergeant Derek DeCambra leaned against a Maui County rescue vehicle and looked up at one of his men perched on the wrecked plane.

"Sure as we can be, Sarge. Me and Glenn went up and down those aisles half a dozen times. And Ortize even crawled down and checked out the baggage compartment. I'm telling you that there's nobody else in here — dead or alive." The young firefighter climbed onto a ladder that had been set against the aircraft's battered wing.

Sergeant DeCambra wiped his brow with a sleeve. "We're lucky as hell that there wasn't any fire — and I still can't figure why there wasn't."

"Hell, fire! Look at the shape the god damned thing is in. I'll tell you, I want to meet that captain and shake the man's hand. I just can't believe it was even possible for him to fly this bucket of shit anymore. Yeah, whoever he was that brought this baby in is one hell of a hero!" Keoki Machado stepped off the bottom rung of the ladder and instinctively brushed the legs of his jumpsuit, cleaning nothing at all in particular from them.

"Sorry, Keoki, but you're never going to meet him?"

"Oh, shit — do you mean to tell me that he died?"

"No, thank god. But him's a her."

Keoki tilted his head in a way that said he didn't understand.

"Him's a HER! The captain is a woman."

The young man pulled off one of his gloves and reached up to scratch his nose. "No shit? I want to tell you, Sarge, when Ortize and I walked down that aisle, you could feel the entire plane just flexing up and down, up and down. There's no way the son-of-a-bitch should stay together on the ground, let alone while in flight. It must have been a real bastard to fly. Do they have any idea how far she had to go to bring it on in?"

"Must have blown open somewhere over the Alenuihaha Channel, maybe ten miles off Upolu Point."

"Christ! That's better than halfway over to the Big Island. And she got that sucker all the way over here to Maui? They ought to give that woman a medal."

"I imagine they probably will."

"So, what's the casualty list look like?"

The sergeant looked at a small notebook he had pulled from his shirt pocket. "Well, the airline tells us there were eighty-two passengers and a crew of five. So far, we have accounted for seventy-four survivors and have recovered twelve bodies. We've set up a triage area over there and have gotten the most serious cases off to Maui General." DeCambra gestured towards an emergency medical area that had been set up a hundred yards from where the plane had come to rest. "Obviously, we still haven't identified all the bodies, but at least we only have, um..." He quickly added the numbers up in his head. "...just one more person to account for."

"Maybe they went into the drink." He whistled and made a diving motion with his hand.

"Maybe you're right, Keoki, but I'd sure like to finish going over this whole area before it gets dark, anyway — just in case. You know, the damned plane bounced along the ground so hard, it's really not too difficult to figure somebody simply got shaken right on out."

"Hey, Sergeant DeCambra." A voice called out from several hundred feet away. "I'm over this way, Sarge."

Both men looked up, but it was Keoki who immediately located one of his coworkers waving both of his hands over his head. "Hey, it looks like Taguchi, Sarge."

The sergeant raised his voice to a shout. "You find something over there, Taguchi?"

"Sure did!"

The sergeant and Keoki walked over towards the other member of their team. Hoping the last person missing was still alive, DeCambra yelled towards his man. "You need a medical team over there?"

"Too late for that."

As the two men approached, it rapidly became obvious that an entire set of three seats must have been thrown clear of the disintegrating plane as it tumbled across the airfield. Yet even as they came right up behind the large, intact chunk of debris, they were screened from seeing whether or not a body was strapped into the wreckage. Sadly, Taguchi's dire expression seemed to confirm the suspicion.

"I guess it's not too pretty a sight." Keoki decided he had seen enough carnage for one afternoon.

"Yeah, that's for sure, but I just don't know here. It's a really weird ah... weird situation." Neil Taguchi stood with his gloved hands resting on his hips, just staring at his find. "How many bodies d'ya say we're still looking for, Sarge?"

"Only one left that's unaccounted for. And evidently, you got him there, right?"

Taguchi just continued to stand motionless, slowly shaking his head from side to side.

The two got close enough to get around the seat section and join him. There were two corpses locked in an embrace of death. "My god, I see what you mean." The Sergeant shook his head. "Something's just not adding up here. You got TWO more bodies. Maybe there was a stowaway or something. And you know, the guy there looks almost untouched. Evidently, this shrapnel wound in the chest just hit his heart and did it to him instantly. But Jesus..." He temporarily turned away.

"Yeah, but... Oh my god — look at... is it a her? Is that... that thing a woman?" Keoki was fighting the urge to rid his stomach of his lunch.

Sergeant DeCambra ran his open hand forcefully over his mouth. "This is the craziest thing. He doesn't look that old, but... I mean, Jesus... they're wrapped in an embrace that seems hard to imagine. It's just that, ah... you know, people can do some pretty crazy things when they're facing death straight on — really unpredictable. But my god, you wouldn't predict a guy grabbing an ah... an... whatever that thing is."

Taguchi very delicately used his gloved hand to free Ben's face from that of Leilani's. "I don't know what to make of this... it... Until they do an autopsy, who knows? But I'll tell you one thing, she — it — looks as though it's been dead for a long, long time."

"A hell of a lot longer than an hour or two. It looks — smells — like it's... decayed... Oh god no..." Keoki finally surrendered to the sick feeling in his gut and turned away.

"What's he hanging onto so tightly there?"

"I'll check, Sarge." Taguchi pried Ben's hand open and picked up the newspaper. "Just looks like today's paper." He handed it to Sergeant DeCambra.

"Yeah — looks like the *HONOLULU STAR BULLETIN* – I'm amazed it didn't get blown away. Funny — the masthead isn't right. It's somehow different..." He folded the front page open. "Now isn't that just the craziest... The paper isn't yellow at all — it's brand new, but it says Monday, February 11, 1957."

The late afternoon sun was now painting very long shadows over everything. Taguchi looked up from his squat position in front of the two corpses. "You know Sarge, I don't know if your theory's going to wash."

"Theory?"

"Yeah, about these two just reaching out to the closest human and arbitrarily embracing each other out of sheer fear. Hey, I've seen enough people who had been killed in accidents, even murders."

"And?"

"You know just as well as I do that it doesn't always happen that way, but sometimes their facial expressions reflect the exact emotions they had at the time of death.

"I've seen it."

"Well, just look at that guy's face..." He slowly positioned Ben's undamaged face, so he was plainly visible to the other firefighters. "I mean, isn't that really weird?"

Derek DeCambra and Keoki Machado both glanced down to see Ben's face locked into the most genuinely joyful smile imaginable — solidly frozen in place... forever...

EPILOGUE

"E Hoomau Maua Kealoha… May our love last forever."
– Ancient Hawaiian Proverb

Present Day

Wailani let out a deep sigh. "Oh man... I just never... just never knew what she had gone through. And granddad, too. It must have been just as awful."

"I have no doubt it was incredibly painful for them both." Uncle Kapena put his arm around Wailani.

"So obviously, my mom was *hapai* with me when grandpa got on that plane back to the mainland."

"Yeah, Malia was *hapai* alright, though she didn't know it right then."

"Oh, uncle... I am glad to know the whole story, but it is SO SAD!". She sobbed on his shoulder.

"Maybe you need to get back to today, young *wahine*. Maybe turn your phone back on – that will snap you out of the 1950s." Kapena knew she needed to come back to today.

Wailani smiled at him and kissed his cheek. "Thanks for telling me that story, uncle." She reached for her bag and started to pull her phone out. "But one last thing... what did you say back at the beginning about granddad – or the Kealohas – and my smartphone?"

Uncle Kapena gently took her phone and raised it up. "Don't you see, Wailani?"

"The Alpha-Max 2000 – the first talking smartphone?"

Uncle Kapena just smiled. His eyes turned to the *pueo* that had remained perched on the old post for the longest time. The bird fluffed his wings and gracefully flew off towards the setting sun beyond Mauna Kea.

ABOUT THE AUTHOR

Dan Churach was born in Pottstown, Pennsylvania. He earned his Bachelor's degrees at Benedictine University in Illinois and the University of Hawaii at Hilo, his Masters at the University of Rhode Island and PhD at Curtin University in Perth.

Dan and his wife Karn are explorers, from Philadelphia to Hawaii in America, from Broome to Perth in Western Australia, they embrace transitions from urban to rural and back again, always with gusto. *BACK TO PARADISE* is his second published novel dealing with a pre-statehood Hawaii Territory. The beauty and legend of Hawaii are featured in a love story that spans decades.

A career university lecturer and a high school teacher, Dan believes that a good educator must be a good storyteller. His constructivist approach to education recognizes that all new knowledge is built upon the learner's existing experience and that storytelling enhances this process. With a formal background in science and academic research, Dan assures the reader that his fictional writing is strongly based on a foundation of scientific reality.

Dan and Karn live with pups Rocky and Bomber in Leeming, Western Australia, but always keeping a keen eye out for what is around the next corner.

PROOF!, Back to Paradise, FEVER and DREAMS are also available from Amazon.com.

Check Dan's website at www.churach.com.

DAN CHURACH

Printed in Poland
by Amazon Fulfillment
Poland Sp. z o.o., Wrocław

61044875R00186